"We need to set some ground rules."

David Prescott's hard blue eyes dissected Diana. "First, the furniture in the carriage house—I expect it to be left in the same condition you find it."

"What do you think I'm going to do? Gnaw on it?"

The look he gave her was corroding. "Lock the gate behind you whenever you go out or come in. That's not just a suggestion. That's an order." He tossed her a large key.

Diana considered flinging the key back at him. This man was insufferable!

His eyes swept over her, missing nothing. "And one final point . . ."

"Yes, what is it *now?*"

"I don't care much for insolence, either."

Shannon Waverly lives in Massachusetts with her husband, a high school English teacher. Their two children are both in college. Shannon wrote her first romance at the age of twelve, and she's been writing ever since. She says that in her first year of college, she joined the literary magazine and ''promptly submitted the most pompous allegory imaginable. The editor at the time just as promptly rejected it. But he also asked me out; he and I have now been married twenty-one years.''

Books by Shannon Waverly

HARLEQUIN ROMANCE
3072—A SUMMER KIND OF LOVE

NO TRESPASSING
Shannon Waverly

Harlequin Books

TORONTO • NEW YORK • LONDON
AMSTERDAM • PARIS • SYDNEY • HAMBURG
STOCKHOLM • ATHENS • TOKYO • MILAN

ISBN 0-373-03150-5

Harlequin Romance first edition September 1991

NO TRESPASSING

CHAPTER ONE

THE CLOSER DIANA GOT to Newport the more apprehensive she became. Vague intuitive fears feathered through her stomach and tied her muscles into knots.

She knew she was being ridiculous, and she told herself so repeatedly. She was merely on her way to Rhode Island to spend the next eight weeks tutoring one sweet nonthreatening fifteen-year-old who'd failed sophomore English—and that was all.

But no matter how often she tried to reassure herself, she knew that was *not* all. From the moment she'd accepted the position, she had been hearing things, catching strange innuendos....

"YOU'RE GOING TO BE tutoring the Osborne girl this summer?" Grace Mathias exclaimed not an hour after Diana had left the headmistress's office. Grace was an art instructor at Fairview Academy, the private boarding school in Vermont where Diana had been teaching for three years.

Diana dropped a heavy stack of final exam papers on the lunch table and smiled. "Pretty great, isn't it!" Cissy Osborne had been one of her favorite students the previous year, and the prospect of spending a summer with her—and getting paid for it—cheered her immensely. In addition, she'd be staying in historic Newport, Rhode Island, a place she'd always wanted to visit. Of course, there were other reasons for her wanting to get away from Vermont this summer. But she wouldn't let herself even think about those for fear they'd register on her face.

"Well, my, my!" Grace said. "My, my, my!" Then she strolled out of the faculty room, leaving Diana staring after her in bewilderment.

She poured a cup of coffee and glanced over at Mildred Price, a fellow English teacher. Mildred was at the table having lunch. "Do you have any clue what that was all about?"

"Must have something to do with the fact you'll be living with Cissy's family."

"Oh." Diana's puzzlement deepened. "But I won't really be living *with* them. They have a few rooms over their garage they're letting me use."

As Mildred chewed on her sandwich, frowning thoughtfully, Diana felt a growing uneasiness.

"Did Carrington tell you anything about them?" Mildred asked.

"A little. Cissy's an only child, and her mother's divorced. They live in Manhattan, but in the summer they go to their house in Newport. Actually, it's not Mrs. Osborne's house. It's her uncle's." Diana opened the refrigerator, found her brown bag and sat opposite Mildred.

"Did she mention that this uncle's house..."

"Cliff Haven?"

"What?"

"Cliff Haven. The house has a name." Diana smiled. She liked that idea, of naming houses. She and Skip would have to come up with a name for the farm, something more poetic than White's Dairy.

"Yes, well... did she bother to tell you that Cliff Haven is one of the Newport mansions?"

Diana had just taken a bite of her ham-and-cheese, but suddenly her jaw turned to stone.

"Surprise, surprise," Mildred said, unsmiling.

Diana took a sip of coffee and finally got the food down. "I expected something nice. I mean, most of the girls here are... Are they *that* well-to-do?"

"I expect so. They're Prescotts, you know. Osborne is Cissy's mother's married name."

"Prescotts?"

"Mm. The *steel* Prescotts."

Diana suspected she still looked baffled.

"Honestly, Diana, sometimes I wonder where you've been all your life!"

Lost within the pages of literature, she thought to say but didn't.

Neither of them was aware that Dr. Wilson, sitting in a wing chair by the window, had been listening to their conversation.

"Prescott," the old history teacher murmured, puffing on his pipe. "Now there's a name I haven't heard in a while."

Diana turned, bristling with attention. "You know these Prescotts, Doc?"

The old man chuckled. "Lord, no! Their name used to be in the papers a lot, that's all. Not that I found much in it myself, but stories about people like that sell papers, I suppose."

"People like what?" She was definitely uncomfortable now.

"Oh, you know. Wealthy people. Society people. No matter what little thing they do, it comes out looking bigger than life, doesn't it?"

Wealthy people? Society people? Diana rewrapped her sandwich and slipped it back into the bag.

"You don't hear much about them anymore, though," he continued. "Not since the old man died and there was all that infighting over—" Abruptly, he focused on her with new interest. "You say you're going to be staying with those people this summer?"

"Y-yes. Cissy failed English this term, though for the life of me I can't figure out why." For a moment, Diana's thoughts drifted back to her concern about the girl. "Anyway, her mother's asked if someone could tutor her at their summer home. It's more convenient than having her attend summer school and a lot more sensible than doubling up her English courses next year."

"Well, watch out for yourself, little lady. They spin in a whole other orbit from ordinary people like us. Of course, I could be wrong. They haven't made the news in a long time. But when they did, it was usually bad news. And that one in Newport, the uncle you mentioned—what's his name?"

"I . . . I don't know."

"Well, he always seemed to be front and center of every story. I'd give him a wide berth if I were you."

DIANA TOLD HERSELF that listening to rumor was silly. Still, during the two weeks between school closing and her leaving for Newport, she couldn't help recalling the conversations and wondering what she was getting into.

For the most part, she was barely aware of her students' backgrounds. All that really mattered was what went on in her classroom, not how much money their parents had or how many titles. She'd been raised by proud hardworking people to believe she was as good as anybody else—"and better than most," her father would always add.

And yet her imagination, which her brothers claimed would eventually be her undoing, kept getting the upper hand. There were days when, like Scott Fitzgerald, she believed rich people really were different, and that she, the gauche outsider, would spend the entire summer tripping and lost amidst their smooth sophistication.

She was ashamed of herself for giving in to such stereotypical nonsense. Not only was it uncharacteristic of her to be insecure, but it was unfair to these unknown people who would probably turn out just fine. People usually did.

She only wished the other teachers hadn't reacted so strangely. It was as if they knew something that she didn't—and should. Often she tried to recall her interview with Ms. Carrington, searching for something that might shed light on the matter. But all she remembered the headmistress saying about Cissy's family was that they were quiet private people who preferred to keep to themselves. Then she'd urged Diana to respect their desire for privacy and keep to herself, too.

"They won't even know I'm there." She nodded in complete accord.

"Good. I'm glad you understand."

But even now, paying the toll to cross the Newport Bridge, Diana still did not understand. Not fully. The only thing she was sure of was her growing uneasiness.

She shifted her red Toyota into gear and entered the flow of traffic crossing the high sweeping arc. Below her, boat-cluttered Narragansett Bay was a lifeless shade of pewter, reflecting a heavy gray sky. The hot humid day lay on Acquidneck Island like a bad mood. Before nightfall there would surely be a storm.

Diana was exhausted. Not only had she been on the road for five hours, but her brothers had kept her up well past midnight instilling innumerable fears about her spending a summer away from home. *They* had called it a going-away party.

As if she hadn't developed enough apprehensions all on her own, their gifts to her included telephone numbers of emergency ambulance services in Newport, just in case she fell seriously ill; a map of the city, all the police stations circled in red; extra money; the strongest sunscreen on the market; warnings about undertow; and to top it all off, a can of Mace because Newport was a big place, with lots of summer transients, and who knew what characters she might run into! And they said *she* had an imagination!

They meant well, all five of them, but there were times when she wished they were a little less protective. That was another reason she'd accepted the position so readily. The time had come to cut the cord. This summer would prove she could survive alone. It would also prepare them for the news she had to tell them when she returned, that she had already signed a lease on her own apartment.

She would miss Skip tremendously. They were the last two left in the farmhouse where their parents had raised them all, but it was time she moved on, away even from him. He would be marrying in the fall, and though he and Vicki pleaded with her to stay, she couldn't help feeling like extra baggage.

She supposed her brothers' protectiveness was natural, she being the only girl in the family and the youngest child, besides. Added to that, she knew she'd given them reason—like all the school-yard fights they'd rescued her from, all that misdirected anger the year their mother died.

And then there was the more recent matter of Ron Frasier. Even now, a year after he'd left her, she still felt a stab of embarrassed pain when she thought about Ron.

How could she have been so wrong about another human being? It wasn't as if she'd been a total innocent, falling for the first guy to pay her attention. She'd gone out with lots of guys. But she'd really thought this relationship was special. It was the mature relationship she'd always dreamed of having after college, after she was settled into a career.

She'd been teaching at Fairview for half a year when they started dating. He was something of a local luminary, with his drop-dead smile, his "power" wardrobe, and his ability to climb the management rungs of the largest bank in the area. Six months later, he'd asked her to marry him.

She glanced in the rearview mirror as she swung off the bridge. Her face looked strained and too pale.

Well, at least he hadn't left her standing at the altar. At least he'd had the decency to call a week ahead of time to let her know he was bowing out. She winced, remembering the shock she'd felt as his words sank in, that panicky bottoming-out feeling in the pit of her stomach.

He'd said he was sorry, but they really weren't cut out to be married to each other. What they wanted from life was just too different; *they* were too different, and she would thank him some day. Then he'd left town for a few weeks, leaving her to unravel a wedding that had taken almost a year to arrange. That was one time, she supposed, when she'd been lucky to have such a large meddlesome family. Somehow, they got her through the ordeal.

A short while later school reopened and plunged her into its blessedly hectic routine. And after a couple of months she realized with relief and surprise that she was over Ron. She even reached the point where, seeing him dash around town in his three-piece suits and rented Mercedes, she wondered why she'd ever fallen for him. He was right. They weren't suited to each other. The woman he started dating right after their split—or maybe even before—was far more his type. She was older, higher up the corporate ladder, and a much quicker route than Diana to the life-style he obviously thought he deserved.

Getting over Ron hadn't turned out to be half the problem she'd originally envisioned. The problem that did develop, though, was everyone's subsequent attitude toward her. Poor Diana! Left in the lurch while Ron paraded around town with his new woman! She might be over the love she'd felt for him, but this pity, encountered almost every day, would not let her get over her anger or embarrassment.

Even more upsetting than the pity was everyone's concern over her empty love life. In this matter her brothers were the chief offenders. She'd started dating, but they were sporadic experimental excursions at best. Each time, she'd returned home convinced she wasn't ready to get involved again. Then Andy had arranged a date with one of his work buddies, and George had invited her over to meet his unmarried neighbor. Soon life became a gauntlet of blind dates. She felt a pressure to be happy, happy with some man. But why did her brothers assume she couldn't be happy alone? Did they think she was turning into an old maid, an old spinster schoolteacher?

Funny thing was, lately she was beginning to believe it herself. Many of the men she'd dated were quite nice, and she'd tried to like them. But by the second or third date, she'd known their relationship had no future. She'd felt herself pulling away, shutting them out. The whole ordeal of dating seemed, well, ridiculous to her, distasteful. She wanted nothing to do with it. Maybe she was just shell-shocked and in time would get over her distrust and this numbness she felt toward the opposite sex. But in the meantime, all she wanted was to be left alone.

When Ms. Carrington offered her the job in Newport, Diana saw it as a godsend. It was the perfect escape from her worrying hovering family—and exactly the right place to ride out the anniversary of her almost-wedding. She needed time alone to heal.

Diana pulled to the side of the road and checked her map. She would be arriving a day or two before the family, but she preferred it that way. She wanted to be fully settled in and ready to start lessons as soon as Mrs. Osborne gave the nod. She'd been assured that a housekeeper who lived at Cliff Haven year-round would be there to meet her.

Having found her bearings, she eased back into the traffic. Within minutes, she'd reached the busy harbor district. Its shops and restaurants looked very festive in spite of the gloomy weather, which was growing gloomier by the minute, but Diana was a little too tired to fully enjoy her surroundings.

She turned up a hill, away from the harbor, and headed for Bellevue Avenue. She'd done a lot of reading about the famous Newport "cottages" since accepting this position, but driving along the tree-lined avenue, she realized how unprepared she was for the real thing. Built during the Gilded Age, they were veritable palaces of marble and granite, surrounded by lush parklike grounds. Many of them had been turned over to the Preservation Society and were open to the public, yet most were still privately owned by an elite summer colony. The Prescotts among them? she wondered. Is this what Cliff Haven would be like?

She glanced down at her rumpled khaki shorts and white tank top, clinging to her body with the muggy heat. How could she arrive at such a magnificent estate looking so bedraggled? A long filmy chiffon garmet beaded with pearls would be more appropriate. Hair done up in an elaborately coiled design—not this messy French braid hanging damply down her back. She choked out a nervous giggle.

Bellevue Avenue ended at a sharp turn and became Ocean Avenue, also marked on her map as Ten Mile Drive. Her heartbeat quickened; Cliff Haven was somewhere on this road. Appropriately enough, the ocean came into view, unbroken as far as the eye could see. Unlike the calm harbor on the other side of the island, the water here was unnervingly choppy, crashing and spraying over the huge boulders that littered the shoreline. The road was quite narrow and winding, at times bordered by a lonely stretch of marsh, an intriguing gate house or mysterious drive.

Diana could see several more mansions ahead of her, but they looked different from the ones she'd just left behind. Or was it only the harsh landscape here that made them appear so? They seemed more rugged, more like castles or fortresses, having to face the onslaught of the wind and sea so directly.

A heavy mist now blurred her windshield. The sky was bearing down hard. Somewhere in the distance, thunder rumbled. She clutched her steering wheel with fingers that had gone white, trying to keep her sense of reality from fleeing completely. It seemed that somewhere along this narrow coastal road she had lost the twentieth century—indeed, had lost America as she knew it—and had plunged into a time and place that were totally unreal.

Suddenly she spotted it, the high iron gate with the name Cliff Haven scrolled into its fretwork. Perspiration beaded on her forehead.

The house itself stood far out on a promontory overlooking the sea, a solitary bastion brooding in the mist. From the road it looked as if it were part of the cliff, having risen there at the dawn of time, stone from stone. Several tall chimneys grazed the sky, reaching up from a steep slate roof. Narrow gabled windows glinted among its towers and parapets. An English design was Diana's first impression. Rather Gothic, she thought next. No, it was downright eccentric, she concluded with a shudder.

She pulled off the road and got out of her car. This wasn't the kind of place she'd imagined. This was something else entirely. It was smaller than the grand palaces she'd glimpsed on Bellevue, darker, more isolated, and the grounds were hardly parklike. Weeds were even growing through the asphalt drive.

"They're quiet private people," Ms. Carrington had said, but now Diana wondered if the headmistress realized what sort of privacy she'd been alluding to.

Diana tried the gates, but they were firmly locked. Just above eye level, a sign stared down at her: Private Property—Keep Out—Trespassers Will Be Prosecuted. As if soundly reprimanded, Diana took an obedient step back.

With a feeling of growing helplessness, she glanced around. The estate was surrounded by an eight-foot-high wall marked at several spots with clearly lettered plates warning of electronic surveillance. Private people, indeed! She never ignored her intuition. More often than not, it proved right. And the bad feeling seeping into her bones right now was simply too real not to heed. Again she wished she knew something about Cissy's family. What had they done to be in the news? Why should the old man who owned this house be given "a wide berth"?

About ten feet inside the gate stood a sign that read Beware of the Dogs. A few feet beyond that was another, just in case some bold intruder missed the first. Ordinarily Diana loved dogs, but these persistent warnings did nothing for her sense of well-being. Trying to look as nonchalant as possible, she searched the underbrush at the base of the wall for a rock or stick, just in case one of the huge fanged three-headed creatures her imagination had spawned suddenly leapt out at her.

Then she remembered the present her brother George had given her last night. She hurried to her car and took the small can of Mace from the glove compartment. The thought of hurting an innocent animal bothered her, but if she was confronted by a pack of vicious watchdogs, perhaps the Mace would protect her.

She returned to the gate. Okay, she sighed, what next? The house was too far away for her to call out. Should she try to scale the wall? Go back to civilization and find a phone? She turned her head and quite by accident glimpsed an intercom installed in the gatepost. But of course! In order to get into a place like this, one had to announce oneself through an intercom!

Light-headed with relief, she pressed the button. She stared at the small square grille for a moment, then pressed the button again. After five minutes and several more tries, she lowered her head and groaned. Either the contraption was broken or no one was home to answer it. In her frustration, she grabbed the gate and gave it a hard angry shake.

She didn't hear the motorcycle advancing up the road, and became aware of it only when it roared off the macadam and skidded to a heart-shattering stop behind her. She spun around in blind panic just as its tall dark rider vaulted off. He flung his helmet down and started coming toward her.

In the space of a heartbeat, she took in the huge black Harley and the equally sinister-looking man it belonged to. He was over six feet tall and deceptively lean. His black T-shirt and worn jeans were molded revealingly to a hard muscular body. His wind-whipped hair was black as night, his eyes shielded by intimidating reflector glasses. A coarse stubble accentuated his features, hard features that included an almost imperceptible scar on his upper lip. But Diana saw it clearly enough. All her senses were heightened in that electrified split second. And this man, this dark fierce stranger, was coming straight for her with malice in every taut muscle of his body.

Without a doubt, she had never been in such a vulnerable position in her life. It was a living nightmare, plucked straight out of her brothers' fertile imaginations. Her back pressed into the gate, and her heart lodged in her throat. Not a single coherent thought could be found in her entire brain. Suddenly, instinctively, she raised the can of Mace and pressed the button.

The next moment, her would-be assailant was doubled over, gasping and coughing. He tore off his glasses and dug at his eyes with his fists. "Damn it!" he sputtered. "What did you do? What the hell *was* that?"

Diana stood frozen with a mixture of fear and fascination. She had immobilized him, this terrifying stranger who looked about three times her size. She'd done it!

But even as she was congratulating herself, her brain was telling her to move, to run to her car and speed away before he recovered.

She hadn't taken two steps, however, when the intercom crackled to life. "Yes, may I help you?" came a metallic female voice.

Diana hesitated. Her gaze raced from her car to the man, who was still coughing and rubbing his streaming eyes. Then, aiming the can as if it were a gun, she backed up to the intercom.

"This is Diana White," she said in a badly wavering voice. "I'm the tutor Mrs. Osborne hired for her daughter. Is it possible for you to open the gate? And please, could you hurry?"

Before Diana could receive a reply, the man she thought she was holding at bay crossed the distance that separated them and knocked the can from her grasp. Her mouth opened but she was too terrified to scream. She felt as if she were about to faint. Well, that was probably for the best, she thought through the mists fogging her brain. If she was about to be raped or murdered, she'd rather not be conscious to know about it.

His hands dug into her shoulders—hard powerful hands. She could feel their strength clear down to her toes as they roughly moved her aside.

"Abbie!" he snarled into the intercom, still blinking away tears from his eyes. "I'll take care of the gate."

Diana's breath stopped in her lungs. Her eyes widened, and a feeling of dread far worse than anything she had experienced so far that day crept under her skin.

"Oh, I didn't realize you were there, too," the voice from the intercom answered. "All right. See you in a few minutes, Mr. Prescott."

The first drops of rain began to fall, hissing on the scorched road like the sound of snakes.

CHAPTER TWO

"YOU CAN'T BE!" Diana whispered. "*You're* Mr. Prescott? *You're* the owner of this place?"

He turned on her angrily, still blind with pain. "And *you're* the tutor my sister invited here without consulting me?" His voice resonated like the thunder overhead.

She swallowed hard. Rain was falling steadily now, running in rivulets down his face. "Y-yes. Diana White." She couldn't take her eyes off him, even though looking at him made her heart race. Where had she got the idea that Mr. Prescott was an elderly gentleman? Hadn't the headmistress said he was Mrs. Osborne's uncle?

Or had she merely said "her" uncle, meaning Cissy's, and Diana had misunderstood? Well, whomever he belonged to, this man wasn't a day over thirty-five! He was no gentleman, either, not with that fierce stubble-darkened face and those scruffy clothes!

Yet, even while these thoughts coursed through her mind, he seemed to pull an invisible cloak of dignity around himself, like a man accustomed to authority and respect, rendering his outfit immediately irrelevant.

Her shock over his identity gave way to the horror of what she had just done to him. She glanced at the Mace can lying on the ground and cringed.

"Mr. Prescott, I'm sorry. Are you all right?" She stepped closer, sincerely wanting to help in spite of the irrational sense of danger she felt when she looked at him.

"Of course I'm not all right. What the hell was that, tear gas?"

Diana shrank back. "No, Mace." She watched him lift his constricted face and blink against the cleansing rain. A flash of lightning illuminated his features, making stark his agony and anger. "I really am sorry. I was told that the family wouldn't be here yet, so I didn't have the slightest notion who you were."

"Oh? And is that supposed to be an excuse?" He pulled a handkerchief from his back pocket and wiped his eyes. "Tell me, Miss White, do you make a habit of incapacitating every stranger who has the misfortune to cross your path?"

"No," she offered weakly. "But..." But what? Could she ever come up with an adequate excuse for her reaction? "You frightened me," she said simply, lowering her eyes. Even though his skin looked leather-tough, it was becoming inflamed where the Mace had hit. She could only imagine what would have happened if he hadn't been wearing glasses.

"Good. Then maybe you'll think twice before you go rattling people's gates as if you were trying to break in."

"Break in?" Diana glanced up, wringing her hands. "I wasn't... The gate was locked and the intercom... I didn't think it was working. Listen, this is crazy, Mr. Prescott. Shouldn't we go inside so you can be tended to properly?"

"Wait a minute!" he barked. "Evelyn may have hired you, but that doesn't mean you have to stay hired."

Diana reared back. Whoever or whatever this man was, he certainly didn't mince words.

He wiped his eyes again, then squinted at her with an intensity that made her suspect he was seeing her for the first time. In the downpour, her tank top and shorts had become plastered to her body. She knew it wasn't an outstanding body; in fact, being five foot seven and not exceptionally curvy, her figure had often been described as boyish. Still, it was a frame that wore clothes well, and so far no one had ever said it was inadequate.

She knew she wasn't exactly pretty, either. Her lips were perhaps too thin, and a small bump marred the line of her nose. And unless she was tanned or wore a bit of blush, her cheeks could run to sallow. Yet she knew she had nice eyes, large chocolate-brown eyes with long lashes and lots of expression, and her dark brown hair was thick and healthy. She suspected she let it grow so long—it was now below midback—to compensate for the features that were less than perfect.

Under Mr. Prescott's cold stare, however, her usual confidence wilted. His eyes were hard and judgmental with none of the approval she usually saw in men's eyes.

"Good Lord! How old are you?"

"Nearly t-twenty-six." Her voice was thin and unsure.

One dark eyebrow lifted in surprise. "And where did Evelyn dredge you up?"

"Evelyn. Is that Cissy's mother?"

He barely nodded.

"From F-Fairview." What was happening to her? She didn't ordinarily stammer. "Didn't she tell you?"

"Yes, of course," he said, contradicting himself. His eyes began to stream again, and it was a while before he continued. "But not till yesterday when it was too late for my input. I didn't even know my niece was having trouble with school. So, you're twenty-*five* and from Fairview. I suppose that means you've been teaching all of, what, four years?"

She gulped. "Three."

The look on his face left no doubt about what he thought of her brief career.

With a trembling hand, she wiped the rain from her eyes. "I can assure you, Mr. Prescott, you won't find anyone more hardworking than I am. I'm fully qualified. I've almost finished work on my master's degree. I've received nothing but commendable reviews whenever I've been observed, and..."

She paused in midstream as a wave of resentment coursed through her. Who did this guy think he was, interrogating her in that ridiculously arrogant pose? And what was she doing, thinking she had to justify herself to him?

"Mr. Prescott, I don't see how my credentials can be any of your business. Fairview felt confident enough to recommend me for this position, and your sister was sufficiently satisfied to hire me. In my estimation, that should end the matter. Besides, it's *raining!*"

But his hard-planed face didn't waver from its expression of indurate displeasure. "Don't tell me what *is* and what is *not* my business, Miss White. No one walks into a job here without being interviewed."

Diana's breathing became like a bellows. Never had she met a more insufferable man.

"Now," he went on, feet planted aggressively apart, looking perfectly comfortable in the storm, "I hear that my sister has offered you the rooms over the carriage house."

"That's what I hear, too."

"I hope you realize that if she had asked me, I never would have agreed to this arrangement."

Diana summoned all her dignity. "Then you should have called me. If I had known they weren't available, I would have saved myself a lot of trouble and stayed in Vermont."

His eyes narrowed, dissecting her. "I didn't say they weren't available. I just wanted you to know I'm not happy about the arrangement, that's all, and we should get a few ground rules straight before we proceed."

They stared hard at each other, blinking away the rain, oblivious to the thunder crashing around them. Their hair, nearly identical in color, was now sculpted to their heads. He had such strange eyes, Diana thought. Intelligent sharp eyes. Yet they were hooded, cautious, masking whatever soul lay beneath them. But what arrested her most was the fact those eyes weren't black, as she'd first assumed, given the rest of his coloring, but blue, the blue of the sky on only the best of days. And though she knew perfectly well that eye color had nothing to do with one's character, she couldn't help feeling here was a color that belonged in the eyes, not of this intimidating brute, but of a kind sensitive man.

Suddenly, Diana felt heat rushing to her cheeks for reasons she couldn't fathom. She spun around and looked unseeingly through the gate. "W-what ground rules?"

He cleared his throat officiously. "Well, first of all, the furniture in the carriage house is hardly precious. Still, I expect it to be left in the same condition you find it."

Diana's head swiveled, her wet braid flying out behind her. "What do you think I'm going to do? Gnaw on it? Stuff it into my Toyota and take it back to Vermont?"

In any other man, she would have interpreted the tightened mouth as a suppressed smile, but Mr. Prescott seemed totally unacquainted with humor.

"Secondly," he continued, "while you're on the grounds, please confine your activities to the carriage house. That includes my niece's lessons, too. I'm a busy man, Miss White. Most of the time I'm away on business, but when I am here, I don't want to be bumping into strangers whenever I turn a corner."

Diana could feel her lips disappearing. "I don't have to be told what any polite person would take for granted."

"Fine. Then it's needless to say you're not to bring friends onto the grounds. Friends are to be met in town and left in town."

"I'm from Vermont. I have no friends here. I don't know anyone but your niece." He must be aware of that, she thought. So why burden her with yet another rule, unless he was obsessed with exercising authority?

None of her daggered looks affected him, however. "Another thing, my staff here is old line—loyal, you know? And as long as you're here, I expect you to be the same. Whatever goes on within these walls is not to be gossiped about outside. Do you hear?"

Diana couldn't help smirking at his ridiculous "lord of the manor" attitude.

"Do you hear?" he bellowed.

She snapped, "Yes, sir!" and clicked her heels with military smartness.

The look he gave her was corroding. "I don't care much for insolence, either."

"And when I decide to live under a dictatorship, I'll move to Iran!"

"I'm warning you, your job could depend on it."

"Is that supposed to be a threat?"

"Damn right! And one you'd better heed."

She took a reckless step forward, uncaring that even from her height she had to look up. "Might I remind you that I'm not working for *you?*"

"And might I remind you that you're living on my property?"

"Mr. Prescott?" She could feel her blood racing. "You can stuff your precious property." With that, she stormed off toward her car, her feet squishing noisily in their wet sneakers.

Effortlessly he reached out and caught her upper arm. "One more thing, Miss White," he continued as smooth as ice. "Don't go poking into places you don't belong. I don't like snoops, and I swear I'll personally skin the next maid or gardener—or tutor—who turns out to be a reporter."

Diana gasped. "Mr. Prescott, let's get one thing straight," she said, yanking free of his hold. "I'm not the slightest bit interested in you or your... your estate. I came here to tutor Cissy and that's all. I'm a professional, I always conduct myself in a professional manner, and I don't take kindly to being treated otherwise. Is that clear?" He didn't answer. "Now, are you through?"

Silence spun out for a few long seconds before he replied, "Not yet." He removed a large key from a ring on his belt, then walked to the gate and inserted it into the lock. The gate swung in with a whine.

"Here," he called, casually tossing her the key as if knowing all along she wasn't going to leave. She caught it against her breast. "Lock the gate behind you whenever you go out or come in. That's not just a suggestion. That's a hard and fast order."

She stared at the key and considered flinging it back at him, but suddenly she remembered something, something that had been preying on her thoughts just before his arrival. "Do you let your dogs run free?"

He squinted at her through the rain, a puzzled expression lining his leathery face.

"Your dogs. As in 'Beware of the.'" What an insufferable bully this man was, with his dogs and rules and signs—and that motorcycle! Now she understood why her colleagues had felt so uneasy about her coming here.

He swung one long sinewy leg over the machine and straddled it aggressively. "My last dog died three years ago."

He kicked the bike into thundering life. "Miss White!" he called over the roar.

"Yes-s-s, what is it *now?*"

His mysterious blue eyes swept over her slowly, missing nothing. "Welcome to Cliff Haven." Then he went streaking through the gate, leaving her behind trying to catch her breath.

DIANA DROVE HER CAR through the gate, stopped, got out and locked the gate, just as Mr. Prescott had instructed. She was still trembling through every inch of her body.

The long driveway opened out onto a wide cobbled courtyard in front of the main house. Perhaps in fair weather she would feel better about it, but at the moment it seemed such a forbidding place.

Diana stopped her car in the middle of this dismal rain-pounded square and glanced around. Mr. Prescott's motorcycle was parked beneath the portico, but he himself had disappeared. To her right stood a smaller two-story stone structure she assumed was the carriage house. Having abandoned her, did Mr. Prescott expect her to let herself in?

Just then, the front door opened, and a tall dark-haired woman in a plastic raincoat came crinkling out. She was built like a rampart, but as she got closer, Diana realized she was old. Her face was mapped with creases, and her hair had obviously been dyed. Still, she was smiling, and the harshness of her hair did not diminish the softness in her eyes.

"Hello!" It was the same voice Diana had heard over the intercom. "Ungodly weather to be arriving in. The garage doors are open. Go park inside, and I'll meet you there."

Diana headed into one of the wide stalls. She switched off the engine and quickly surveyed her surroundings. There were none of the mile-long limousines she'd expected, just an old truck and a sporty-looking sedan.

The elderly woman came lumbering through the doorway, and Diana got out of her car, wishing her legs weren't still so wobbly.

"I'm Mrs. Burns, the housekeeper. But call me Abbie, or I'll get very cross with you."

"Diana White." She held out her hand, and the woman grasped it warmly in both of hers.

"What a treat to have you with us this summer!" Though she looked fairly strong, Diana noticed her head shook with a slight palsy. "Oh, child, you're soaked to the skin."

Diana felt her cheeks warming. "I—I met Mr. Prescott at the gate, and we talked for a while."

"Yes, I know." The humor left the housekeeper's eyes, making Diana wonder if she'd overheard any of the ruckus through the intercom. "If you don't mind my asking, what did you do to the poor devil? He came into the house in a terrible state. He hollered that you were here and I was to get myself outside to meet you. Then he tore straight up the stairs and slammed shut his bedroom door."

"I—I sprayed him with Mace," she offered softly.

The old woman's eyes narrowed. "You what?"

"I sprayed him. With Mace. You see, I was at the gate when he came up out of nowhere. He scared the life out of me, so..."

"You sprayed him."

Diana nodded, wondering if the housekeeper was framing a stiff tongue-lashing, being "old line" and "loyal," as Mr. Prescott had phrased it.

But then a smile broke over Abbie's frown. "Well, good for you. That's what he deserves for going around looking like a hooligan and driving that hooligan machine."

Diana relaxed a little. "The effects should wear off soon, but maybe somebody should tend to him."

Abbie waved dismissively. "David could be dying and he wouldn't let anyone tend to him."

David. So his name was David.

"Abbie, I hate to pry, but is he always so... odd?"

The housekeeper seemed to be weighing her reply. "He's just been cooped up with his accountants for the past two weeks. The end of the fiscal year, you know. He's unwinding." Then she snorted. "Big deal! He comes here, doesn't say anything worth a plug nickel, doesn't do anything but read and walk back and forth to the seawall—and ride that infernal machine. Then he goes back to work all rested, as if he's been on a cruise to the Bahamas. I tell you, sometimes he makes me so mad..." Her face screwed up with exasperation. "Maybe I should get myself some Mace, too, and then when I want to get his attention, all I'll have to do is squirt." Suddenly she laughed and Diana couldn't help joining in. "C'mon. Let's take your bags upstairs and get you settled. And don't you give another thought to young David. He'll get over your Mace. He's gotten over worse."

Diana followed Abbie up a flight of narrow stone stairs that hugged the outside of the building. The apartment smelled musty, having been closed up for some time, but it was spacious and comfortably furnished in a delightful jumble of late Victoriana and Art Deco. It consisted of a living-dining area, a kitchen and a bedroom.

"This is really cute." Diana smiled, setting down her bag.

"I've always liked it, too. My husband and I lived here ourselves when we first came to work for the Prescotts."

Diana didn't have to ask. She knew by the woman's expression that Mr. Burns was deceased.

"Oh, my, but these windows are dirty!" Abbie cried, lifting aside the lace curtain. "I used to do them twice a year, but the big house is about all I can handle these days."

"Surely you don't take care of the whole place yourself?"

"In the off-season I do," she asserted proudly. "It isn't hard. Nobody's here to muss the place, except David once in a while, but he comes and goes like a ghost. Doesn't even leave laundry."

"Still, the house is enormous!"

"Eighteen rooms!" She paused and studied Diana's expression. "Oh, I know what you're thinking. You're thinking Abbie's getting too old to take care of the house the way she used to." Her head was shaking more noticeably now. "Well, maybe. I'll turn seventy-five two weeks from next Friday. But I'm not ready to be put out to pasture yet."

Diana gazed out the window toward the ivy-bearded mansion across the way. "I'm sure you're very capable," she murmured, wondering if there was someone in the old woman's life who didn't think she was.

They carried her bags into the bedroom, then explored the kitchen until Diana was familiar with the quirky old appliances. When she opened the refrigerator to turn it on, her eyes widened. Not only was it already cold, but someone had stocked it with food.

"I didn't think you'd feel up to going shopping after such a long drive."

Diana felt a rush of affection for the old woman, especially after just having met the ogre she worked for. "Thanks, Abbie," she said, giving her arm a friendly squeeze.

"If it was up to me, I'd have you over to the house for your meals, but . . ." She lifted her shoulders in an eloquent shrug.

"That's okay. I understand."

Abbie looked at her thoughtfully, nodding to some inner voice. "Yep, Mace. That's what we all need." And they both laughed again.

"Oh, before you go..." Diana said. "Has Mrs. Osborne arrived, by any chance?"

"No. She'll be coming in tomorrow. Which reminds me, tell me about our little Celia. What's she done to bring you here?"

"She failed English this year."

Abbie wagged her head. "Now, why'd she go and do a foolish thing like that?"

"I've been wondering about it myself." Diana hesitated. "Maybe she was in love."

"Maybe," Abbie murmured doubtfully.

Diana glanced up sharply. "What do *you* think her problem was?"

The woman's gaze seemed to turn inward. "The poor child probably couldn't study for wondering what's to become of... of her summers after her uncle's gone and sold this place."

"Mr. Prescott is going to sell Cliff Haven?"

Abbie nodded indignantly. "After it's been in the family for four generations, too."

Diana felt the imprudent stirrings of concern and she paused. But only for a moment. "Abbie, how long have you worked here?"

"Oh, let's see. It'll be fifty-seven years come October."

Diana's eyes snapped wide open.

"I've known them all, even Zeke, the one who built the place. But he was real old, died the year after I came. Then Kate and Justin took over. David's grandparents." Abbie's eyes brightened. "Those were grand days! We had a staff of twenty people then, even though it was the depression. Parties on weekends, all the bedrooms full of guests.''

"Sounds exciting.''

"Oh, it was. Things got a little quieter during the last reign,'' she continued, fondly mocking a family she obviously loved. "There were still parties, but Miss Loretta was a lady,'' she pronounced with significant dignity.

"David's mother?''

Abbie nodded. "She was the most beautiful woman in all society. I used to tell my Andrew she had royal blood in her. She and Walter made a dashing couple. He was very handsome, too. Like all the Prescotts, don't you think?''

Diana was confused by the heat flushing her face. She had to admit that the Prescott she'd just met had, well, riveting looks. But *handsome?*

"How about the present reign? What are they like?''

"They? Why, there's only David and Evelyn now.''

"David never married?'' Diana blushed harder, hearing the curiosity that had unwittingly slipped into her tone.

"No.'' Abbie answered simply, yet almost evasively, Diana thought.

"So, not much goes on here anymore?''

"No. They…they have their lives.…'' Abbie shuffled to the door. Diana followed, lost in speculation.

"Now, listen, child. If you need anything, don't hesitate to come over to the house and give a holler.''

"Thank you,'' Diana said, though she had no intention of going anywhere near the house while David Prescott was in it. "And you be careful on those wet stairs.''

As soon as the housekeeper was gone, Diana put her mind to settling in. It was a cute little place, a place that would provide peace and solitude for nearly two months. And she would be hanged before she'd let anyone turn it into a prison!

CHAPTER THREE

DIANA AWOKE to the crashing of waves, the caw of gulls, the smell of wet grass and pungent salt air. She blinked open her eyes and then remembered. She was in Newport.

She slipped out of bed and went to the window. The sun was shining brightly, turning the lingering beads of rain on her screen into jewels. She leaned on the sill and let all the new sights and sounds and smells wash over her. This morning she was definitely glad she'd come to Newport.

She only wished she felt more rested. Unfortunately, she'd tossed and turned for too many hours. David Prescott seemed to be sitting there all night long, right behind her eyes, reminding her she was not welcome here.

She'd tried to feel sorry for him. Her unexpected and undoubtedly painful attack had given him every reason to be angry. But nothing she told herself worked. She could only continue to see him as a cold insulting brute!

The best thing, she decided, was simply to forget him. He had nothing to do with her duties here. Besides, he'd probably be leaving on one of his business trips soon, and with any luck, she'd never run into him again.

She left the window and padded out to the kitchen to make herself some coffee. She wished she could call Skip and tell him she'd arrived safely, but she knew from her search last night that the carriage house had no phone.

Feeling rather cut off from the outside world, she went into the bathroom and turned on the shower. At least she had hot water!

By ten o'clock, she had her hair blow-dried and arranged in a neat chignon. She'd applied her makeup lightly but carefully, and slipped on a proper little dress of cream-colored linen. She'd even struggled into nylons. Nervously, she decided she was as ready for the day as she would ever be. Now she could only hope that Mrs. Osborne wasn't a female version of her overbearing brother!

She settled into a chair overlooking the courtyard and opened her copy of *Moby Dick,* the first novel she and Cissy would be tackling. But after reading the same passage three times, she tossed the book aside. She longed to get outside and take an exploratory walk around the grounds. She longed to breathe the fresh salt air. But, considering the narrow parameters Mr. Prescott had set for her, she immediately dismissed the idea.

Damn the man and his stupid rules! And damn him doubly for continually intruding on her thoughts after she'd vowed to ignore him.

Well, he certainly couldn't object to her making a simple call home, she thought, rising determinedly from her chair.

Nevertheless, her legs felt like rubber as she crossed the courtyard. After taking a deep calming breath, she lifted the brass door-knocker and let it fall.

"Yes?" It was Mr. Prescott, sharp and impatient. Diana glanced up and around the shadows of the portico, wondering where his voice was coming from. "Yes, what do you want, Miss White?"

"Sorry to disturb you, Mr. Prescott." She felt a bit like Dorothy standing before the gates of Oz. "Mr. Prescott, may I use your phone for a quick call home?" She wondered if he could hear the hammering of her heart.

"Yes, yes." Abruptly he cut their connection. Diana stared at the door uncertainly. Was he coming to meet her? Was he sending someone else? The next moment, the intercom hummed back into life. "Well, are you going to stand there all day? Let yourself in, Miss White." Then he was gone again.

She opened the heavy door and inched into the cool marble-floored foyer. His voice drifted from a room to her left. The door was open. She peeked in. A library.

He was pacing across a red Persian rug, a phone to his ear. Lines like quotation marks furrowed his brow. "If you can bring the cost down to two dollars a unit, we'll take the lot. Otherwise, I'm afraid we'll have to look elsewhere."

When he noticed Diana, his pacing stopped, and just for a moment he looked a bit off balance. She supposed she looked different today—efficient, professional, maybe even pretty.

But if *her* appearance surprised him, *his* completely bowled her over. She knew she was staring but she couldn't stop. It was amazing what a shower and a shave could do for a man. His hair was brushed back in a semblance of civility, and in place of yesterday's scruffy clothes, he now wore a blue cotton sweater and pleated white trousers, looking for all the world as if he'd just stepped out of a glossy yachting magazine.

Yet, in spite of this new image, she realized he still made her shiver with an intimation of danger. She felt an almost physical release as he returned his attention to his phone conversation.

"Good. My representative will meet with you next Thursday then... Nice talking to you, too." He put the phone down on the desk and stared at it for a moment, lost in thought.

"Mr. Pres—"

"Just a moment." He lifted the receiver again and punched out a number. Diana huffed and decided to sit down.

"Max. Hi. David..."

Diana's attention shifted to his face. Lean, determined, the face of a winner. It was also the face of someone you wouldn't want to cross.

"I'm sending Lou out to Stuttgart next week, but I want you to go with him... Exactly. That factory doesn't have a chance unless we get those parts on our terms." He was pacing nervously again although his voice still ran smooth and strong. "Sure enough. See you Monday." He put down the phone and finally turned to Diana, though it was a moment before his thoughts seemed to catch up to him.

She rose from her seat. "I'm really sorry to disturb you, but I promised my brother I'd call him when I got here."

He went around his cluttered desk and collapsed into the cracked leather chair behind it. His stare was unnerving. Cool, judgmental. Nevertheless Diana felt her cheeks warming uncomfortably. "Sure. But make it brief. My sister should be here any minute."

She walked to the desk and picked up the receiver, glancing meaningfully in his direction, but evidently he had no intention of leaving the room. Instead, he picked up a newspaper, the *Sunday New York Times,* and rustled open the business section. For a person so hung up on privacy, he certainly didn't think much about hers.

"Hi, Skip? It's me... Yes, I got here just fine..."

As she talked, she noticed David's eyes lift from the paper occasionally to flick over her, and she was dismayed to realize that her own eyes were fixed on him each time. But for the life of her, she still couldn't stop staring. Not that he was a man she could actually be attracted to. A man had to be warm, sensitive, have a sense of humor. And as far as she could see, David Prescott possessed none of these qualities. But she had to admit Abbie was right. He really was handsome. Objectively speaking, of course.

She could hear voices over the phone. "Is that Dan and Sylvia? Are you people heading out to church together?... I won't keep you, then... Oh, is Robin there, too?... Yes, put her on... Hi, Robin. How's my punkin today?"

Over the rim of the paper, she noticed Mr. Prescott's face screw up with disgust. Well, excuse *me!* Did he think that every call a person made had to determine the fate of whole factories? Again his eyes met hers, seemingly drawn by her thinking about him. Disturbingly blue, they became like physical prods, hurrying her conversation along.

Luckily, Skip came back on the line then and asked for a number where she could be reached. She began to read it off the phone, only to have a hand come down over it swiftly.

"Skip, don't call here. I'll call you... Yes, I've got to go, too."

She almost slammed down the receiver. "Thank you," she said tightly.

"That's an unlisted number, Miss White." He sat back, folded the newspaper and flung it onto a nearby window seat. Next to it, like alien visitors from the future, stood a new fax machine and a large computer. "I think you and I ought to have another talk," he said.

Diana felt her palms go clammy. She was Dorothy again, about to confront the fire and roar of the Great Oz. But she would *not* let him know that.

"Sure." She pulled a chair closer and sat before he could invite her to. She lifted her chin confidently, and when he opened his mouth to speak, she beat him to it. "I'm glad to see you suffered no lasting effects from our meeting yesterday." His lips parted again, but again she interrupted. "I'm sorry. It was a terrible thing to do, but I was *so* nervous about your watchdogs..."

"Mace has no effect on dogs," he finally slipped in.

"It doesn't? Oh." That slowed her momentum.

"I'm not condemning you for carrying Mace, Miss White. A person can never be too cautious. Just keep it away from me. Okay?"

Diana waited to see if he would apologize in turn. But obviously he didn't see anything wrong with his abrasiveness yesterday. "Is there anything else you wanted to talk about?" She managed a small smile.

"Uh, yes," he said vaguely, sounding a bit like someone who's lost his train of thought. "I'd like to know how long this tutoring of yours is going to take."

"About eight weeks."

"That long? Hmm. Can it be hurried up a bit?"

Diana was about to say maybe. "No."

"Hmm." He touched his fingertips together as he rocked back and forth in the creaking old chair, thinking. It was then that Diana noticed the papers on his desk. They looked familiar. It was downright uncanny but...yes, they *were*. They were her records! Transcripts of grades, applications, letters of recommendation, department reviews. Within seconds, her blood was roiling. Where did he get them? Who was this man that he *could* get them?

Before she could say anything, however, two cars pulled into the courtyard.

"That's probably my sister now."

Diana rose from her chair uncertainly. "Are you going out to meet her?"

"No. I have a few more calls to make."

So she'd have to go out and introduce herself. She was sure her eyes were spitting fire by now, but he merely reached for the phone and began to dial—telling her in his inimitable way that she was dismissed.

By the time she reached the portico, she'd managed to swallow her anger. Car doors were already opening and people were piling out. Diana froze in her tracks. *That* was not the Cissy Osborne she remembered. The Cissy she knew opted for neat preppy outfits with a wholesome outdoorsy look. The Cissy she knew smiled interminably and wore her shiny brown hair in a bouncy bob. But the girl slouching out of the station wagon down there in the courtyard made Diana want to cry.

She'd clipped her hair scalp-close over one ear and shaved a lightning bolt into it. The other side, left chin-length, was streaked with green dye. Her face was powdered white, her lips painted stark red, and she was wearing a skintight tube top and jeans torn in all the most unlikely places. It wasn't so much the outfit that got to Diana. She'd seen the punk look before, even at Fairview. It was just that it seemed such a drastic change for Cissy.

"Hi, Cissy. Good to see you again." Diana approached the girl with a smile, determined to hide her reaction.

Cissy's eyes darted up and back to the ground. "Hi, Miss White." A pink wash of embarrassment shone through her ghostly makeup. Diana's heart went out to her. Something was definitely wrong.

"Miss White?"

Diana turned reluctantly toward the voice. A thin dark-haired woman was holding out her hand. "I'm Evelyn Osborne, Cissy's mother."

"Oh. Pleased to meet you."

"Have you been here long?"

"I just got here yesterday."

"Well, I'm certainly glad you agreed to join us this summer. It's a real break for Cissy." It was impossible not to notice the helpless look the woman cast in her daughter's direction. "I'm pleased we managed to get someone from Fairview, too. I have a high regard for all the instructors there. I went there myself when I was a girl."

"Which was only a couple of years ago, I'll have you know," said a robust middle-aged man unlocking the back of the station wagon.

Evelyn laughed, easing the worry lines from her thin face. "Miss White, this is Emmet Thorndike. He was kind enough to make the trip with us from New York."

Diana shook his hand. He was handsome, with smiling green eyes and a personality that seemed cheerful and relaxed. He had red hair, peppered with gray, and wore a plaid shirt and bright green golf pants—an oddball, she decided, among all these dark gloomy people.

A moment later, the courtyard was full of activity. Two extra maids, up from New York for the summer, had emerged from the second car, and Abbie had come out of the house, accompanied by a short gnarled man of about sixty who Diana soon learned was the caretaker, James. Then they were all hugging each other and shaking hands and saying how good it was to be back at Cliff Haven.

All but David Prescott, that is. He preferred to stay inside. Making business calls. On Sunday morning. What could his heart be made of? she wondered. Though she'd accepted this job partly to get away from her overbearing brothers, now she couldn't help thinking of them—and how much they could teach Mr. Prescott about simple courtesy.

"Have you met my brother yet?"

Aware that she'd been gazing at the library window, she turned in time to notice Mrs. Osborne swallow uncomfortably.

"Uh, yes." That's all she could say without revealing her own discomfort. "Mrs. Osborne, I was wondering," she went on quickly, "if it would be all right if I had a phone installed."

"Oh, of course." But then the woman paused. "I suppose I should clear it with David first."

Diana frowned. It seemed even Mrs. Osborne had to get his permission before making the simplest of decisions.

The trunk lid was lifted and soon everyone was pitching in to unload luggage. "When would you like me to start Cissy's lessons?" Diana asked, gripping the handle of a large case with Cissy's name on it.

"Let's see, tomorrow's the Fourth of July. Tuesday? Is that convenient for you?" Although Mrs. Osborne resembled her brother physically, she had none of his aloofness or acerbity. On the contrary, she seemed eager to please, insecure, even nervous at times, causing Diana to wonder if this house was filled with nothing but problems and enigmas.

"Tuesday's fine with me. Okay, Cissy? Nine a.m., up in my apartment?"

"Sure." The girl tried to smile but only managed to look mildly nauseated.

Together, Diana and her young pupil carried the case up the steps. At the front door, she hesitated. Should she go in? Did she have his majesty's okay? Immediately, she realized how absurd the thought was. Why shouldn't she go in? How could she not? Even Abbie was working. Besides, she wanted to spend a little time with Cissy, to establish a bond as soon as possible. Diana wasn't sure what was bothering the girl, but she did know she wanted to help.

David Prescott came to the library door as they were passing, and her heart began pounding unnaturally.

"Hey, Uncle David." Diana was amazed to see Cissy smile.

"Hey, kid." She was equally amazed that he didn't comment on his niece's hair. But then she realized he probably hadn't even noticed it. His eyes hadn't left Diana for a second.

She lifted her chin and walked on with as much dignity as she could muster, although her knees were dangerously weak. She wished she knew why she was reacting this way; it was so unlike her....

Cissy led her across the marbled foyer and into an enormous sitting room. Tall French doors at the opposite end opened onto a terrace. In the adjacent dining room, Diana caught a glimpse of a gleaming cherrywood table that could easily accommodate a party of twenty guests, and beyond that...a billiard room? In the other direction was a music room, oval in shape and half glassed-in by ornately beveled windows. Sunlight, caught in their facets, danced upon a grand piano and across the parquet floor.

The staircase was to the right of the sitting room. It was a dramatic marble affair, curving up to a horseshoe balcony that overhung the room below. Off the balcony were the bedrooms, with their pale Aubusson rugs, mantels shipped from castles in Europe, wall silks from France, and adjoining baths carved out of marble.

Cliff Haven was little short of fabulous. It was the definitive summer place, built for guests, meant for entertaining. Yet, as Diana walked its tapestry-hung halls, she got the oddest feeling she was wandering through a lifeless shrine to the past. The antiques, though quite valuable, she was sure, were a jumble of differing styles. The wall coverings and draperies looked dingy and worn. She felt sorry for the old place. Apparently its owner couldn't have cared less about it, and hadn't for quite some time.

"This is my room," Cissy finally announced with a sigh of boredom.

"How beautiful, Cissy!"

"It used to be my mother's when she was young. It's always been 'the girl's room,'" she drawled with mocking gravity as they lowered the case. Finally free of her burden, Cissy kicked off her sandals and plunked herself down on the bed.

Diana walked to a window and gazed out on the back lawn. The grass was vibrantly green after yesterday's rain, and the gardens were blooming. There was a gazebo down by the seawall, a three-tiered fountain in the center, though she suspected it was broken, and way to the left, a boarded-up stable. Beyond all this was the ocean, glittering like endless silver dust. Whether she liked Cliff Haven or not, Diana had to admit it was worth a fortune for its view alone. She turned. Voices drifted from other rooms along the corridor. Abbie's voice. Evelyn Osborne's.

"Your mother's very nice," she commented casually.

Cissy just shrugged. "What do you think of David?"

Diana felt her pulse jump again, as it always did when he was mentioned. "I don't think your mother cleared my coming here with him."

"Why? Did he give you a hard time?"

"Slightly."

"Don't take it personally." Cissy paused, eyes lost to inner thoughts. "And don't be upset with my mother. She didn't tell him about you till the last minute because she didn't want to give him the chance to veto you. And he most likely would have, too. He doesn't like anybody but us staying here, and she knew I absolutely had to get tutored this summer. It took a lot for her to do that." Cissy pulled a tissue from a dispenser on her nightstand and began to rub off her makeup.

Diana returned to gazing out the window, her frown deepening. "Who's Emmet Thorndike?"

After a heavy pause, "Nobody."

Diana swiveled around, one eyebrow arched in a stern question mark.

"He's the president of one of my uncle's plants."

"Is that all?"

Cissy's lips pressed into a hard bloodless line. "Yes," she said, and Diana knew that was not all. An inner voice, which sounded remarkably like Mr. Prescott's, reminded her not to go prying where she didn't belong, and yet her instincts told her the time was right. Besides, if it concerned Cissy's well-being, she *did* belong.

"Is he dating your mother?"

Cissy snorted contemptuously.

"I see. And you don't approve?"

"At their age? It's ridiculous."

"It must be difficult. You've had your mother all to yourself for the past eight years."

Cissy averted her peevish eyes. "I don't really care, Miss White."

"Well, hang in. Things'll work out." Diana knew she'd pressed far enough. For now, anyway. "I should be going. You must have a lot to do, first day here and all." She crossed the room to check the time on a porcelain clock on the fireplace mantel. "You'll be wanting to have lunch soon, too." She was about to turn away when she spotted a small framed photograph beside the clock. She picked it up before any inner voice could warn her not to.

"Cissy, who are these children? Is this your mother and David?"

The girl glanced over. "Uh-huh. Walter, too. My mother's other brother."

Diana looked closer. She hadn't realized there *was* another brother. The three youngsters, all with similar features and the same dark hair, were sitting on a blanket in bathing suits. Evelyn was the oldest, a teenager at the time.

As usual, David was scowling. Even at the age of ten or eleven, he looked haughty and detached. Beside him was the younger boy, slim and tanned and brightly smiling, one arm linked affectionately through his sullen older brother's, the other wrapped around the neck of a huge wet Labrador. Sunlight streaked his raven-smooth hair and gleamed within his clear trusting eyes.

"Your Uncle Walter sure was cute."

"Walter?" Cissy hopped off the bed.

"Mm. This adorable child with his arm around the dog."

Cissy threw back her head and hooted with laughter. "Miss White, that isn't Walter."

"It isn't?" Then color flamed in Diana's cheeks. She felt it creep right up to her scalp.

Cissy stared at her with an awkward quivering smile, and perhaps thinking she had dealt her tutor's composure a mortal blow, she also blushed and began to stammer. "H-he's the youngest, David is. We don't see Uncle Walter anymore. Not since he and David... I mean... He lives in Pennsylvania with Aunt Glenda and their two boys. I don't know them. We don't visit. Uncle David and Glenda..."

Diana looked up, sharply curious, but Cissy had gone silent, her eyes fixed on a point somewhere over Diana's shoulder.

On a sudden wave of dread, Diana spun around. There stood David Prescott, looming on the threshold like a huge dark storm about to break.

"I'm sorry," she whispered, not knowing what she had done, only that something was terribly wrong. Unsteadily, she placed the frame back on the mantel.

"What's up, Uncle David?" Cissy sounded unnaturally cheerful.

But he didn't answer. He just went on glaring at Diana until she thought she would die.

"Well, if that's all I can help with, Cissy..." She took a step toward the hall.

"Where are you going, Miss White?"

"I'm sorry. I have to go. I ... There are errands I have to run in the city. Excuse me," she said, her voice growing fainter. But David Prescott refused to move. She glanced up, her eyes defenseless against his.

Was this really the same person she had just seen in the photograph? Were these the same eyes that had once looked out on the world with such openness and love? At the moment they looked more like the eyes of an animal—an animal who has been whipped until it's grown irrevocably mean.

"Please," she begged weakly.

After what seemed an eternity, he stepped aside. She was barely down the stairs before tears flooded her vision.

CHAPTER FOUR

DIANA CLOSED THE DOOR of her apartment and turned the lock. She told herself she wasn't going to cry, but the tears kept coming. She felt miserable, and the worst part was she didn't have the foggiest idea why. David Prescott hadn't said a word. It was only that she'd never seen a look like that before, so angry, so pained. What had she done?

True, he'd told her to confine her activities to the carriage house, and just this morning she'd used his phone, met his family and staff, and gone up to one of the bedrooms. But did actions as ordinary as these really warrant such a reaction?

No, intuition told her it had more to do with that photograph. Had she stumbled across a family skeleton? The estranged brother perhaps? What had David done to the poor guy?

Diana blew her nose, still denying that she was crying. Something was definitely rotten in this state of Denmark, and if she had any sense at all, she would let it lie. Not only was it none of her business, but she had enough problems of her own.

She picked up her handbag, checked her appearance in a mirror by the door and headed down the stairs. The time was ripe for getting away and doing some sightseeing. With any luck everyone would be asleep when she returned.

She backed her car out of the garage and turned it around in the courtyard. But just as she was about to head down the drive, the front door of the main house opened and David Prescott stepped out. Diana's lungs felt on fire. He looked directly at her as he descended the stairs. She had the oddest feeling he wanted to speak to her.

Well, David Prescott could go straight to hell. She'd had enough of him for one day. She stepped on the gas so hard her tires squealed and left a black scar on the bricks.

FOR HOURS THAT AFTERNOON Diana walked the narrow streets of the harbor district, admiring the beautifully restored homes of the colonial era. And when she tired of that, she wandered down America's Cup Avenue to the wharves, lined with countless little shops. In spite of the emotional turmoil that had driven her here, she realized she was famished. She found a cheerful outdoor café where she ordered a hamburger and listened to a trio of country fiddlers.

Feeling infinitely better, she continued on her way. She ended up buying a bag of peach potpourri to chase away the mustiness at the carriage house, five plants because the place was in dire need of something green and alive, and a bag of exotically flavored jelly beans simply because she couldn't resist them.

Then, since she still wasn't ready to face Cliff Haven again, she drove to the Bellevue Avenue area in search of The Breakers, the seventy-two-room Vanderbilt mansion styled after an Italian palazzo. When that tour ended, she zipped down the road and visited Rosecliff, a replica of the Grand Trianon at Versailles.

Somehow, she managed to stay out till nearly eleven o'clock, but she could forestall the inevitable no longer.

How dark Cliff Haven was after the bustle of the harbor! Nothing stirred. Only the ocean, rushing and retreating over the rocky shore below the cliff.

Diana washed quickly and settled into bed with *Moby Dick*. Totally exhausted from her busy day, she fell asleep with her light still on. But in the middle of the night she awoke again. She sat up, suddenly fully alert and listening. Her travel alarm read two forty-five.

She slipped out of bed and made herself a cup of hot milk, but it did little to calm her restlessness. She wandered to the window and stared at the main house sleeping across the way. The next minute, she tied on her sneakers, threw a sweater over her nightgown and slipped out the door. She glanced at the house once again and frowned, remembering the unreasonable emotions its owner had aroused in her that day. He was an autocrat, that's what he was. And autocracy was meant to be defied!

She found her way around the carriage house and crossed the back lawn. Before long she reached the seawall. It was a beautiful soft night. Below her, waves were rolling in, just a glimmer of stars sparkling over their foam.

And then her heart stopped. She clutched the wall and leaned forward, squinting. No, her eyes were not deceiving her. There really was someone out there.

A stairway led from the lawn, down the cliff to a pier of some sort, and at the end of that pier, with dark waves surging all around, stood a solitary man. From his size and build, it was unmistakably David Prescott.

What in heaven's name was he doing out there at three in the morning, gazing at the ocean and looking so... so lost? Was he communing with the night? Pining for lost love? Was he plotting some ungodly business takeover? What was going on inside that head, behind those gorgeous frightening blue eyes?

Diana knew she should get back to the carriage house. He would be angry if he discovered her wandering the grounds. Besides, he wasn't worth her curiosity. He was nothing but a ... a businessman, an ill-mannered bad-tempered one at that.

But still she lingered, drawn to watching him as if he were a mystery just beginning to unfold. In fact, she watched until David himself turned and began to tread up the pier. And if she went back to her bed imagining there was more to him than met the eye, well, that was an indulgence she supposed she could tolerate for one night.

EARLY THE NEXT MORNING Diana heard movement in the garage below. She was already dressed and busy, even though it was a holiday. The carriage house was passably clean, but not as fresh as she would have liked it, and she'd decided to spend the day scrubbing—and trying not to think about the Fourth of July cookout back home, or the annual softball game, or the family from whom she was supposedly here to declare her independence.

Again the noise. Mildly curious, she put down her scrub brush and went to the window. The blue sedan was pulling out of the garage. It stopped at the main house and James got out to lift the hood. At the same time David Prescott appeared, briefcase in hand. He was wearing a dark suit, white shirt and conservative navy tie. Even from a distance, Diana was impressed. The suit hugged his lean powerful body with subtle sensuality even while presenting the most proper business form.

Could this really be the same man who had roared up on a Harley just two days before? she wondered. She wished she weren't so intrigued, but he was such a study in contradictions.

When she realized he was staring up at the carriage house, she jumped back from the window, her heart lodged in her throat.

Get back to work, you idiot! she told herself. She resumed washing the floor, but it wasn't long before she was peeking over the sill again.

He was pacing the courtyard while the caretaker tinkered with the engine. He looked preoccupied, one hand occasionally combing through his hair. Suddenly he paused and Diana's heartbeat seemed to pause along with him. Then, as if powered by some momentous decision, he loped toward her stairs. In less than a second, it seemed, he was at the door, peering down at her through the screen. She got up and wiped her hands on her shorts. She couldn't find her voice as she opened the door.

And for a while it seemed neither could he.

His high cheekbones and straight, perfectly arrogant nose were brushed-stroked with sun, and he exuded a clean masculine fragrance that momentarily derailed her train of thought.

"Good morning," he finally said.

The only reply she could muster was a confused nod.

"I just came over to see if everything was all right here. For my niece's lessons, I mean."

"Yes, fine." She regained enough presence of mind to remember to scowl.

He nodded with a serious businesslike economy. At the same time, though, she was aware of his eyes traveling over her with an interest she found disturbing, taking in her long loosely tied hair, the heightened color of her cheeks, the snug fit of her cutoffs.

"Well, if there's anything you need..."

"No, nothing."

His gaze finally released her and roamed to the curtainless windows, over the stacked furniture and new plants, and back down to the pail of sudsy water at her feet. For a moment, Diana felt sure he was going to sail into her for up-ending the place. His eyes narrowed and he shook his head slightly as if in exasperation. But that was all.

Diana didn't know what to say, and her speechlessness confused her. Why couldn't she just boot the man down the stairs as he deserved, instead of standing here feeling self-conscious and uncomfortable and so very *aware* of him? She didn't understand this one bit. She thoroughly disliked him, and he disliked her. So why was she feeling these stirrings of femininity under his gaze? This was the wrong time, the wrong place and he was most definitely the wrong man.

"The car's all set, Mr. Prescott," the caretaker called.

"Be right down." He turned back to Diana and the hardness that usually rendered his face unreadable seemed to drop for a second. A look that resembled frustration troubled his eyes. "I also came over to say—"

"Your plane's leaving in fifteen minutes. Really, sir, we've got to hurry."

"Damn!" she thought he whispered. He raked Diana's features with a thoroughness that left her slightly breathless. "Well, take care. And stay out of trouble while I'm gone, hm?"

Diana nodded, blinking at him with wide incredulous brown eyes. His appearance was hard enough to handle this early on a Monday morning, but this sudden overture of . . . of what? Why *was* he here? she wondered.

He said nothing more. He simply turned and hurried down the stairs, moving with a masculine sensuality that finally made her realize why he'd frightened her so much.

DIANA WAS HANGING curtains over a makeshift line in the bathroom when Evelyn Osborne knocked on her door.

"What *are* you doing?" the older woman exclaimed.

"Oh, hi." Diana came out to the front room. "I hope you don't mind."

"No, of course not. But you should have said something if you didn't find the place adequate."

"Oh, but I did. I do." Diana tugged the old vacuum cleaner aside. "I get a kick out of cleaning, that's all. Not everyday drudge cleaning, mind you, but I love to turn a house inside out occasionally. Come in."

"Thanks. I won't be long. I just came to ask if you'd like to watch the Bristol Parade with us. Emmet is sailing us over."

Diana guessed she looked confused.

"Bristol isn't far, but the traffic's horrendous on the Fourth. Going by boat is the fastest way to travel. Come on, Diana. It's a fabulous parade, the oldest in the country. It takes hours and hours to watch. Besides, you can't spend the holiday cleaning."

Diana began to smile. She loved parades. So much for not having anything in common with "wealthy society people."

"I'd love to. Let me change."

"Great. Mind if I stay? There's something else I'd like to talk about. Go ahead. I'll talk through the door."

Diana hurried to her room, intrigued.

"I heard about your little melee with my brother at the gate."

Through the door, Diana heard the woman's soft chuckle. "It wasn't funny, Mrs. Osborne."

"No, I don't suppose it was. If there's anything David can't abide it's feeling vulnerable. And please, call me Evelyn."

Diana slipped on a corn-yellow blouse and a pair of matching trousers. "He's a hard person to understand, Mrs.—Evelyn."

"That's for sure! In an article *Fortune* did a few years ago, he was described as industry's lone hawk, King Midas, a white knight with an assassin's stare..." She paused and chuckled. "His inscrutability drives people batty, especially reporters searching for metaphors. And his competitors."

Diana opened the door. "Evelyn, something tells me he wouldn't approve of our talking about him."

"You're right again. There isn't much he values more than his privacy. But I don't want you going through the summer hating him, or misunderstanding, and that's why I'm going to talk anyway."

"What's to misunderstand?" Diana picked up a brush and hastily pulled it through her hair.

"Everything, if you don't really know David." Evelyn sighed and walked to the window. "He wasn't always so difficult, Diana. Believe it or not, he was once a pretty terrific kid—cheerful, loving, certainly the smartest of us three. I have another brother, you know," she admitted hesitantly. "Walter."

"Yes. Cissy mentioned him briefly." Diana put down the brush and left her room to come sit on the couch.

"Mm. David was so bright, always taking things apart to see how they worked, always inventing things..." She sighed as if under the weight of too many memories. "He was a lot like my mother. They were very close. She taught him how to ride. They played tennis..." Evelyn's brow furrowed as she gazed out the window. "Sometimes I can still see them sitting together at the piano. Even when he was practically a baby and couldn't really play yet, she loved to hear him bang away and sing. She would laugh so hard..." Evelyn was quiet a long fragile moment.

"Walter, on the other hand, was my father's favorite," she continued in a firmer voice, moving from the window to pace restlessly. "He was named after him, talked like him, even walked like him. But being the firstborn male and all that chauvinistic nonsense..." She waved her hand dismissively. "The point I meant to make was simply that David was an open loving person at one time, and I'd like to think he still is, deep down.

"But when he was sixteen, my mother died. I promised myself when I was walking over here I wouldn't get maudlin about it, and I won't." She lifted her chin and attempted to smile. "Let me just say that she died in a plane crash. My father used to fly his own plane back then, and one Saturday morning they were coming into Newport and the engine failed."

"I'm so sorry, Evelyn."

"Somehow, my father managed to survive, but he was never as vigorous as he'd been before the accident. He died five years later." Evelyn came to sit on the couch beside Diana.

"What a dreadful experience. For you all."

"But for David especially. You see, he'd gone to the airport to meet them. He'd just got his license and was eager to show them how well he could drive."

Diana clutched her hands tightly in her lap. "You mean, he saw the crash?"

Evelyn nodded, and something inside Diana pulled tight, like a fist clenching.

"He was so young and, as I said, very close to my mother. I can't imagine what he went through, being right there, being the one to call the ambulance, and to face the police and all the insanity of the press. But whatever it was, he suffered it silently, all the while taking charge with a strength and self-possession I couldn't pull off even now."

Diana watched a patch of sunlight dance across the floor. Though she still didn't feel any sympathy for the man who'd bullied her at the gate, she felt a kind of heartbreak for the boy in Evelyn's story.

"After the funeral I insisted he come live with me for a while. I'd recently married, and my home was a slightly happier place than Maplecroft in those days."

"Maplecroft?"

"Mm. Our house in Pennsylvania. Walter and Glenda live there now." Diana saw a shadow trouble the woman's expression, and again she wondered about this Walter and why he seemed to disturb everyone so. And Glenda. What part did she play in all this? Her name, so fleetingly mentioned, nonetheless burned in Diana's thoughts as if branded there.

"David stayed with me for two years. It was fun, except...well, I don't know what I expected. Maybe to see him bounce back to the carefree teenager he'd been before the accident. But he'd changed, and there was no going back.

"Oh, everything seemed normal on the surface. He finished school with honors and went on to Harvard. But the David I knew, that open loving boy, had retreated into himself, and he kept on retreating with every..." Her voice trailed off evasively. "Let's just say that David's life hasn't been a smooth one. My mother's death was only the first setback. He's become a cautious, tough and very independent man, Diana, some might even say bitter and disillusioned. But as I said, he wasn't always this way."

Diana sat very still, contemplating Evelyn's words. "I guess this is supposed to have some bearing on my run-in with him, isn't it?"

Evelyn nodded. "Cliff Haven used to be a marvelous place when we were kids. It was David's favorite spot in all the world. And my mother's. But her death changed everything. We came here occasionally after she was gone, but never for long. We sold the horses, all our boats, we cut back the staff. Needless to say, there were no more parties, and we stopped inviting friends. After the accident, the house just sort of went to sleep. Cissy and I started coming back a few summers ago because, frankly, I missed the old place and the happy times. But I guess David's grown accustomed to it lying fallow, so to speak. It's been eighteen years, after all, and any change here upsets him.''

"I see. Especially the kind that comes wielding Mace?"

"That kind especially." Evelyn smiled and got to her feet. "Well, we'd better be getting over to that parade. I guess my story can't make living with David any easier. He is what he is, and I suppose he'll never change. But I was hoping you'd find it in your heart to forgive.''

Diana had the oddest feeling she already had.

CHAPTER FIVE

DIANA'S FIRST TWO WEEKS at Cliff Haven passed pleasantly enough. The only incident that marred the time was Abbie's falling ill. For some reason, the woman went on a house-cleaning binge and then had to be confined to bed for three days. Diana felt terrible. She couldn't help thinking it had come as a direct result of her own cleaning spree at the carriage house.

For the most part, Cissy was a cooperative student. She zipped through grammar and essay lessons with the ease Diana remembered her showing the previous year, and though she didn't like *Moby Dick* very much, at least she was trudging through it with a minimum of complaints.

She was usually happy, too. She spent most of her free time at a nearby yacht club and constantly regaled Diana with stories about her friends there and the comical things they did at sailing lessons.

But she wasn't happy all the time. It was fairly obvious that her relationship with her mother wasn't good, though from scattered comments, Diana surmised that it once had been. Almost every day they went their separate ways, Cissy to the yacht club and Evelyn to visit with friends. When they did find the time to be together, Diana sensed they didn't know what to do with it. Evelyn looked uncomfortable; her conversation sounded stiff and solicitous. Cissy, on the other hand, became critical and sarcastic.

Fridays were the worst, and it didn't take much for Diana to put two and two together and come up with Emmet Thorndike. He usually arrived on Friday to visit for the weekend.

She tried not to think about it, but the situation saddened her nonetheless. She really liked Emmet. She joined him and Evelyn for a round of golf one morning, and it was then that she noticed how easily he could lift the worry lines from Evelyn's face.

Cissy, however, continued to resent him. One evening Evelyn invited Diana to the main house for dinner, and though Emmet tried to joke and cajole away the tension that hung over the table, Cissy's rebellious mood won out.

Later that evening, Evelyn came to the carriage house to apologize. That afternoon she'd told Cissy that Emmet had suggested setting a firm date for a wedding. "I don't know what I'm going to do, Diana. I love both of them so much. But of course, Cissy comes first. If it comes to a choice..." Tears welled up in Evelyn's dark blue eyes. Diana felt so bad for her, for them all, and she wondered if David Prescott had any idea what was happening within his family.

He was gone the entire two weeks, but hardly a day went by that Diana didn't think about him. She thought too about the effect his mother's death had had and often found herself wondering what David felt when he came to Cliff Haven. Did he think about that tragic day when he was sixteen? Is that what he associated Cliff Haven with? Or did he come here to remember how it used to be, those happy summer days before the plane crash? Is that why he'd let the place become frozen in time, like Sleeping Beauty's castle?

She wondered, too, about Evelyn's vague hint of other problems contributing to his remoteness. More than ever she suspected they involved the mysterious Walter, maybe even Walter's wife, Glenda.

But what Diana wondered about most was the Sunday morning David left for the airport. Why had he come up to the carriage house? What would he have said if he hadn't been in such a hurry? And why did he have such a disturbing effect on her? Inexplicable though it was, she'd felt real sparks of attraction flying between them.

In retrospect she supposed it was understandable; he'd looked fairly dynamic that morning, and she had simply responded the way any normal healthy female would. She should be relieved. She was coming back to life after the blow Ron had dealt her.

But . . . she wasn't relieved. Good Lord, David Prescott? The idea was absurd!

Maybe she'd let down her guard and allowed herself to be attracted to him precisely because he *was* so unapproachable and incapable of responding in kind. Or maybe it was just this place, this fairy-tale setting, which bore so little resemblance to the reality of her life back home.

But no matter what the reason, she knew these stirrings of attraction meant nothing. She still wasn't ready to trust anyone enough to get involved again. Maybe she would change her mind some day, but the man who caused the change would surely be someone a lot more human than David Prescott.

THE WEEKEND finally came around again and with it another invitation to go sailing on Emmet's boat. Diana was glad to learn that Cissy had agreed to join them.

Wearing a long loose blouse over her simple black maillot, Diana met Evelyn and Cissy on the back lawn precisely at noon. They were to meet Emmet down at the pier below the cliff. Diana had been sailing only the one previous time, on the Fourth of July, and frankly she was still nervous.

"Oh, did I mention that David is back?" Evelyn said as the three descended the stairs down the cliff. "Emmet has actually convinced him to come along, too."

Diana's head jerked up and her heart began to race. She glanced out to the small white craft bobbing on the waves, and sure enough, there he was. Who else was so tall, had hair that dark or a back so smoothly muscled?

"And he's got Barbara with him." Cissy sounded as if she were squealing on a naughty brother.

"That's enough, young lady." Evelyn's comment was soft but sharp.

Diana searched the boat. Yes, a third person was indeed with them, a blonde, dressed in a white bikini, sunning herself on the bow.

Diana didn't want to go any farther. David would be angry. This was a private outing. She had no business tagging along. The last person he'd want to see today was *her*, the idiot who'd introduced herself to him with a blast of Mace.

Yet she had no choice but to continue.

David was busy removing sail covers. He was wearing only jeans, tight-fitting faded denims and a pair of scuffed deck shoes. His broad muscled back gleamed like mahogany as he worked. Though he was a tall man, he moved with amazing agility. He turned and his eyes linked with hers. The roar of the ocean died away, and all she heard was the thundering of her heart. She knew what he was thinking: here she was again, the constant intruder!

What *she* was thinking, however, was that she'd never seen such a ruggedly handsome man in all her life. Two weeks had done nothing to put her attraction into perspective. Here under the open sky, he took her breath away.

"Hello, David," his sister said, greeting him warmly. "Welcome back. I hope your trip went well."

He nodded fractionally, his eyes finally leaving Diana's.

"Hello, Emmet." Evelyn climbed down into the boat and shyly kissed his cheek. "Diana, this is Barbara Benedetto, an old friend of ours," she continued, squinting up at Diana, still rooted to the pier. "Barbara, Diana White, a teacher from Fairview who's staying with us this summer."

The look Diana got from Barbara was cool and appraising. "Hello," was all she said. She was attractive and darkly tanned, her long straight hair perfectly streaked by the sun. Diana glanced at David again. She should have known there would be a woman in his life, but why was the reality making her stomach knot up so tight?

Cissy made an ordeal out of getting on the boat, probably because it was Emmet's. First she emptied her duffel bag on the dock, looking for some vague treasure. Then she insisted on brushing her hair.

"Well, are you coming or not?" David finally asked. It was a moment before Diana realized he was looking at her, not his niece.

"Sorry." She took a deep breath and glanced around for something to hang on to. "I—I'm not much of a sailor." It was painfully obvious David didn't want her aboard.

"Here, let me give you a hand," Emmet said graciously, managing not to draw attention to her insecurity. The bow rocked under her feet, causing her stomach to rise and fall.

"Hang in, you'll get used to it," Cissy called, tossing her bag down. Then at David's nod, she unwound a rope from the mooring and leapt aboard like a young gazelle.

Diana found what she thought was an unobtrusive spot, yet she still seemed to be in everyone's way. "Excuse me," they said, stepping over her legs. "Sorry," they murmured climbing over her shoulders. By the time they were out of the slip, she was sorry she'd agreed to come along. She felt like the proverbial fifth wheel, unneeded and unwanted.

Out on the open water, the wind caught the sails and they were off, skimming so fast she lost her breath. Unneeded, unwanted, and now terrified!

"How are you doing?" an exhilarated Cissy called, forgetting she was supposed to be a rebel.

"Okay, I guess." An expert skier, Diana was hardly a stranger to speed and danger. Surely she could adjust herself to this. She glanced up at David and Barbara, so adept at what they were doing. She ached with envy—and admiration. Two more perfect bodies you couldn't find! David glanced back at her as if he'd sensed her attention, and she averted her eyes, feeling painfully self-conscious.

The boat sliced through the water, into the bay, past Jamestown Island and on past Prudence. Diana's blouse was now drenched with spray, and her skin tingled from sun and wind and drying salt.

"Looks like you've found your sea legs," Evelyn called happily from the bench on the opposite site of the cockpit. Diana laughed, realizing she was no longer clinging, white-knuckled, to the gunwale.

They eventually dropped anchor in a quiet cove. Cissy peeled off her T-shirt and immediately dove overboard for a cooling swim while the others lounged in the sun, sipping exotic rum drinks that Emmet had concocted down in the galley.

What David was doing wasn't actually lounging, though, Diana thought. He was sitting slightly apart from the group, as if denying he was part of the social gathering, his whole body alert and restless. He didn't even appear to be listening to the conversation.

But he was. Diana sensed he was taking particular note of the familiarity with which she, Emmet and Evelyn spoke to each other. His jaw became harder with every joke Emmet cracked about Diana's golf game.

Suddenly, doubts about the wisdom of her being aboard returned to torment her. What was she doing here? She didn't belong with these people. Not with *that* person, anyway. Though he hadn't said one word to her since she'd come aboard, she'd been conscious of his attention all afternoon. It was almost a tangible connection, singing like a telegraph line between them. She'd tried to block him out, but it was impossible. She remained as uncomfortably aware of him as he was of her, she was sure.

"Anybody else care to go for a swim?" Barbara yawned and stretched her golden body.

"Looks inviting, doesn't it?" Emmet drawled.

"Sure does." Barbara stepped onto the bobbing bow.

"I've been hoping someone else would want to go in." Evelyn sprang up eagerly. "Diana?"

"Me? Oh, no. I'll pass." Diana was only a fair swimmer, but worse than that, she had no idea how she would get from the boat into the water. Somehow, through all the grueling sessions at the Y and all the summers spent with her brothers down at the pond, no one had ever been able to teach her to dive.

She noticed David get up and gather empty glasses. Then he disappeared below. With him gone, she breathed a little easier. Evelyn and Emmet dove in, sure and graceful, and began to swim toward Cissy who was floating on a rubber raft nearby.

"So, how long are you going to be at Cliff Haven?" Barbara asked. Oddly, she was still standing on the bow.

"Till the end of August." They were the only ones topside now.

"That long, huh? Lucky you."

Diana shrugged. "It's a job."

The blonde smiled coolly. "In case you're wondering, the answer is yes. David and I *are* seeing one another. We have been for three years."

Diana's dark eyes widened. "I wasn't... that's none of my..."

"Sure it is. You've been trying to figure us out all afternoon."

Diana knew she was right. "Whew! Three years! Are you planning to be married soon?"

Barbara choked out a laugh. "Now what would I do with a husband? I've had two of them already. No, no. David and I have something better than a marriage. We have an understanding."

Diana fixed her attention on a distant motorboat, hoping her feelings weren't showing. Not that she understood what those feelings were exactly. They were too numerous and jumbled to sort. The one thing she did know, though, was that they were upsetting.

"It's a wonderful arrangement," Barbara continued. "Whenever either of us needs an escort, we're there for each other. He knows I'm not out for his money, and he's not out for mine. And neither of us is looking for emotional complications. Basically we're both too independent, the no-strings-attached type. Which is probably the reason we've stayed together so long. What about you? Are you interested in David?"

Barbara's forthrightness had Diana spinning. She began to stammer a denial.

"It's okay if you are—honestly. As I said, there are no strings. Only, you'd better be tougher than you look." Barbara's mouth curled in a small pitying smile. "Because David doesn't have romances, honey. He only has affairs."

"I'm really not interested in him in that way." Diana tried to sound sincere, offended even.

The blonde shrugged. "Sorry to have brought it up then. Well, I'm going in. Coming?" Without waiting for an answer, she dove, slicing through the water with hardly a ripple. Diana wished she could do the same, but for heaven's sake, she'd grown up on a dairy farm in landlocked Vermont! Oh well, maybe this time it would turn out all right.

With her heart in her mouth, Diana lurched forward. There was the familiar moment of weightlessness, and then cold water was rushing over her head and up her nose. She panicked and flailed her arms, not knowing which way was up or down. Salt burned her eyes. Her lungs felt crushed. Hell, this wasn't worth it. Pride be damned!

Just then, she felt an arm around her waist—Barbara to the rescue, no doubt. But the arm was too thick and strong, pulling her up to the surface with an ease few women could manage. When Diana shook the water from her eyes, she was startled to find it was David Prescott. Water was streaming down his black hair and glittering on his long spiked lashes.

"Are you all right?" he asked gruffly.

Diana coughed and nodded. He was holding her tightly, crushed against the hard wall of his chest. "I can swim," she said, coughing again.

The corners of his mouth tightened. "Could've fooled me."

Diana pulled back her head as far as his hold would allow and squinted into his eyes. "Where did you come from so fast?"

"I was coming up from below when I saw you hit the water, and since you looked about as graceful as an egg-beater..." He shifted his hold, bringing his right arm more firmly around her waist.

The embarrassing intimacy of being held so close by a man who obviously found her to be the biggest irritant in his life made her indignant. "I told you, I know how to swim."

"Then why the hell did you make me jump in after you with my pants still on?"

"Oh, no! You still have your pants on?"

"Yes, I still have my pants on," he mimicked.

"*Shoot!* I've done it again, haven't I?"

"Done what?"

"Ruined your day."

"Seems so."

"Hey, you two!" Barbara called. "What are you doing, a water ballet?"

Even with ears clogged with water, Diana caught the annoyance in her voice. She flicked a look at David's dark angular face, only inches from hers. Although the water was cool, his muscular chest felt hot beneath her hands. Suddenly it seemed as if she might explode with the emotions churning inside her. She pushed hard and broke away. With short choppy strokes, she struck out for the horizon. She didn't need this; she didn't need to be out on any damn boat; she didn't need a jealous female on her back; and she certainly didn't need a sarcastic malcontent chipping away at her ego and making her feel unwelcome and self-conscious.

When she had nearly exhausted herself—and her anger— she turned and swam back. Streaming water, she mounted the ladder, which, unfortunately, she hadn't seen before her dive. She knew her eyes were blazing with independence. Everyone else was waiting for her. A vague tension filled their silence, as if they'd only that moment stopped talking about her. She chafed her wet arms, feeling a chill that went clear through to her bones. Her heavy tangled hair stuck to her back. Over Cissy's shoulder, she caught the smug smile on Barbara's lips. She obviously found Diana highly amusing.

Well, the hell with Barbara! The hell with all of them! She didn't need any of this.

David had evidently just come aboard, too. He'd thrown a towel over his head and was briskly rubbing the moisture out of his thick hair.

"Let's take her in," he said to Emmet.

Exhausted, wet and cold, Diana slumped to the deck. She drew up her legs and lowered her forehead to her knees. Goose bumps ran up her arms.

As he walked by, David looked down at her, paused and casually dropped his towel. Then he strode off.

Diana picked up the towel—it was quite wet—and glared at his broad tanned back. "How magnanimous!" she drawled. Then, in a rush of anger, she threw it at his head.

Her aim was off, though, and the towel sailed on by and landed in the water. Color immediately flamed across her already sunburned face.

David froze, watching the towel sink out of sight. Then he turned, stiffly.

"I ought to make you go get that," he said, dangerously quiet. Disturbing lights were dancing in his eyes.

Diana had had enough. Her teeth were grinding so hard she feared they'd crack. She noticed another towel slung over a rail not two feet away, and without thinking, yanked it free and sent it flying overboard, too. "Make me! I dare you!"

David's hands bunched into fists, his jaw hardened, and Diana began to think he was going to accept her dare.

But then a strange expression quivered over his lean face, and the hard edges of his features softened. His stern mouth lifted tentatively at one corner, then curved into a smile. The smile broadened, and he threw back his head and laughed. Not a laugh of mockery or derision, it was just . . . a laugh.

Diana stared at him, openmouthed. She didn't know whether he had gone over the edge or what! He had a brilliant smile, a wonderful set of teeth and—yes—even dimples. And his eyes, they crinkled so delightfully.

He suddenly became aware of everyone's fascinated gaze, and as abruptly as the laughter within him had arisen, it ended. He turned and made himself busy, and for the rest of the journey back, Diana was sure she had imagined the whole thing.

CHAPTER SIX

BUT OF COURSE IT HAD happened, and Diana knew her attitude toward David Prescott would never be quite the same. There was a chink in his armor, a soft spot on his heel. He was human after all, perhaps even pleasantly so. She might be dead wrong, but she hoped not, and suddenly she didn't want to give up trying to find out.

They docked the boat at the yacht club, then returned to Cliff Haven in Emmet's car, detouring on the way to drop Barbara off at her condominium.

Once home, Cissy dashed straight into the house in search of a shower, complaining that she was going to be late for a dance back at the club, and Evelyn and Emmet, trying to ignore her continued attempts to rile them, went into the house to see about dinner.

Left alone in the garage with David, Diana's heart pounded unnaturally. He was taking an inordinately long time unloading his belongings from the car, and she wondered if perhaps he hadn't really minded their brush with communication on the boat. Maybe now was the time to share the concerns she had about his family. They'd been troubling her since the day she'd arrived. Maybe this was the moment he'd listen.

"Mr. Prescott?"

"Yes?"

"Would it be too much of an inconvenience if...I mean...could I talk to you for a minute?" Her mouth was so dry her lips were sticking to her teeth.

"What about?"

"Your family."

His eyes narrowed. "What do you mean?"

"Well, there are some problems here you might not be aware of, coming and going the way you do." His scowl became almost too much to bear. "Cissy, for instance. I'd like to talk to you about...her lessons," she finally said, turning coward. She held her breath, expecting him to laugh her right out the door.

"Can it wait till I've cleaned up?"

She gasped audibly in surprise. "Oh, sure. I'd like to shower, too...get all this salt out of my hair."

Still studying her warily, he nodded. "All right. In a couple of hours?"

"I can fix us a light supper if you'd like." The boldness of her offer startled her. Why had she said that? What had possessed her? Now he was really going to laugh.

But he didn't. She couldn't tell what he was thinking. His face was utterly unyielding as he surveyed her, from her sneakers up to her long damp hair. Then he amazed her with a taciturn nod. "Seven-thirty?"

"Seven-thirty."

When she got upstairs, she closed the door and butted her head against it until it hurt. Dear Lord, what had she done? She fell back, disconsolate, onto the couch.

She knew precisely what she'd done. She had just arranged a date for herself with David Prescott!

She sat up and tried to compose herself. So what if she had asked David Prescott over? *He* certainly wouldn't see it as a date. Besides, it wasn't! She really needed to talk to him about Cissy's antagonism toward Emmet and Evelyn's inability to connect with her daughter. She had to let him know about Abbie's fear of growing old and the effect his decision to sell Cliff Haven was having on her. So many problems beleaguered his household—quiet under-the-surface problems that might go undetected if one just flew in for the occasional weekend. David should be told. Maybe he could help.

As Diana glanced at her watch, a whole new anxiety assailed her. It was already six-fifteen, and she didn't even know if she had the ingredients in her kitchen for a peanut-butter sandwich. She jumped off the couch and flew to the refrigerator. All that stared back at her was half a pound of hamburger and a small steak. She pulled open the crisper, yanking so hard it fell right out, spilling its contents. In her frenzy, she left everything on the floor and flung wide a cupboard.

After a thorough search of what was on hand, she decided maybe she would pull this off, after all. She could throw together an Oriental dinner of thinly sliced beef and stir-fried vegetables, served on a bed of rice. She set to work and within twenty minutes had everything sliced, measured and ready for cooking. Then she dashed for the tub.

Miraculously she was ready with ten minutes to spare. Her heart was racing, though, and she wondered how she was ever going to eat. All her former trepidations came flooding back, intensified. What in heaven's name did she think she was doing, inviting David Prescott over for dinner? They had absolutely nothing in common—except their mutual animosity. What would they ever talk about once she'd filled him in on his family's problems, which would take all of about five minutes considering his guarded nature. How would they ever make time pass?

Suddenly there was a firm rap on her door. A wave of nausea washed through her.

"Come on in. Door's open," she called as casually as possible.

Still, when David walked in, she was standing in anything but a casual stance, rooted stiffly by the table, twisting her formal pearls round and round her fingers.

She was surprised to see he was wearing a jacket and tie. He looked casual enough, she supposed. His tan jacket was lightweight cotton and unconstructed, and his pants were brown denim. And yet...

"I brought over some wine. Rosé. Is that all right?"

"Perfect. Thank you."

He walked to the table, looking unfairly tall and assured, and set the bottle down.

"I have some wine open already," she said. "Only half a bottle actually. I'm glad you brought this over. Would you like a glass now?" *She* could surely use one.

"Yes. Thanks."

Diana ducked into the kitchen.

"This place looks different," David called.

She peeked over her shoulder. He was strolling about the living room, picking up framed photos of her family.

"It isn't, honestly." She returned and handed him a glass.

"I wasn't trying to accuse you of anything. Honestly." His gaze met hers, and she realized how automatically she'd become defensive. They each sipped their wine uneasily.

"I hope you don't mind being put to work." The thought of having David Prescott help with the cooking had never crossed Diana's mind before that moment, but suddenly it seemed a wonderful way to defuse the tension between them. "I've got everything ready. It just has to be cooked."

"What are we having?"

"Just a simple stir-fry dinner, I'm afraid. Beef, broccoli, mushrooms, that sort of thing."

"Sounds good. What can I do?" His eyes had a softness to them she'd never noticed before, his eyebrows raised in an arch that gave him an unexpected openness.

"Well, come on into the kitchen. Once the oil is heated, maybe you could stir the vegetables. You can handle that, can't you?"

"If I can't, I'm sure you'll be glad to show me how."

Diana shot him a wary glance, but small mocking lights were dancing in his blue eyes.

"Meanwhile, what are *you* going to do?" he asked.

"Don't worry, I wasn't planning to be idle." As she lit the burners under the fry pan and the rice water, David loosened his tie and undid the top button of his white shirt. "Good idea," she murmured, kicking her high heels off into a corner. "I hope you don't mind refrigerator biscuits. I would've run out for fresh bread if I'd had—"

"Diana, will you please stop apologizing. I'm not fussy."

Diana? He'd called her Diana? She didn't know where to settle her gaze.

"This looks a lot better than my own cooking, and light-years away from the junk I eat on the road."

She glanced up curiously from the sticky biscuit dough. "Do you do a lot of cooking for yourself?"

"Yes, though my talent lies more with Italian dishes."

"Really! Mine ends at tinned spaghetti sauce and a can opener. You can toss in that beef now." She handed him a long wooden spoon, then reached across him to cover the pot of rice. When she did, her arm brushed his shirt front, and the contact, brief as it was, rattled her composure. Good Lord, but this kitchen was tiny!

She sneaked a peek at his face and bit her lip. With his thick dark hair falling attractively over his brow and his skin wind-whipped to a deep healthy bronze, he exuded a masculine appeal she was finding harder and harder to ignore.

"You know," she said, "it's never even occurred to me—I don't know where you live. Where *do* you do all this cooking? You can't be staying in hotels all the time you're away."

"I do much of the time—you'd be amazed. But home, I suppose, is my apartment in New York." His voice was flat and unenthusiastic.

"Why New York?"

He scooped the beef into a bowl and added the broccoli to the pan. "It's home base for all my businesses. The corporate offices are there."

"Really!" She added sliced carrots to the pan and slipped the biscuits into the oven. "For some reason I imagined the steel industry being run from someplace in Pennsylvania."

"Steel?"

Diana glanced at his handsome puzzled face. "A-aren't you the steel Prescotts? Isn't your family—"

"My brother, Walter, controls that end of the business, not me. I'm into other things."

"Oh." Diana stared at the steam rising from the pot of rice for a long quiet time.

Finally he nudged her arm. "Well, aren't you going to ask what kinds of things?" His eyes seemed to bore into her with their bright taunting lights.

She smiled, warming to his unexpected teasing. "What sort of person do you think I am? I don't pry into other people's affairs."

David laughed attractively. "Are you sure you don't want to ask? I'm a fascinating guy. Into everything from racehorses to computer chips."

Diana lowered her eyes. He didn't have to tell her how fascinating he was. Her preoccupation with him these past two weeks had nearly driven her crazy.

"I think everything's ready," she said softly.

At the table David opened the wine he'd brought and re-filled their glasses. Diana lit the candles, and the soft glow wrapped them in a warm intimate circle. He pulled out her chair for her.

"Evelyn lives in New York, too, doesn't she?" Diana asked, trying to hide her reaction to his small kindnesses.

He sat. "Yes, a few blocks from me."

"Oh, how nice. Being close, I mean."

"Except that we don't get to see each other that often. We're all busy." He ladled hot rice onto Diana's plate be-fore serving himself. "But enough about me. Let's talk about you for a while."

She swallowed her wine with a loud gulp. "Me?"

He nodded, smiling a small tilted smile of amusement. "Who are you, Diana White, bane of my life?"

Diana felt prickly heat at the back of her neck. Did David suspect how conscious she was of him? Was he feeling any of that uncomfortable physical awareness himself? Maybe she shouldn't have worn this red dress with the halter top that bared so much of her shoulders. Maybe she shouldn't have left her hair hanging loose.

"I heard you mention a brother once," he prompted.

"I—I don't have a brother, David." She finally found the courage to say his name and almost stopped right there. "I have five."

He put down his fork and stared at her incredulously.

"We grew up on a beautiful dairy farm in central Ver-mont just a few miles north of Fairview. It's something of a local landmark. You can see the silver silos for miles around. Only Skip and I live there now—everyone else is married. But Dan still comes over to help Skip work the dairy."

David seemed to miss most of this. "Five?" he repeated, stupefied.

She laughed. "Uh-huh. And all older."

He whistled. "Poor kid!"

"Worse than you can imagine. All my life, I've had five extra parents." Her expression became serious. "They're the ones who insisted I bring that Mace to Newport. In case I ran into trouble." David's smile dropped. "I'm really sorry I did that to you, David."

"I survived. But it wasn't a funny stunt to pull."

"I didn't mean it to be. I was terrified." She heard him mumble something. "What did you say?"

"I said I'm sorry, sorry I frightened you." He looked aside, and Diana's heart lurched. It must have taken a great deal for a proud aloof person like David to say those words. She didn't imagine he said them too often.

"Let's... let's just put the whole incident behind us, okay?"

She nodded.

"So, tell me more about yourself. This is really delicious, by the way. What ever made you decide to become an English teacher?"

Diana watched the candlelight flickering in his blue eyes. "This is going to sound like a cliché, but it was a teacher I had. In seventh grade." She paused and let her thoughts tumble backward.

"Go on," he coaxed gently.

"I was having trouble in school at the time. Actually, I was failing." Failing, losing weight, getting into school-yard fights. The year she'd lost her mother had been the most painful time in her life, and Mrs. Connelly had realized it and offered to tutor her. Diana knew that had she been kept back, her anger would only have deepened.

But Diana kept the story simple. "She came to my house every afternoon that spring to help me. She was great. She's the one who turned me on to reading. *Anne of Green Ga-*

bles. The Secret Garden. I adored those books. She made me keep a journal, too. I'm still amazed by how much a person can learn about herself by keeping a journal.''

David's attention was locked on her face, taking in every shift of expression, every nuance of her voice. ''It can be quite cathartic, too,'' he said.

She shifted uneasily in her seat, suddenly feeling as transparent as glass.

''So, Diana, bane of my life—'' his deep smiling voice lifted her out of her uneasiness ''—how did you get that bump on your nose?'' He poured her more wine.

She touched a hand to it self-consciously. ''Is it all that obvious?''

He shook his head. ''Quite charming, actually.''

She felt herself blush. ''Well, it goes this way: once upon a time I got a notion to play Senior League ball.''

''Senior League?''

''Yeah, I know. My brothers thought I was crazy, too. Pulling a feminist stunt, they said. But I wasn't. Skip was on the team, George coached, and my other brothers always came to watch. I just wanted to be part of it, that's all.''

''You *are* as crazy as I thought. Teenage guys can get pretty rough.''

She nodded ruefully. ''One day I was waiting in the batting circle and the kid up hitting swung and let go of his bat.''

David drew in his breath with a grimace.

''Yep. Wham! Right here.''

''Did you continue playing?''

''Not that night.'' Diana realized she loved hearing him laugh and so provoked it as often as possible. ''I did finish the season, though, but most of the time I was scared witless.''

''Your brothers must have been glad when you quit.''

"Very. They're the kind of guys who used to come home with ruffled organdy dresses for me when I was a kid."

"Your mother died when you were young?" It was more a statement than a question.

"Yes." Diana lowered her eyes. She wanted to tell him she knew he'd lost his mother, too; she knew how hurt he'd been and how deep the scars still ran. But she also knew he never discussed his private life with outsiders.

"I . . . my mother died . . ." he began haltingly.

Diana's eyebrows shot up, and time seemed suspended on that precarious moment.

"My mother died when I was sixteen. In a plane crash. I know how tough it can be." That's all he said, but with that brief admission, Diana felt he'd taken a giant step. Her heart swelled and ached for him. Without thinking, she reached across the table and covered one of his hands with hers.

She realized it was a mistake when David froze. Quickly she drew back her hand.

"Would you care for some coffee, David?"

"Uh . . . no, thank you." He folded his napkin and placed it alongside his plate.

"So, is there anything else you want to know?" she asked. "Who my favorite authors are? When I lost my baby teeth?"

But David no longer seemed interested. He pushed back his chair and got to his feet. "That was delicious, Diana," he said perfunctorily. Inside her, something budding and vital felt crushed. What had she done? Had that simple touch been all that inappropriate? Did he really dislike her so much that he couldn't wait to get away?

She rose quickly and in her agitation toppled her nearly full glass of wine. Immediately, David snatched up his napkin and started mopping up. She felt her cheeks flaming and tears about to spill over.

"What an oaf! What a clumsy stupid oaf!" she muttered as she dabbed her own napkin over the spreading stain.

"Diana, stop it. Spilled wine is supposed to mean good luck."

"Good luck? Is *that* what you call good luck?" She pointed as the wine dribbled off the table and down his pant leg.

She ran to the kitchen for a towel and knelt to wipe at his shoe. "I'm sorry, David. It seems every time you and I get together, something awful happens, and usually you're the one who gets the worst of it."

"Diana, will you stop it!" He gripped her by the arms and hauled her up from her frenetic mopping. She squirmed unthinkingly, and he held her tighter, closer to him now. Finally she calmed down and dared a look up into his dark enigmatic eyes.

She was amazed by how warm he felt, this man who always appeared so hard and glacierlike. She could feel the heat of his body all down the length of her own. She smelled the clean masculine scent of him, felt the beating of his heart under her sensitive palm, and something coursed through her, a fiery urgency she thought had died forever—only now it seemed brand-new and so much more exciting than she remembered. In the soft candlelight, his thick luxuriant hair glimmered with highlights she longed to touch. His face lost its hardness. His mouth became sensuous and intriguing.

But what frightened her most was the realization that he was looking at her the same way she was looking at him. Something mysterious was passing between them, making them forget who they were, how different their backgrounds, how much they didn't get along. All that mattered was that they were alone together, linked by some powerful wordless bond. Breathlessly, she waited and saw his head lower, and not for a second did she want it any other way.

His lips found hers, brushing them softly at first, tantalizingly. They were warm and tasted of wine. His breath escaped raggedly and became one with hers, and a shudder ran through his body. "Diana," he whispered just before his mouth fell on hers in a deep urgent kiss.

Diana's hands worked their way up his chest and around his broad muscled shoulders, pulling him closer still. His hands moved hungrily over her back, his fingers entwined in her long silken hair. Gently, he pulled back her head and brushed his lips along the smooth pulsing curve of her neck. Then his mouth returned to hers, searing her with a passion she had never known.

When he finally drew away, she was so weak her knees actually buckled and only his arms kept her standing. His heart was beating hard against her cheek. His body, molded to hers, was taut and throbbing.

Her mind was awash, and it was David who finally broke away. He did it so abruptly that she nearly fell over. He turned from her and strode to the door, staring out at the dark night. "I'm sorry, Diana. That wasn't very smart."

As the sensual feelings he'd ignited in her ebbed, an ache gradually took their place. Her throat constricted painfully. Incomprehension filled her eyes.

"Honestly, I didn't plan that," he went on, his voice searching for a cool distant tone. "I make it a rule never to mix my personal life with business. I just lost my head for a minute. I'm sorry."

Oh, was that what she was? Business? One of the hired help? She paused, dumbstruck with the realization that he was right, of course.

"No, David," she said in a proud but breaking voice, "I'm the one who's sorry. Now, you'd better go before I do something really stupid and try to throw you out of your own property."

DIANA AWOKE with a headache. She stumbled to the bathroom, reached for the aspirin, pulled back her tumbled hair and squinted at her reflection. "Diana, you look like hell!" she moaned.

But what did she expect after spending half the night beating her face into the pillow? She hated him. She *hated* him! He had no right to humiliate her—kissing her the way he had and then just dropping her as if he were appalled by the squalid little deed!

It wasn't very smart, he'd said. He'd lost his head. Well, she guessed she had lost her head, too. She swallowed the aspirin with a shudder. She didn't even like David Prescott. He was the coldest, most humorless, unappreciative man she'd ever met. Time and again he'd let her know she wasn't welcome here, not on his property and not in his life. Well, fine! She didn't want him in her life, either.

And yet, there were all those little incongruities that kept pulling her back, whispering in her ear that there was more to him than met the eye. The more she thought about him, the more his cold dictatorial personality fit like a badly cut coat. For a while last night he'd become so easygoing and likable. And when he'd taken her into his arms, she'd wanted to be there more than any other place on earth. Somehow, he, of all people, had turned a key....

She buried her face in her hands and rubbed her swollen eyes. No! The situation had all the potential of a major disaster. She needed to cut him out of her life right now.

He confused her too much. Last night, for instance, she hadn't even broached the subject of his family's problems, and that had been the whole point of his visit, hadn't it? But somehow, caught up in getting to know him, she'd never found the opportunity, and now those problems would only intensify. She should have kept a clearer mind. And he should have remembered to ask. But what really frightened her was the suspicion that neither of them had even tried.

It was a quiet Sunday, muffled by a cool fog. Diana spent two hours of it curled in a chair talking to her brothers. For some reason, their voices sounded rather comforting this gray troubled morning. When she finally got off the phone, she straightened the apartment and gathered a basketful of laundry. Then, dressed in jeans and a red sweatshirt, she hurried across the damp courtyard with her load, taking in deep breaths of the invigorating salt air.

Before she could duck around to the service side of the house, however, the front door opened and she made the mistake of looking back. David was just stepping out. Their eyes linked immediately. He was dressed as he had been the last time he'd left on business, in a suit and tie. From sailing, his skin glowed red-bronze, accentuating the blueness of his eyes.

Diana stumbled to a halt. As if it were happening all over again, she felt the humiliation of being aroused by him and then coldly rejected.

But David was right. Their becoming involved was definitely a mistake. She shifted the weight of the laundry basket, lifted her chin and continued on her way.

"Diana!"

She drew in her breath and slowly turned. He looked tall and calm and utterly aloof. She hoped she looked the same. "What is it?"

A few long strides brought him to her. "I have to leave. I have to go to Michigan for a while."

She was tempted to ask why, but didn't, and just stared at him as dispassionately as possible. "Well, have a good trip."

The corner of his mouth tightened. "Listen, while I'm gone..." He raked back his neatly combed hair from his forehead and paused, thinking. Then, abruptly, he set his briefcase down, took the basket from her arms and set it alongside. "Come on, let's go for a walk." He took Diana by the arm before she had time to protest and propelled her down the path.

"David!" she objected.

"David!" he mimicked with a glint in his blue eyes. She looked at him with a mixture of surprise and alarm. "Come on. It won't take long. I should be out of here already."

On the far side of the house, up a path and half-hidden by vines, stood a small greenhouse. Its glass panes were milky from years of neglect.

"Careful." David held her arm as they stepped over exposed tree roots. He nudged open the reluctant door, then took her hand to lead her through. As he did, a disturbing warmth tingled up her arm and radiated through her body. Her eyes flew to his to see if he felt any of her reaction, but David was a master at concealing whatever was on his mind.

"What *is* this, David?" she asked, forcing her own features into a mask of indifference.

He let go of her hand and slowly surveyed the long wooden benches lined with clay pots. The air was warm and close and smelled of earth.

"Last night I couldn't help noticing how many plants you have. And, well..." He shrugged, looking slightly uneasy, she thought. "We have all these garden tools. If you have any use for them..."

Diana didn't know what to think of David anymore. Just when she decided she had him pegged, he went ahead and surprised her. Her anger began to slip, in spite of her efforts to hang on to it.

She looked up at his sun-bronzed face. They were standing so close she could feel the warmth of his body even through the thickness of his suit. Her breath seemed impossible to catch. Such fathomless eyes! she thought, peering into their blue swirling depths. What was he thinking? Was he remembering last night and the way she'd felt in his arms? Was he thinking of kissing her again?

She couldn't tell, but suddenly she realized she hoped he would. She wanted David to kiss her more than anything else in the world.

But, as if reading her thoughts, he wrenched his eyes from hers. "Diana, about last night..." The tone of his voice sent her emotions plummeting. "It didn't occur to me until later that I probably confused you, maybe even hurt your feelings."

In a flash, Diana realized here was the real purpose for this walk to the greenhouse. And in the same instant she remembered something else, something so obvious she wondered how it could have slipped her mind. "Barbara Benedetto!"

"What?"

"Barbara. Aren't you and she...?"

"Good Lord, no! Barbara and I are just friends."

Diana couldn't look at him. She bent her head and ran shaky fingers along the bench, over a yellowed seed catalog from 1973. "Aren't the two of you...involved?"

"Not romantically."

"I know. I understand." She tried to keep her voice steady. "But you are carrying on an affair."

"Not the last time I looked."

Diana turned to eye him him warily. "Are you sure?"

"Yes, quite. I'll admit we did at one time. Between her marriages. But that was years ago, over and done with."

"And you're not involved with anyone else?" She hoped her lips weren't quivering.

"No!" He thrust his hand impatiently through his hair, mussing it over his forehead.

"Then it's me." As soon as she'd said it, she kicked the ground in disgust. Why had her tone been so peevish? And why did she feel so hurt?

"Diana!" He gripped her arm. "There's nothing wrong with you. Just the opposite. I think you're absolutely..." He let go of her and turned away. He seemed to be silently berating himself. Finally he looked back, once again composed. "I'm just not the kind of guy you'd want to get involved with. I don't have the time or the inclination for romantic involvement. When I do take someone out, it's mostly companionship I'm seeking. That's all. And the women I take out know that clearly."

"And you think I wouldn't understand?"

He studied her features cautiously. "I wasn't sure."

"Thanks, but you don't have to worry. I don't believe much in romance myself."

"No?"

"Trust me, David, if there's anything I don't want in my life right now, it's a relationship."

He expelled a long breath. "Well, that's a relief!"

"That's one of the reasons I was so happy to get a job away from home this summer. My brothers got on a kick of setting me up on blind dates." She lowered her eyes. "We made a mistake last night, but I'm willing to forget it if you are."

"A deal." He held out his hand and she placed hers within it.

She was doing and saying all the things she believed. She was glad they'd had this opportunity to clear the air. And yet why didn't her words ring true, even to herself? Why did she want him to keep holding her hand?

But he didn't. He released it and moved toward the door. They retraced their steps along the path and returned to his abandoned briefcase and her laundry basket, sighing similar deep sighs as they picked them up.

"I have to go."

"Yeah." She looked away. Looking at *him* was too difficult. "Well, have a good week." Or two or three.

He gazed down into her face and for a moment an expression of melancholy seemed to flicker across his handsome guarded features. Gently his hand caressed the side of her face. "You, too." Then he turned and disappeared around the corner of the house.

Diana stared after him for a long time. Her heart was pounding like a frightened animal's. No matter what they had avowed back at the greenhouse, this thing between them wasn't over yet.

CHAPTER SEVEN

CISSY HAD SCOOPED UP her books and was already half out the door when Diana remembered. "Before you go, Cissy, do you realize this Friday is Abbie's birthday?"

"Is it?" The girl paused. "How old will she be, do you know?"

"Seventy-five."

"Wow! I had no idea."

Diana bit her lower lip, hesitating. "I don't know if you people celebrate birthdays in any special way, but I was thinking . . . I would love to throw her a little party. Here, at the carriage house," she emphasized quickly.

Cissy began to nod with growing interest. "Yeah, that would be fun. Turning seventy-five deserves a celebration."

"Of course, I'll clear it with your mother first and assure her it won't be anything extravagant. I'll just bake a cake and invite Abbie over for a visit. It doesn't even have to be a surprise." She didn't expect David to be back. The last time he'd left, he'd stayed away for two whole weeks. Still, she didn't want rumors of a party reaching him. "Does Abbie have any relatives I should invite?"

"Not that I know of."

"Oh, well." Diana shrugged. "I guess it's just us then," she said with a grin. "Oh, I can't wait. Abbie's such a peach."

THE WEEK PASSED in relative calm, except for Wednesday when Emmet came for a visit. He had four tickets to a tennis match at the Newport Casino and insisted that Diana and Cissy accompany him and Evelyn. Diana was thrilled to finally be visiting the Bellevue Avenue landmark. It was the site of the very first tennis court in America.

Cissy, on the other hand, couldn't have cared less.

"But it's the Virginia Slims, Cissy!" Diana coaxed. "Some of the biggest names in tennis are going to be there today!"

"So what! I'm going to miss my sailing lesson." That afternoon, Diana was convinced the girl was an incorrigible brat.

The Casino was lovely with its latticed Victorian porches, flapping canopies and thirteen manicured grass courts. Diana found it easy to imagine she'd traveled back in time to another era, one that was slower, more graceful, and far more peaceful.

The game, however, was anything but slow or peaceful. Diana, who played a little tennis herself, was astounded by the speed and accuracy of a ball hit by a professional. She was enjoying herself so much that she wasn't even aware of the scene developing at her elbow.

She finally did look over, though, as Evelyn's voice rose in frantic whispers. Cissy had removed her shirt, revealing not only a skimpy tank top, but the most hideous tattoos Diana had ever seen. All up her arms and across her shoulders—logos of heavy metal bands, snakes, skulls. Several people were casting discreet, though obviously appalled, glances in her direction. Diana became quite alarmed. She'd passed a tattoo parlor in town...

But on closer inspection she realized the designs weren't permanent.

Smiling smugly, Cissy pulled her shirt back on. Although nothing more was said, the rest of the afternoon was a washout. They didn't go to dinner as planned, and Emmet left for New York right after dropping them off.

THE FOLLOWING FRIDAY afternoon, Diana and Cissy drove to a stationery store in town to pick up balloons and streamers for Abbie's party. Traffic was heavy, it now being late July, and Diana was glad to get back to Cliff Haven.

As her Toyota approached the courtyard, however, every nerve in her body seemed to snap to. David was home. Oddly her first reaction upon seeing him was one of joy, but that passed quickly as all the ramifications of his being back dawned on her.

"Hey, it's Uncle David!" Cissy cried. "I didn't know he was coming home today."

"Neither did I. Oh, Cissy, tonight's Abbie's party, too! What are we going to do?"

"Invite him?"

"Glad to see you think my predicament's so funny."

"What predicament? Why are you so nervous?"

Diana cast her pupil a baleful look. "Cissy, your uncle is hardly a fan of parties, especially parties held at Cliff Haven, and when he finds out I'm the perpetrator, he's going to throw a fit." She peered through the windshield as David crossed the courtyard. Another man, carrying a clipboard and a camera, was with him.

"I don't know how you expect to keep it from him," Cissy said.

Diana sighed disconsolately. "I guess I can't."

"Diana, this is Mr. Sloane, a real-estate appraiser," David explained as she got out of her car. "He's going to take a look at the carriage house. Do you mind?"

Obviously it didn't matter if she did. A week of being away had evidently erased her from his memory. His personality had regained all the crispness of dry toast. Her eyes traveled over his face, searching for a trace of the warmth and humor she'd discovered the previous weekend, but it was gone.

She was furious at herself for being disappointed. What had she expected, anyway? Hadn't they both agreed that their kiss was a mistake? Hadn't they both promised to forget it had ever happened? David was acting the sane one here, and she would be wise to take her cue from him.

"No problem," she answered, tossing her hair with cool indifference. "By the way, I'm having a small get-together tonight for Abbie. It's her birthday." Somehow his coolness gave her the courage—or perhaps the anger—to face him squarely. "You're welcome to come, if you have the time."

He cleared his throat officiously. "Sorry. I'm already locked in to taking Mr. Sloane to dinner. But thanks for asking."

Diana wasn't fooled by his polite phrasing. Ice frosted each and every word.

"You're welcome," she responded in kind. "Follow me, Mr. Sloane."

ABBIE CAME OVER with James at seven forty-five, protesting all the way. "Such a fuss, just because of a silly birthday!" Still, Diana could see she was pleased. The two maids were already there, helping concoct a strong fruity punch.

Diana ladled out five cups and passed them around, keeping one for herself. "Happy Birthday, Abbie," she said, raising her glass. Before she could sip from it, there were more footsteps on the stairs.

"Happy birthday to you, happy birthday to you..." sang a pair of discordant voices. "Happy birthday, dear Abbie. Happy birthday to you." Out on the stair landing, Cissy and a young man took a deep bow. Abbie beamed until her face looked stretched.

They wandered in, and Cissy planted a kiss on the old woman's cheek. "Abbie, this is a friend of mine from the yacht club, Steven Clark." Then she glanced at Diana. "You don't mind, do you?"

"Of course not. Hi, Steven. Come in, make yourself comfortable. But unless you're twenty-one and have a cast-iron stomach, don't try this punch."

A few minutes later, Evelyn and Emmet arrived.

"Miss Evelyn!" Abbie cried in soft astonishment.

Diana carried a tray of drinks across the room. "Thank you for coming, Evelyn. I don't think she expected you. You must know how much it means to her."

"Nonsense. I wouldn't miss this for the world. There hasn't been a party at Cliff Haven in, well, you know. It's wonderful, Diana."

Suddenly the small living room was bursting at the seams with people. Diana smiled. A party! This was turning into an honest-to-goodness party! Well, what was she doing sitting in a corner? she asked herself excitedly. What this room needed was a little music!

They had a perfectly wonderful time. Abbie opened her presents and made a fuss over every one. Then as evening deepened into night, she got to telling stories about the past, stories of rumrunners hiding in the cellar at Cliff Haven during Prohibition, stories about the terrible hurricane of thirty-eight. And when she tired of talking, they put on more music, old brittle records that had been stored there years before—Glen Miller and Bing Crosby, Harry James and several other favorites from the big-band era. Emmet was out of his seat immediately, twirling Evelyn around.

"This is the jitterbug," he announced for the edification of the younger people in the room. "The *real* jitterbug. The one we used to dance to when this music was all the rage."

"Emmet! We're not that old!" Evelyn panted, swinging out limply at the end of his firm grasp.

As Diana slipped quietly into the kitchen to get the cake, she happened to catch a glimpse of Abbie. She was sitting a little apart from the rest of the gathering, a sad smile quivering along her lips. Diana crept back into the room.

"What's the matter, Ab?" she whispered, leaning over.

"Nothing. What could possibly be wrong, child?" But Diana could see moisture glistening on the woman's thin gray lashes. "It's a lovely party. Lovely. Thank you so much. It's just the thing to remember Cliff Haven by when I'm not here anymore."

"Not here? What are you talking about?"

"Well, when David sells this place, what do you think's going to happen? Do you think the new owner is going to want an old hag like me hanging around?"

Diana pressed her lips together tightly as she recalled the appraiser who'd roamed the estate all afternoon. His appearance had undoubtedly made the sale of Cliff Haven a painful reality for Abbie. Unfortunately she could find no words of comfort, only anger toward the man who was at the bottom of this devoted hardworking woman's insecurity.

A peek out the window confirmed that David had returned from his dinner engagement. The sedan was parked beneath the portico.

"Excuse me. I'll be right back," she whispered.

No one except Abbie noticed her slip out the door. She hurried across the courtyard in a defiant long-legged stride, her navy blue dress snapping crisply about her knees. And with every aggressive step she took, she became more convinced that she and the almighty David Prescott were about to lock horns once again!

She gripped the heavy brass knocker and let it fall.

"Yes?"

She jumped. David was the only person who used the intercom. She had forgotten about its existence. "I-it's me, Diana," she stammered. "May I speak with you a moment?"

"I'm pretty busy, Diana."

She summoned her most assertive voice. "I won't be long. It's very important."

Even over the intercom she heard his impatient sigh. "All right. Let yourself in. I'm in the library."

David was sitting in a pool of lamplight, reading at his desk. His white shirt was rumpled and opened at the collar. His dark hair fell untidily over his brow as if he'd passed his fingers through it again and again.

"Don't just stand there," he muttered, flicking a quick glance her way. His gaze ricocheted back almost immediately and swept over her with an attention that made her self-conscious in every fiber of her being. She knew this particular shirtwaist made the most of her tall slender figure. And her hair, which she'd taken time to curl tonight, tumbled in soft waves from two tortoiseshell combs.

"Have a seat," he said, regaining his impassivity almost immediately.

The leather crackled as she lowered herself into it. She folded her hands and watched him sit back, guardedly assaying her. Light from the lamp angled over his face and deepened the stern creases alongside his mouth. Involuntarily she remembered how that mouth had kissed her a week ago, how those eyes had looked down at her, half-closed and drugged with desire.

"Yes?" he prodded. "What did you want to speak to me about?"

"Abbie. Her b-birthday party," she said, her voice wavering.

"Mm. I can hear it clear across the courtyard."

She was about to apologize but then decided not to. The party was on her turf, after all.

"David, what I came over here to say is, Abbie is worried sick about your selling Cliff Haven."

The creases on his brow deepened. "What do you mean?"

"Well, with that realtor showing up, today of all days . . . She's seventy-five, David. That should explain it all."

"I'm afraid it doesn't."

Diana bit back her irritation. "She's worried that she's too old to be of any use around here."

"That's nonsense. She takes care of the place just fine."

"Yes, she does. But the effort exhausts her. She should have more help."

"Is that what you came over to tell me—to hire more help?" He looked at her with infuriating hauteur, suddenly making her want to shake him senseless.

"Yes. No! I mean, Abbie thinks that if you sell the estate, she's going to be out of a job. She figures the new owner won't want her, and she assumes the old one doesn't, either." She examined the clutter on his desk rather than meet his eyes. "Well, is it true?" she finally asked when the silence grew uncomfortable.

He didn't answer except with a disquieting stare.

"She's been here an awfully long time. Over fifty years. I brought up the subject of retirement once, but she got too agitated to talk. This is the only home she knows. She has no children, no place to go..."

"Well, there isn't much anybody can do about that now, is there?"

Diana stared at him, dumbfounded. "How can you be so dispassionate? After all the years she's worked for your family, there must be something you can do! Surely you can tell her that you'll find her a comfortable place to live. If nothing else, you can put her mind at ease about her financial future."

The room rang with David's silent anger. She knew he wanted her to leave. She'd said enough. She began to get up, then abruptly sat down again.

"I guess that's not really why I came over. For some odd reason, which I will never understand, that old woman loves you. And sometimes," she continued softly, "being loved in return is better than all the monetary assurances in the world."

"So, what do you suggest?" he drawled sardonically. "You seem to have all the answers."

Diana took a deep fortifying breath. "Well, for starters, you could come over to the carriage house. Everyone but you is there."

"Let's just say I don't take too seriously invitations extended at the very last minute."

Diana lowered her eyes. "I'm sorry I didn't invite you sooner, but I didn't think you'd be exactly thrilled about my throwing a party."

He swiveled away from her and walked to the window. Light was spilling from the carriage house. Voices and music rode the breeze. "It's all right. I probably wouldn't have gone, anyway, even if I'd been the first invited."

"Are you sure? I know she'd love to see you."

"Diana!" It was almost a plea. "I have work to do."

She stared at the rigid muscles of his back for a long silent moment. Then, realizing he considered the discussion closed, she rose and went to the door.

A strap seemed to cinch her lungs as she crossed the courtyard. She felt awful—for Abbie, of course, but also for herself, for being so foolish as to think she could get through to that man. At the moment she had serious doubts there was anything to get through to!

Back at the carriage house, the party went on. She lit the candles on the cake and carried it out to the living room, and as she placed it on the table, everyone began to sing.

She was just slicing into it when suddenly something caught her eye—a dark figure out on her stair landing. She flew to the door and opened it wide.

"Come in, David," she said. Her voice had gone breathless.

CHAPTER EIGHT

"UNCLE DAVID! What are you doing here?" Cissy cried.

Diana sensed the others were equally surprised, but mature enough not to express it so vocally. David ignored them and went straight to Abbie.

"Happy birthday," he said, leaning over to kiss her. "How's my favorite girl tonight?"

Diana returned to cutting the cake but cast a glance up to see Abbie's eyes fill with tears. She had a hard time keeping her own from doing the same.

David sat on the arm of Abbie's chair and handed her a present. Carefully she removed the paper and opened the box. Then the tears that had been shining in her eyes finally spilled over.

"What've you got there, Abbie?" Emmet asked.

With badly shaking hands, she lifted out a large silver frame and turned it for everyone to see.

"Why, that's you and Andrew, isn't it?" Evelyn exclaimed.

"Our fifth anniversary, it was." Abbie wiped her cheek and laughed. "Where did you ever get this picture, David? I don't even remember posing for it."

He grinned. "I have my sources."

Diana could see that the framed photograph had been professionally touched up and enlarged from an old snapshot. This was not a gift hastily dug out of a back closet within the past few minutes. Just then his eyes happened to meet hers, and she hoped he saw how sorry she was for her outburst.

Abbie held the frame in both her hands and beamed at it through her tears. "Don't we look grand, though, me and Andrew? I couldn't have weighed more'n a hundred pounds there. And him, with those fancy spats!" She placed it on the coffee table where she could look at it the rest of the night.

The party finally broke up around ten. Diana watched everyone leave from the top of her stairs. David was with them, his arm linked with Abbie's, his head bowed in quiet conversation.

Still stunned, she went back inside and distractedly picked up a few glasses. The living room seemed to echo with conversation and laughter. It had been a wonderful evening, full of surprises.

Suddenly there was a light tap at her door. "Need any help?"

Her heart leapt as she recognized David's deep voice. He strolled in and, without waiting for her okay, began to pick up plates.

She was about to ask what he was doing, but for some inspired reason didn't. This was an overture of some sort. "Sure, I'd love a little help."

In no time at all they had the place straightened. David filled the dishpan in the kitchen and began to wash.

"David?"

He looked up from his scrubbing.

"David," she began again, "I want you to know that what you did tonight was pretty nice."

"No big deal." Then after a short silence, "What you did, having this party, was pretty nice, too."

"You don't mind?"

He shrugged. "Whether I do or not doesn't seem to matter. You go right ahead and do what you want, anyway." Before she could decide if he was reprimanding her, he reached out and dabbed a mound of soapy foam on her nose. He smiled, and the smile transformed his whole face. "I'm not trying to make excuses for myself but, well, I have thought about Abbie. I've thought about bringing new people in to help, but I've always been afraid she might think I was trying to replace her. Same reason I never asked her to retire."

"Oh, David. I'm sorry."

"Don't apologize. I didn't realize she was so worried until you told me."

"And now that you do?"

"I offered her the position of head housekeeper at my apartment in New York. I know she'd prefer to live out the rest of her life here, but it's the best I can do. And she seemed happy enough with the arrangement."

How easily David had found a solution! A very personal solution, too. And all it had taken was a little nudge. In her elation Diana wrapped an arm around his neck and gave him a tight spontaneous hug. He looked uneasy and set to scrubbing a glass with unnecessary vigor. Still, he wasn't stiffening the way he had last weekend when she'd reached across the dinner table to touch his hand.

Before long the dishes were done and they were walking into the living room. "Thank you, David. I really appreciate your help. Would you care for a cup of coffee?"

He paused at the screen door. "No, thanks. I've got to get back to my work." He rested a hand on the door latch and sighed with reluctance.

"Nice night, isn't it?" Diana peered into the hot humid darkness. Crickets were chirruping in the shadows below the stairs. The surf was a low distant roar.

"Well..." David stepped onto the landing and glanced up at the full yellow moon.

"Good night, David, and thanks again."

Suddenly he was back in the room. "Diana, are you very tired?"

"Not really." Her pulse began to race.

"Great! Let's go for a sail."

"W-what?"

"I've had too much coffee, I'm restless as hell, and the last thing I want to do is go back to those damn books. Let's go for a sail."

"Where? How?"

"In my new boat." He laughed with boyish glee. "I didn't realize how much I missed sailing until I went out on Emmet's."

"So...you bought a boat?"

He nodded. "It was an impetuous thing to do, I know, but I didn't go out and get anything big or elaborate."

"But...I don't feel like going sailing. I don't even like sailing."

"That's just because you don't know how. Go on, go change into something more comfortable."

Openmouthed, Diana stared back at him over her shoulder as she hurried to her room. Telling herself that she'd lost her mind, she slipped out of her dress and into jeans and a T-shirt.

"But it's nighttime," she protested, even as David propelled her down the stairs. "Isn't it dangerous to go sailing at night?"

He arched his eyebrows in a comic leer. "Extremely." Inside the garage, he walked right by the sedan and headed for his motorcycle.

Diana's feet riveted to the cement floor. "Do we have to go on that thing?"

He nodded.

"But why?"

"But why?" he mimicked.

"Don't make fun of me!"

"Wouldn't dream of it. Here." He lowered a helmet over her head and gently tucked her hair inside.

"I'm not getting on that thing!"

"Okay. You can run alongside." With that, he swung his leg over the bike and started it up.

By the time they reached the yacht club, Diana was thoroughly shaken. "You drive like a maniac!" she hollered.

"I beg your pardon!" he said, feigning mild affrontery. In his eyes small flames danced like devils.

"You must have been doing seventy around some of those curves!" She pulled off her helmet and flung it at him.

"Admit it, you loved it." He turned and strode down the dock without waiting for her. With disconcerting agility, he leapt onto his sleek new boat and held out a hand. Diana's stomach turned over.

"No, David. Forget it."

He retracted his hand and dragged it through his hair. "What is it now?"

"Sailing at night is dangerous, isn't it? I want you to really level with me."

He shook his head. "The water's calm as glass, the wind's only about three knots, and I could navigate these waters with my eyes closed. If that's not enough, there are six life jackets on board, and you can wear them all, okay?" He held out his hand again and his dark brilliant gaze locked with hers. "Trust me," he said in a low whispery voice.

Though her knees were knocking, Diana let him take her aboard. He started the engine, and slowly the graceful white hull backed away from its mooring and headed toward the open bay.

"Di, come here a minute," he called. "I want to teach you how to hoist a sail."

Di? Her heart leaped inexplicably. Her brothers sometimes called her Di. Close friends did, too. Had David unwittingly crossed a threshold into their ranks? Was he feeling so comfortable with her that the nickname had just slipped out?

They sailed a slow arc around the island, following the mansion-studded coast. When they passed Cliff Haven, David pointed it out to make sure she didn't miss it. Moonlight glazed the entire estate. More than ever, it looked like Sleeping Beauty's castle.

"It's awfully impressive, isn't it?" she said softly, surprised by the depth of fondness she felt for the place. She looked into David's face. He was sitting close enough to reach over if necessary and adjust the rope she was holding. His closeness was reassuring. "David, why do you want to sell Cliff Haven? It's so beautiful, and it's been in your family since it was built."

She could almost feel the tension rise like a tide up his body.

"Sorry. I guess it's none of my business." She lowered her eyes, hoping she hadn't spoiled the good mood that had opened up between them tonight. Besides, she already suspected the reason. The bad memories he associated with Cliff Haven apparently outweighed the good. Selling the place would be an emotional unburdening.

"Okay," he finally conceded. "I'm selling Cliff Haven because... because it's not cost-efficient."

Diana's breath exploded in an abrupt little laugh. "It's what?"

"I'm serious. It's far too expensive for what I get out of it. I rarely use it during the winter, yet it has to be heated. Taxes are atrocious. There's a never-ending upkeep bill, and even during the summer I'm too busy to spend any significant time here."

"Oh, so it's just a matter of balance."

"Of what?"

"Balance. In other words, if you got more out of the place, then it would be worth the expense?"

"Don't put words into my mouth. I never said that." He reached around her and adjusted the rope she held. For a moment, the brush of his body against hers made the simple act of speaking impossible.

"B-but it's true, isn't it?" she resumed with difficulty. "If you stayed longer, went sailing and played tennis, entertained clients here, got a few horses..."

"Hey! Slow down!"

She tensed again. "Sorry. I run off at the mouth sometimes. I realize I have no right arguing the pros and cons of selling Cliff Haven with you. It's your house, your life..."

"Exactly."

It was a crisp reply, and she knew she was pressing her luck by adding, "Forgive me?"

"No!"

"It's going to be a pretty long night unless you do."

David threw up his hands. "All right! Forgiven. Just as long as you shut up!" And then he erupted in an involuntary laugh. Diana laughed, too. She liked this bantering far more than the aloofness he'd tried to affect earlier in the evening.

With her tentative help, David headed up into the Sakonnet River along Acquidneck's east coast. She felt heady with a sense of accomplishment. Soon the river narrowed. Farmlands and pastures rose up from grassy marshes to meet moon-washed barns and old New England homes.

"It's so peaceful here," she commented. David, who was busily taking down the sails, smiled, and it seemed to her that a quiet pride entered his eyes. He'd probably sailed these waters innumerable times, as a boy growing up, as a daring teenager.

"Di, lower the anchor for me, will you?"

Di again. The name sounded so personal, so intimate, coming from him. She blinked. "The anchor? Why?"

"Because if you don't, the boat will drift off while we're swimming."

"Who said anything about swimming?"

"I did. You don't happen to be wearing a bathing suit under those clothes?" he asked, giving her jeans and T-shirt a quick but decidedly approving glance.

"No. But that's perfectly all right. I don't feel like swimming, anyway," she said, watching the dark current slide by the boat.

"Of course you do. On a night like this, the river's probably like bath water. As still as a Vermont cow pond, too."

"Cute." She tried to look vexed, but he was slipping off his pants, and her eyes couldn't help skimming over the corded muscles of his long legs.

"Di, don't get all excited now, but I didn't bring a suit, either.

"You . . . you're not!"

Off came the shirt, and suddenly David was standing there just in his underwear. His chest was broad, his stomach hard and flat. For a moment the air seemed insufficiently thin as she tried to catch her breath.

She chided herself for reacting to him this way. All night she had kept a firm rein on her emotions, knowing there was nothing she needed less in her life than a man—especially this man! But for a moment, watching him remove his clothes, reason had abandoned her.

"Don't go any further." She pointed an unsteady finger at him.

"Wasn't planning to—though it's a perfect night for skinny-dipping. Now, what are we going to do about you?"

"Nothing. I'm staying right here, thank you."

"I wouldn't suggest going in wearing those jeans. They'd get too heavy."

She was about to protest again, but he'd already stepped to the edge of the bow. Then in perfect form, his magnificent body arced forward and sliced through the dark surface.

Diana peered over the side with growing anxiety. Eventually he emerged, yards away, his dark hair sleeked back from his high forehead, his strong muscled shoulders gleaming like polished mahogany. For a moment, her heart stopped. A sea god—that's what he reminded her of. Neptune rising from the ocean depths. She could feel a small bemused smile chasing her vexation.

"I can't describe it, it's that good," he called out. "Come on, jump in or I'll throw you in myself."

"No! I'll go in on my own!" She kicked aside her sneakers and pulled off her jeans—but she would keep on her long T-shirt no matter what he said. She inched to the edge of the prow and raised her arms over her head.

But when she peeked down at the water, panic took hold of her. "I can't."

David swam toward the boat. "You can't? What are you talking about? You're a good swimmer."

"It isn't that." She hesitated. "I . . . I can't dive."

David was silent one brittle moment, then he began to laugh. She regretted the day he'd first laughed at her because, having started, he seemed to indulge in it every chance he got.

"It's not funny!"

"Can you jump in?"

"That's a little easier, though I still get that feeling in the pit of my stomach. You know, like riding down sixty stories in an express elevator. Once I'm under, I begin to think I'm never going to find the surface. And at night . . ." She shivered.

David blinked up at her. His lashes were incredibly long and silvered with water and moonlight. Did he understand? If only he could see her ski, she thought. She'd learned at four. Took the women's downhill two years in a row at college.

But as soon as the thought struck her, she wondered why it had. What was this urgent need to shine in his eyes?

"I'll be right here," he reassured her. "If you can't find the surface, I'll haul you up by your hair. How's that?"

Diana rolled her eyes. "Terrific!"

"Trust me," he said, smiling rakishly. "I'll be right here."

Her toes curled over the side. Then, with a sudden surge of adrenaline, she dove into the water. She emerged, spluttering, about two feet from David. Her thighs were stinging.

"How'd I do?"

"I'd forget the Olympics if I were you. But for one July midnight on the Sakonnet River, it wasn't too bad."

Just as he'd promised, the water felt wonderful, like warm silk against her skin. It didn't take much to persuade her to swim to a tiny island nearby. It was only about thirty yards, he said, and the current was with them.

When they finally reached the island, though, she felt a rush of relief. She staggered forward, muscles quivering, and collapsed onto a patch of thin grass. Her shirt clung uncomfortably, and the night air, humid as it was, felt cold on her skin.

David sank down beside her and was quiet while she caught her breath. Lying on his back, he stared up at the hazy moon through the thin leaves of a sapling. A breeze rustled over the water and raised a chill on Diana's body.

"Cold?" he asked softly. She nodded. He lifted himself up on one elbow and rubbed her wet arms, trying to warm her. It was an innocent-enough gesture, she supposed, but it made her much too conscious of herself as a woman and of him as an extremely desirable man.

She sat up. "We should be getting back," she said nervously. Swimming out to this island with him had been foolhardy.

"Let's wait. The tide will be changing soon and the current will be in our favor again."

"How long?"

"An hour. Maybe a bit more."

"You don't know, do you? For all you care, we could be stranded here forever."

His mouth curved into a soft amused smiled. "Don't you ever shut up?" he said lazily. "Here we are alone on an island, the moon couldn't be bigger if it tried, and all you can think about is what time the tide is changing." He shook his head disparagingly.

Diana swallowed hard, staring into his heavy-lidded languorous eyes. And what might he be thinking about? she wondered.

As if reading her thoughts, David reached up and caught a handful of her long wet hair and slowly pulled her down to the grass beside him. All the air seemed to be sucked out of the night. She couldn't breathe, or speak, or think. All she knew was that his arms were wrapping around her, gathering her close. Their bodies pressed together, and then he was kissing her, exquisitely, passionately, the way no man had ever kissed her before.

Reluctantly he raised his head and looked into her eyes. She smiled. It felt so right, so natural to be in his arms. Ever since the previous weekend when he'd kissed her, she'd been able to think of little else. They may have claimed it was a mistake, but she'd known even then that theirs was an attraction too strong to forget. Not even David, who commanded an iron will over his emotions, could ignore the chemistry that flared between them. It frightened her. It was blind unreasoning attraction. But it was also thrilling. She felt heady and alive in a way she never had before.

She reached up and buried her fingers in his hair, pulling his head down. Her lips parted and his mouth touched hers once more in a deep probing assault that toppled the last of her reservations and turned her bones to water.

She could feel his body becoming insistent. He moved over her, his weight pressing her to the ground. His long legs entwined with hers.

"Diana," he said, his sensuous whisper sending small waves of heat licking through her body. She gazed lovingly at the black hair framing his leathery face, ran a finger down his beard-coarsened cheek to the mouth that now looked so sensitive and passionate. He kissed her fingertips.

"David, I don't understand this." Her voice was a helpless whisper.

"I know. When I went away last weekend, I was so sure I could ignore you the rest of the summer, but you have an insidious way of getting under my skin."

"Thanks. You make me sound like a disease."

"You are. A very dangerous one, too." His eyes smoldered as they traveled across her face. His hand ran lightly over her wet hair, smoothing it. "Why you?" he whispered almost to himself. "What's so special about *you* that made me come running back home two weeks before I intended to, hm? I don't even like you." His mouth curved in a sensuous half-smile. "You're a smart-mouthed nuisance who insinuates her way into everybody's business, invited or not. You talk too much, and you can't dive worth a damn.''

Diana curled closer into his embrace, drugged by his low soft voice. "Maybe it's not to understand," she answered. "Maybe we shouldn't even try."

David's face went deadly serious. Then he pulled her into the warmth of his body and kissed her until neither of them was capable of logical thought.

After a few minutes, nothing mattered. Nothing and no one existed beyond the small private world that enveloped them. Their bodies lifted toward each other, tightening into knots that strained to be released.

David's hands roamed over her freely, spreading waves of heat wherever they went. When he worked his way under her shirt and found the firm swell of her breasts, the heat between them leapt into flame.

Suddenly voices were whispering in her ear, voices she didn't want to hear. David was a man who never got involved. He didn't have the time for love. He only had affairs. But even if his intentions *were* noble, she had nothing in common with him. They came from different worlds. When her work was done at Cliff Haven, their paths would never cross again. And if she got too close, if she opened her heart too wide, she was bound to get burned.

"David, please, let's stop," she murmured against his lips.

"Di, I want you. More than I've wanted anything for a long time. Please..." His hand moved slowly from her breast down to her waist and over the smooth length of her thigh. A wave of debilitating heat washed through her. Still, she managed to sit up.

"No! This is crazy!" she said as firmly as she could.

He rolled away from her and lay still for a few seconds. "Why not?" His voice was tight with frustration.

"Because I don't want to."

"Don't lie." He shielded his eyes with his arm as if he didn't want her to see whatever lay within them. The gesture tugged at her heartstrings.

She stroked his hair lightly, only to have him shake her off with a hurt angry snap of his head. She curled up her legs and wrapped her arms around them. "David, you don't understand." Her voice was husky with impending tears. "I do want to make love. I'm very attracted to you." She was appalled by the easy way she was admitting to him what she'd been unable to admit to herself. "But we hardly know each other, and when the summer's over, we'll never see each other again. It would just be an impetuous physical affair, a one-night stand, simply because we happen to be alone under a full moon. And I can't live with that. When I make love, I expect love and commitment to be involved, too." She paused. "Are you listening to me?"

He sat up and gazed at the water gently lapping at their feet. "Commitment," he repeated sardonically. "And by that I suppose you mean a marriage license."

"Yes. Or the prospect of one in the near future."

He picked up a pebble and flung it into the water. "I told you last week how I feel about all that. I don't have time for emotional complications, Diana." He reached over and stroked her back. "What a pity," he murmured. "We're so naturally attracted to each other, too. I bet we'd light up the sky with our lovemaking."

He lifted aside her hair and ran his warm lips over her shoulder. Diana trembled with reaction. Then he turned her to face him and kissed her so persuasively that she almost changed her mind. But she knew she'd be sorry if she did.

Powered by a strong sense of self-preservation, she pulled away and stared levelly into his half-closed eyes. "No,

David!'' Her hands on his bare chest rose and fell with his heavy breathing.

"You know it wouldn't be hard for me to take you by force."

"I know. You're a lot bigger and stronger than I am. But even though I haven't known you long, I know you'd never do a thing like that."

He swallowed with difficulty. "How can you be so sure?"

"You don't play the tyrant very well." She smiled, letting her head fall so that his lips were on her forehead. "David, all night you've asked me to trust you, and I have. I was afraid to come sailing tonight. I was afraid to dive off the boat, afraid to swim to this island. But I did. I did it all, not to provoke you, but simply because...because you asked." She finished softly, her voice trembling with sincerity. "Now I'm asking something of you." She raised her head so that their eyes met. "Don't press me into making love. I'm not ready."

His dark eyebrows nearly met in puzzlement.

"You see, last year just about this time, I was supposed to be married, but a week before the wedding, my fiancé called it off. To make a long story short, I got burned. To a crisp. I lost a whole lot when we split up—my pride, my self-esteem and confidence, and I've been unable to get involved since. I guess I'm scared of being hurt again. So I have to be very careful. And I have been. I haven't become involved with anybody so far. Though, to be perfectly honest, nobody has come along who's interested me. Until now." She paused, wondering what it was about this man that prompted her to bare her soul. He himself was the most uncommunicative person she'd ever met. "David, I feel very close to you right now. Already I feel more for you than..." She paused. No, she couldn't possibly mean to say Ron, though that was the name on her lips. "But I can't make love with you. For one thing, it's not in my nature to have a casual summer affair. But more importantly, even it it were, I'm not ready. I'm scared . . .''

At that moment, there wasn't a single barrier between her and David. He was listening to every word she said, his eyes so clear she was sure she could see right through to his soul. And what she saw was an understanding and compassion so deep it momentarily startled her.

He tucked her close and rested his cheek on the soft crown of her hair. And there she sat, wrapped in the protective warmth of his arms, until she began to think he would never let her go.

CHAPTER NINE

"THERE'S A POT in here, but I can't find the coffee," Diana called from the galley.

"Are you decent?"

"Always." When David looked in, she twirled around. His warm fisherman's knit sweater swung about her knees.

"Lovely." He winked and ducked into the cramped quarters. "It's in the cupboard over the sink. Here, let me get it."

A few minutes later, they were sitting across from each other at the small table with steaming mugs in their hands.

"So, this creep...Ron? How do you feel about him now?"

"Still a bit angry."

"That all?"

She thought awhile. "Uh-huh. Funny, isn't it? Last year my world revolved around him and now—" she shrugged "—nothing."

"It happens."

Diana glanced at David curiously. "To you? Have you ever been jilted by someone you really cared about?"

"Of course not. Not me." He reached across the table for her hand and touched it to his lips.

Diana felt light-headed with the easy intimacy that flowed between them. It seemed like they'd been friends forever.

"I've been dying to ask you something, David. How did you get that little scar on your lip?"

He laughed quietly, squeezing her hand. "You're probably hoping I'll reveal a dramatic tale about a fencing duel or something, but it's nothing like that. I just fell down a flight of stairs when I was two."

"Eow!"

"But if you want me to embellish it, I could tell you my brother probably pushed me."

Diana's attention sharpened.

"It was all Evelyn's fault, though. She used to pay too much attention to me, constantly dressing me and brushing my hair as if I were one of her dolls. I think Walter was secretly jealous." Although the story was supposed to be amusing, David's smile faded. He retracted his hand and stared at his coffee mug.

"You and Evelyn have a special relationship, don't you?"

He looked up, his eyes still slightly unfocused. "Why do you say that?"

Diana's heart beat with anxiety. Yet she felt they'd grown closer tonight, and she could say almost anything to him. "She...she told me what you went through when your mother died."

David's shoulders tightened perceptibly. "Oh."

"She mentioned that you went to live with her, too."

"Yes. I'll never forget her kindness."

"David? Can I ask you something else? What kind of relationship do you have with your brother?"

David sipped his coffee meditatively. It was none of her business and he was probably thinking as much. But then he shrugged. "What can I say? When I was growing up, I idolized him. He was my big brother."

"But you don't see each other anymore..."

"Damn right we don't." Bitterness hardened his mouth.

"Well, that's what I'm asking, I guess. What happened between you two?"

"You don't know?"

"No."

"Honestly?"

"No!"

He subsided with a sigh of resignation. "After my father died, Walter and I came to blows over settling the estate."

"Wasn't there a will?"

"Yes, but my father wasn't himself toward the end, and to this day I believe Walter had too much of a hand in drawing up that will. I was in college at the time, so I was unaware of what was actually happening, whereas Walter was in the perfect position to exert his influence. The will gave him full authority over the disposition of the estate. And while I didn't mind Walter naming himself chairman of the holding company, I can't imagine that my father really wanted him to have seventy percent of the stock." David's eyes still looked painfully angry, and Diana could only wonder what he'd felt at the time of the argument.

"Of course," he went on, "Walter graciously conceded ten percent to me and Evelyn, with the remaining stock being in the hands of shareholders. Evelyn got an additional cash settlement, and I got the rest of my father's interests. But they were just a handful of tired old factories that Walter had no interest in and were about to fold anyway."

"And Cliff Haven?"

"And Cliff Haven, which is a barn compared to our house in Pennsylvania."

"Which Walter kept for himself."

"Right. That really knocked the wind out of me, being railroaded by my own brother. It certainly opened my eyes. No matter what you've been told, Diana, the meek do not inherit the earth."

"So, what happened after that? What did you do after you found out you'd been cheated?"

A muscle along his jaw twitched. "In spite of a lengthy court battle, there wasn't much I could do. I finished school and then went to work on those wrecks Walter generously let me have." In the silence that followed, he slowly began to smile. "Funny things, those wrecks..."

Diana didn't like the way he was smiling. It was an expression she imagined *Moby Dick*'s Ahab capable of. "They're the ones you still own today, aren't they?"

He nodded with immense satisfaction. "And Walter's blue-chip stocks have been dropping ever since!"

Diana didn't like the sound of his laugh, either. David had undoubtedly been deeply hurt and as a result had turned bitter and perhaps vengeful.

"So you haven't spoken since?"

David was quiet a long time, his eyes fixed on the table-top. Watching him, Diana got the strangest feeling there was something else lying back there in the past, something he was thinking about right now. But as close as they'd become, he wasn't about to tell her.

"No, we haven't spoken," he finally said.

"Don't you ever miss him? I mean, gosh, he has a wife, two boys who are your nephews..."

A curious shadow passed over his features and he blinked a few times. But then he lifted his chin with unyielding pride. "No. They mean nothing to me." And the subject was dropped.

THANK HEAVEN it was Sunday! Without even bothering to remove David's sweater, Diana fell into bed and went to sleep. When she awoke, her clock confirmed that it was just before noon. With a small contented smile, she wrapped the thick sweater closer and breathed deeply of a fragrance that was distinctly David's. Then she arose, feeling remarkably refreshed, and took a long hot shower.

She was combing the last tangles out of her hair when there was a knock at her door. It was David, leaning cavalierly against the door frame. "Hi." He smiled through the screen.

"Hi, yourself." She was amazed at how happy she was to see him again. "What are you doing up so early?"

"Diana, it's almost one o'clock!"

"Sure. But when you go to bed at five a.m., one is early."

"May I come in, or do you have a thing about talking through screens?"

Diana giggled and opened the door. Much to her surprise, he brushed a light kiss across her lips. Because it seemed so unthinking, she found it utterly endearing.

"I don't suppose you've had breakfast yet?"

"Uh-uh. What's that you're carrying?"

"Croissants. If you'll put on some coffee, I might even let you have one."

"You've got yourself a deal, mister." Diana fairly danced into the kitchen.

They decided to make a picnic of it, changing into swimsuits and taking the croissants and coffee down the cliff to a small sandy cove. Sitting cross-legged on her blanket, feeling the hot sun on her back, Diana nearly purred with contentment.

"I feel positively hedonistic," she confessed, wiping the last crumbs off her thighs.

David watched her with a small pleased smile. "You do have a knack for making feasts out of simple pleasures."

"They're the best kind."

The dark hair on his chest glistened in the sun. She studied the way it ran down to his hard flat stomach and disappeared in a vee at the waistband of his trunks. He had an incredible body. It was no wonder she had reacted with such volatility to him last night out on the river.

She tried to clear her mind of that disturbing memory by reaching for the book in her canvas bag.

"What are you reading?"

"Stendhal. *The Red and the Black.*"

"Oh, nothing to do with Cissy's work, then?"

"No. Just for my own pleasure."

"Have you reached the part where Julien has been caught with the mayor's wife and is running across the yard with the watchdogs at his heels?"

Diana shook her head.

"It's priceless. I've always thought it would make a hilarious scene in a movie." He paused, his eyes growing wary. "What's the matter?"

"You! When did you ever read Stendhal?"

"What? Don't you think I know how to read?"

"Well, when I was in school, I wasn't always that sure about you people in business."

"What a snob!"

"I am not!"

"You are. But that's beside the point. Where'd you get the idea I took a business degree?"

"Well, I . . . what *did* you study?"

"You ask too many questions." He sat up and removed a hairbrush from her bag. "Turn around." He positioned her between his legs and began to brush her hair. Diana closed her eyes and succumbed to the relaxing sensation washing over her.

"You have terrific hair, y'know that?"

Diana wasn't sure if her goose bumps rose from the gentle stroking or from the compliment. With surprising adeptness, he braided her hair and secured it with an elastic. When he finished, he planted a light kiss on each of her bared shoulders, then turned her around in his arms. The closeness of his lips made her mind reel.

"Archaeology," he whispered.

Diana blinked through her languor. "What?"

"Archaeology. That's what I studied."

"You're kidding!"

"Uh-uh. I was going to travel the world uncovering lost civilizations."

"Really?" She lifted her fingers to his forehead, brushing aside the breeze-tossed hair. "It doesn't seem fair, your life being rerouted just because of Walter's greed."

He leaned into her soft caress. "I made my own choices. I don't blame him for *that*."

"Do you miss it, the archaeology?"

"No. It was a fascination of my youth. Like love." He closed his eyes as she traced a pattern around his lips. Finally he grabbed her wrists. "Diana, for heaven's sake. I'm only human. Stop teasing."

Her cheeks warmed. "I... wasn't aware..." She moved away and wrapped her arms around her knees. "So, back to archaeology. Are you sure it was just a fascination? I hate to see people trapped in occupations they don't like."

"I do, too. That's why I'm in business. I may have fallen into it by default, but I've stayed in because I discovered I love it."

"I don't know, David—all that corporate raiding that's going on today, junk bonds and mergers..."

"I agree. It's pretty empty. That's why I'm not into any of that."

"Then, what...?"

He laughed in exasperation at her persistent questioning. "Manufacturing, pure and simple. I love producing things. Come on. Let's go for a swim."

The surf was strong, and David taught her how to catch the waves just as they were peaking and ride them all the way to shore. In the water, he became uninhibited and boyish, whooping with joyous expectancy as each new wave was about to curl over him. Diana had never imagined he could have so much fun.

Finally they dragged themselves up from the surf and collapsed on the blanket, exhausted and tingling all over. She turned to look at him. His eyes were closed, his dark hair sleeked back. Water was drying on his cheek.

"By the way, how's Cissy doing these days?" he asked, interrupting her quiet admiration.

"Fine, as far as her schoolwork is concerned." She sat up and sifted sand through her fingers. "David?"

"Mm." His voice was deep, sleepy, sexy.

"Have you noticed the tension between Evelyn and Cissy lately?"

He opened one eye and frowned. "Is there tension?"

"Uh-huh. And I think that's why Cissy failed English this year."

He sighed resignedly and sat up. "Am I about to hear another one of your theories about my household, Miss White?"

"But I was right about Abbie, wasn't I? *Wasn't* I?"

He nodded grudgingly. "So, what do you think Cissy's problem is?"

"Well, it all stems from the fact that Evelyn and Emmet want to get married, and Cissy feels that she's—"

David's hand suddenly clamped over her arm. "Get married? Evelyn and...? Whoa! Back up, Diana."

She stared at him incredulously. "Didn't you know?"

"Would I be making such an ass of myself if I did?" He loosened his hold and turned his dazed blue eyes on the horizon. "Married. Well, I'll be damned!" But almost immediately he swung back to her. "How is it that *you* know what's going on and I don't?"

"Because you're always too busy to open your damn eyes!" The vehemence of her answer dismayed her. He'd take offense.

"I know I'm busy, but I never figured..." He paused, lost in thought. "You say Cissy's not too crazy about this upcoming marriage?"

"Right. Of course, she won't always admit it in so many words..."

"It just sneaks out in failing grades."

"Right again. She's had her mother's undivided attention for so long, I guess she feels threatened now. She has to win back that attention any way she can, even if the means are self-destructive." She paused and lowered her eyes. "That's my opinion, anyway."

"Sounds plausible. The outrageous makeup, the pouting..."

"It's usually when Emmet's around, too. She loves to do things that cause him misgivings about becoming her stepfather."

David's lips tightened. "You know, I think you're right."

"I think so, too," she said. "But the biggest danger I see in this war she's waging is that she and her mother might drift so far apart they won't know how to get back together again."

David rubbed the side of his face. "Do you have any suggestions?"

She didn't like the flinty look in his eye. "I wouldn't feel right suggesting anything. It isn't my place."

"But if it were?"

"Well—" she sighed "—Evelyn and Cissy should spend more time together, and maybe the summer isn't enough. As

I see it, the problem might be eased if . . . if Cissy didn't go to boarding school.''

"Prescott kids have always gone to boarding school.''

"So? Maybe it's time to break with tradition. If she were living at home, at least she'd be part of her mother's new life instead of feeling shut out.'' Diana felt uneasy. David was looking at her with the same angry expression he'd worn the first time they'd met. "I'm sorry. Maybe we should drop this whole subject.''

"Yes, maybe.'' He stood up, frowned at her a moment, and then walked off with slow contemplative strides. Diana rolled onto her stomach and buried her face in her arms. Why couldn't she ever leave well enough alone? Why did she always have to go running headlong into other people's problems?

The answer wasn't hard to find. The truth was, she was as meddlesome as her brothers. They were all cut from the very same cloth. Only three weeks into the summer and already she felt too fond of the people at Cliff Haven, already too enmeshed in the everyday events of their lives. But she couldn't help it. That was just the way she was. Naturally she couldn't help feeling pain when they hurt. Neither could she keep from wanting to help.

But David didn't want her involved, and he certainly didn't invite her help. Perhaps because of his past, he trusted only himself to handle his affairs or those of his family.

Just then she felt the coolness of a shadow across her bare back. She swung around and looked up at David's towering figure. A tear trickled down her cheek.

He was about to say something when he noticed. "Aw, don't do that. Diana, for heaven's sake! I'm not mad at you.'' He thrust a hand through his damp hair. "It's me! How the *hell* could I let that happen? How could I lose touch with the people who mean the most to me?'' His shoulders rose and fell with sharp angry breaths. Finally he lowered himself to the blanket. "Okay. I'll do what I can. As head of this poor excuse for a family, I guess I should. I'll make the time."

Diana rested her forehead against his shoulder. "Thank you."

"No. Thank *you*." He raised her chin and stared into her eyes. He was going to kiss her, she thought. Small candle-flames of desire were burning in his eyes, and his mouth had a serious hungry curve to it. But then he looked away, took a deep breath, and when he looked back, the moment was gone. He leaned across her and lifted his watch from the folds of his shirt. Suddenly an unexpected dread gripped her heart.

"What's up?"

"I have to catch a plane back to New York at six o'clock."

"Oh." That's what she'd suspected. "Well, that still gives us a couple of hours." She blushed almost immediately. What if he wanted to spend the rest of his time here alone— or, worse, with someone else?

"Mm, but I should be packing." He seemed hesitant. "What did you have in mind?"

She sat up, equally hesitant. "Would you care to go into town? There's always something to do there." She waited for his excuse, sure that he would make one.

David sighed thoughtfully. "Would you like us to take your car? You don't seem too crazy about my bike."

Diana was afraid she would laugh out loud in her relief. "No, your bike's fine. Much better actually. Parking's horrendous on Sundays." She got to her feet and tugged on her beach robe. Going into town with David would be so much fun. Suddenly there wasn't a moment to waste.

David seemed stiff at first as they explored the gift shops along the harbor, and Diana noticed he never took off his dark glasses. As for herself, she was having a ball. She'd walked through these very same shops several times before, but with David along, they seemed transformed. The afternoon was charged with a special excitement.

Later they strolled out to Christie's Landing for something to eat. A Dixieland band was playing, and people were dancing right on the wharf. They sat at an umbrella-shaded table and ordered lobster rolls and frosty mugs of beer. The surrounding waters were jammed with boats, from multi-million-dollar schooners to humble dinghies. The sounds of their horns and bells punctuated the air, enhancing the harbor's holiday mood.

Diana happened to glance at her watch as they were eating. Immediately she jumped to the edge of her seat. "David! It's quarter to six!"

He nodded, smiling his endearing, slightly crooked smile.

"Don't you have a plane to catch?"

"I think so," he answered calmly.

Of course, it couldn't mean anything, she told herself shakily. So what if David had decided to miss his plane? And so what if he was looking at her as if she were a large part of the reason?

He glanced away. "I...I'd like to stick around Cliff Haven one more day. See if I can talk to Evelyn about Cissy."

"Oh." Diana felt ridiculous for having assumed what wasn't there. "Oh, of course. Good." She had to remind herself that David had been seeing someone else for three years, someone who provided everything he wanted in a relationship. Why would he want to get involved with her? He didn't have the time or inclination for emotional involvements. For that matter, neither did she.

But the plain truth was that it was happening, anyway, whether she ranted against it or not. She was attracted to David to a degree that stunned her, and what was perhaps even more alarming, she was beginning to realize she liked him, too. She really liked him, liked doing things with him, liked sharing his company and conversation.

But how did he feel about her? What purpose was she serving in his life? Diana gazed at his dark chiseled features and wondered for the thousandth time what was going on behind those blue eyes.

He sipped his beer and leaned forward, staring at her with unnerving interest. "So, Diana—" the corner of his mouth lifted into that roguish smile she was learning to love "—as long as I'm going to be here..."

"Yes?"

"Have you ever been to jai alai?"

"No." She was becoming increasingly light-headed.

"Me, neither. And I was just thinking I'd love to go tonight. How about you?"

DIANA WAS IN an abstracted state all through Cissy's lesson the next morning. David's being home on a weekday was such a novelty. She watched the clock with mounting anticipation.

They'd had a wonderful time at jai alai. David had been hilarious, refusing to place even a two-dollar bet until he'd had a chance to watch a few games and size up the players. Diana, on the other hand, had exasperated him by picking her tickets from the numerals in her birth date. But when she won a fifty-four-dollar quinella, he'd tossed his program into the air in disgust and started betting her way.

Midnight had found them at a pancake house. By one they were home. He didn't kiss her, but she knew he'd wanted to. Ever since she'd told him about Ron and her fear of being hurt again, he'd held back. But she sensed it was a control that wasn't coming easy. He had to work at it, as she did, and she wondered if he had any idea how quickly her fear was disappearing, or how much she wanted him to forget his chivalrous concern.

She'd had lunch and corrected Cissy's work before David finally came over. "I really can't stay, Di. Already my secretary had to cancel a conference this morning." He stood by the door, hand on the latch.

"When will you be back?"

"I'm not sure."

Diana didn't know what to say. Thank you for a lovely weekend? Please don't go? She felt sad and confused. She glanced up and noticed that David looked just as distressed. Suddenly he pulled her into his arms and kissed her the way she had been hoping and dreaming he would ever since she'd asked him to stop. Only now, the reality far surpassed her dreams.

Finally he drew his head back and breathed a long shaky sigh as if he had felt something he hadn't counted on, either. Then with an effort he pushed himself away and stepped out to the stair landing. He didn't say anything else, just gave her one last smile that reached down to the deepest part of her, and was gone.

THE NEXT AFTERNOON, Diana was just coming back from hiking the Cliff Walk, a three-mile path that ran behind some of the grandest mansions in Newport, when Abbie came lumbering over from the main house.

"You have a letter," she called, waving the envelope.

Curious. Diana had received mail here before, from school, from her family, but Abbie's eyes had never looked so mischievous.

"It came by special courier."

"Thanks, Ab." She took the envelope and glanced at the return address. It was from David. Immediately her heart was thundering.

Upstairs, she dropped her purse and camera on the couch and tore open the envelope.

"Dear Diana," the typed letter began. It was on crisp company stationery. "Included with this letter you'll find a couple of tickets to the Newport Folk Festival, which is this upcoming weekend." Diana began to smile. "I noticed your collection of tapes last Sunday and came to the conclusion there's no type of music you don't like, which leads me to think you'll really enjoy the festival. I wish I could be there to enjoy it with you . . ."

Diana's eyes swam out of focus. *Wish I could be there . . . ?*

"Unfortunately I'll be in Atlanta. But I've called an old friend in Newport who says he'd be delighted to take you. His name is Stan Hillman."

David was setting her up with somebody else? She couldn't believe what she was reading.

"I thought you might enjoy getting to know someone in Newport outside our family. Stan's a terrific guy. He's thirty years old, teaches art history at a nearby college and drives a funky old Aston Martin. I have a feeling you two are really going to hit it off."

There was a hastily scrawled signature—and nothing more.

CHAPTER TEN

DIANA LOWERED HERSELF shakily to the couch and stared at the letter. What had happened? Hadn't David held her in his arms just yesterday? Why was he pushing her toward another man? And pushing it was. She could interpret it no other way.

Had he suddenly remembered she was just an employee? Had he decided she'd become too familiar with him and his family and had better transfer her interest somewhere else?

Perhaps he'd come to the conclusion she simply wasn't worth his time. If there was no chance of having an affair with her, as she had told him, why should he bother with the tiresome preliminaries?

Or was she just so pitiful that everybody who came in contact with her felt the need to arrange a blind date for her with the nearest bachelor?

Whatever had prompted this letter, Diana was certain of one thing: she'd been crazy to let herself get involved with David Prescott. She'd spent the past twelve months guarding so carefully against the possibility of being hurt again. Why, then, had she been so ready to throw caution to the wind with David? Had this fairy-tale place lulled her into believing that what happened here really didn't matter? Had this summer out-of-time tricked her into thinking the pain really wouldn't hurt?

She was still sitting there staring at the letter when her phone rang.

"Is this Diana White?"

"Yes."

"Hi, my name is Stan Hillman..."

Diana covered her eyes with an unsteady hand. "Oh, yes. I just got David's note."

"Good, that saves a lot of explaining." He had a nice voice, rich and melodious, and Diana wondered what he looked like. She hoped he was terribly unattractive. Then she'd know David had merely wanted her to have an escort to the festival.

"Diana, I hope you don't mind this. I mean, I don't usually let my friends arrange my social life, either, and if you'd like to call it off, I understand."

"Listen, Stan, I honestly don't know what I want to do. I haven't had much time to think about David's letter."

"If you want to know the truth, I didn't trust his call myself. I wondered if maybe you and he were an item and he was trying to get you off his hands."

Diana's spine straightened. "Why? Is that what he usually does when he gets sick of someone?"

Stan chuckled. "We've been known to come to each other's rescue upon occasion. But he assured me that wasn't the case this time. He said there was nothing between you. You were simply a guest in his house."

"I tutor his niece." Diana's throat was growing so tight she was surprised she didn't croak.

"Yes, and he feels concerned that you might be getting bored."

"Well, isn't that decent of him."

There was a pause. "Are you sure I'm not stepping on anybody's toes here?"

"Positive."

"Okay, that's the last time I'll ask. Now about Saturday..."

"The folk festival. Sure, I'd love to go with you, Stan." Though her voice was even and friendly, her right hand was crushing David's letter into a hard ball. A moment later she pitched it across the room. "Dinner Thursday? That sounds terrific... Fine. See you at seven." She hadn't the foggiest idea who this Stan Hillman was, but she was determined to have a ball. And David and his unpredictable mood swings could go straight to hell!

WHEN STAN STEPPED from his sports car Thursday evening, Diana was peeking out her window, chewing her nails. He looked up and she dropped her hand—and then her jaw. He was gorgeous!

Stan turned out to be a wonderful person, as well. He was so unlike David that she had trouble believing the two were friends. Where David was reticent and distrustful, Stan was outgoing and gracious. Even physically he was different, with his blond Robert Redford looks and dazzling smile. And one more thing—David was right; she and Stan hit it off immediately.

They had dinner at the elegant Sheraton on Goat Island and later retired to a top-floor lounge where they danced till midnight. Across the harbor, the boats and buildings of Newport seemed strung with fairy lights. She hated to leave but knew if she didn't get some sleep, Cissy's lesson tomorrow would be a waste.

The Newport Folk Festival, two nights later, was held on the grounds of Fort Adams, a formidable-looking fortification built in the early 1800s at the mouth of the harbor. Stan's and Diana's seats were perfect, dead center and six rows from the stage, but then she didn't suppose David ever settled for anything less.

The program started, and she was enthralled—but only for a while. She was dismayed to find herself thinking increasingly about David. She didn't understand why the blasted man still filled her thoughts or why her heart raced when his image crossed her mind. He obviously considered her just an encumbrance, someone he had to unload on a friend. And yet she couldn't free herself from thoughts of him. He wouldn't give her peace.

The concert passed in a blur and, before she knew it, was over. On the way home, Stan suggested they stop by his place for a drink. He wanted her to listen to a CD he had of one of the guitarists who had performed that night. Diana was beginning to feel that the only place she wanted to be was back at the carriage house, but it was Saturday night and perhaps too early to go home just yet.

Only when she was there did she realize what an imprudent decision she'd made. She was alone with Stan, in his apartment, and she didn't have any way to get home. And though he had been nothing but a gentlemen all evening, she knew she was, in a way, at his mercy.

He put on the CD she'd supposedly come to hear and fixed a couple of drinks. When he sat beside her, he sat very close.

"I really can't stay long, Stan."

"No problem. Whenever you want to go."

He was really a nice person, she told herself, and they were just doing what most other people did after a date. Still, she couldn't help feeling uneasy, the way she'd felt with every other man she'd tried to date that year. And instead of being flattered whenever he put his hand on her arm or leaned closer, she only felt an irrational urge to slap him away.

It didn't make sense. Stan was Mr. Perfect, yet something was wrong. She felt no attraction, no chemistry.

It was nearly one-thirty and he was insistently putting on another piece of music when the telephone rang. He swore under his breath as he yanked the receiver off the hook.

"Oh—hello! ... Uh, yes, she's here ... Yes, of course ... No, that's not necessary ... Honestly, David, you don't—" He held out the receiver and stared at it a moment before hanging it up.

Diana's heart thudded alarmingly. "David's home?"

"Sure is. Diana, are you certain there's nothing going on between you and him?"

She felt herself flushing. "Why would he arrange for you and me to go out if he and I ... ?"

"I don't know." Stan frowned. Then shrugging off the thought, he sat again, letting his arm drift across her shoulders. When he began to play with her hair, she'd had enough. She stood up.

"Stan, I've had a wonderful time—I really have—but I've got to go."

He looked offended. "Sure, but do you mind waiting a little while? David's on his way over."

Diana's strength drained. "He's coming here? Now?"

"Yes." Evidently it never occurred to Stan to say no to David. His concerned gaze traveled over her expression. "I thought so." He lifted her chin so that she had to look at him. "Oh, be careful, Diana."

She answered sulkily, "I know."

"Do you?" His eyes drilled into her. But before either of them could say another word, there was a buzz at the door. "Cripes! He must have phoned from the booth on the corner."

A moment later, David was standing there, and if Diana's pulse had been racing before, it was now completely out of control. As soon as he entered the room, his eyes sought her out and swept over her with an odd combination of hunger and concern. Then he smiled. Her face suffused with hot color as she smiled back. Almost as an afterthought, he said hello to Stan.

"I hope you don't mind my stopping by."

"Why should I mind? You were just in the neighborhood, right?" Stan's tight smile hardly disguised the irritation beneath it. "Would you care for a drink?"

"No, thanks." David's gaze returned to Diana, again roaming over her like a physical caress. It made her feel alive and utterly feminine.

She didn't have the vaguest idea why he had dropped in at a friend's at nearly two in the morning, but she was thrilled that he had. In fact, she could barely contain her sudden joy. It made no sense. For most of the week she'd been furious with him, but looking at him now, she realized his presence filled her senses, her spirits soared, and she forgave and forgot whatever had made her angry in the first place.

"I stopped by to see if I could save you a trip out to my place, Stan. As long as I'm here, I can give Diana a ride back."

Stan sipped his drink, eyeing David over the rim of the glass. "That's not necessary."

"I know, but it's the least I can do. You were nice enough to take her to the festival."

Diana's eyes flew from one man to the other. Competitive tension was crackling just beneath the surface of their politeness.

"I honestly don't mind the drive," Stan returned. "Actually, I'll rather enjoy it."

"I'll take her home," David said quietly.

Diana stood up and scooped up her purse. "Stan, thank you. I had a marvelous time. But David is right. I'll hop a ride with him and save you the trip."

Stan sighed and threw up his hands. "Okay, if that's what you want." And giving David a look of grudging admiration, "Take care, David, you hear?"

In silent accord, they hurried down the stairs. David handed her a helmet, mounted his bike, and waited for her to climb on behind. A moment later they were streaking down the road, Diana clinging to his waist and feeling distinctly like war plunder.

They roared through the night without speaking. The beaches and mansions whizzed by with the beautiful illogic of a surrealistic landscape. The wind whipped at her hair, but she wouldn't let go of David even to tuck it back.

The night was deafeningly quiet when he finally turned off the engine. They got off the bike and walked to the carriage-house steps. There they paused, standing so close she could see the spikes of color in his eyes. How she'd missed him! And how happy she was now! It was almost too much emotion to bear.

Suddenly she was in his arms without knowing how she got there, and he was lifting her off her feet in a fierce embrace. "Oh, Di! I thought this week would never end! It's so good to be home! How are you?"

She could barely speak for lack of breath. He set her down, and she nodded, somehow conveying that she was all right. He touched her lips, her cheek, her hair, smoothing its wind-whipped tangles. His eyes gleamed as they studied her. Then they both seemed overwhelmed by another flood of emotion. He pulled her close and kissed her. Her lips parted and matched his ardor with a fire of their own. Her hands slid under the silky warmth of his jacket and reveled in the hard strength of his back. His hands caressed her hips, drawing her closer, molding her to him. His kiss deepened until she moaned. When he finally released her, she felt airborne. She clung to him, her head resting under his chin, listening to his racing heart.

She had been warned to be cautious of David—she could never say she hadn't. But there was something at work here that was headier than reason, a force even stronger than her sense of self-preservation.

She shrugged from his embrace and took his hand. "Let's go upstairs." They climbed hand in hand and, at the top, closed the door against the rest of the world.

In the dim light of a small lamp, David gathered her back into his arms. Beneath the soft cotton of his shirt, he was whipcord lean and hard, and just the light touch of her palms brought a weakness to the pit of her stomach.

"I've been thinking of holding you like this all week," he murmured, brushing his lips over the crown of her head. "I'm sorry about this thing with Stan. Did everything go all right?" His voice was low and languid with desire.

She nodded, nestling closer. He scooped her up into his arms and walked to the couch. There he lay her down and sat beside her.

"Why did you do it, David? Why did you set me up with him?"

He looked away. "I thought it would be good if you met someone else who could take you out. But then, once it happened, the idea drove me crazy. I'm afraid I made a fool of myself tonight, barging in on the two of you like that."

Diana laughed softly. "Did you think I was being ravished?"

"Well, if anyone's got the moves, it's Stan Hillman. When you didn't come home right after the concert, I got worried."

"You're as bad as my brothers." She brushed a finger lightly over his firm thin lips. She'd never felt so complete or so at peace as she did now, locked within the world created by his concentration on her.

"Di, the real reason I arranged this date with Stan…" His brow furrowed. "When I left here Monday, I started thinking about the wonderful weekend we'd spent, and I got scared. I don't know how it happens, but when we're together, things get sort of crazy. I do things I never intended…"

"And that scares you?"

"To death. All my adult life I've worked at being independent and in control. That's all I've ever wanted. Am I making any sense?"

"I think so. I make you feel vulnerable."

He nodded solemnly.

"So you fixed me up with the nicest, most attractive guy this side of Mars, thinking I couldn't help but fall for him."

"I didn't mean to push you into anything you couldn't handle. I know what you went through last summer."

"You just wanted to push me away from *you*."

He stroked her face, the look in his eyes so tender Diana felt weightless. His head lowered and his mouth touched hers, gently, savoring the softness of her lips. Then he made his way to her eyes, kissing each lid as lightly as a breath. "Di, if he happens to call again, don't go out with him."

"I never intended to." The last syllables were all but smothered under the warm pressure of his lips. This time they parted hers with a hot insistence that sent her into a mindless tailspin. Soon all she wanted was to lose herself in the fire of his body.

But David surprised her by sitting up. "There's nothing I'd rather do right now than carry you off to the bedroom, but we both know that would be a mistake."

Diana lay beside him, trembling under the light touch of his hands on her arms. No, not a mistake, she wanted to say.

Making love with this wonderful man suddenly seemed the best, most natural thing to do, and she wondered why she'd never felt this way before, not even with Ron. And as she watched him watching her, the answer quietly entered her heart. She was in love with David. For the first time in her life, she was totally, madly, in love.

"Something wrong, Di?" he whispered.

"No. Yes." She didn't know whether to laugh or cry.

David pulled her into his embrace, his chest rumbling with laughter. "Exactly how I feel."

Was it? she wondered. Did he have any idea what she'd just discovered about herself? As much as she wanted to believe he was in love, too, she didn't dare. They'd grown close, but she was painfully aware that he still kept a guard on the innermost tickings of his life. And when two people loved, there were no secrets.

"I should go." He kissed her quickly and wrenched himself up from the couch. "I can't be compromising the reputation of the local schoolmarm now, can I?"

Be my guest, she thought, rising also. "No, I suppose not. Everybody's giving me strange looks as it is."

"I know what you mean. Do you have plans for tomorrow?"

"No."

"Want to sail out to Nantucket?"

"Sounds great."

"Good. See you around nine, then."

"Good night, David." His gaze washed over her and again she was a lost drowning woman.

THE ROCK MUSIC pulsing from Diana's radio wasn't having the effect she'd hoped. She still felt miserable. And confused. She dropped her sunglasses into the bag she was packing for the sail to Nantucket and then fell back on her bed. As soon as David had left last night, the reality of her predicament had set in, and she'd thought of little else since.

Falling in love was not what she'd set out to accomplish this summer. It was precisely what she'd wanted to avoid. She hadn't fully healed from the last disaster yet, had she? Where would she find the strength to survive another? And it *would* come, just as surely as the seasons changed and her days here in David's world would run out. But even if she and David did have endless time, he'd told her repeatedly he wasn't interested in a serious relationship.

Then what was all this running back to her on weekends? Why the jealousy over Stan? Was it just a physical hunger she'd aroused in him? She wanted to believe she'd touched him more deeply than that, that she'd somehow broken through the barricade he held between himself and the world, but she suspected she'd only be kidding herself if she did.

She sat up, admitting she had no answers.

She was stuffing a towel into her bag when the telephone rang.

"Hello?"

There was a slight pause, then, "Diana, are you all right?"

"Hi, Stan. Yes, I'm fine." She guessed her hello had been rather flat.

"No, really. How *are* you? I hardly got any sleep last night worrying about you. I never should have let David whisk you off like that. I'm sorry."

"I'm just fine." She tried to sound upbeat this time.

"Well, I hope so. You're too nice a person. I'd hate to see you get hurt."

She tensed. "What makes you think I might get hurt?"

"Because David is what he is—a user."

"Stan!"

"Don't get me wrong. He's a wonderful guy when he's in your corner. The best. It's just when it comes to women...well, you know. Ever since that incident with Glenda... We can all try to pretend it never happened, like he does. But it did, and it changed him."

Diana's heart seemed to constrict as Stan's words sank in. There had been an incident with Glenda? Walter's wife? From the offhand way Stan mentioned it, he evidently assumed the "incident" was common knowledge.

"I'm sorry, Stan, but you've lost me. I know he and his brother don't speak because of the disagreements they had settling their father's estate. But Glenda...I'm not sure I know which incident you're referring to."

"David's being dumped, of course. What else?"

Diana sank into the nearest chair. "Oh, that. Yes, of course."

Stan was quiet a long while. She wondered if her voice had conveyed any of the hysteria she was feeling.

"I'm sorry, Diana," he finally said in a low apologetic tone. "I thought you knew."

She was too embarrassed to say anything and the silence spun out.

"David and Glenda went together years ago," he explained hesitantly. "Actually, they were engaged."

David had once been engaged. He'd been that close to another woman? Diana trembled, realizing how little she knew about the man she loved.

"And...what did you say? *She* broke up with *him?*"

"Uh-huh. And married Walter instead. David's never been quite as, well, considerate of women since."

"Glenda," she repeated dazedly. "You mean she's the reason he doesn't let himself get involved with anyone?"

"Afraid so."

She hadn't seen a single picture of the woman anywhere in the house, nor had she heard any conversations about her. Yet this mysterious Glenda had once wielded such power over David that her leaving him had soured him forever on romantic involvement?

"She hurt him pretty badly, I take it."

"Yes, pretty badly."

"She must have been some woman."

"She . . . yes, she was. I've seen David go through lots of women since, but none of those relationships were nearly as serious."

That wasn't what Diana had wanted to hear. She blinked rapidly and tried to swallow the lump in her throat. No wonder David considered a reconciliation with his brother impossible. More stood between them than just a stolen steel empire.

"That's why I'm calling," Stan continued. "To make sure you don't become one more casualty."

"I appreciate your concern, Stan, but I'll be all right."

"I hope so."

"I will. I wish I could talk longer, but I really have to run."

"I won't keep you then. But do me a favor—don't toss out my number just yet, okay?"

"I won't."

Diana hung up the phone and gazed out the window. David was coming through the front door of the main house. "I'll be all right," she repeated in a shaky whisper, but she already knew she didn't believe a word of it herself.

CHAPTER ELEVEN

"...JUST THE WAY we did yesterday with 'Birches.' Let your mind float free through all the possible connotations of the image— Hold on!" Diana threw down her book and went to the window. "What *is* that racket?"

"Oh, Uncle David's having the gazebo repaired," Cissy informed her. "The floor's rotted in a few places."

"Really? And he's actually taken the time to notice!" Her voice grated as if David had planned the repair expressly to irk her. Ever since he'd left for New York three days ago she'd been in a foul mood. It had started on the drive to the yacht club Sunday morning.

"Awfully quiet today," David had commented. "Anything wrong?"

She'd shaken her head and looked out the window, sinking further into the sullen speculations that had begun with Stan Hillman's call.

David had then pulled to the side of the road. "Don't tell me there's nothing wrong. I've never seen you this quiet before."

"Everybody's entitled to a bad mood once in a while."

He'd flicked off the ignition and given her a look that told her they would be going nowhere until she talked.

"David, do you like me?"

"What?"

"Do you like me? Do you consider me a friend?"

He'd laughed. "Yes, of course."

"Then why is it you've never told me about Glenda?"

For the rest of her life, Diana was sure she'd never forget the look that had come over David's face. "The first time we met," he'd said icily, "I gave you a lot of orders. Most of them were silly and embarrassing, but there's one thing I'll never retract—don't go prying into my personal business!"

Diana had flinched. Lately she'd begun thinking she *was* his personal business.

"Damn it, Diana! Why are you so fascinated with my past? It's gone. Ancient history."

"Is it?" she'd accused. "Is it really?"

"And what's that supposed to mean?"

"It means I think the past is very much alive and festering inside you, David. Losing your mother, what Walter did, Glenda's defection. You won't let any of it go. Any of it. It's turned you bitter and distrustful and it's robbing you of a future, but still you won't let go." Diana hadn't realized she'd been harboring so many opinions, and as they'd poured out, she'd become almost as shocked as David. Still she'd continued, "You dwell on your anger, David. It's what drives you. To work like a madman. To succeed beyond anyone's wildest dreams. To make those who hurt you pay, with their envy and regret and—"

"Enough!" That one command had carried such menace she hadn't dared say another word. "I think we ought to forget sailing today," he'd muttered, turning the key so hard the ignition ground. Then he'd sped back to Cliff Haven, back to its locked gates and No Trespassing signs, and within an hour was gone.

Diana had seen him angrier but never quite as defensive. It reminded her again how little she really knew him—and how strongly he wanted to keep things that way.

"I'm glad it's being fixed," Cissy said. Diana shook her head, trying to remember what they were talking about. "In the past that gazebo was used as a bandstand at parties. There used to be lots of parties here, though I don't remember them, of course. They were all before I was born. But we have tons of old pictures."

Diana returned to the table. "Let's get back to Robert Frost."

Twelve o'clock came around slowly. Normally Diana loved tutoring, but since her argument with David, she seemed to have lost interest in everything. She had an unappetizing cup of yogurt for lunch and then forced herself to read a grant proposal Evelyn had written for an adult-literacy project she was involved with in New York. When she'd jotted down a few ideas of her own, she took the proposal over to the main house. It was Cissy who came to the door.

"Oh, hi! I'm glad it's you, Miss White. Come here." She took Diana's arm and hauled her in, through the foyer and into a receiving room. Stacked on the settee were several satin-covered books.

"These are the family albums I mentioned this morning. I love looking through them." She patted the seat beside her.

"I just came over to return something to your mother."

"Sure, but you *have* to see this. Aren't these outfits too much?"

Diana was curious. She sat and within seconds was hooked. The photographs were priceless, capturing an era the way no textbook ever could, from the Gilded Age, through the raucous twenties, right up to the recent past. Diana looked at them all, and what she saw was a summer home alive with activity and happy social gatherings. She also saw a warm fun-loving family, for generations back, that proud aristocratic beauty marking the features of every one. In fact, she saw too much.

David's youthful handsomeness was so poignant it brought a tightness to her throat. He was in dozens of pictures, horseback riding with his mother, sailing with his sister, helping Abbie's husband tend a clambake. As he grew into his teens, however, another person appeared with increasing frequency, a blonde with delicate porcelain features and huge cornflower eyes. Even from across the span of time, Diana could see they were very much in love.

She knew Cissy was watching her and had been for some time. "That's Glenda, my uncle Walter's wife," the girl finally said. "She went out with David first, before Walter. They were even engaged for a while."

Diana tried to contain her reaction but knew it was overwhelming her. "How old were they?"

"In that picture? I'm not sure. Young. They started dating at fifteen, broke up about six years later."

Fifteen. Diana hadn't realized all that trouble had occurred so long ago. "Do you have any idea what happened between them?"

Cissy shrugged. "One day Glenda decided she didn't love him anymore. Sad, isn't it? I'd just die if somebody jilted me like that." She lifted another album off the floor, a scrapbook filled with newspaper clippings. She flipped through the pages until she found the items she wanted. Without saying a word, she placed the album on Diana's lap and stood up. "Y'know, I haven't even had lunch yet. I get so engrossed."

"Cissy, no..." If David didn't want her poking into his background, he certainly wouldn't want her looking at these clippings.

"I'll be right back as soon as I've had a sandwich. Can I get you anything?"

Diana shook her head. She considered leaving, but as soon as the girl was gone, she began to read. She couldn't resist.

Just as old Doc Wilson back at school had said, the Prescott family had indeed been in the public eye. But the longest, most detailed articles always seemed to involve David— the plane crash, his romance with Philadelphia socialite Glenda Hughes, the bitter dissension and court battles between him and Walter, and finally Glenda's marriage. David was prominent in each account. Diana no longer wondered about his obsession with privacy. His youth had been a nightmare of publicity.

Throughout the years, the press had followed the vicissitudes of the Prescotts as if they were royalty. Everything they did was a new installment in an ongoing public saga, each generation providing a few new chapters. Evidently, by the time David and Glenda arrived on the scene, people were ready to perceive them as society's crowned prince and princess. Reporters followed them everywhere, ever hungry for a glimpse into their glittering privileged lives.

Diana thought her heart would break for David—or at least for the David she saw in these yellowed clippings. He looked so happy, this coltish nineteen-year-old on the slopes of Gstaad where he and Glenda had just announced their engagement. How much older he looked only two years later as he hurried down the steps of a New York courthouse!

Diana flipped the pages with mounting agitation. She had to find more about Glenda. What had ever possessed the girl to break up with David? And when, *when* had this actually happened?

Suddenly it was all there, right at Diana's fingertips.

"Diana? Are you still here?"

Diana wiped her eyes quickly. "Y-yes."

Evelyn entered the room hesitantly. "I see Cissy's been at the old albums again." She sat beside Diana.

"I hope you don't mind. I came over to return your proposal, and I got sidetracked."

"Of course not." Evelyn's smile faded, though, as she recognized the album on Diana's lap. She picked up a loose clipping—Walter and Glenda's wedding—and skimmed the print. "But the topic that dominated most conversations this afternoon," she read sardonically, "was the conspicuous absence of the groom's brother and sister." She shook her head sadly as she replaced the article.

"He was put through the ringer, wasn't he?" Diana said.

"David? Ah, yes."

"Glenda broke off their engagement after it became evident he wasn't the Prescott who was going to inherit the family's steel interests, right?"

Evelyn sighed. "Oh, she denied it to the end, but it was pretty obvious. Why else would she break up with David? He adored her, and he had so much going for himself. And to this day I still believe she loved him, too. But apparently not as much as she loved the Prescott fortune. As if that weren't bad enough, he had to suffer it all in the limelight of the press."

Diana hunched over the album, lost in speculation. *He adored her,* she repeated silently. *He adored her.* She could understand how being betrayed had made him bitter. But was it also possible that Glenda had left an emptiness in his life no one was able to fill? Suddenly, Diana panicked. After all these years, was David still carrying a torch for Glenda?

No. The thought was absurd. Not even David could be so singleminded of purpose. Could he?

Cissy entered the room just then, and in silent accord they let the conversation drop. Evelyn picked up one of the albums lying on the floor.

"Good heavens! Is that really me under that huge hairdo?" she cried, making room for her daughter on the settee.

Diana leaned in to better see a picture captioned Family Reunion, 1962. "Those people aren't all Prescotts, are they?"

"They sure are. Cousins, aunts, uncles."

"And I thought I came from a large family." Diana's smile faded as she remembered the people she'd left behind in Vermont, people who, unlike the Prescotts, still gathered to take pictures like these. But then, they hadn't been tested the way the Prescotts had, by tragedy, by greed and deceit.

Cissy expelled a sigh that seemed to come from her toes. "Gosh, I have relatives I don't even know. Why don't we ever get together anymore?"

Evelyn swallowed with difficulty. "Oh, probably 'cause Kate and Justin are gone. My grandparents—that's who we all had in common."

Cissy sighed again, probably recognizing a poor excuse when she heard it, and opened a different book.

"Which one's that?" Evelyn asked.

"The one with Grandma Kate's big gala—1924."

Diana leaned in again, full of curiosity, as Cissy turned the pages.

"I wish we could throw a party like that," the young girl said. "Just once in my life, a real dressy affair, with tuxedos and ball gowns and flowers everywhere."

Evelyn glanced up. "Celia Osborne, the day you trade in those blue jeans for a gown I'll eat my hat."

"But I would, for a party like that."

Her mother chuckled. "It's too bad sweet-sixteen parties aren't in style anymore. Your birthday would be the perfect excuse. It's probably the last chance we'll get, too, if your uncle goes ahead and sells Cliff Haven."

"But sweet-sixteen parties *are* back in style. Where have you been, Mom?" Cissy's sun-browned face suddenly beamed with hope. "Oh, do you think we could?"

"You know we can't. Your uncle would never allow it."

Cissy sank back, sulking for a moment. "But we don't know that for sure. He's been doing an awful lot of strange stuff lately. Let's call him. He's probably in his office right now."

"Oh, honestly! You can be the most exasperating creature!" But there was something in Evelyn's voice that betrayed a fascination with the idea. "Let's think this through first. For instance, who would we invite?"

"Well..." Cissy sat forward. "I'd like my friends from the yacht club and maybe a few girls from school. About ten in all. That's not many, is it?"

"No, but if I know you, the figure will double by sundown."

"You could invite friends, too. Actually, this could be your party. The fact that it's my birthday can be secondary. I won't even complain about the music if you get one of those awful ballroom bands."

"Ballroom bands! Who said anything about music?" Evelyn laughed. "Will you listen to us! We're talking about this as if it's actually—"

"A small party then?" Cissy pleaded eagerly. "With records for music and potato chips for hors d'oeuvres?"

Evelyn fell reflectively quiet. "That's hardly what my sixteenth was like. What an affair that was! I'll never forget the gown I wore. It was from Paris, Cissy. Paris!"

"That's it." Cissy jumped to her feet. "I'm calling Uncle David. We'll never know unless we try. On second thought, let's have Diana—I mean Miss White—call him. She seems to have a way with him that we don't."

Diana's heart leapt to her mouth. She hadn't seen this coming. Evelyn and her daughter had been so engrossed she'd begun to think they'd forgotten she was even there. "No, Cissy!" she cried, but the teenager was already dashing across the foyer to the library phone.

"Cissy, wait!" Diana sprang out of her immobility. "I can't ask your uncle—"

"Sure you can," Cissy insisted.

"But what'll I say?" she asked no one in particular. "What'll I do?"

It was too late. "Hi, Mrs. Slater? This is Cissy Osborne. May I speak to my uncle, please?... Yes, it's very important." She covered the receiver and giggled. "Oh, no! She's ringing the conference room, and uh— Oh, hi! Uncle David?... No, nothing's wrong. How are you?... No, this won't take long. Somebody wants to talk to you. Wait a sec." With that, she thrust the receiver toward Diana. "Here. He's really busy. Better not keep him waiting."

Diana's legs turned to rubber as she took the phone. How was she ever going to do this? Her heart still ached over his angry refusal to talk about Glenda, his shutting her out from that part of his life as if it were sacred territory, and he was undoubtedly still angry at her for her persistent meddling.

"David?" Her voice was high and thin.

"Yes...Diana? Is that you?"

"I know you're busy. I won't keep you long."

"That's okay. What's up?" His voice was hesitant, guarded. Still, Diana loved hearing it again. The timbre of it brought his face to mind distinctly.

Evelyn took her daughter's arm. "Cissy, let's let Miss White handle Uncle David alone."

Diana returned a smile of gratitude as they left the room. "David, I . . . we . . ." How was she ever going to ask his permission to throw a party at Cliff Haven? It went against every grain of his character. "David, your sister and I have just been discussing a matter that needs your approval. It concerns Cissy's birthday."

"Oh, yes, that's in August sometime."

"Right. In two and a half weeks. She'll be sixteen, David, and we were wondering if we could have a little party for her."

"Sure." He seemed to be shedding some of his wariness.

"But we were wondering if it could be a little more momentous than just a cake and ice-cream affair."

David's sigh crackled over the wire. "Exactly how momentous?" he asked suspiciously, but she could almost see the mocking glint in his eyes. She smiled through her trepidation.

"The details haven't been worked out yet but . . . oh, David, this would be such a great opportunity for Cissy and Evelyn to get to know one another again. There will be so much to do during the next two weeks they'll be forced to spend hours and hours together planning and shopping and whatnot."

"Hm, it's the whatnot that's got me worried. What exactly do you have cooked up?"

Diana couldn't believe how receptive he was being. Perhaps he was trying to make amends for storming off three days ago. "Well, basically it'll be an outdoor party in the late afternoon or early evening, fifteen or twenty guests. Of course there'll be refreshments, probably a buffet," she improvised, "and a little music."

"This is beginning to sound highly suspicious."

"We're not asking you to do anything except give your permission. Evelyn will handle all the details and expenses. If you really feel uncomfortable about it, you don't even have to attend." She paused, biting her lip. "Well, can I tell her it's on?"

David drew in his breath. "I don't know, Di."

"Please, David. Cissy is so excited. If you could see her face, you'd know how much it means to her. It'll hardly raise a ripple on the surface of your life, but to her and Evelyn it may be a turning point." She waited. She could hear him nervously tapping on a tabletop.

"Evelyn will arrange the whole thing?"

"Uh-huh."

"And you'll make sure there are no press releases, no society columnists?"

"Of course."

He sighed, long and deep. "I must be clear out of my mind, but all right. Tell her it's fine with me."

Diana laughed with relief.

"What are you laughing at, troublemaker?" he drawled in a low sensuous voice. "If this thing gets out of hand, I'm holding you responsible."

"Me!"

"Yes, you, you little witch."

"David, aren't you in the middle of a conference?"

He chuckled. "Yes. As a matter of fact, I am."

"Then you'd better go. And thank you. Cissy's going to be thrilled."

"Di, wait!"

"Yes?"

She heard the rustling sounds of movement, a door shutting, and then a sudden quiet.

"About last Sunday..."

She held her breath. "I know. You're sorry. So am I."

"You *are* a witch. Now you're even reading my mind."

They both laughed, and suddenly Diana knew everything was all right between them again.

"Not as well as I'd like. When will you be coming home?"

"Not fast enough." His voice was a heart-stopping whisper. "I'll see what I can do to trim my schedule, but the way it looks now, I won't be back from Japan till a week from Friday."

"Japan!" Diana sank into his desk chair. "Oh, David!" That's all she could say. She wanted to cry. Each time he went away, time seemed to shift into a slower gear, until now ten days seemed an eternity.

"My sentiments exactly. Di?"

"Yes," she choked out.

"Can you forgive me for being such a jackass?"

Diana felt tears gathering in her eyes. "There's nothing to forgive. I'm the one who went prying into a sensitive area. I had no right." She waited, hoping he would refute her and say she had every right, hoping he'd take the time to talk about Glenda. But he didn't.

All he said was, "And I had no right getting angry."

"Maybe," she began hesitantly, "we can talk about it when you return?"

"I think not. It's done. Let's forget it, okay?"

Diana frowned. "Sure."

"You understand, don't you? I'm sick to death of the past. I hate dragging it up. It's tiresome. It's boring."

She paused, believing that he did indeed hate dragging up the past, but not because it was boring. "Sure, I understand."

"Good. Well, I'd better get back to my meeting."

"Right. Well, have a safe trip, David."

"See you soon, Di."

Diana hung up the phone, quietly rejoicing over their having made up. Still, what did it mean? Was she any more certain now where this summer was taking her than she'd been before the call? Had he said anything to make her believe his feelings for her were anywhere near what hers were for him? Her smile faded. For all she knew she was still just playing at romance, riding a one-way train straight into heartbreak.

FROM THAT DAY ON, Cliff Haven buzzed with excitement. Cissy and Evelyn were constantly going off shopping together. Abbie was turning storage closets upside down looking for linens and silver that hadn't been seen in years, and James groomed the grounds from sunup to sundown. As for Diana, she seemed to be doing a little of everything.

They were all having a great deal of fun. Yet Diana was becoming wary. In no time at all, a simple buffet had mushroomed into a dinner. Single buds on each table blossomed into whole bouquets, and the music was a live five-piece band. She helped write the invitations and was alarmed when she counted thirty-two. And every day Cissy or Evelyn thought of someone else who would just die if left out. Now there was talk of renting a tent.

With so much going on, Cissy had trouble concentrating on her schoolwork. She talked about dresses and how to do up her hair, which, luckily, had grown in enough over the summer to style. She became inordinately jumpy, too. She bit her nails, dashed to the mail as soon as it arrived, fell on the phone whenever it rang, and on more than one occasion was overheard muttering, "I hope things turn out all right."

Diana sympathized, but she knew she had to bear down now more than ever. Cissy had worked very hard, so hard that she would probably finish everything before the party.

Still, she had a long exam to take, and Diana didn't want her to jeopardize all that effort at the last moment.

She heard from David twice that week, but each call only left her feeling lonelier and emptier. It was unfair that love could do that to a person, she thought. Each night, she crossed off another day on her calendar, then went to sleep wondering what she was going to do with all this love when he finally did come home.

Two days before the party, Diana was kneeling within the border of perennials that edged the courtyard when the family car came up the driveway. Actually the plants were so overgrown she hadn't realized they formed a border until James told her.

As soon as he'd heard about the party, he'd begun to trim and weed, but he was getting on in years and the grounds were too extensive for him. Diana didn't know if her efforts were making any difference, but she was giving it a shot, anyway.

As the car approached, she stood up, clutching the straw hat Abbie had plopped on her head. Her arms were sunburned and two fingers had poked through her gardening gloves. Suddenly her heart raced with joy. The car stopped alongside her, David got out and waved James on. Then he stood there, staring at her with a look capable of melting steel. His gaze slid over her dirt-smudged clothing and back up to her eyes, and his mouth lifted at one corner into that little smile she found so maddeningly sexy.

She hadn't seen him in almost two weeks, but never for a minute had he left her thoughts. She'd missed him so much it had become a physical ache. She had so much to say, but at the moment she couldn't get even a syllable past her lips. All she could do was run, arms outstretched, and leap into his embrace.

He held her tight. She could barely breathe, but she didn't care.

Slowly, he eased his hold. "That's the sweetest hello a man could ever ask for." His lips found hers in a long urgent kiss. "And getting sweeter by the minute." he murmured against her mouth.

How was this possible? she wondered vaguely. In his embrace less than a minute and she was on fire. She'd never known such desire for a man. But then, she'd never known such love, either. It was deep, abiding, all-consuming in its power.

"It's so good to have you home, David."

He swept her into his arms and effortlessly carried her up the carriage-house stairs. "Good to be home," he said, smiling devilishly as he kicked the door closed behind them. Then he kissed her with the hunger of a starving man. Slowly, still kissing her, he set her down on her feet and pulled her closer. Diana's head was spinning, her body turning to a river of heat.

How strange life could be! How wonderfully, awfully strange! When she'd first met David she'd considered him the coldest man she'd ever encountered.

She still had no illusions that this fire in him was love. He was a virile man who had certain obvious needs—but emotional need was not among them. He'd been scarred by too many events and by too many people, and he'd disciplined himself against intimacy so he'd never be hurt again.

Neither did she believe she still had a chance of getting away with her heart intact. She loved David far too much for that. She feared for herself, but right now the fear wasn't quite enough. She didn't care if she got hurt. Right now David was more important.

She ached as if the injustice he'd suffered in the past were her own. She wished she could lift the pain from his heart—

the dark shadow of the plane crash, the wound where Walter had thrust his greed-driven deceit—and leave him free to love again and be happy. But most of all, Diana longed to erase the memory of Glenda, the beauty he'd courted for six ardent years before she'd tossed him aside in favor of wealth. Diana held him close, trembling with the desire to burn away those evil haunting memories, yearning to set him free with the heat of her love—even if only for a little while.

"Di, what's the matter?" David cradled her head in his hands, his worried gaze taking in her expression.

"Nothing." Her voice wavered as she took his hand. He looked at her questioningly. She returned a small shy smile and then gave his hand a tug as she led him toward her room.

CHAPTER TWELVE

THEIR LOVEMAKING was exquisite torture. David took such gentle care with her, such slow pleasure, she almost couldn't bear it. She felt her whole life had been a preparation for this moment; her existence had no other reason. Every part of her, body and soul, ached to join him, to fulfill him and be fulfilled.

When it was over, she felt nerveless, as if she'd had an out-of-body experience and somehow found a way to remain there, floating among the stars. She reached for the sheet, drew it over them and, with a contented sigh, drifted into dreamless sleep.

She thought she'd awakened into an impressionistic painting, the afternoon light seemed that unreal. Beside her, David lay sleeping, his arm across her waist. His face looked peaceful and so much younger than she remembered. Trying not to wake him, she ran her fingers through the thick black silk of his hair, remembering how tenderly he'd made love to her an hour before.

His eyelids fluttered. He looked around with momentary confusion and a defensive tension that tugged at her heart. But when he realized where he was, he relaxed and smiled. His gaze melded with hers, enclosing them within the small private world they could create whenever they were alone together. "How are you doing?" he whispered.

She smiled dreamily, still finding it hard to believe she'd taken this momentous step. "I feel . . . wonderful!"

He nodded and smiled as if he understood.

"But scared, too, as if I've just stepped off into space." She leaned up on one elbow. "What have we done, David? What are we doing?"

He smoothed back her hair, a quiet intensity in his eyes. "Having regrets already?"

"No. None. Never. It's only, well, we come from different worlds, and . . . and I'm not sure I know how to fit into yours."

"That makes two of us then."

"I'm serious, David."

"So am I. If you're concerned about my family, or the staff here, friends or associates, Diana, you get along with them better than I do. You're personable and bright, and you're genuine. You have a gift for fitting in."

She cast her eyes down and was quiet a moment. "Maybe that's not what I was really asking." How was she ever going to phrase this? How could she ask if she fit into *his* life?

"David, after I leave here . . ."

"Yes."

"We're never going to see each other again."

"Why not?" The corner of his mouth lifted. "Because of a few hundred measly miles?"

Diana lay very still, afraid to break the spell of this magic moment. He wanted to keep seeing her? Was he actually saying they had a future?

David sat up, pulling her with him, and propped the lace-edged pillows behind him. "So, tell me, Diana White, bane of my life, what's been happening around here while I've been gone."

Diana nestled into the warm crook of his shoulder, feeling incredibly happy and content. She told him all about the party and how it had grown. She didn't want to keep anything back. When she mentioned that a tent had been raised, he slipped from between the sheets and went to the window.

"Good Lord, it looks like a circus has come to town!"

"We didn't know what else to do, David. What if it rains?"

He turned, sunlight playing over his bronzed musclecorded body, and he smiled one of his endearing crooked smiles. "So, what other damage have you done?"

"The fountain out back is working again. Oh, and I painted the gate. Did you notice?"

"You did that? I suppose you're the one who pulled up the Beware of the Dog signs, too?"

"Oh, David, I couldn't leave those horrid things there. What a way to greet guests!"

The mattress gave with his weight as he sat beside her. "This is going to be some bash, isn't it?"

"Afraid so."

"Are you going?"

"Yes. You?"

"Looks like I have no choice."

Diana bit her lip. "Are you angry?"

"Angry? No, just terrified."

"It's only a bunch of teenagers. Some family and friends. No one to get nervous over. I wrote out the invitations myself." But even as she spoke, Diana realized how glib she sounded. For David, a party at Cliff Haven undoubtedly set off emotional echoes that even she couldn't fully understand.

He pulled on his pants brusquely and sat down again. "You were right, you know. The last argument we had, you were right about my living in the past. I do. Or at least I used to. It gave me a reason, an order..." His voice thinned. "But I get the feeling everything's slipped out of control this summer. I've lost my grip..."

"Good," Diana whispered.

"Maybe." He stroked her cool bare arm. "But what did I expect, letting you into my life, hm? First time we met, you blinded me, crippled me, brought me to my knees." Grinning wickedly, he pushed her back into the soft pillows and leaned over her. Diana smiled with the realization that he wasn't brooding on the past anymore—or on anything else for that matter. He kissed her, and kept on kissing her, until neither of them was thinking about anything but making love again.

EARLY THE NEXT MORNING, a landscaping crew arrived. Cissy was sitting at Diana's kitchen table, engrossed in her final exam. Diana's heart went out to the girl. She was so nervous her hands were shaking as she wrote. Diana put down the book she was reading and went to the window. David and Evelyn were out there, talking to the men.

"Well, I'll be!" she whispered. So David was getting into the swing of things, too. But then she'd already sensed his mood changing last evening as they'd walked the grounds. Standing at the fountain, watching the setting sun enflame the tumbling water, she had almost heard his pride kicking in.

Diana instructed Cissy to leave the exam on the table when she was done and ran down to meet them.

"How's everything shaping up?"

"Good morning, Diana," Evelyn said, her eyes shifting from Diana to David with a merry twinkle. "I thought we were doing just fine until David stuck his two cents in. I told him it was too late, but do you think he listens? He's brought fourteen men to work on the grounds. Fourteen! And inside we have eight more washing windows and—"

"You only have yourself to blame. You started it. I'm just making sure it's done right." His eyes crinkled as he looked at Diana.

"So—" she smiled back "—what can do? I'm free for the rest of the day."

Diana ran errands all that morning. David, who had been helping the landscapers, joined her for lunch. Then together they carried china and crystal from the pantry out to the tent. Much to everyone's dismay, a heavy drizzle began to fall.

"This looks more like a wedding than a birthday party for a sixteen-year-old," he complained.

Evelyn ignored him as she continued to count place settings. "I hate to say this, Diana, but we could use one more table."

"Do you have any more?"

"We should. Out in the stable." Evelyn seemed tired, but as time-consuming and expensive as the party had turned out, it had done wonders for her relationship with her daughter.

"I'll go take a look."

"Would you? David, go with her and help. Four more chairs, too, please."

The air inside the stable was close and dusty. Yet the beauty of the building shone through—the clerestory windows, the intricately lathed posts of the stalls. It was a pity that David was going to sell Cliff Haven, but Diana supposed she understood. While it contained the best of his memories, it also contained the worst. This estate was his most tangible link to the past. Cut this . . . and he was free! Still, it was a pity.

They found the tables and chairs up in the otherwise empty loft. But David didn't seem in a hurry to carry them down right away. Instead, he stepped to the two haymow doors and pushed them open. A tide of misty light swept past him. He lowered himself to the floor and rested against the door frame.

"This is a lovely view. You can see all of Cliff Haven from here." Diana could tell that he was trying to speak without emotion, like the person he had been at the beginning of the summer, but he failed miserably.

Gingerly, Diana sat opposite him. Her gaze roamed over the estate, out to the muted gray sea. When she looked back, she was startled to find David's eyes on her, so still, so serious!

"Di, do you like it here?"

"Yes. Very much." She held her breath.

"So do I." With those few words she knew years of denial had just been reversed. "I think I'll hang on to the place a while longer. Besides, the interior of the house really needs an overhaul. I shouldn't try to sell it the way it is. What do you think?"

"That . . . that would be wonderful." Her throat was so tight with joy, her voice was barely audible.

His eyes traveled over her face, down her body to her legs, which she'd crossed at the ankles. A mixture of admiration and wistfulness filled his expression. "Di, talk to me," he said.

"Talk to you? About what?"

"Anything. I just love to hear your voice."

Diana cleared her throat. She paused, then cleared her throat again. For once in her life, she couldn't think of a single thing to say. She smiled diffidently.

"You know, you have a beautiful smile. It's so unaffected and warm. I bet you're going to have the loveliest lines in your face when you're old."

Diana looked down at her nervously interlacing fingers. She had made love with this man only yesterday, yet now she felt shy and a little frightened—as if they were on the edge of something immense.

"Di, I know I'm a difficult person to be with sometimes, and I know my work has..."

From where she sat, Diana could see the front gate open. A moment later, a car came up the drive. David looked out, too, and whatever he was about to say was momentarily forgotten. The car came toward the house so slowly it looked positively hesitant.

"Can that be the florist already?" Diana asked.

"I doubt it. Unless he's taken to driving a Mercedes lately." David's forehead puckered.

The car glided to a stop under the portico, and after a tense moment, two people got out. From the driver's side emerged a tall man with graying hair dressed in a light summer suit; from the other, a blonde who seemed to have stepped off the cover of *Vogue*.

"Oh, Lord!" David whispered, ashen under his tan. "Oh, dear Lord!" He trembled before his color came surging back. He leapt to his feet.

"David, what's the matter?" Just watching him, Diana was in a panic.

But he didn't answer and she suspected he hadn't even heard her. All he did was stare at the couple, as he stood there poised like a tiger about to pounce from his perch.

She turned and looked at them again, and suddenly awareness of who they were jolted through her. "That's your brother and Glenda, isn't it?" But David was still wild-eyed, breathing hard.

The couple walked to the front door, looking around slowly. Before they had a chance to knock, Cissy opened the door and let them in. Diana glanced at David. A vein was throbbing along the side of his taut face.

"Isn't that the strangest thing? Did you know they were coming?" Immediately she felt foolish.

He wheeled around and glared at her. His eyes, so loving just a minute ago, were now like hot coals, burning with the blackest anger she'd ever seen. Her nerves shattered.

"How could you do this to me? Diana, why did you invite them here?"

"But I didn't!"

"What did you tell them?" he went on, deaf to her. "We couldn't have a party without their hallowed presence?" His words came out stark and tight, through teeth that wouldn't unclench.

"But, David, I didn't!" She was so stunned by his accusation, she could barely speak.

"How could you do this to me?" he repeated, slamming the wall with his fist.

"David, please! I—I'm as surprised as you are."

He glowered down at her. "Are you? Well, somehow I find that hard to believe." He paced the floor, clenching and unclenching his fists as if he wanted to hit something again. "Damn it! Damn it!"

Watching him, Diana thought he looked rather like an animal pacing in a cage. Was he afraid of seeing Walter again, the brother who had shamelessly cut him out of his rightful inheritance?

Or... or was it Glenda? Was she the cause of this emotional maelstrom in David's soul? Diana's blood ran cold. Recently she'd wondered about David's feelings for Glenda—if he still carried a torch for her, deep down in some secret part of himself. But whenever the thought reared its head, she just as quickly denied it.

What a fool she'd been! What a stupid blind fool! Glenda was the first woman he'd ever let himself love, and he had loved her completely. "Adored her" were the words Evelyn had used. Glenda was also the only woman who'd ever been able to hurt him. Now as Diana stared at David, she realized that after all these years, David still loved his brother's wife. After all these years he was still open to being hurt by her.

David stopped his pacing and cast Diana a bitter look. "Why did I ever let you talk me into this damned party? You've changed everything. Why did I ever let you in here?"

Diana's throat constricted painfully. She couldn't believe how unfair he was being. Evidently the intimacy they'd shared meant nothing to him. One turn of events, and he was ready to hate her. There *was* no life for them in the future. The idea was absurd—and always had been. The only thing that loomed in her future was heartache and loneliness. David wanted no part of her, and never had. Not seriously.

Well, if that was the position he was determined to take, there was no use in trying to defend herself. There wasn't enough time left to the summer to do that. All she could do now was try to escape with a little of her dignity intact.

She stood up, straighted her back and lifted her chin. "I think I'd better go."

"Don't bother!" There was only contempt in his voice as he headed for the stairs.

"David, you aren't going to cancel Cissy's party because of this, are you? She'd be crushed if you did. She's been planning it for weeks, night and day."

"Looks like she wasn't the only one who was making plans." He turned stiffly and retraced his steps. "Do you think this is funny?" he said, pointing toward the car under the portico. "Do you think some miracle is suddenly going to happen? A great dramatic spirit of forgiveness embracing us after all these years?"

"No." Diana lowered her eyes. "But... but it would be wonderful if it did. I think you care about Walter more than you know."

"You poor deluded optimist!" His face was as dark as the clouds pressing down from the sky. "Diana?"

She looked up. "Yes?"

"Leave me alone. Please, get out of my life and give me back my peace."

He descended the stairs, his posture wooden and erect. Diana slumped against the wall and listened to him go, her lips trembling uncontrollably.

She watched him cross the courtyard through the drizzle, walking with the purposefulness of a man heading into a duel to the death.

I didn't do it! I didn't ask them here! she wanted to cry out. But he glanced up at her, standing in the hayloft door, and his cold blue eyes executed her on the spot. Her mouth closed and she lowered her head.

CHAPTER THIRTEEN

DIANA CARRIED the table and chairs to the tent, then hurried to the safety of her apartment. But even there, she was pursued by misery. With trembling hands, she set a kettle of water on for tea and forced herself to correct Cissy's exam.

When she was finished, she sat back and thought, well, at least there was one thing to redeem the summer—the girl had passed English with an A. Diana longed to tell her the good news, but she wasn't about to trek over to the main house now. She didn't even have the courage to phone. Heaven only knew what was going on over there or what kind of reception she would get.

With the test corrected, her summer here was done. She had nothing left to do. Nothing, that is, except think about David's unfair accusations and try not to cry. She loved him, more than she'd ever loved anyone in her life, and it destroyed her to be despised in return.

Early in the evening, there was a knock at her door. It was Abbie, florid-faced with excitement.

Diana jumped from the chair where she'd been nervously watching the house. "Abbie, what's going on?"

The old woman rolled her eyes and fell into a chair. "We were all trying to listen from the back hall, but it was hard. There was so much hollering going on."

"They're quarreling?"

"Oh, yes! And poor Celia, curled up in a chair like a mouse in the middle of them all."

Diana moaned. "What's going to happen?"

"I don't know. But if the roof don't blow by tonight, it never will." Abbie tried to laugh but the gravity of the situation defeated her.

"Do you have any idea why Walter and Glenda showed up—*now* of all times?"

"They say they got an invitation to the child's party! Can you imagine! They thought it was from Evelyn, and they figured if she could put aside her pride and invite them to a party, the least they could do was bring the girl a gift. They weren't planning to stay much beyond that."

"But Evelyn didn't send them an invitation. I helped her write them myself." She paused. "Oh, Abbie! You don't suppose . . ."

"That's just what I've been thinking."

"So that's why she's been so jumpy lately. Cissy took it upon herself to send them an invitation in secret! I bet she thought if she got them all together, she could force a reconciliation."

Abbie nodded vigorously. "But if she did, she hasn't owned up to it yet. For some reason, David seems to think you did it. I heard your name mentioned a few times."

Diana closed her eyes and fought back angry tears. "Well, if he insists on blaming me, that's his problem. If it'll keep Cissy out of hot water, I won't try to alter his verdict, either. He's not worth the effort." Diana felt Abbie's keen old eyes on her. "Well, he isn't!"

"Don't give up now, child. You've brought him so far. He'll come around."

Diana shook her head. "Not this time."

"Why do you say that? What's happened?"

Diana thought back to the argument in the stable and the words that had hurt so much. She was also aware of the person whose arrival had prompted those words.

"Abbie, do you think it's possible he's still in love with Glenda?"

Abbie's eyes narrowed. "You know all about that, do you?"

She nodded. She hoped the woman would reply with a ready "Of course not." But she didn't.

"Who can tell? He keeps so much to himself. I don't *think* he loves her. It's been so long."

"But you're not sure..."

"All I know is he loved her once. But she's no good for him. And he's aware of that."

Diana had her answer. But then she'd known it all along. She'd read it in David's face when he'd seen Glenda arrive. She was an obsession with him. She crowded out any possibility of new love ever blooming. Nobody else had a chance.

"The thing to do now is sit tight," Abbie said compassionately. "He still has some anger to work out. But then he'll come around. You'll see."

But Diana had no intention of sitting tight. He didn't want her in his life and never had. Well, she was determined to grant him his wish.

She went to the window dozens of times after Abbie left. The house looked still from the outside, but inside... She didn't want to think about what might be happening inside those thick stone walls. Lights went on, one by one. Then around ten o'clock, the caretaker came out to the Mercedes for a suitcase, and when Diana went to bed at twelve, the car was still under the portico.

SHE COULD TELL it was going to be a perfect day as soon as she lifted her bedroom shade. The drizzle from the day before had washed the world clean. Now the air was hot and dry, and a lovely evening was sure to follow.

Diana surmised the party was still on, in spite of the latest turn of events. Voices drifted from the service side of the house, and on the back lawn, caterers were dashing in and out of the tent.

She went to her closet and pulled out her luggage. She had wanted to attend the party so much, but there was no possible way she could do that now. With an aching heart, she began to pack her clothes. Why she hadn't started last night was beyond her. Maybe she'd been secretly hoping Abbie was right, that David would come over and apologize, talk to her and set everything right between them.

But he hadn't, and now she couldn't pack fast enough. It was time to get out of here, time to return to reality and get on with her life.

She was making her second trip down to her car when Cissy came jogging over. "Hey, what are you doing?"

Diana couldn't meet the girl's eyes. "I don't like to leave things for the last minute. Oh, hey! Happy birthday, sweetheart."

"Thanks. I can't believe I'm finally sixteen!"

"It's a landmark year, kiddo." Diana winked. "By the way, I've corrected your exam. You got an A!"

"An A!" Cissy threw back her head and laughed. "Now the day's perfect. Thanks, Miss White. You've been great."

"So, how is everything else—at the house I mean?"

Cissy grimaced. "Quieter than last night."

"Was it you who sent that invitation?"

Cissy's eyes lowered and she nodded. "I thought the feud had gone on long enough. I wanted the family to be together at my party." She flicked a worried glance over to the house. "I never expected the reunion to be easy, but, cripes, I never thought it would be this hard! I was sent to bed around midnight and they were still going at it!" She sighed wearily. "All I wanted... Well, our family used to be so big once, and happy—like yours—and I guess I just wanted a little of that for myself. Things are better today. I'm still in hot water, but at least everyone's agreed to overlook it till the party's over.''

"*You're* in hot water?''

"Mm. I wasn't going to say anything about sending the invitation, but somehow Uncle David got the idea you'd done it. I waited almost three hours before I did confess, though. I'm sorry.''

"Don't apologize. It doesn't matter what David says or thinks about me. And another thing, don't let him bully you. Your intentions were noble. You acted out of the goodness of your heart.''

"That's what Mr. Thorndike says, too.''

"Emmet? Is he here?''

"Uh-huh. He arrived early this morning.''

Diana couldn't help noticing the look of gratitude on the teenager's face when she mentioned Emmet as an ally.

"I guess he's not such a bad guy, after all,'' Cissy continued. "Oh, I haven't told you the biggest news of all—I won't be going back to Fairview in September.''

"What!''

"Isn't that something? My mother wants me to stay home and help her get adjusted to married life. I'll be attending a school in New York just a few blocks from our apartment.''

"Well, that certainly is something!'' Diana began to smile. How clever of Evelyn to come up with such a brilliant rationale. "I'll miss you, kid. Fairview won't be the same.''

"I'm sure it'll survive. Well, I gotta go. Gotta get my hair done. See you tonight, Miss White.''

Diana waved with a too-bright smile, realizing it was probably the last time she would see the girl.

Packing took longer than Diana expected. She'd accumulated so much junk over the summer. And then she still had to run into town to pick up Cissy's gift at the jeweler's. She'd ordered a silver chain and a charm in the shape of a whale—to remind Cissy forever of her least favorite novel. She would leave it wrapped on the kitchen table along with a note apologizing for her hasty departure.

She'd just returned from running this errand when she glanced out the window and noticed David and Glenda stepping out of the house. They were already dressed for the party, David in a formal black suit, Glenda in a watery champagne silk dress. Diana hadn't realized it was so late. She should have been gone hours ago.

With troubled eyes, she watched them descend the stairs. Glenda was looking up at David and talking animatedly, a smile brightening her beautiful face. Whatever she said made him laugh.

They stopped at the Mercedes for a shawl. David took it from her and carefully draped it over her shoulders. Then they continued on their stroll, oblivious to the bustling preparations all around them.

Diana's insides felt as if they were being ripped to shreds. How many times had those two walked these grounds when they were young and in love? What was to say they weren't in love still? Maybe Glenda realized she had made a mistake in choosing the older brother. Maybe that's what she was telling David now.

Suddenly Diana feared for David, feared a situation that could easily break open into another public scandal, possibly the worst yet. As successful as he had been in downplaying his image over the past thirteen years, there would be no escaping the attention he'd provoke if he chose to pursue his brother's wife. It would be one more installment in the continuing Prescott family saga, moving with satisfying predictability toward the union of their two most glamorous characters. The press wouldn't be robbed of such a fairy-tale story, nor the innumerable spin-off articles that would mawkishly recount the events from the past that had led up to it.

But there was nothing Diana could do about that now. David was a grown man, with a will of his own. If he wanted to go after Glenda, then he obviously considered her worth the consequences. Besides, Diana had to think of a way to get out of here without drawing attention.

But in spite of her growing sense of urgency, she continued to lean on the sill, watching. Cars were pulling into the courtyard, and elegantly dressed people were converging on the back lawn. Orchestra music drifted on the breeze, now loud, then soft, and mingled with fragments of conversation and laughter.

For a moment, she heard David's voice above the others. She searched the gathering and found him, looking every bit the congenial host. What a change from the man she'd met only seven weeks before! He was devastating in dark evening clothes, tall, confident and so at ease. And why not? Glenda, the woman he had chosen to marry years ago was back in his life and smiling at him just a few feet away.

Diana could take no more. She knew what she had to do, and it had to be done immediately.

WITH HEADLIGHTS OFF, she inched her Toyota up the drive, through the gauntlet of cars parked along each side. Behind her, Cliff Haven was a blaze of lights. Music filled the air.

Her duties were over, she told herself, trying to put things into perspective. She had come here to tutor Cissy Osborne, and she had done her job—quite well, too. In the process, she'd put some distance between herself and her brothers, and she'd sailed right on by the anniversary of her almost-wedding without even realizing it. There was no earthly reason to stay in Newport any longer.

Out of habit, her foot moved to the brake as she approached the gate. What a tedious chore that had been—all that stopping and starting and getting in and out of her car just to pass through. But tonight the gates stood wide open and unguarded.

Suddenly she remembered her key. It was still in her handbag! She stopped the car and thought about returning to the carriage house to leave it on the kitchen table, but she didn't want to risk being seen and questioned. Then she thought, wouldn't it be a pleasure just to fling it into the woods! She dug the key out of her bag and stared at it. Slowly she touched it to her lips. No, she wouldn't throw it away. She would keep it as a souvenir and in years to come perhaps have it mounted. "Found art," she would call it, and when someone asked, she'd tell them all about the fairy-tale mansion with its locked gates where she had worked one timeless summer when she was young.

Where she had worked? And what would she tell them about all the love?

She sped up Ocean Avenue as if pursued. In the distance, far out on the promontory, Cliff Haven blazed on. Diana felt empty, empty of everything that really mattered. It was as if she had left her soul behind.

CHAPTER FOURTEEN

THE LAST TIME Diana had phoned her brother Skip, he'd been in the midst of packing for a camping trip. That had been four days ago, so she wasn't surprised to find the farmhouse deserted when she arrived, and the front porch light set on an automatic timer.

She carried her bags into the living room, then sank into an easy chair, letting her gaze roam over the quiet room. She hadn't told Skip that her job was ending a week ahead of time. She hadn't wanted him to change his plans just to be here when she returned, and she knew he would have, too. But now, how she wished she had told him. She needed a strong sympathetic shoulder tonight.

She'd left here thinking she didn't want or need that close familial concern, but she'd been wrong. That was not what independence was all about. Her family's concern had helped her weather so many storms. Even the stupid blind dates they'd arranged after the disaster with Ron had probably helped. They'd forced her to dress up, get out and socialize, and climb out of her occasional depression. Having observed the Prescotts, she now knew she was blessed to have family who cared enough about her to drive her crazy! How awful to have to go through life alone.

But then, she'd probably known that all along, she thought, recalling that the first change she'd made at the carriage house had been the installation of a telephone. No sooner had she arrived than she'd wanted to hear a familiar loved voice. And she had. She'd called everyone, once or twice a week throughout the summer—brothers, sisters-in-law, aunts, uncles. In fact, the phone had become her biggest expense.

She rose, suddenly wanting to call Andy or Mark to let them know she was back. But it was after midnight, and she would undoubtedly be rousing them from sleep.

She paced restlessly. By now the party at Cliff Haven would be long over, and everyone there would know she was missing. She hoped they weren't too angry. She would have to call tomorrow and say her goodbyes properly.

She wandered through the dining room, into the kitchen, flipping on lights as she went. Somewhere she would find comfort within these rooms, among the portraits and knickknacks and overstuffed furniture of her growing-up years.

But all she found was herself, alone. Tonight everything looked unfamiliar. The house had lost its sense of home.

She climbed the stairs to her old room, exhausted and eager to crawl into bed. But even as she pulled back the covers, she knew sleep would elude her. Her mind and heart were too full of Cliff Haven and how it had come to feel like home.

But of course it wasn't Cliff Haven. It was the fact that David was there. She knew she would feel at home wherever he was.

Why had she done it? she asked herself as she lay staring at the dark ceiling. Why had she fled Newport so abruptly? Was she that angry at him for distrusting her? Was she that hurt over his blind obsession with Glenda? That scared of hearing the words "I'm sorry, Diana, it's been fun, but..."?

Yes, she admitted, a resounding YES to it all.

Not that running away had provided an escape. The pain had followed her home, and as she'd suspected, it was far worse than anything she'd ever suffered before. But staying in Newport would only have made things harder. At least this way she'd preserved a modicum of pride.

Besides, it was too late for regrets. She'd done it. She'd left, and David was finally a part of her past, as she'd always known he would be. All she had to do now was figure out how to pick up the pieces of her life.

SHE AWOKE LATE the next morning. Someone was ringing the front doorbell. She hopped out of bed and threw on her robe, wondering if one of her brothers had been passing on his way to church and seen her car.

She peeked out the window and found, not one of her brothers, but a stranger in a uniform. Out in the driveway was a florist's delivery truck. She wiped her smudged mascara and opened the door.

"A delivery for Miss Diana White."

"Thank you." She took the long white box and turned.

"Ma'am? If you'll just wait..."

With stirred curiosity, she watched the delivery man return to his truck. He came back with five more identical boxes.

"Are you sure these are all...?"

"Yes, ma'am."

Stupefied, she waved goodbye and stared at the mysterious boxes stacked on the hallway floor. Almost fearfully she lifted one of the covers. Inside, nestled in green tissue, were a dozen perfect long-stemmed red roses. A card identified the sender simply as "David." Immediately her eyes filled with tears.

She opened the second box to find another dozen roses, the third box and the fourth—until finally six dozen roses scented the air with their heady perfume. She sank to the floor in the middle of them all and clutched her arms tight, holding back a sob. Why couldn't David let her make a clean break? Why did he have to prolong the suffering? Did he actually think that flowers would ease the pain of his dumping her? Did he think he could appease her with a consolation prize?

She picked up a few velvety buds and shakily breathed in their fragrance. She had never seen so many beautiful flowers in one place before. Except at funerals. How apt, she thought, as a tear slipped down her cheek. How perfectly, horribly apt!

Afraid that she was on the edge of completely breaking down, she hauled herself up and took the roses into the kitchen. Best to keep busy, she told herself, as she searched the cupboards for her largest vases. But as she worked, her mind inevitably returned to last evening's party.

As hard as she'd tried, she still couldn't shake the image of David, talking to his guests, with Glenda just an arm's reach away. He'd looked so at peace with himself—as if he'd finally come home to the person destiny had always intended him to love. Even from a distance she'd seen the change in him. Something of his old self was back, the youthful openness and charm, the expectant alertness in his features, as if the most wonderful thing was about to happen.

Diana set a vase in the middle of the dining room table and paused, staring unseeingly at the blooms. No one could fight Glenda, least of all a Vermont schoolteacher just passing through David's life for a summer. Glenda was an ideal of his youth, an ideal grown into obsession.

If only she'd known what she was up against, maybe she would have guarded her heart more carefully. But she hadn't. She'd let herself be carried away, by her surroundings, by David's passion, by her own eternal optimism. And now she was paying for it. Would she never learn?

She was just returning to the kitchen to fill yet another vase when the house began to vibrate with a loud clamor. She stopped in her tracks, startled, as the noise grew louder. Soon it was thunderous, banging on the windows and setting the jars in the spice rack to rattling. "What in the world?" she whispered.

She ran to the front door to see what was happening, only to be thrown back by the sting of wind and sand. She ducked inside again and chose to investigate from behind a closed window. What she saw made her mouth drop. There, right on the front lawn, was a small helicopter, its rotors slicing the sunny August morning with slowing revolutions.

Then she noticed the tall raven-haired man at its controls, and the morning became a bright swirling blur. David leapt down to the lawn and strode up to the front door without the slightest hesitation in his gait. He flicked a glance at the address, then rang the bell.

Diana fell back against the wall clutching her racing heart. What was she going to do? What should she say? But her mind was in such a fever she couldn't think. All she could do was open the door and stare up into David's arrogant sun-bronzed face—the most wonderful face she had ever known.

He didn't say anything at first, either. He just looked at her grimly, his shoulders rising and falling with his angry breathing. Then, "Diana, what the hell do you think you're doing?"

She reared back. "Well, good morning to you, too."

He brushed past her and stepped into the hall. "That was some stunt you pulled last night. Very dramatic!"

His attitude stung and brought her to life. "Oh, really! I didn't think you'd notice." She lifted her chin as defiantly as she could, aware of still being barefoot and dressed in a nightgown and robe. She hadn't even combed her hair.

But then, it didn't look as if David had gotten around to shaving, either. His hair was in disarray and he was wearing his worn jeans and a plain white T-shirt. He reminded her a lot of the man she'd met seven weeks ago outside the gates of Cliff Haven, a man trying to act tough and in command, even while suffering near-total incapacitation.

"And what's that supposed to mean, you didn't think I'd notice? Everybody noticed! You had a lot of nerve, that's all I can say, stranding me at that party, leaving me to fend for myself." His voice sank, and as Diana peered into his eyes she got the strangest feeling he was far more disarmed now than he'd been when she'd sprayed him with Mace.

"David, why are you here?" she asked squarely.

He looked aside, frustration tightening his features. Had Abbie been right when she'd said David would come around? Did Diana dare let herself think that the flowers he'd sent were not about death but about life and new beginnings?

Suddenly he gripped her arms, his fingers pressing into her soft flesh almost painfully. "Di, you have to come back with me."

Her eyes widened. "Why? Is something wrong at Cliff Haven?"

"Yes, everything—now that you're not there." Then he pulled her against him and kissed her with a fierceness that caused reverberations all the way down to her toes.

"Di, we have to talk," he whispered when he finally lifted his head.

Limp as a rag doll, she nodded and wondered where her anger had gone. "Let's go sit outside," she suggested, reaching for his hand.

They walked out to the porch swing and sat. Her hand, gripped within his, rested on his hard thigh.

"First of all," he began, "I have to apologize for everything I've ever said or done to hurt you. I put you through hell this summer." He laughed bitterly. "I still don't believe how I treated you when we first met. How pompous and—"

"David, please. That's history."

He nodded with strong conviction. "Yes. It is. But I still feel the need to apologize. For other things, too. The way I constantly shut you out whenever you tried to help, and then the other day at the stable, accusing you of inviting Walter, and those things I said..." He looked away, his eyes narrowed as if in pain.

In spite of his apparent contrition, she dredged up yet one more scowl. "Yes. You really outdid yourself that time, David. Though I suppose you had good reason to suspect me," she admitted, relenting a little. "I was the one who pushed the idea of the party on you. I was the one who sent out the invitations. It was a logical assumption."

His eyes raced over her face, seemingly trying to measure the depth of her sincerity. But even as she watched him, his expression changed.

"Lord, but you're beautiful!" he said.

Diana blushed right up to her hairline with the unexpectedness of the compliment.

Then his lips tightened into a grimace. "I no more want you out of my life than I want to stop living."

Diana lowered her head to his shoulder with a small shuddering sigh.

"It's just that a lot happened to me this summer," he explained, stroking her hair, "and I always seemed two steps behind, trying to adjust. But I did, always. Sometimes it took a few days, but I always came back. Didn't I?"

Diana raised her head and nodded thoughtfully.

"Having Walter and Glenda show up was obviously the biggest shock. Everything inside me short-circuited."

"That's what you get for letting unresolved problems fester too long. As maddening as my brothers can get, that's one thing I love about them. They've always made me talk about my problems, cry, scream, whatever it took."

"You're right. Walter and I should've had it out years ago."

"I'm always right. Haven't you figured that out by now?"

A tentative smile flickered across his handsome features. They sat quietly for a moment, listening to the thin creak of the swing as it rocked.

"David?" she finally said. "Why didn't you come to the carriage house yesterday and say all this?"

He frowned. "I figured you wouldn't talk to me." He turned to look at her, a glimmer of a smile in his eyes. "I did venture over in the afternoon, though, but you weren't around. So I decided to wait for the party. The plan was, I was going to dazzle you into forgiving me, sweep you off your feet with my charm and sparkling conversation..."

He paused and his expression darkened again. "Why did you do it, Di? Why did you leave?"

Diana suddenly realized how uncharacteristic this conversation was. David was doing almost all the talking, all the reaching out. Things had indeed turned around in the past few weeks.

"Did you decide you'd had enough of me? Did you give up?" he went on, his face grim, ready to hear the worst.

She lifted her chin stoically, pulling in a fortifying breath. "It...it was Glenda."

David sat silent for one brittle moment. Then, "What?" he said, his voice an octave higher than normal.

"It's okay. I understand," she said, squeezing his hand. "You don't have to pretend anymore. I know all about her. I saw the family albums. I read the newspaper clippings. I know how much you loved her and how you've suffered since she left you for Walter." An ache was tightening across her chest. "I also know she's been the driving force behind your success. You've amassed a fortune of your own to impress her and show her what she gave up. She's the reason you refuse to get involved with any other women."

David took her by the shoulders, turning her to face him. "But I am involved with another woman."

"Are you?" Her breath trembled.

His eyes narrowed, and his jaw set into a hard line. "Go on. What else do you know about me and Glenda? I'm dying to hear this."

She lowered her eyes. "Well, it's pretty obvious you're still carrying a torch for her. If you could have seen your face when she and Walter arrived, you'd know what I mean."

He let her go and sat forward, resting his elbows on his knees. "For heaven's sake, Di! Those two people betrayed me, humiliated me. They rearranged my entire life. And suddenly there they were after a thirteen-year cold war. You may have seen something in my face, but believe me, it was nothing more than an urge to maim."

"But . . . but I saw you walking with her the next day."

He laughed bitterly. "And could you also hear our conversation?"

"No, but you certainly looked happy and content." Her throat was tightening up on her, and speaking was becoming painful.

"Right again, Miss Know-It-All! But it was only because I'd finally aired all the ugly feelings I'd been harboring toward her and my brother—something I never would have done even a month ago, I should add. I felt free, released.''

''That's all?''

''Yes.''

Diana still wasn't completely convinced. ''So, have you reconciled?''

''I'm not really sure. They apologized to me and Evelyn, which came as no little shock, and Walter's invited me down to Maplecroft. Maybe we were just being polite for Cissy's sake. I don't know. Time will tell.'' He paused and slowly a smile entered his deep blue eyes. ''So, you think I've been languishing for my brother's wife all these years?''

''Yes, I do.'' Diana looked away, chewing her lip nervously.

''Okay, I'll admit she had an effect on me. I was hurt when we broke up, and I was madder than hell. I became bitter and started down a road of meaningless affairs. But it was a short road. It ended. Unfortunately a lot of people like to keep a reputation alive. But honestly, I'm not like that anymore. I haven't been for years. What I have been, I'll admit, is very guarded. And sure, Glenda is part of the reason, but just a small part. I simply reached the point where I didn't want *anyone* to get close.

''In any case, I don't ever want you thinking you're playing second fiddle to some ghost from my past. I got over Glenda years ago—quite thoroughly, too.''

''Well, how was I supposed to know? You never told me. You refused to talk about her.''

He blew out a sigh of frustration. ''I know. But I hope you'll understand. I stopped talking about my private life long ago. My late teens, early twenties—that was a terrible time for me, very emotional. I used to talk to reporters back then, but things always seemed to get misquoted or distorted. And even when they were right, I found it hurt to have my private life played out in public. I found it debasing, putting my feelings out there for everyone to discuss. I soon became defensive whenever anyone questioned me on a personal matter. Eventually I got downright nasty. What I didn't realize was that my defensiveness would cause such misunderstanding between you and me. I'll never shut you out again. I promise. Hey!'' He lifted her chin so that she had to look up at him. "If you thought I was languishing for Glenda, what did you think was happening between you and me?''

"I wasn't sure. Sometimes I let myself believe it was real. Most times, though, I followed the general consensus—that you don't get involved romantically. You said it yourself, remember?''

"Sure do.''

"And it's okay if that's the case. I don't want you cushioning the blow because of guilt or a sense of obligation. I'm a big girl. I can handle it.'' She hoped he didn't notice her lips trembling.

David gazed at her a long quiet time. "How about a lifetime commitment? Can you handle that, too?''

Diana opened her mouth and some sort of sound came out, but she was sure it was nothing decipherable.

"Di, I love you! I love you so much. Please, don't *ever* leave me again!'' His voice vibrated with tenderness and longing. Suddenly she was in his arms and they were clinging to each other as if they would never let go.

"I love you, too, David. I always will.'' She'd never had the chance to say those words aloud before, and as she did now, a tide of happiness engulfed her.

David sat back and reached into his jeans pocket. From it, he pulled out a blue velvet ring box. It swam out of focus as she gazed through her tears.

"I was planning to give you this last night—one of the reasons I apparently looked so happy yesterday." Irony seasoned his words.

Diana peered into his eyes, stupefied. The boyish eagerness she'd seen in his face, the easy charm, the peace—it had all been because of her?

He opened the box and took out a large emerald-cut diamond. "Will you marry me, Di? Will you *please* marry me and put me out of my misery?"

She laughed and sobbed, wondering if he believed she might actually consider saying no.

"Yes, I'll marry you."

He slipped the ring on her finger, then gathered her into his arms. "You've made me the happiest man alive," he said, laughing with relief. "I don't mean to rush you. I know you went through this whole wedding thing just last summer."

"I beg your pardon, but I'll rush if I want to." She wrapped her arms around his neck as tight as she could, drinking in the musky scent of his hair, the warmth of his rough cheek.

"Do you mean that?"

"I certainly do. I have one question, though. You *are* going to keep the house in Newport, aren't you?"

"Do you really have to ask?" He undid the belt around her waist and slipped his hand under her robe.

She tried to control her reaction, because there was still so much to talk about, but she knew he could feel her shudder. "David, would you mind if I kept teaching after we were married? Not here at Fairview…" She had to stop talking; his caresses were robbing her of her breath.

"Go on," he whispered, kissing her ear.

"N-not here. In Newp-port. I was thinking... Oh, David!" She dug her fingers into his hair, drawing him into a kiss.

When his lips finally released hers, there wasn't a coherent thought left in her head. And when he murmured, "Sure, anything you say," she had no idea what he was referring to.

"I think we ought to go inside, Di, unless you have very liberal-minded neighbors." He smiled as he nibbled the corner of her mouth.

"Yes, yes, of course." Diana clung to him as they rose from the swing. But as they were passing through the door, she grabbed the lintel and spun around.

"David, what are you doing with a helicopter?"

"Oh, do you like it? I was going to surprise you. It's for commuting. I plan to cut back on my business trips—send other people in my place. But I'll still have to show up at the office occasionally. I figure we can build a helipad at Cliff Haven easily enough. What do you think?"

"I..." She began to laugh. "I think I can't wait to get back."

"We can be there in an hour." He glanced into her eyes and began to smile wickedly. "Better make that two hours," he said, pulling her against him.

Just as his lips touched hers, however, a car turned into the driveway. Then another.

Diana groaned. "No, love. I'd say we're not going to get out of here for at least another three days. You're about to meet my brothers."

PENNY JORDAN

Sins and infidelities...
Dreams and obsessions...
Shattering secrets
unfold in...

THE HIDDEN YEARS

SAGE — stunning, sensual and vibrant, she spent a lifetime distancing herself from a past too painful to confront... the mother who seemed to hold her at bay, the father who resented her and the heartache of unfulfilled love. To the world, Sage was independent and invulnerable— but it was a mask she cultivated to hide a desperation she herself couldn't quite understand... until an unforeseen turn of events drew her into the discovery of the hidden years, finally allowing Sage to open her heart to a passion denied for so long.

The Hidden Years—a compelling novel of truth and passion that will unlock the heart and soul of every woman.

AVAILABLE IN OCTOBER!
Watch for your opportunity to complete your Penny Jordan set.
POWER PLAY and SILVER will also be available in October.

HIDDEN

Fall in love with

 Harlequin Superromance®

Passionate.
Love that strikes like lightning. Drama that will touch your heart.

Provocative.
As new and exciting as today's headlines.

Poignant.
Stories of men and women like you. People who affirm the values of loving, caring and commitment in today's complex world.

At 300 pages, Superromance novels will give you even more hours of enjoyment.

Look for four new titles every month.

Harlequin Superromance
"Books that will make you laugh and cry."

HARLEQUIN

Romance

**This October,
travel to England with
Harlequin Romance
FIRST CLASS title #3155
TRAPPED
by Margaret Mayo**

"I'm my own boss now and I intend to stay that way."

Candra Drake loved her life of freedom on her narrow-boat
home and was determined to pursue her career as a company
secretary free from the influence of any domineering man.
Then enigmatic, arrogant Simeon Sterne breezed into her life,
forcing her to move and threatening a complete takeover of her
territory and her heart....

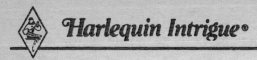

NINA HARRINGTON

My Greek Island Fling

HARLEQUIN®
entertain, enrich, inspire™

Recycling programs
for this product may
not exist in your area.

ISBN-13: 978-0-373-17832-2

MY GREEK ISLAND FLING

First North American Publication 2012

Copyright © 2012 by Nina Harrington

www.Harlequin.com

Printed in U.S.A.

Nina Harrington grew up in rural Northumberland, England, and decided at the age of eleven that she was going to be a librarian—because then she could read *all* the books in the public library whenever she wanted! Since then she has been a shop assistant, community pharmacist, technical writer, university lecturer, volcano walker and industrial scientist, before taking a career break to realize her dream of being a fiction writer. When she is not creating stories that make her readers smile, her hobbies are cooking, eating, enjoying good wine—and talking, for which she has had specialist training.

Books by Nina Harrington

WHEN CHOCOLATE IS NOT ENOUGH
THE BOY IS BACK IN TOWN
HER MOMENT IN THE SPOTLIGHT
THE LAST SUMMER OF BEING SINGLE
TIPPING THE WAITRESS WITH DIAMONDS
HIRED: SASSY ASSISTANT
ALWAYS THE BRIDESMAID

Other titles by this author available in ebook format.

PROLOGUE

'MUM—I'm here,' Lexi Collazo Sloane whispered as her mother breezed into her room, instantly bringing a splash of purple, bravado and energy to the calm cream and gold colour scheme in the exclusive London hospital.

'I am *so* sorry I'm late, darling,' her mother gushed, shaking the rain from her coat and then planting a firm kiss on Lexi's cheek. 'But our director suddenly decided to bring the rehearsal of the ballroom scene forward.' She shook her head and laughed out loud. 'Pirate swords and silk skirts. If those dresses survive intact it will be a miracle. And don't talk to me about the shoes and wigs!'

'You can do it, Mum.' Lexi chuckled, folding her pyjamas into her overnight bag. 'You're the best wardrobe mistress in the theatre business. No worries. The dress rehearsal tomorrow will be a triumph.'

'Alexis Sloane, you are the most outrageous fibber. But, thanks. Now. Down to more important things.' She took a breath, then gently put a hand on Lexi's shoulder and looked into her eyes. 'How did it go this morning? And don't spare me. What did the specialist say? Am I going to be a grandmother one of these fine days?'

Lexi sat back down on the bed and her heart wanted to weep. Time to get this over and done with.

'Well, there's some good news, and some less-than-good news. Apparently medical science has advanced a little over the past eighteen years, but I don't want you to get your hopes up.' She reached out and drew her mother to sit next to her on the bed. 'There is a small chance that I might be able to have children, but...' she caught her breath as her mother gasped '...it would be a long, tough process—and there's no guarantee that the treatment would be a success in the end. According to the specialist, I'd only be setting myself up for disappointment.'

She braved a half smile and squeezed her mother's hand. 'Sorry, Mum. It looks like you might have to wait a lot longer before I can give you those grandchildren after all.'

Her mother exhaled loudly before hugging her. 'Now, don't you worry about that for one more minute. We've talked about this before. There are lots of children out there looking for a loving home, and Adam is happy to adopt. You *will* have your own family one day—I just know it. Okay?'

'I know, but you had such high hopes that it would be good news.'

'As far as I am concerned it *is* good news. In fact, I think we should splash out on a nice restaurant this evening, don't you? Your dad will insist,' she added, waggling her eyebrows. 'It seems the photography business is paying well these days.'

Lexi touched her arm and swallowed down the huge lump of anxiety and apprehension that had made an already miserable day even more stressful. 'Is he here yet, Mum? I've been nodding off all afternoon and now I'm terrified that I might have missed him.'

But her mother looked into her face with a huge grin. 'Yes,' she replied, clasping hold of both of Lexi's hands. 'Yes, he *is* here. I left your dad back in the car park. And he is so different. He really does want to make up for lost time. Why else would he pay for this lovely private hospital at the first mention that you needed treatment? He knew how scared you must be after the last time. Everything's going to be just fine. You wait and see.'

Lexi's heart started to race. 'What if he doesn't even recognise me? I mean, I was only ten the last time he saw me. That was eighteen years ago. He might not even know who I am.'

Her mother patted her cheek, shaking her head. 'Now, don't be so silly. Of course he'll recognise you. He must have albums filled with all of the photos I've sent him over the years. Besides, you're so lovely he'll spot you in an instant.'

She pressed her cheek against Lexi's as she wrapped her in a warm hug. 'Your dad has already told me how very proud he is of everything you've achieved in your life. And you can tell him all about your brilliant writing over dinner tonight.'

Then she patted her hair, snatched up her bag and headed into the bathroom. 'Which means I need to get ready. Back in a moment.'

Lexi smiled and shrugged her shoulders. As if her mother could ever be anything other than gorgeous! She'd aways been so irrepressible, no matter what life had thrown at them. And all she'd ever wanted was a large family around her whom she could shower with love.

Lexi wiped away a stray tear from her cheek. It broke her heart that she wouldn't be able to give her mother grandchildren and make her happy. Just broke her heart.

Mark Belmont stabbed at the elevator buttons, willing them to respond, then cursed under his breath and took off towards the stairs.

The logical part of his brain knew that it had only been

seconds since he'd thanked his mother's friend for keeping vigil in that terrible hospital room until he arrived. The steady weeping hadn't helped him to keep calm or controlled, but he was on his own now, and it was his turn to make some sense of the last few hours.

The urgent call from the hospital. The terrible flight from Mumbai, which had felt never-ending, then the taxi ride from the airport, which had seemed to hit every red light in London on the way in.

The truth was still hard to take in. His mother, his beautiful, talented and self-confident mother, had taken herself to a London plastic surgeon without telling her family. According to her actress friend she had made some feeble joke about not alerting the media to the fact that Crystal Leighton was having a tummy tuck. And she was right. The press were only too ready to track down any dirty secrets about the famously wholesome English movie star. But to him? That was his mother the tabloids were stalking.

Mark took the stairs two at a time as his sense of failure threatened to overwhelm him.

He couldn't believe it. They'd been together for the whole of the Christmas and New Year holiday and she'd seemed more excited and positive than she'd been in years. Her autobiography was coming together, her charity work was showing results and his clever sister had provided her with a second grandchild.

Why? Why had she done this without telling anyone? Why had she come here alone to have an operation that had gone so horribly wrong? She'd known the risks, and she'd always laughed off any suggestion of plastic surgery in the past. And yet she'd gone ahead and done it anyway.

His steps slowed and he sniffed and took a long breath, steadying himself before going back into that hospital room where his lovely, precious mother was lying comatose, hooked up to monitors which beeped out every second just how much damage the embolism had done.

A stroke. Doing what they could. Specialists called in. Still no clear prognosis.

Mark pulled open the door. At least she'd had the good sense to choose a discreet hospital, well-known for protecting its patients from prying eyes. There would be no paparazzi taking pictures of his bruised and battered mother for the world to ogle at.

No. He would have to endure that image on his own.

Lexi had just turned back to her packing when a young nurse popped her head around the door. 'More visitors, Miss Sloane.' She smiled. 'Your dad and your cousin have just arrived to take you home. They'll be right with you.' And with a quick wave she was gone.

'Thank you,' Lexi replied in the direction of the door, and swallowed down a deep feeling of uncertainty and nervousness. Why did her father want to see her now, after all these long years? She pushed herself off the bed and slowly walked towards the door.

Then Lexi paused and frowned. Her cousin? She didn't have a cousin—as far as she knew. Perhaps that was another one of the surprises her dad had lined up for her? She'd promised her mother that she would give him a chance today, and that was what she was going to do, no matter how painful it might be.

Taking a deep breath, she straightened her back and strolled out into the corridor to greet the father who had abandoned her and her mother just when they'd needed him most. If he expected her to leap into his arms then he was sorely mistaken, but she could be polite and thank him for her mother's sake, at least.

If only her heart would stop thumping so hard that she

could hardly think. She'd loved him so much when she was little—her wonderful father had been the centre of her world.

She braced herself and looked around. But all was calm, restful and quiet. Of course it would take a few moments for him to get through the elaborate security checks at the main desk—designed to protect the rich and famous—and then take the elevator to the first floor.

She was just about to turn back when she caught a movement out of the corner of her eye through the half-open door of one of the patient's rooms identical to the one she had just left, but tucked away at the end of the long corridor.

And then she saw him.

Unmistakable. Unforgettable. Her father. Mario Collazo. Slim and handsome, greying around the temples, but still gorgeous. He was crouched down just inside the room, under the window, and he had a small but powerful digital camera in his hand.

Something was horribly wrong here. Without thinking, she crept towards the door to get a better look.

In an instant she took in the scene. A woman lay on the hospital bed, her long dark hair spread out against the bleached white sheets which matched the colour of her face. Her eyes were closed and she was connected to tubes and monitors all around the bed.

The horrific truth of what she was looking at struck Lexi hard and left her reeling with shock, so that she had to lean against the wall to stay upright.

The nurses wouldn't have been able to see her father from the main reception area, where a younger man she had never seen before was showing them some paperwork, diverting their attention away from what was happening in this exclusive clinic under their very noses.

When she found the strength to speak her words came out in a horrified shudder. 'Oh, no. No, Dad. Please, no.'

And he heard her. In an instant he whirled around from where he was crouching and glared at her in disbelief. Just for a moment she saw a flash of shock, regret and contrition drift across his face, before his mouth twisted into a silent grin.

And her blood ran cold.

Mario Collazo had made a name for himself as a celebrity photographer. It wasn't hard to work out what he was doing with a camera inside the hospital room of some celebrity that he had stalked here.

If that was true… If that was true then her dad hadn't come to see *her* at all. He had lied to her warm-hearted mother and tricked his way into the hospital. None of the security officers would have stopped him if he was the relative of a patient.

Ice formed in the pit of her stomach as the hard reality of what she had just seen hit home. Her dad never had any intention of visiting her. The only reason he was here was to invade this poor sick woman's privacy. Lexi had no idea who she was, or why she was in this hospital, but that was irrelevant. She deserved to be left alone, no matter who she was.

Lexi felt bitter tears burning in the corners of her eyes. She had to get away. Escape. Collect her mother and get out of this place as fast as her legs could take her.

But in an instant that option was wiped away.

She had waited too long.

Because striding towards her was a tall, dark-haired man in a superbly tailored dark grey business suit. Not a doctor. This man was power and authority all wrapped up inside the handsome package of a broad-shouldered, slim-hipped man of about thirty. His head was low, his steps powerful and strident to match the dark, twisted brow. And he was heading straight for the room where her father was hiding.

He didn't even notice she was there, and she could only watch in horror as he flung open the door to the woman's room.

Then everything seemed to happen at once.

'What the hell are you doing in here?' he demanded, his voice furious with disbelief as he stormed into the room, pushed aside the visitor's chair and grabbed her father by the shoulder of his jacket.

Her breath froze inside her lungs, and Lexi pressed her back farther against the wall.

'Who are you, and what do you want?' His voice was shrill and full of menace, but loud enough to alert the receptionist at the desk to look up and lift the telephone. 'And how did you get a camera in here? I'll take that, you parasite.'

The camera came flying out of the door and crashed against the wall next to Lexi with such force that it smashed the lens. To Lexi's horror she saw the young man at reception reach into his pocket and pull out a digital camera and start to take photographs of what was happening inside the room from the safety of the corridor. Suddenly the stillness of the hushed hospital was filled with shouting, yelling, crashing furniture and medical equipment, flower vases smashing to the floor, nurses running and other patients coming out of their rooms to see what the noise was all about.

Shock and fear overwhelmed her. Her legs simply refused to move.

She was frozen. Immobile. Because, as if it was a horrible train wreck, she simply could not take her eyes away from that hospital room.

The door had swung half closed, but she could see her father struggling with the man in the suit. They were fighting, pushing and shoving each other against the glass window of the room. And her heart broke for the poor woman who was lying so still on the bed, oblivious to the fight that had erupted around her.

The door swung open and her father staggered backwards into the corridor, his left arm raised to protect himself. Lexi covered her mouth with both hands as the handsome stranger stretched back his right arm and punched her father in the face, knocking him sprawling onto the floor just in front of her feet.

The stranger lunged again, pulling her father off the ground by his jacket and starting to shake him so vigorously that Lexi felt sick. She screamed out loud. 'Stop it—please! That's my dad!'

Her father was hurled back to the ground with a thud. She dropped to the floor on her knees and put her hand on her father's heaving chest as he pushed himself up on one elbow and rubbed his jaw. Only then did she look up into the face of the attacker. And what she saw there made Lexi recoil in horror and shock.

The handsome face was twisted into a mask of rage and anger so distorted that it was barely recognisable.

'Your *dad*? So that's how it is. He used his own daughter as an accomplice. Nice.'

He stepped back, shaking his head and trying to straighten his jacket as security guards swarmed around him and nurses ran into the patient's room.

'Congratulations,' he added, 'you got what you came for.'

The penetrating gaze emanating from eyes of the darkest blue like a stormy sea bored deep into her own, as though they were trying to penetrate her skull. 'I hope you're satisfied,' he added, twisting his lips into a snarl of disgust and contempt before looking away, as if he couldn't bear the sight of her and her father for a second longer.

'I didn't know!' she called. 'I didn't know anything about this. Please believe me.'

He almost turned, but instead shrugged his shoulders and returned to the bedroom, shutting the door behind him and leaving her kneeling on the cold hospital floor, nauseous with shock, fear and wretched humiliation.

CHAPTER ONE

Five Months Later

GOATS!

Lexi Sloane pushed her designer sandal hard onto the brake pedal as a pair of long-eared brown and white nanny goats tottered out in front of the car as she drove around a bend, and bleated at her in disgust.

'Hey, give me a chance, girls. I'm new around here,' Lexi sang out into the silent countryside, snorting inelegantly as the goats totally ignored her and sauntered off into the long grass under the olive trees on the other side of the road.

'Which girls? Lexi? I thought you were working.' Her mother laughed into her earpiece in such a clear voice that it was hard to imagine that she was calling from the basement of an historic London theatre hundreds of miles away. 'Don't tell me. You've changed your mind and taken off with your pals on holiday to Spain after all.'

'Oh, please—don't remind me! Nope. The agency made me an offer I couldn't refuse and I am definitely on Paxos,' Lexi replied into the headset, stretching her head forward like a turtle to scan the sunlit road for more stray wildlife. 'You know how it goes. I am the official go-to girl when it comes to ghostwriting biographies. And it's always at

the last minute. I will say one thing—' she grinned '—I
stepped off the hydrofoil from Corfu an hour ago and those
goats are the first local inhabitants I've met since I left the
main road. Oh—and did I mention it is *seriously* hot?'

'A Greek Island in June… I am *so* jealous.' Her mother
sighed. 'It's such a pity you have to work, but we'll make
up for it when you get back. That reminds me. I was talking to a charming young actor just this morning who would
love to meet you, and I sort of invited him to my engagement party. I'm sure you'd like him.'

'Oh, no. Mum, I adore you, and I know you mean well,
but no more actors. Not after the disaster with Adam. In
fact, please don't set me up with any more boyfriends at
all. I'll be fine,' Lexi insisted, trying desperately to keep
the anxiety out of her voice and change the subject. 'You
have far more important things to sort out without worrying about finding me a boyfriend. Have you found a
venue for this famous party yet? I'm expecting something
remarkable.'

'Oh, don't talk to me about that. Patrick seems to ac-
quire more relatives by the day. I thought that four daugh-
ters and three grandchildren were more than enough, but he
wants the whole tribe there. He's so terribly old-fashioned
about these things. Do you know, he won't even sleep with
me until his grandmother's ring is on my finger?'

'Mum!'

'I know, but what's a girl to do? He's gorgeous, and I'm
crazy about him. Anyhow, must go—I'm being dragged
out to look at gothic chapels. Don't worry—I'll tell you
all about it when you get back.'

'Gothic? You wouldn't dare. Anyway, I look terrible in
black,' Lexi replied, peering through the windscreen and
slowing the car at the entrance to the first driveway she'd

seen so far. 'Ah—wait. I think I've just arrived at my client's house. Finally! Wish me luck?'

'I will if you need it, but you don't. Now, call me the
minute you get back to London. I want to know everything
about this mystery client you're working with. And I mean
everything. Don't worry about me. You just try and enjoy
yourself. *Ciao,* gorgeous.'

And with that her mother hung up, leaving Lexi alone
on the silent country lane.

She glanced up at the letters carved into a stone name-
plate, then double-checked the address she'd noted down
over the phone while waiting for her luggage to come off
the carousel at Corfu airport, some five hours earlier.

Yup. This was it. Villa Ares. Wasn't Ares the Greek
god of war? Curious name for a house, but she was here
and in one piece—which was quite a miracle.

Checking quickly for more goats or other animal resi-
dents, Lexi shifted the hire car into gear and drove slowly
up a rough gravel driveway which curved around a long,
white two-storey house before coming to a shuddering halt.

She lifted off her telephone headset and sat still for a
few minutes to take in the stunning villa. She inhaled a
long breath of hot, dry air through the open window, fragrant with the scent of orange blossom from the trees at
the end of the drive. The only sound was birdsong from
the olive groves and the gentle ripple of water from the
swimming pool.

No sign of life. And certainly no sign of the mystery
celebrity who was supposed to have sent a minion to meet
her at the hydrofoil terminal.

'Welcome to Paxos,' she whispered with a chuckle, and
stepped out of the car into the heat and the crunch of rough
stone beneath her feet.

The words had no sooner slipped from Lexi's lips than

the slim stiletto heel of her favourite Italian sandal scraped down a large smooth cobblestone, her ankle twisted over, and she stumbled against the hot metal of her tiny hire car.

Which left a neat trail of several weeks' worth of grime and bright green tree pollen all down the side of the Italian silk and linen jacket.

Oh, no! Grinding her teeth, she inspected the damage to her clothing and the scrape down her shoe and swore to herself with all of the fluency and extensive vocabulary of a girl raised in show business. The dark red leather had been completely scraped into a tight, crumpled ball down the heel of her shoe.

This project had better be a real emergency!

Even if it was so *totally* intriguing.

In the five years that she'd worked as a contract ghost writer this was the first time that she had been sent out on a top-secret assignment on her own—so secret that the publisher who'd signed the contract had insisted that all details about the identity of the mystery author must remain under wraps until the ghost writer arrived at the celebrity's private home. The talent agency was well-known for being extremely discreet, but this was taking it to the next level.

She didn't even know the name of her client! Or anything about the book she would be working on.

A tingle of excitement and anticipation whispered across Lexi's shoulders as she peered up at the imposing stone villa. She loved a mystery almost as much as she loved meeting new people and travelling to new places around the world.

And her mind had been racing ever since she'd taken the call in Hong Kong.

Who *was* this mysterious celebrity, and why the great secrecy?

Several pop stars just out of rehab came to mind, and

there was always the movie star who had just set up his own charity organisation to fight child trafficking—any publisher would be keen to have that story.

Only one thing was certain: this was going to be someone special.

Lexi brushed most of the pollen from the rough silk-tweed fabric of her jacket, then straightened her back and walked as tall as she could across the loose stone drive, the excitement of walking into the unknown making her buzz with anticipation.

A warm breeze caressed her neck and she dipped her sunglasses lower onto her nose, waggling her shoulders in delight.

This had to be the second-best job in the world. She was actually getting paid to meet interesting people in lovely parts of the world and learn about their lives. And the best thing of all? Not one of those celebrities knew that she used every second of the time she spent travelling and waiting around in cold studios to work on the stories she *really* wanted to write.

Her children's books.

A few more paying jobs like this one and she would finally be able to take some time out and write properly. Just the thought of that gave her the shivers. To make that dream happen she was prepared to put up with anyone.

Magic.

Swinging her red-leather tote—which had been colour-matched to her now-ruined sandals—she shrugged, lifted her chin and strode out lopsided and wincing as the sharp stones of the drive pressed into the thin soles of her shoes.

Hey-ho. They were only sandals. She had seen too much of the flip side of life to let a little thing like a damaged sandal annoy her. Meeting a client when she didn't even know their name was a drop in the ocean compared to the train wreck of her personal history.

It was time to find out whose life she was going to share for the next week, and why they wanted to keep their project such a secret. She could hardly wait.

Mark Belmont rolled over onto his back on the padded sun lounger and blinked several times, before yawning widely and stretching his arms high above his head. He hadn't intended to fall asleep, but the hot, sunny weather, combined with the latest bout of insomnia, had taken its toll.

He swung his legs over the lounger, sat upright, and ground the palms of his hands into his eyes for a few seconds to try and relieve the nagging headache—without success. The bright sunlight and the calm, beautiful garden seemed to be laughing at the turmoil roiling inside his head.

Coming to Paxos had seemed like a good idea. In the past the family villa had always been a serene, welcoming refuge for the family, away from the prying eyes of the media; a place where he could relax and be himself. But even this tranquil location didn't hold enough magic to conjure up the amount of calm he needed to see his work through.

After four days of working through his mother's biography his emotions were a riot of awe at her beauty and talent combined with sadness and regret for all the opportunities he had missed when she was alive. All the things he could have said or done which might have made a difference to how she'd felt and the decision she'd made. Perhaps even convinced her not to have surgery at all.

But it was a futile quest. Way too late and way too little.

Worse, he had always relished the solitude of the villa, but now it seemed to echo with the ghosts of happier days and he felt so very alone. Isolated. His sister Cassie had been right.

Five months wasn't long enough to put aside his grief. Nowhere near.

He sniffed, and was about to stand when a thin black cat appeared at his side and meowed loudly for lunch as she rubbed herself along the lounger.

'Okay, Emmy. Sorry I'm late.'

He shuffled across the patio towards the stone barbecue in his bare feet, watching out for sharp pebbles. Reaching into a tall metal bin, he pulled out a box of cat biscuits and quickly loaded up a plastic plate, narrowly avoiding the claws and teeth of the feral cat as it attacked the food. Within seconds her two white kittens appeared and cautiously approached the plate, their pink ears and tongue a total contrast to their mum. Dad Oscar must be out in the olive groves.

'It's okay, guys. It's all yours.' Mark chuckled as he filled the water bowl from the tap and set it down. *'Bon appétit.'*

He ran his hands through his hair and sighed out loud as he strolled back towards the villa. This was *not* getting the work done.

He had stolen ten days away from Belmont Investments to try and make some sense of the suitcase full of manuscript pages, press clippings, personal notes, appointment diaries and letters he had scooped up from his late mother's desk. So far he had failed miserably.

It certainly hadn't been *his* idea to finish his mother's biography. Far from it. He knew it would only bring more publicity knocking on his door. But his father was adamant. He was prepared to do press interviews and make his life public property if it helped put the ghosts to rest and celebrate her life in the way he wanted.

But of course that had been before the relapse.

And since when could Mark refuse his father anything? He'd put his own dreams and personal aspirations to one side for the family before, and would willingly do it again in a heartbeat.

But where to start? How to write the biography of the woman known worldwide as Crystal Leighton, beautiful international movie star, but known to him as the mother who'd taken him shopping for shoes and turned up at every school sports day?

The woman who had been willing to give up her movie career rather than allow her family to be subjected to the constant and repeated invasion of privacy that came with being a celebrity?

Mark paused under the shade of the awning outside the dining-room window and looked out over the gardens and swimming pool as a light breeze brought some relief from the unrelenting late-June heat.

He needed to find some new way of working through the mass of information that any celebrity, wife and mother accumulated in a lifetime and make some sense of it all.

And one thing was clear. He had to do it fast.

The publisher had wanted the manuscript on his desk in time for a major celebration of Crystal Leighton at a London film festival scheduled for the week before Easter. The deadline had been pushed back to April, and now he would be lucky to have anything before the end of August.

And every time the date slipped another unofficial biography appeared. Packed with the usual lies, speculation and innuendo about her private life and, of course, the horrific way it had been brought to an early end.

He had to do something—anything—to protect the reputation of his mother. He'd failed to protect her privacy when it mattered most, and he refused to fail her again. If anyone was going to create a biography it would be someone who cared about keeping her reputation and memory alive and revered.

No going back. No compromises. He would keep his promise and he was happy to do it—for her and for his family. And just maybe there was a slim chance that he would come to terms with his own crushing guilt at how much he had failed her. Maybe.

Mark turned back towards the house and frowned as he saw movement on the other side of the French doors separating the house from the patio.

Strange. His housekeeper was away and he wasn't expecting visitors. *Any* visitors. He had made sure of that. His office had strict instructions not to reveal the location of the villa or give out his private contact details to anyone.

Mark blinked several times and found his glasses on the side table.

A woman he had never seen before was strolling around inside his living room, picking things up and putting them down again as if she owned the place.

His things! Things he had not intended anyone else to see. Documents that were personal and very private.

He inhaled slowly and forced himself to stay calm. Anger and resentment boiled up from deep inside his body. He had to fight the urge to rush inside and throw this woman out onto the lane, sending her back whence she came.

The last thing he wanted was yet another journalist or so-called filmmaker looking for some dirt amongst his parents' personal letters.

This was the very reason he'd come to Paxos in the first place. To escape constant pressure from the world of journalists and the media. And now it seemed that the world had decided to invade his privacy. Without even having the decency to ring the doorbell and ask to be admitted.

This was unacceptable.

Mark rolled back his shoulders, his head thumping, his hands clenched and his attention totally focused on the back of the head of this woman who thought she had the right to inspect the contents of his living room.

The patio door was half-open, and Mark padded across the stone patio in his bare feet quietly, so that she wouldn't hear him against the jazz piano music tinkling out from his favourite CD which he had left playing on Repeat.

He unfurled one fist so that his hand rested lightly on the doorframe. But as he moved the glass backwards his body froze, his hand flat against the doorjamb.

There was something vaguely familiar about this chestnut-haired woman who was so oblivious to his presence, her head tilted slightly to one side as she browsed the family collection of popular novels and business books that had accumulated here over the years.

She reminded him of someone he had met before, but her name and the circumstamces of that meeting drew an annoying blank. Perhaps it was due to the very odd combination of clothing she was wearing. Nobody on this island deliberately chose to wear floral grey and pink patterned leggings beneath a fuchsia dress and an expensive jacket. And she had to be wearing four or five long, trailing scarves in contrasting patterns and colours, which in this heat was not only madness but clearly designed to impress rather than be functional.

She must have been quite entertaining for the other passengers on the ferry or the hydrofoil to the island from Corfu that morning.

One thing was certain.

This girl was not a tourist. She was a city girl, wearing

city clothes. And that meant she was here for one reason—
and that reason was him. Probably some journalist who had
asked him for an interview at some function or other and
was under pressure from her editor to deliver. She might
have come a long way to track him down, but that was her
problem. Whoever she was, it was time to find out what
she wanted and send her back to the city.

Then she picked up a silver-framed photograph, and
his blood ran cold.

It was the only precious picture he had from the last
Christmas they had celebrated together as a family. His
mother's happy face smiled out from the photograph, complete with the snowman earrings and reindeer headset she
was wearing in honour of Cassie's little boy. A snapshot
of life at Belmont Manor as it used to be and never could
be again.

And now it was in the hands of a stranger.

Max gave a short, low cough, both hands on his hips.

'Looking for anything in particular?' he asked.

The girl swung round, a look of absolute horror on
her face. As she did so the photograph she was holding
dropped from her fingers, and she only just caught it in
time as it slid down the sofa towards the hard tiled floor.

As she looked at him through her oversized dark sunglasses, catching her breath unsteadily, a fluttering frag-
ment of memory flashed through his mind and then wafted
out again before he could grasp hold of it. Which annoyed
him even more.

'I don't know who you are, or what you're doing here,
but I'll give you one chance to explain before asking you
to leave the same way you came in. Am I making myself
clear?'

CHAPTER TWO

LEXI thought her heart was going to explode.

It couldn't be. It just could *not* be him.

Exhaustion. That was the only explanation. Three weeks on the road, following a film director through a series of red-carpet events across Asia, had finally taken their toll.

She simply had to be hallucinating. But as he looked at her through narrowed eyes behind rimless designer spectacles Lexi's stomach began to turn over and over as the true horror of the situation hit home.

She was standing in front of Mark Belmont—son of Baron Charles Belmont and his stunningly beautiful wife, the late movie actress Crystal Leighton.

The same Mark Belmont who had punched her father in that hospital on the day his mother had died. And accused *her* of being his accomplice in the process. Completely unfairly.

When she was a little girl she'd had a recurring nightmare about being a pilgrim sent to fight the lions in some gladiatorial arena in Rome.

This was worse.

Her legs were shaking like jelly, and if her hand held on to her bag any tighter the strap would snap.

'What—what are you doing here?' she asked, begging and pleading with him in her mind to tell her that he was a temporary guest of the celebrity she had been paid to work with and that he would soon be leaving. Very soon. Because the other alternative was too horrible to imagine.

She'd thought that she had escaped her shameful connection to this man and his family.

Fate apparently had other ideas.

Fate in the form of Mark Belmont, who was looking at her with such disdain and contempt that she had to fight back the temptation to defend herself.

With a single shake of the head, he dismissed her question.

'I have every right to be here. Unlike yourself. So let's start again and I'll ask you the same question. Who are you and what are you doing in my house?'

His house? A deep well of understanding hit her hard and the bottom dropped out of Lexi's stomach.

If this was his house—was it possible that Mark Belmont was her celebrity?

It would make sense. Crystal Leighton's name had never left the gossip columns since her tragic death, and Lexi had heard a rumour that the Belmont family were writing a biography that would be front-page news. But surely that was *Baron* Belmont, not his business-guru son?

Lexi sighed out loud. She was jumping to conclusions— her imagination was running ahead of itself. This was a big house, with room for plenty of guests. It could easily be one of his colleagues or aristocratic friends who needed her help.

And then the impact of what he was asking got through to her muddled brain.

Mark had not recognised her. He had no clue that she was the girl he had met in the hospital corridor only a few months earlier.

They had only met for a few fleeting moments, and she

had certainly changed since then. They both had. And her sunglasses were a genius idea.

She inhaled a couple of breaths, but the air was too warm and thick to clear her head very much. It was as though his tall, powerful body had absorbed all the oxygen from the room.

A flicker of annoyance flashed across his full, sensuous mouth before he said, 'I don't take kindly to uninvited guests, so I suggest you answer my question before I ask you to leave.'

Uninvited guests? Oh, God, the situation was worse than she'd realised. He didn't seem to be expecting a visitor—any visitor. He had no idea that his publisher had sent a ghost writer out to the island! No wonder he thought that she was some pathetic burglar or a photojournalist.

Okay, so he had treated her unfairly in the worst of circumstances, but she was here to do a job. She glanced down, desperate to escape his laser-beam focus, and her eyes found the image of a happy family smiling back at her from behind the glass in the picture she had almost dropped.

It could have been a movie set, with a perfect cast of actors brought in for the day. Gorgeous film-star mother, handsome and tall aristocratic father, and two pretty children—with the cutest toddler on the planet waving at the camera. All grouped in front of a tall Christmas tree decorated in red and gold and a real fire burning bright in a huge marble fireplace.

What did Mark Belmont know about broken families and wrecked dreams?

Guilt about the pain her father had caused the Belmont family pinched her skin hard enough to make her flinch. But she ignored it. What her father had done had never been her fault, and she wasn't going to allow the past to ruin her work. She needed this job, and she'd be a fool to let her father snatch away the chance to make her dream come true.

Lexi opened her mouth as if to speak, closed it again, and then pinched her thumb and forefinger tightly against the bridge of her nose.

'Oh, no.' She shook her head slowly from side to side, eyes closed. 'The agency would *not* do this to me.'

'The agency?' Mark asked, his head tilted slightly to one side. 'Have you got the right villa? Island? Country?'

She chuckled, and when she spoke her voice was calmer, steadier.

'Let me guess. Something tells me that you may not have spoken, emailed or in some other way communicated with your publisher in the past forty-eight hours. Am I right?'

For the first time since she had arrived a concerned look flashed across his tanned and handsome face, but was instantly replaced by a confident glare.

'What do you mean? My publisher?'

Lexi dived into her huge bag, pulled out a flat black tablet computer, and swiped across the screen with her forefinger—being careful not to damage her new fingernails, which still carried the silver and purple glitter that had been the hit of the last show party in Hong Kong.

'Brightmore Press. Sound familiar?'

'Maybe,' he drawled. 'And why should that matter to me?'

Lexi's poor overworked brain spun at top speed.

He was alone in the villa. This was the correct address. And Mark *was* familiar with Brightmore Press. Lexi put those three factoids together and came up with the inevitable conclusion.

Mark Belmont was the mystery celebrity she had been assigned to work with.

And the bubble of excitement and enthusiastic energy that had been steadily inflating on the long journey from Hong Kong popped like an overstretched balloon.

Of all the rotten luck.

She needed the job so badly. Running a home in central London wasn't cheap, and this bonus would have made a big difference to how quickly she could start the renovations. All her plans for the future relied on having her own home office where she could write her children's books full-time. Walking away from this job would set her back months.

She stared at him wide-eyed for a few seconds, before sighing out loud.

'Oh, dear. I hate it when this happens. But it does explain why you didn't meet me at the harbour.'

Mark shifted his legs shoulder-width apart and crossed his arms. 'Meet you? No, I don't think so. Now, let me make myself quite clear. You have two minutes to explain before I escort you from my private home. And please don't think I won't. I've spent more time than I care to think about giving press conferences. My office has a catalogue of past interviews and press statements, covering every possible topic of conversation. I suggest that you try there—because I have absolutely no intention of giving you an interview, especially when you seem intent on damaging my property. Am I getting through to you?'

'Your property? Oh, I'm so sorry,' she murmured, scrabbling to pick up the picture and brushing off any dust from the silver frame. 'I did knock, but there was no answer, and the door was open. This is a lovely family photo and I couldn't resist peeking at it, so...' She gave a quick shrug of the shoulders and lifted her chin slightly. 'You should be more careful about security.'

'Really?' He nodded, his voice calculating and cool enough to add a chill to the air. 'Thank you so much for the advice, but you aren't in the city any more. We don't lock our doors around here. Of course if I'd *known* I was to have visitors I might have taken additional precautions. Which brings us to my earlier question. Who are you, and why are you here? I'm sure the two charming police officers who take care of this island would be delighted to meet you in a more formal setting. And, as you have probably realised, Gaios is only about three miles from here. And they are the proud owners of both a police car and a motorcycle. So I would suggest that you come up with a very convincing excuse very quickly.'

Police? Was he serious?

She looked warily into those startling blue eyes. Oh, yes, he was serious.

Her chest lifted a good few inches and she stared straight at him in alarm. Then she sucked in a breath and her words came tumbling out faster than she would have thought possible.

'Okay. Here goes. Sorry, but your peeps have *not* been keeping you up to date on a few rather crucial matters. Your Mr Brightmore called my talent agency, who called me with instructions to get myself to Paxos because one of their clients has a book to finish and they—' she gestured towards his chest with her flat hand '—are apparently a month past the final deadline for the book, and the publishers are becoming a little desperate. They need this manuscript by the end of August.'

She exhaled dramatically, her shoulders slumped, and

she slid the tablet back into her bag with a dramatic flourish before looking up at him, eyebrows high, with a broad grin.

'Right. Now that's out of the way I suppose I should introduce myself. Alexis Sloane. Otherwise known as Lexi. Ghost writer *extraordinaire*. And I'm here to meet a client who needs help with a book. I take it that would be you?'

'Well, of *course* I didn't tell you what the publisher had organised, darling brother, because I knew exactly what your reaction would be.'

Mark Belmont sat down hard on the end of the sun lounger, then immediately stood up again and started pacing up and down the patio, the sun-warmed stone hot under his bare feet. The temperature was a perfect match for his mood: incendiary. His emotions boiled in a turmoil of resistance, resolution and defiance touched with fury. Cassandra Belmont had a lot to answer for.

'Cassie,' he hissed, 'I could strangle you. Seriously. How could you do this to me? You *know* that this biography is too personal, too close to home, to ask anyone to help. Why do you think I've come all the way to Paxos to work on the book on my own? The last thing I need is some random stranger asking questions and digging into places I don't know I want to go myself. Communication is a wonderful thing, you know. Perhaps you've heard of it?'

'Relax.'

His sister's voice echoed down the phone, and he imagined her curled up on the sofa in Belmont Manor while her two small sons played havoc around her.

'Lucas Brightmore recommended the most discreet agency in London. Their staff sign cast-iron confidentiality agreements and would never divulge anything you tell them. I think it could work.'

'Cassie, you are a menace, I don't care how discreet this…*secretary* is. If I wanted a personal assistant I would have brought one. I have excellent staff working for me. Remember? And I would never, *ever* invite them here to the villa. I need privacy and space to get the work done. You know me.' His voice slowed and dropped lower in pitch. 'I have to get my head into the detail on my own before I can go public with anything. And I need peace and quiet to do that.'

'You're right. But this is not a business project you are evaluating. This is our mother's life story. It has to do her justice, and you're the only person in the family with the faintest bit of creativity. I know I couldn't do it in a million years. I don't have nearly enough patience. Especially when it comes to the difficult bits.'

Cassie took a breath and her voice softened.

'Look, Mark, this is hard for all of us. And it's incredibly brave of you to take over the project. But that makes it even more important to get the job done as quickly as you can. Then we can all get on with our lives and Dad will be happy.'

'Happy?' Mark repeated with a dismissive cough. 'You mean like he's happy about my plans to renovate those derelict cottages on the estate into holiday lets? Or the restructuring plans for the business that he's been blocking since Christmas?'

'Probably not,' Cassie answered. 'But you know as well as I do that it isn't about you or me. It has a lot more to do with the fact that he's ill for the first time in his life and he's just lost his wife in a surgical procedure she never even told him about. He doesn't know how to deal with that any more than the rest of us.'

Mark ran his tongue over his parched lips. 'How is he today?'

The delay before Cassie answered said more than the sadness inherent in her reply. 'About the same. This round of chemotherapy has really knocked him back.' Then her steely determination kicked back in, tinged with concern. 'You don't need to put yourself through this. Hand back the advance from the publisher and let some journo write Mum's biography. Come home and run your business and get on with your life. The past can take care of itself.'

'Some journo? No, Cassie. The press destroyed Mum's last chance of dignity, and I don't even want to *think* about what they'd do with a true-life *exposé* based on lies, innuendo and stupid gossip.' He shook his head and felt a shiver run down his spine despite the heat. 'We know that her friends have already been approached by two writers for hire looking for dirt. Can you see the headlines? Read All About It: The True Sordid Past of the Real Crystal Leighton Belmont.' He swallowed hard on a dry throat. 'It would kill him. And I *refuse* to let her down like that again.'

'Then finish the book our mother started. But do it fast. The agency said they were sending their best ghost writer, so be nice. I'm your sister, and I love you, but sometimes you can be a little intense. Oh. Have to go. Your nephews are awake and need feeding. Again. Take care.'

'You, too,' Mark replied, but she had already put the phone down.

He exhaled slowly and willed his heart rate to slow.

He had never been able to stay angry with Cassie. His sister had been the one constant in his father's life ever since their mother had died. She had her own husband, a toddler and a new baby to take care of, but she adored the manor house where they had grown up and was happy to make a home there. Her husband was a doctor at the local hospital whom Cassie had met when she'd taken their father for a check-up. Mark knew that he could totally rely on her to take care of their father for a few weeks while he took time out of the office.

She had even taken over the role of peacemaker on the rare occasion when he went back to Belmont Manor.

But she shouldn't have talked to the publisher without telling him about it.

Suddenly the decision to come to Paxos to finish the biography seemed ridiculous. He'd thought that being on his own would help, but instead he'd become more agitated and irritable by the day. He needed to do things. Make things happen. Take responsibility just like he'd always done. It infuriated him that he'd found it impossible to focus on the task he had set himself for more than a few minutes without having to get up and pace around, desperate for an opportunity to procrastinate.

Cassie was right. This biography was too close. Too personal.

His mother had always been a hopeless housekeeper, and organisation had never been one of her strong points. She'd liked the creative world, and enjoyed making sense of the jumble of random photographs, letters, newspaper clippings and memorabilia.

And he was just the same. An artist in many ways. His natural inclination was to push through the boundaries of possibility to see what lay beyond and shake things up. Little wonder that he was increasingly at loggerheads with his father's almost obsessive need to keep things in order. Compliant. Unchanging. Private and quiet.

Or at least that had been the case until six months ago. But now?

Now his father was on his second round of chemotherapy, his beloved mother had effectively died on a plastic surgeon's operating table, and his on-off girlfriend had finally given up on him and met someone she actually seemed to love and who loved her in return.

Mark felt as though the foundations on which he had based his entire life had been ripped out from under him.

His fingers wrapped tightly around the back of the chair until the knuckles turned white with the pressure.

No. He could handle this trauma. Just as he had abandoned his own life so that he could take his brother's place in the family.

There was no point in getting angry about the past.

He had given his word. And he would see it happen on his own, with the privacy and the space to work things through. The last thing he needed right now was a stranger entering his private space, and the sooner he persuaded her that the publisher was wrong and she could head off back to the city the better.

Think. He needed to think.

To stop herself shaking Lexi gripped her shoulder bag with one hand and pressed the other against the back of the leather sofa. She couldn't risk ruining her carefully contrived show of being completely unfazed as she looked at Mark Belmont, pacing up and down the patio next to the swimming pool, her cell phone pressed to his ear.

Only this was not the business-guru version of The Honourable Mark Belmont that usually graced the covers of international business magazines around the world. Oh, no. She could have dealt with that stiff, formally dressed office clone quite easily. *This* version was an entirely different sort of man: much more of a challenge for any woman.

The business suit was gone. Mark was wearing a pair of loose white linen trousers and a short-sleeved pale blue striped polo shirt that perfectly matched the colour of his eyes. His toned muscular arms and bare feet were tanned as dark as the scowl he had greeted her with, and the top two buttons of his shirt were undone, revealing a bronzed, muscular chest.

His dark brown hair might have been expertly cut into tight curls, but he hadn't shaved, and his square jaw was covered in a light stubble much more holiday laid-back than designer businessman. But, Lord, it suited him perfectly.

She knew several fashion stylists who would have swooned just at the sight of him.

This was a completely different type of beast from the man who'd defended his mother so valiantly in the hospital. This was Mark Belmont in his natural setting. His territory. His home.

Oh, my.

She could lie and pretend that her burning red neck was simply due to the heat of a Greek island in late June and the fact that she was overdressed, but she knew better.

Her curse had struck yet again.

She was always like this around Adonis-handsome men. They were like gorgeous baubles on display in a shop window. She could ogle them all day but never dared to touch. Because they were always so far out of reach that she knew she would never be able to afford one. And even if she could afford one it would never match the disorganised chaos of her life.

This particular bauble had dark eyebrows which were heavy and full of concern. He looked tense. Annoyed and anxious.

It had seemed only right to ring the publisher for him. Just to clarify things.

Only judging by the expression on his face the news

that her assignment was not a practical joke after all had not gone down well.

Normally her clients were delighted that a fairy godmother had dropped into their world to help them out of a tricky situation.

Apparently Mark Belmont was not seeing his situation in quite the same way.

She had to persuade him to allow her to stay and help him with…with *what?* She still had no idea what type of book Mark Belmont was writing. Business management? A family history? Or…she swallowed…the obvious. A memoir of his mother.

Lexi looked up as Mark turned towards her from the door, lowering the phone, and searched his face for something—anything—that would help her make the decision.

And she found it. In his eyes of frosty blue.

The same eyes that had looked at her with such pain mixed with contempt on that terrible day in the hospital. When his heart had been breaking.

Decision made. If he could survive writing about his late mother then she would do her best to make the book the best it could be. Even without his help.

She could make this work. It would take a lot of effort, and she would have to be as stubborn as a stubborn thing in Stubbornland, but she could do it. She had stood her ground before, and she'd do it again.

Mark stood still for a moment, eyes closed, tapping the cell phone against the side of his head.

'If you're quite finished with my phone, Mr Belmont?' A sweet, charming voice echoed out from behind his back. 'It tends not to function very well after being used as a percussion instrument.'

Mark opened his eyes and stared at the offending cell phone as though he had never seen it before. He'd never used a purple phone in his life and he was extremely tempted to throw the offending article into the pool and leave it there. *With its owner. The hack writer.*

Fortunately for the phone, good manners kicked in and, holding it between his thumb and forefinger, he turned and extended his arm towards Lexi.

To her credit, she was not wearing a self-satisfied smirk but the same look of professional non-confrontational indifference he was used to seeing from city suits around the boardroom table where some of his riskier ideas were discussed.

Except for him this was not a job. It was very personal. And even the idea of sharing his deepest concerns and emotions about his parents made him bristle with resentment and refusal to comply.

He hadn't built a venture-capital company from the ruins of his father's business without taking risks, but they had been calculated risks, based on information he had personally checked and worked on until he'd known that the family's money would not be wasted on the investment.

This girl—this woman—in this ridiculous outfit had arrived at his home without his approval.

His sister might have confidence in the talent agency, but he knew nothing about the plan, and if there was one thing guaranteed to annoy him it was things being planned behind the scenes without his knowledge.

Cassie was perfectly aware of that fact, but she'd done it anyway. Her intentions might be excellent, but the reality was a little difficult to stomach.

A light tapping broke Mark out of his reverie, and he flashed a glance at the girl just in time to see her keying furiously into the cell phone, her sparkly purple-painted fingernails flashing in the sunlight. Although how she could see through those huge sunglasses was a mystery to him.

In the living room she had been more stunned than stunning, but in the bright white light reflected back from the patio her skin appeared pale and almost translucent, as though she hadn't seen sunlight for quite some time. The contrast between her English-rose complexion and the startlingly bright scarves wrapped around her neck was so great that it distracted him for a moment from the fact that she was talking.

'I'll be with you in a moment, Mr Belmont,' she said away from the phone. 'I'm just trying to find out the location of the nearest hotel on the island. Unless, of course, you can recommend one to me?'

She looked up and gave him a half smile—a pink-cheeked, polite kind of smile that still managed to brighten her whole face, drawing his full attention.

'I apologise for not booking accommodation before I arrived, but this assignment was rather last-minute. I'll need to stay somewhere close by, so I don't waste too much time travelling back and forth. Don't worry,' she added, 'I'll be out of your hair within the hour.'

'A hotel? That is quite out of the question,' he answered.

'Oh?' She raised her eyebrows and her fingers stilled. 'And why is that?'

Mark pushed his hands into his pockets to keep them from fastening around that pretty pale neck and squeezing hard.

'Well, for one thing there is indeed a small hotel in Gaios. But it is currently closed for over-running refurbishments. And secondly...' He paused before saying the words. 'Paxos is a very small island. People talk and ask questions. I hardly think it would be appropriate for you to stay in rented accommodation while you're working on a confidential project for the Belmont family. And I'm afraid that you certainly don't *look* like a package holiday tourist.'

To her credit, she didn't look down at her outfit to check if something was amiss. 'I don't? Excellent. Because I have no intention of looking like a tourist. I want to look like me. As for confidentiality…? I can assure you that I'm totally discreet. Anything you tell me will be in strict confidence. I've worked on many confidential projects, and none of my previous clients ever had any problems with my work. Now, is there anything else you'd like to know before I head to town?'

He lifted his chin and dropped his shoulders back, chest out, legs braced, creating the sort of profile his media consultants had recommended would be perfect to grace the covers of business magazines. Judging by the slight widening of her eyes, it was equally effective on the patio.

'Only this. You seem to be under the illusion that I've agreed to this arrangement. That is not the case. Any contract you might have is between my publisher and your agency. I certainly haven't signed anything. And I have a big problem with being railroaded. Which is exactly how I'm feeling right now. I dislike surprises, Miss Sloane.'

She lifted her chin, and instantly the firmness of the jawline on her heart-shaped face screamed out to him that this was a girl who rarely took no for an answer.

'It's unfortunate that you weren't expecting me,' she replied with a tight smile, 'but I can assure you that I have no plans to return home before this assignment is completed.'

She reached into the tiny pocket of her jacket, pulled out a small business card and presented it to him. 'I've just survived two long international flights, one hour on the hydrofoil from Corfu, and twenty minutes negotiating car hire with the charming Greek gentleman at the port to get here. I don't intend to leave until my boss instructs

me to. So. May I suggest a compromise trial period? Let's
say twenty-four hours? And if you don't find my services
valuable, then I promise to jump into my hire car and get
out of your life. One day. That's all I'm asking.'

'One day?' Mark echoed through gritted teeth.

'Absolutely.'

A smile warmed her lips, and for the first time since
they'd met it was a real smile. The kind of smile that made
the Cupid's-bow curve of her full lips crinkle girlishly at
the edges and the pink in her cheeks flush with enjoyment.
She was enjoying this. And she was clearly determined to
make him do all the work.

'Very well. Twenty-four hours it is. In which case there
is only one possible option,' he continued. 'You will be
staying here at the villa with me until I decide whether I
need your help or not, Miss Sloane.'

CHAPTER THREE

'You want me to stay here at the villa?' Lexi looked around the patio, then back towards the house. 'You did say you lived here alone, Mr Belmont? Is that correct? I'll take your silence as a yes. In that case, aren't you worried about what your wife or girlfriend will think about the arrangement? A single man living here alone suddenly has a young lady houseguest? There are bound to be questions.' Lexi glanced at him. 'Perhaps you have nieces?'

'I'm afraid not. Two nephews. Both under five. Go by the names of Charles and Freddie.'

'Shame.' She nodded and screwed up her face. 'How about cousins? Old schoolfriends? Casual acquaintances that just happen to pass by?'

'No subterfuge will be necessary, Miss Sloane. You can call yourself a business colleague or personal assistant for as long as you stay here. Take your pick.'

'Business colleague it is. Personal assistant smacks too much of a girl who organises your dry-cleaning, runs your office and buys presents for your lucky lady-friends—of which I'm sure there are many.'

Lexi leaned forward slightly towards Mark.

'I don't actually perform those particular duties, by the way. In case you're wondering. Ghostwriting. That's it. Okay? Splendid. Now, seeing as I'll be staying here, would you mind helping me with my suitcases? I do have quite a few.'

'What do you mean a few?'

Mark strolled over to the edge of the patio and stared at the tiny hire car. Lexi tottered past him and descended the two low steps that curved down to the driveway.

'You men have it easy.' She laughed, opening up the boot and heaving the two massive matching cases out onto the pebble driveway. 'A couple of suits and that's it. But I've just spent three weeks on the road with different events every evening.'

A cabin bag and a leather Gladstone bag followed.

'Clients expect a girl to wear different outfits for each film launch to keep the photographers happy,' she added, walking around to the passenger door and flinging it open. The top garment bag had slipped a little down the back of the driver's seat, so she tugged it free and folded it over one arm before grabbing hold of her travel bag with one hand and slinging the shoulder strap of her overnight case across the front of her jacket.

Lexi pushed the car door closed with one foot and looked around for Mark. He was standing open-mouthed, still watching her from the terrace as though he could hardly believe what he was looking at.

Lexi rolled her eyes, took a firmer hold of her bag and tottered across the pebbles of the car park onto the patio steps. 'Don't worry about me,' she said, 'I've left the heavy bags down by the car. Any time today will be good.'

'No problem,' Mark murmured under his breath. 'The porter will be right with you.'

He reached for his shoes, which he had stashed under the lounger. Unfortunately, as he bent over, Lexi tottered past his very fine rear end in her high-heeled sandals, and as he stood up his elbow jogged the overnight bag she was carrying.

At exactly the same moment the slippery silk fabric of her garment bag slipped down her arm. She snatched at it with the hand holding the travel bag, twisting her body round to stop it from falling to the ground.

And she took one step backwards.

The stiletto heel of her right sandal hit the smooth marble edge of the swimming pool, her right leg shot forward, she completely lost her balance and instinctively flung both arms out to compensate.

For one millisecond she was airborne. Arms twirling around in wide circles, both legs in the air, luggage thrown out to each side and the thin silk fabric of her overdress inflated up to her waist as a parachute.

She squeezed her eyes tight shut and prepared herself for a dunking in the swimming pool. But instead her feet lifted even higher off the ground as a long, strong arm grabbed her around the waist and another arm swept under her legs, taking her weight effortlessly.

Lexi flashed open her eyes, gave a high squeak of terror, and flung both her arms around Mark's neck by sheer instinct, pressing herself tight onto his shirt. Unfortunately she forgot that she was still clutching her travel bag for dear life, and succeeded in hitting Mark on the back of the head with it.

To his credit, he gave only a low, deep sigh instead of yelling like a schoolboy.

She opened her mouth to apologise, then closed it again. Her lungs seemed to have forgotten how to work and her breathing had become a series of short panting noises—which would have been perfect for a spaniel but which, from her lips, managed to sound both pathetic and wheezy at the same time.

She had *never* been picked up before.

And the last time she'd been this close to a handsome man had been on Valentine's night, when her ex-boyfriend had confessed he'd been sleeping with a girl she'd thought was her friend. So it would be fair to say that it hadn't ended well.

This, on the other hand, was turning out to be a much more positive experience.

Below his loose blue shirt Mark was muscular, warm and solid against her body, and in the position he was holding her their faces were only inches apart. His eyes locked onto hers, and suddenly it made perfect sense just to lie there in his arms while he took her weight.

Up close, she could see that his eyes were not a perfectly clear blue, as his mother's had been, but were flecked with slivers of darker blue and grey, so that under the shade of the terrace they looked like a cloudy summer sky.

His wiry dark brown hair was curled at the base of his neck with the heat of the afternoon, and she inhaled an intoxicating aroma of some fragrant shampoo or shower gel, freshly laundered linen shirt and something much deeper and muskier.

She had no clue what it was, but that extra something had the power to make her heart beat faster than was probably safe. So fast that it was all too easy to recall that she was here to work. Not to cuddle the client or to partially strangle him with her arms after trying to knock him out.

'I should have warned you about the pool. Are you okay now?' he asked, his voice low with concern.

She swallowed, and gave a smile and a short nod. Instantly the arm around her waist slackened and her brief adventure came to a halt as he slowly lowered her back down and her sandals made contact with solid ceramic tile.

Strange how her arms seemed reluctant to lose contact

with Mark's shirt and practically slid the full length of his chest—before the sensible part of her brain took over and reminded her that her agency contract included some rather strict rules about fraternising with the clients.

Lexi tugged down on the hem of her dress and pretended to be straightening her clothing before daring to form actual words.

'No problem. I prefer not to go swimming fully clothed, so thanks for saving me from a dunking. And sorry about the bag.' Her fingers waved in the direction of his head.

'Well, at least we're even,' Mark replied, gesturing with his head towards the swimming pool, where her garment bag was floating on the surface and making small glugging noises.

'Oh, drat,' Lexi replied and her shoulders slumped. 'There go two cocktail dresses, a business suit and a cape. The dresses I can replace, but I liked that cape.'

'A cape?' Mark repeated, strolling down the patio and picking up a long pole with a mesh net on the end.

'One of my previous clients started life as a professional magician, entertaining passengers on a cruise ship,' Lexi replied, preoccupied by watching Mark try to guide the wayward luggage to the side of the pool. Every time he got close the filter pump blew it back towards the deep end.

She winced the second time he almost had it close enough to reach.

'Fascinating man. He told me he'd kept the cape just in case he ever needed to earn a few dollars. I pointed out that after forty years in Las Vegas the chances of that happening were slim.' Lexi sniffed and gave a low chuckle. 'The rascal gave me that cape the day of the launch party for his autobiography. He'd decided that his pension didn't need boosting after all, and that at ninety-two he might be a little rusty. So we had one final performance. I was his glamorous assistant, of course. He supplied the top hat, plastic flowers and scarves. The full works. Then he patted my bottom and I threatened to cut him in half.'

She grinned. 'Happy days. It was a great party. What a shame that a vintage cape like that is going to be ruined after all of those years in showbiz…' Her eyes tracked slowly from the bag across to Mark, then back to the bag again, and she gave a dramatic sigh just to make sure that he'd got the message.

'Are you always so much trouble?' Mark asked, rolling up his trousers to reveal a surprisingly hairy pair of muscular legs before descending the steps into the shallow end of the pool and dragging the soggy garment bag onto the side.

'Oh, no,' Lexi replied in a totally casual, matter-of-fact voice as she grasped the handle and sloshed the bag farther onto the terrace, to join the other pieces of luggage she had abandoned there. 'I'm usually a lot more trouble than this. You should be grateful it was the shallow end. But these are early days.'

His reply was a snort and a brief smile illuminated his face. It was the first time she had seen Mark smile, and even in the hot afternoon sunshine she felt the warmth of it on her face. And was instantly filled with remorse.

She paused and focused on her bags before breathing out slowly, eyes down.

It was time. If she was going to do this then she had better do it now and get it over with.

Mark frowned and strolled over towards her. 'I'm sure you have enough dry clothing to last a few days. Is there something else I can help you with?'

Lexi looked up at him reluctantly and licked her lips, which were suddenly bone dry.

'Actually, there is one more thing I need to clear up

before we start working together. You see, we have met before. Just the once. In London. And not in the best of circumstances.'

She whipped off her sunglasses and hung them over the breast pocket of her jacket, looked up into his startled face.

'We weren't formally introduced at the time, but you'd just met my father in your mother's hospital room and you were rather preoccupied with escorting him out. Does that jog your memory?'

Mark paused, hands on hips, and looked at her. So they *had* met before, but…?

The hospital. Her father. Those violet-grey eyes set in a heart-shaped face.

The same eyes that had stared up at him in horror and shock after he'd punched that slimy photographer.

'Get out,' he said, cold ice reeling in his stomach, fighting the fire in his blood. 'I want you out of my house.'

'Just give me a minute,' she whispered in a hoarse, trembling voice. 'What happened that day had nothing to do with me. My father is completely out of my life. Believe me, I am only here for one reason. To do my job. As a writer.'

'Believe you? Why should I believe a single word you say? How do I know you're not here spying for your paparazzi father? No.' He shook his head, turning his back on her. 'Whoever is paying you to come here to my home has made a very grave mistake. And if you ever come near me or my family again my lawyers will be called in. Not to mention the police. So you need to leave. Right now.'

'Oh, I'll go.' She nodded. 'But I have no intention of leaving until we've cleared up some of these facts you're so fond of. Just for the record. Because I want to make something very, very clear,' she hissed through clenched teeth as she crammed every piece of clothing she could find from the soaked luggage into her handbag and vanity case.

'My parents were divorced when I was ten years old. I hadn't seen my father, the famous Mario Collazo—' she thumped the cape several times as she stuffed it farther down into the bag '—for eighteen years, until he turned up out of the blue at the clinic that morning. He'd begged my mother to give him a chance to make amends for his past mistakes and to rebuild some sort of relationship with me. And like a naive fool—' her voice softened '—no, make that a lovely, caring and heartbroken naive fool, she took the time to talk to him and actually believed him.'

Lexi shook her head and sniffed.

'She spent years sending me birthday and Christmas presents pretending that my dad still loved me. She mailed him photos and school reports every single year. And this year she'd also let him know that I was waiting for hospital treatment and asked him to come and see us when he was in London. And what did he do?'

Lexi threw her bag onto the patio floor in disgust and pressed a balled fist to each hip, well aware that she was being a drama queen but not caring a bit.

'He abused her confidence. He took advantage of a caring woman who wanted her daughter to have a relationship with her father. And she never even suspected for one moment that he'd set me up in that particular clinic on that particular day because he already knew that Crystal Leighton was going to be there.'

She lifted her chin.

'And I fell for his story just the same as she did. So if you want someone to blame for being gullible I'm right here, but I am *not* taking responsibility for what happened.'

Mark glared at her. Lexi glared back.

'Finished yet?' His voice was ice, clashing with the intense fire in his eyes. The same fire she had seen once before. It had terrified her then, but she *wasn't* finished yet.

'Nowhere close. My mum is a wonderful dress designer and wardrobe mistress. It took her years to rebuild her career after my dad left us with nothing. Her only crime—her fault—was being too trusting, too eager to believe he'd changed. There was no way she could have predicted he was using her. Oh, and for the record, neither of us got one penny of the money he got from selling those photos. So don't you *dare* judge her. Because that is the truth—if you're ready to accept it.'

'And what about you?' he asked, in a voice as cold as ice. 'What's your excuse for lying to me from the moment you arrived at the villa? You could have told me who you were right from the start. Why didn't you? Or are *you* the one who's unable to accept the truth?'

'Why didn't I? But I *did* tell you the truth. I stopped being Alexis Collazo when I was sixteen years old. Oh, yes. I changed my name on the first day that I legally could. I *hated* the fact that my father had left my mother and me for another woman and her daughter. I despised him then and I think even less of him now. As far as I'm concerned that man and his new family have nothing to do with my life, and even less to do with my future.'

'That's ridiculous,' Mark sniped back at her, quick as a flash. 'You can't escape the fact that your family was involved.'

'You're right.' She nodded. 'I've had to live under the shadow of what my father did for the last five months. Even though I had nothing to do with it. That makes me *so* angry. And most of all I hate the fact that he abused my mother's generous, trusting spirit and used me as an excuse to get into that hospital. If you want to go after someone, go after him.'

'So you didn't benefit at all?'

'We got nothing—apart from the media circus when your lawyers turned up and hit us with a gagging order. Are you starting to get the picture? Good. So don't presume to judge me or my family without getting your facts straight. Because we deserve better than that.'

Mark pushed both hands deep into his trouser pockets. 'That's for me to judge,' he replied.

Lexi hoisted the suitcases upright, flung on her shoulder bag and glanced quickly around the patio before shuffling into her sandals.

'I'm finished here. If you find anything I've left behind feel free to throw it into the pool if it makes you feel better. Don't worry about the cases—I'll see myself out. Standard social politeness not required.'

'Anything to get you out of my house,' Mark replied, grabbing a suitcase in each hand as if they weighed nothing. 'Rest assured that if we should ever run into each other again, unlikely though that may be, I shall not try my best to be polite.'

'Then we understand each other perfectly,' replied Lexi. 'As far as I'm concerned, the sooner I can be back in London, the better. Best of luck writing the biography—but here's a tip.'

She hoisted her bag higher onto her shoulder and nudged her sunglasses farther up her nose.

'Perfectly happy people with perfect families living perfect lives in perfect homes don't make interesting reading. I had no idea you were my client when I came here today, but I was actually foolish enough to hope you'd be fair and listen to the truth. I even thought we might work together on this project. But it seems I was wrong about that. You won't listen to the truth if it doesn't suit you. Apparently you're just as cold, unreasonable, stubborn and controlling as the tabloids claim. I feel sorry for you.'

And with that she grabbed the vanity bag and tottered across the patio. She was already down the steps before Mark could reply.

Mark stood frozen on the patio and watched the infuriating girl teeter her way across the crazy paving, the flimsy silk dress barely covering her bottom. How dared she accuse him of being cold and stubborn? That was his father's speciality, not his. It just showed how wrong she was. How could she expect him to believe her story and put aside what he had seen with his own eyes? Mario Collazo being comforted by his daughter on the floor after Mark had knocked him down. Those were the facts.

He had recognised who she was the second she'd taken off her sunglasses. How could he forget the girl with the palest of grey eyes, filled with tears, looking up at him with such terror?

He had frightened her that morning, and in a way he regretted that. He wanted no part of his father's arrogant, bullying tactics. But at that moment he had allowed anger and rage to overwhelm him. Justifiably. It had still shocked him that he was capable of uncontrolled physical violence. He'd worked long and hard to make himself a different man from his father and his brother.

Edmund wouldn't have wasted a moment's thought before knocking any photographer to the floor and boasting about it later.

But he was *not* his older brother, the golden boy, his parents' pride and joy, who had died falling from a polo pony when he was twenty-five.

And he didn't want to be. Never had.

Mark wrapped his fingers around the handles of the

wet luggage, his chest heaving, and watched the small
figure in the ridiculous outfit struggle with the door handle on the car before lowering herself onto the seat with
an audible wince as her bottom connected with the hot
plastic. Seconds later her legs swung inside and the door
closed.

So what if she was telling the truth? What if she *had*
been used by her father that day, and was just as innocent
a victim as his mother had been? What if her turning up
at the villa really was a total coincidence?

Then fate had just kicked them both in the teeth. And
he had handed that monster an extra set of boots.

But what alternative did he have? He knew what the
response would be if his father or even his sister found
out that he'd been sharing precious family memories and
private records with the daughter of the stalker who'd destroyed his mother's last day alive. It would be far better
to forget about this fearless girl with the grey eyes and
creamy skin who'd challenged him from the moment she
arrived. A girl whose only crime was having the misfortune to be the daughter of a slimeball like Mario Collazo.
And she had defended her mother from an attack on her
reputation. In anybody else that loyalty was something
he would admire.

Oh, hell!

He'd spent the last seven years of his life trying to prove
that he could take his brother's place, and then his father's
as head of Belmont Investments. He took risks for a living and he liked it. And now this girl turned up out of the
blue and accused him of being cold and unreasonable and
unwilling to listen to the truth because it didn't agree with
his pre-established version of the facts.

Mark dropped both suitcases on the patio. Perfect families living perfect lives. Was that what she really thought the Belmont family was like? Perfect?

Hardly.

He looked up. The hire car hadn't moved an inch. How did she do it? How did she make him feel so angry and unsettled?

And about to make a potentially very dangerous decision.

Lexi collapsed back against the driver's seat and was about to throw her luggage onto the passenger seat when something moved inside the car. She froze, and for one fraction of a millisecond considered screaming and running back to Mark as fast as her legs could carry her.

But that would make her wimp of the week.

Hardly daring to investigate further, Lexi slowly looked sideways and blinked through her blurred vision in disbelief at the two white faces with pink ears staring back at her.

One of the kittens yawned widely, displaying the cutest little pink tongue, stretching his body out into a long curve before closing his eyes and settling down to more sleep on the sun-warmed passenger seat. The other ball of white fluff washed his face with his paw, then curled back into a matching position.

A low chuckle started deep inside her chest and rambled around for a few seconds before emerging as slightly manic strangled laughter, which soon evolved into full-blown sobbing.

Lexi closed her eyes, slumped back against the headrest and gave in to the moment. She could feel the tears running down her cheeks as the deep sobs ripped through her body, making her gasp for air. *This was not fair. This was totally not fair.*

Swallowing down her tears through a painful throat, Lexi slowly cracked open her eyes and took a firm hold of the steering wheel with both hands, curling her fingers tightly around the hot plastic as if it was a lifeline to reality.

It took a moment to realise that with all the sniffing she had not heard the gentle crunch of Mark's footsteps on the gravel driveway.

She stared straight ahead at the olive and lemon trees as he slowly strolled over to the side of the car, then leant his long tanned forearms on the open driver's window and peered inside without saying a word.

They stayed like that for a few seconds, until the silence got too much for Lexi.

'There are cats. In my car. I wasn't expecting cats in my car.' She sniffed, and then flicked down the sun visor and peered at herself in the vanity mirror.

'And look at this.' She released the steering wheel and pointed at her eyes. 'It took me an hour to put this make-up on at the airport. And now it's totally wrecked. Just like the rest of me.'

She slapped her hands down twice on the dashboard, startling the cats, who sat up and yawned at her in complaint. 'Now do you understand why I never mention my dad when I'm working? Just the mention of his name makes me all...' She waved her arms towards the windscreen and waggled her fingers about for a few seconds before dropping them into her lap.

'I noticed,' he murmured, in a calm voice tinged with just enough attention to imply that he was trying to be nice but struggling. 'And, by the way, allow me to introduce Snowy One and Snowy Two. They live here. And they tend to snuggle on warm car cushions, towels, bedding, anywhere soft and comfy. You might want to think about that when you're working outside.'

Her head slowly turned towards him so that their faces were only inches apart. And his eyes really were sky blue.

'Working?' she squeaked. 'Here?'

He nodded.

'I don't understand. A minute ago you couldn't wait to see the back of me.'

'I changed my mind.'

'Just like that?'

He nodded again.

'Have you considered the possibility that I might not want to work with you? Our last conversation was a little fraught. And I don't like being called a liar.'

'I thought about what you said.' His upper lip twitched to one side. 'And I came to the conclusion that you might have a point.'

'Oh. In that case I'm surprised it took you so long.'

Mark stared back at her with those wonderful blue eyes, and for the first time she noticed that he had the kind of positively indecent long dark eyelashes of which any mascara model would be envious.

They were so close that she could see the way the small muscles in his cheeks and jaw flexed with the suppressed tension that held his shoulders so tight, like a coiled spring.

Mark Belmont was a powder keg ready to blow, and like a fool her gentle heart actually dared to feel sorry for him. Until she remembered that he had been doing all the judging and, until now, she had been doing all the explaining.

'I'm never going to apologise, you know,' she whispered. 'Can you get past that?'

'Strange,' he replied, and the crease in his brow deepened. 'I was just about to say just the same thing. Can *you* get past that?'

'I don't know,' she replied, and took a breath before chewing on her lower lip.

Time to make her mind up. Stay and do the work or cut her losses and go. Right now.

She felt Mark's eyes scan her face, as though he were looking for some secret passage into her thoughts.

Her fingers tapped on the dashboard, but his gaze never left her face, and she could hear his breathing grow faster and faster. He was nervous, but did not want to show it. And she needed this job so badly.

'Okay,' she whispered, her eyes locked on his. 'I am going to give you another chance.'

He exhaled low and slow, and Lexi could feel his breath on her neck as the creases at the corners of his eyes warmed, distracting her for a second with the sweet heat of it. Time to get control, girl!

'Here's what's going to happen,' she continued, before Mark had a chance to answer. 'First I'm going to drag what's left of my luggage back inside your lovely villa and find a nice bedroom to sleep in. With a sea view. And then we're going to write your mother's biography to celebrate her life. And when we're finished, and it's totally and absolutely awesome and amazing, and you're standing at the book launch with your family all around you, *then* you're going to say that you couldn't possibly have created this best-seller without the help of Lexi Sloane. And that will be the end of it. No more recriminations and no more blame. Just a simple thank-you. And then we get on with our respective lives. Do you think you can do that, Mr Belmont?'

'Miss Sloane…'

'Yes?' she muttered, wondering what conditions and arguments he was going to wrap around her proposal.

'My cat has just peed on your shoe.'

She looked down just as Snowy One shook his left leg

and then clawed his way back onto the car seat without the slightest whiff of contrition.

'Can I take that as a yes?' she huffed.

'Absolutely.'

CHAPTER FOUR

MARK woke just as the morning sunlight hit that one perfect angle where it was able to slant around the edge of the blackout blind and shine a laser beam straight onto his pillow.

He groaned and blinked several times, turning to glance at the wristwatch he wore 24/7. It was set to tell the time in each of the main financial markets as well as local time on Paxos. And at that moment they were all screaming the same thing. He had slept for a grand total of four hours since forcing himself into bed at dawn.

By 9:00 a.m. on a normal weekday Mark would already have showered, dressed, had breakfast and coffee and been at his desk for three hours. Insomnia had been his faithful companion for years—he'd hoped that being back on Paxos would help him to catch up on his sleep.

Wrong again.

Pushing himself up on the bed, which was a total wreck, Mark reached across to his bedside table for his glasses and tablet computer and quickly checked through the emails his PA had filtered for him. London was an hour behind Paxos, but the financial markets waited for no man and his team started early and worked late. They earned the huge salaries he paid them to make Belmont Investments one of the most respected London financial houses.

Ten minutes later he'd sent replies to emails that needed his personal attention and forwarded others to the heads of department to action.

Then he turned to the real nightmare. The restructuring plans which would secure the long-term stability and profitability of the company. It was going to be tough convincing his father that these difficult measures needed to be taken, and they had already been delayed for months following his mother's death and his father's illness.

But the real problem was his father. He had built up Belmont Investments by taking a low-key, low-risk approach that had worked well years ago. Not any longer. Not in today's financial market.

Mark flicked over to his own plan—the plan he'd been working on in the early hours of the morning when sleep had been impossible. It was dynamic, modern and exciting, and until now this plan had been a dirty secret that he hadn't shared with anyone else.

His father would hate it. But he had to do something to save the business. Even if it meant breaking through the unwritten rules his father had laid down—rules which came with all the obligations attached to being the next Baron Belmont.

Mark quickly scanned through one of the key implementation plans, and had just started to work on the projected time schedule, looking for ways to bring it forward, when he heard strange, cooing baby-love sounds below his bedroom window.

And they were definitely human.

Mark closed his eyes, dropping the tablet onto his knees with a low sigh.

Of course. Just for a second he'd forgotten about his uninvited and very unexpected houseguest. Miss Alexis Sloane.

No doubt fresh as a daisy, bursting with energy, and ready to get started on ripping his family history apart so she could collect her fee and head back to civilisation as fast as her cute, shapely and very lovely little legs could carry her.

A whisper of doubt crept into his mind.

What if he had made a mistake when he'd asked her to stay?

What if this was all some elaborate ruse and Lexi truly was intending to leave with all the Belmont family secrets tucked under her arm, neatly packed up to pass on to her paparazzi father?

For all Mark knew he could be handing Mario Collazo all the ammunition he needed to twist Crystal Leighton's life story into some sordid tabloid hatchet-job.

He slipped out of bed and padded over to the window to peek out onto the patio.

Lexi was bending down and was rubbing her fingers together in front of Emmy and Oscar, the feral cats who called this villa home and whose kittens had invaded her car. The cats clearly couldn't decide whether this replacement for Mark's soft-hearted housekeeper was friend or foe, and were taking the 'feed me and I'll think about it' approach. But at least she was making an effort to be friendly.

Mark almost snorted out loud. He'd made the mistake of bringing his one-time fiancée here for a weekend break. She'd been horrified that he allowed 'vermin' so close to the house, and actively shooed the cats away at every opportunity in case they contaminated her clothing—which had confused Emmy and Oscar so much that they'd kept coming back to find out what was going on.

She'd lasted three days before stage-managing an emergency at the bank.

Pity he hadn't picked up on the clue that the beautiful girl had enjoyed the kudos of being the future Baroness Belmont a lot more than she'd liked him and his ordinary life.

He pulled back the blind just an inch and watched Lexi dangle a piece of ribbon up and down, inviting the cats to play with this strange new toy. Her childlike laughter rang out in the sunshine and was so infectious that he couldn't help but smile in return.

It struck him all at once that his life revolved around people who were very different from the girl he was looking at now. Lexi was pretty, dynamic and confident enough to challenge him and defend herself against what she saw as unfair treatment.

If this was an act, then she was playing her part very well indeed.

The girl he was looking at—okay, ogling—seemed to have no off button. No dial he could turn to slow her down and make her start conforming a little to other people's expectations.

She had surprised him by telling him who her father was before they'd started work.

A shrewder person might have kept quiet about that little bombshell until the cheque had cleared.

Honesty and integrity. He admired that. Even if she *was* the daughter of a man he despised. And, unless he had lost his knack of judging people, she was telling the truth about not knowing she'd be working with Mark.

Overall, a fascinating, intriguing and very unsettling package. Who probably didn't realise that as she bent over the back of her hipster slim-fit trousers, which were probably extremely fashionable in the city, had slid way down past her hips, exposing the top of what passed for her underwear. And providing him with a splendid and tantalising view of a smooth expanse of skin divided by a tiny band of what appeared to be red lace.

Considering the hot weather, and the tightness of her trousers, it was just about as uncomfortable and unsuitable a combination as he could imagine.

But if her intention was to make a man's heart pound rather too fast, she had succeeded brilliantly.

She was skipping across the patio now, perilously close to the swimming pool where he had held her so close against his body—and had enjoyed every second of it. Enjoyed it rather too much for comfort.

That was it. She made him feel…uncomfortable.

Of course that had been until he'd looked into those remarkable violet-grey eyes and instantly been transported back to the horror of that morning in a London clinic when his world had collapsed around him. And that was not uncomfortable. It was damning.

Mark released the blind and took off his glasses.

Perhaps it was just as well that he knew who her family were. She was way too attractive to ignore, but that was as far as it went—as far as it could ever go.

There was no way around it. Lexi Sloane was part of his past. The question was, would she be able to help him get through this project so he could move on to his future?

Because if he had made the wrong choice, then bringing Lexi into his life could be the worst decision he'd ever made.

Lexi sang along under her breath to the lively trance track blasting her eardrums while she flicked through her cellphone messages, sending off fast replies to the most urgent and deleting what she could.

She was just about to switch to emails when Adam sent her yet another text. That had to be the fourth in the last twenty-four hours.

Please. Call me. We need to talk.

'Oh, I don't think so, loser. You don't tell me what to do. Not any more,' Lexi hissed, moving on to the next message. But the damage was done: her eyes and brain refused to connect and she put down the phone in disgust.

The last time they had spoken face to face had been in the hall of Adam's apartment. Both of them had said things which could not be unsaid. And then she had embarrassed herself by slapping him harder than she'd ever hit anything in her life.

Girls did that when they found out their boyfriends had been cheating on them.

What a fool she'd been to pin all her hopes of happiness on the one man she'd thought was a friend. She should have learned from her mother's experience not to let personal feelings interfere with her judgement. And that was exactly what she'd done. Stupid girl.

She wasn't going to live in Gullible Girl City again. Oh, no. At least not until her home office was ready and her children's books were in the shops.

Then she might think about dating again. If...

She held the thought as she caught a blur of movement in the corner of her eye and turned her head just as Mark strolled into the room. He was wearing loose navy trousers and a very expensive-looking navy polo shirt. His hair was dark and slick, as though he had just stepped out of the shower.

Mark Belmont looked like heaven on legs.

And with one single glance she was instantly hit with a sudden attack of the killer tingles.

The kind of tingles that left a girl feeling hot, bothered, brainless and desperate enough to do something really stupid. Like forgetting that Mark was her client. Like wanting to find out what it felt like to run her fingers through his hair and feel his breath on her neck.

Bad tingles. *Very* bad tingles.

Not ideal qualities for a professional writer.

This was the man who'd accused her of being her father's accomplice and almost thrown her out yesterday. As far as Mark Belmont was concerned she was here to work. And that was all. She had to keep her head together!

It was time to turn on a cheery nonsense gossipy voice and the fixed smile that had become her standard mask to the world. Busy, busy, busy. Chatter, chatter, chatter. That was the role she played. He wouldn't be able to get a word in edgeways, and she could keep her distance.

Deep breath. Cue, Lexi. Action!

'Good morning, Mr Belmont.' She smiled, nervously rearranging the cutlery to hide her complete mental disarray. 'I hope you're ready for breakfast, since I've been on a mission of mercy and made the village baker and shopkeeper very happy. But please don't be worried about your reputation as a ladies' man. I told them I was only here for a few days to help with a business project and I'd be heading back to the office ASAP.'

Oh, and now she was babbling about his love life. Great. Could she be more pathetic?

'My reputation?' Mark repeated, staring at her through those incredibly cute spectacles as he leant against the worktop, his hands in his trouser pockets. Casual, handsome, devastating. 'How very thoughtful of you. But why did you think it necessary to go on a mission of mercy?'

'I was brave enough to rummage around inside your freezer looking for breakfast. Behind the bags of ice cubes were a few ancient, dry bread rolls, which crumbled to pieces in my hands and were only fit for the birds, and an assortment of unlabelled mystery items which, judging by their greyish-green colour, were originally of biological origin. But they did have one thing in common. They were all inedible.'

She stopped cutting bread and looked up into Mark's face. 'It's amazing what they have in small village shops on this island.'

'Food shopping,' he replied, running the fingers of one hand through his damp hair. 'Ah. Yes. My housekeeper stocked up the refrigerator last week, but of course I wasn't expecting visitors.'

'No need to apologise,' she said as brightly as she could. 'But it has been my experience that we can get a lot more work done if we have food available in the house and don't have to run out and stock up at the last minute. And, since the room service around here seems to be a little deficient, some creative thinking was required.'

He peered over her shoulder and the smell of citrus shower gel and coconut shampoo wafted past. She inhaled the delicious combination, which was far more enticing than the food and did absolutely nothing to cure her attack of the tingles.

But as he stepped forward Lexi heard his stomach growl noisily and raised her eyebrows at him.

'It seems that I *could* use some breakfast. Um… What did you manage to scavenge?'

'Since I don't know if you prefer a sweet chocolatey cereal breakfast or a savoury eggs, bacon and tomatoes type breakfast, I bought both. I've already had scrambled eggs and toast, washed down with a gallon of tea.'

'Tea is disgusting. But eggs and toast sound perfect if I can persuade you to go back to the frying pan. I'll take care of my coffee. It's one of my few weaknesses. I'm very particular about what coffee I drink, where it came from and how it was made.'

'Of course, Mr Belmont,' Lexi replied, with no hint of sarcasm in her voice, and turned back towards the cooker.

'It's Mark.'

'Oh,' she replied, whizzing round towards him and making a point of taking out her earphones. 'Did you say something?'

Mark crossed his arms and narrowed his eyes, well aware that she had heard what he said but was making a play of it since she had just scored a point. 'I said, since we will be working together, I would prefer it if you called me Mark.'

'If that is your instruction, Mr Belmont.' She smiled and relaxed a little. 'I'd be very happy to call you Mark. But only if you call me Lexi in return. Not Alexis, or Ali, or Lex, but Lexi.'

Then she turned back to the hob and added a knob of butter to the hot pan before breaking more eggs into a bowl.

'Breakfast will be with you in about five minutes, Mark. I do hope you like orange juice. That was the only—'

The sound of a rock band belted out from her cell phone, and Lexi quickly wiped her hands on a kitchen towel before pressing a few buttons.

'Anything interesting?' Mark asked casually as he reached for the coffee.

'I always receive interesting messages.' Lexi twisted to one side and peered at the display. 'But in this case they were two new messages from my ex-boyfriend, which are now deleted. Unread, of course. Which I find deeply satisfying.'

'I see. I thought you might be a heartbreaking sort of girl.'

'It cannot be denied. But in this particular situation it transpired he was cheating on me with a girl who took great satisfaction in enticing him away from me.'

Mark's eyebrows went skywards and his lips did a strange quivery dance as his hands stilled on the cafetière. 'He cheated on you?' he repeated in an incredulous voice, then shook his head once before going back to his coffee. 'Do you always share details of your fascinating-but-tragic love life with people you've only just met?' he asked with a quick glance in her direction.

Lexi shrugged, and was about to make some dismissive quip when it struck her that he was actually trying to have a conversation this morning.

That was different.

He'd barely said a word over their light dinner of crackers, cheese and sweet tomatoes apart from commenting on the local red wine. The meal had been so awkward that she'd felt she was walking on eggshells every time she tried to break the silence.

She wasn't complaining, and it helped that she now wasn't the only one talking, but she wasn't used to having one-to-one, intelligent, hangover-free conversations with her clients at this time in the morning. Perhaps Mark Belmont had a few more surprises for her?

'Oh, yes,' Lexi replied with a shrug as she added lightly beaten eggs to the sizzling butter in the pan and immediately started working the mix. 'But, if you think about it, my job is to help *you* share details of *your* fascinating-but-tragic love life with strangers whom *you* are never going to meet. This way we are both in the same business. I think it works.'

'Ah.' Mark pressed his lips together and gave Lexi a small nod as he carried the coffee over to the table. 'Good point. I should probably tell you that I am not totally thrilled by that prospect.'

'I understand that. Not everyone is a natural extrovert.' She shrugged just as the bread popped up from the toaster. 'But that's why you called me in.'

'I prefer keeping my private life just that. Private. I would much rather stick to the facts.'

'Are you speaking from past experience?' Lexi asked quietly, flashing him a lightning-quick glance as she quickly tipped hot scrambled egg onto a thick slice of golden toast.

'Perhaps it is,' Mark replied between sips of juice. 'And perhaps it isn't.'

'I see.' Lexi slid the plate onto the table. 'Well, I can tell you one thing. If you want this biography to work you're going to have to trust me and get that private life out for the world to see, Mark.'

His response was a close-mouthed frown which spoke volumes.

Oh, this was turning out so well.

Lexi nodded towards the food. 'Enjoy your breakfast. Then I really do need to find out how much work you've done so far on the manuscript. Perhaps you could show me your mother's study? That'd be a good place to start. In the meantime I'm off to feed the cats. Bye.'

And Lexi waltzed out of the kitchen diner on her wedge sandals, safe in the knowledge that Mark's stunned blue eyes were burning holes in her spectacular back.

CHAPTER FIVE

LEXI followed Mark through a door to a large room on the first floor, looking around in delight and awe.

Crystal Leighton had not had a study. Crystal Leighton had created a private library.

'How did you know my mother even had a study? I don't recall mentioning it.'

Lexi touched two fingers to her forehead in reply to Mark's question. 'Intuition. Combined with the number of rooms in this huge house and the fact that Crystal Leighton was an undisputed artist. Any creative person coming to this island would bring a fine collection of writing materials and reading matter with them. And when it's your own house... She would have a study. Elementary, my dear Watson.' She tapped her nose and winked in his direction. 'But this...' she continued, whistling softly and waving her arm around the room, turning from side to side in delight. 'This is...wonderful.'

'You like it?'

'*Like* it?' She blinked at him several times. 'This is heaven. I could stay here all day and night and never come up for air. Total bliss! I love books. Always have. In fact I cannot remember a time when I haven't had a book to hand.'

She almost jogged across the room and started poring

through the contents of the bookcases. 'Poetry, classics, philosophy, history, languages. Blockbuster fiction?' She flashed him a glance and he shrugged.

'I have a sister.'

'Ah, fair enough. We all need some relaxing holiday reading. But look at this collection of screenplays and books on the theatre. My mother would be so envious. Did I mention that she works as a wardrobe mistress? She loves reading about the theatre.'

'Every school holiday my mother used to stuff a spare suitcase with plays, books, scripts her agent had sent—anything that caught her eye.' Mark gave a faint smile and plunged his hands into his trouser pockets, nodding towards the shelves. 'I spent many wet and windy afternoons in this room.'

'I envy you that. And it's just what I need.' Lexi turned to face Mark, resting her fingertips lightly on the paper-strewn table in the centre of the room. 'Have you ever heard the expression that you can tell a lot about someone from the books they have in their home? It's true. You can.'

'I'm not so sure about that,' Mark replied with a dismissive grunt. 'What about the car magazines, polo-pony manuals and the school textbooks on biochemistry?'

She shook her head and waved with one hand at three particular shelves. 'Theatre history and set design. Fashion photography. Biographies of the Hollywood greats. Don't you see? That combination screams out the same message. Crystal Leighton was an intelligent professional actress who understood the importance of image and design. And that's the message we should be aiming for. Professional excellence. What do you think?'

'Think? I haven't had time to think,' Mark replied, and inhaled deeply, straightening his back so that Lexi felt as though he was towering over her. 'My publisher may have arranged your contract, but I'm still struggling with the idea of sharing personal family papers and records with someone I don't know. This is very personal to me.'

'You're a private person who doesn't like being railroaded. I get that. And I can understand that you're still not sure about my reason for being here in the first place.' She glanced up at his startled face and gave a small snort. 'It's okay, Mark. I'm not a spy for the paps. Never have been. No plans to be one any time soon. And if I was stalking you I would have told you.'

Lexi turned sideways away from the table and ran her fingers across the spines of the wonderful books on the shelves. 'Here's an idea. You're worried about sharing your family secrets with a stranger. Let's change that. What do you want to know about me? Ask me anything. Anything at all. And I'll tell you the truth.'

'Anything? Okay, let's start with the obvious. Why biographies? Why not write fiction or business books?'

She paused and licked her lips, but kept her eyes focused on the books in front of her. To explain properly she would have to reveal a great deal of herself and her history. That could be difficult. But she'd made a pact with herself. No lies, no deception. Just go with it. Even if her life seemed like a sad joke compared to Mark's perfect little family.

'Just after my tenth birthday I was diagnosed with a serious illness and spent several months in hospital.'

'I'm so sorry,' he whispered after a few seconds of total silence.

She sensed him move gently forward and lean against the doorframe so that he was looking at her.

'That must have been awful for you and your parents.'

She nodded. 'Pretty bad. My parents were going through

a rough time as it was, and I knew my father had a pathological hatred of hospitals. Ironic, huh?' She smiled at him briefly, still half-lost in the recollection. 'Plus, he was working in America at the time. The problem was, he didn't come home for a couple of months, and when he did he brought his new girlfriend with him.'

'Oh, no.' Mark's eyebrows went north but his tense shoulders went south.

'Oh, *yes*. I spent the first year recovering at my grandmother's house on the outskirts of London, with a very miserable mother and even more miserable grandmother. It was not the happiest of times, but there was one consolation that kept me going. My grandmother was a wonderful storyteller, and she made sure that I was supplied with books of every shape and form. I loved the children's stories, of course, but the books I looked for in the public library told of how other people had survived the most horrific of early lives and still came through smiling.'

'Biographies. You liked reading other people's life stories.'

'Could not get enough.' She nodded once. 'Biographies were my favourite. It didn't take long for me to realise that autobiographies are tricky things. How can you be objective about your own life and what you achieved at each stage? The biography, on the other hand, is something completely different: it's someone else telling you about a mysterious and fabulous person. They can be incredibly personal, or indifferent and cold. Guess what kind I like?'

'So you decided to become a writer?' Mark asked. 'That was a brave decision.'

'Perhaps. I had the chance to go to university but I couldn't afford it. So I went to work for a huge publishing house in London who released more personal life stories every year than all of the other publishers put together.'

She grinned up at Mark. 'It was *amazing*. Two years later I was an assistant editor, and the rest, as they say, is history.'

She reached her right hand high into the air and gave him a proper, over-the-top, twirling bow. 'Ta-da. And that's it. That's how I got into this crazy, outrageous business.' Lexi looked up at him coquettishly through her eyelashes as she stood up. 'Now. Anything else you'd like to know before we get started?'

'Only one thing. Why are you wearing so much make-up at nine o'clock in the morning? On a small Greek island? In fact, make that *any* island?

Lexi chuckled, straightening up to her full height, her head tilted slightly to one side.

'I take it as a compliment that you even noticed, Mark. This is my job, and this is my work uniform. Office, movie studio, pressroom or small Greek island. It doesn't make any difference. Putting on the uniform takes me straight into my working head—which is what you're paying me for. So, with that in mind, let's make a start.'

Lexi pulled down several books from the shelves and stacked them in front of Mark.

'There are as many different types of biography as there are authors. By their nature each one is unique and special, and should be matched to the personality of the person they are celebrating. Light or serious, respectful or challenging. It depends on what you want to say and how you want to say it. Which one of these do you like best?'

Mark exhaled loudly. 'I had no idea this would be so difficult. Or so complex.'

Lexi picked up a large hardback book with a photograph of a distinguished theatre actor on the cover and passed it to Mark.

She sighed as Mark flicked through the pages of small,

tightly written type with very little white space. 'They can also be terribly dry, because the person writing is trying their hardest to be respectful while being as comprehensive as possible. There are only so many times an actor can play Hamlet and make each performance different. Lists of who did what, when and where are brilliant for an appendix to the book—but they don't tell you about the *person,* about their *soul.*'

'Do you know I actually met this actor a couple of times at my mother's New Year parties?' Mark waved the book at Lexi before dropping it back to the table with a loud thump. 'For a man who had spent fifty years in the theatre he was actually very shy. He much preferred one-to-one conversations to holding centre stage like some of his fellow actors did.'

'Exactly!' Lexi leant forward, animated. 'That's what a biographer *should* be telling us about. How did this shy man become an international award-winning actor who got stage fright every single night in his dressing room but still went out there and gave the performance of his life for the audience? That's what we want to know. That's how you do justice to the memory of the remarkable person you are writing about. By sharing real and very personal memories that might have nothing to do with the public persona at all but can tell the reader everything about who that person truly was and what it meant to have them in your life. That's the gold dust.'

Mark frowned. 'So it all has to be private revelations?'

'Not all *revelations.* But there has to be an intimacy, a connection between reader and subject—not just lists of dry facts and dates.' Lexi shrugged. 'It's the only way to be true to the person you're writing about. And that's why you should be excited that you have this opportunity to make your mother come alive to a reader through your book. Plus, your publisher will love you for it.'

'Excited? That's not quite the word I was thinking of.'

She rubbed her hands together and narrowed her eyes. 'I think it's time for you to show me what you've done so far. Then we can talk about your memories and personal stories which will make this book better than you ever thought possible.'

Lexi sat down at the table, her eyes totally focused on the photographs and yellowing newspaper clippings spilling out of an old leather suitcase.

Mark strolled towards her, cradling his coffee cup, but as she looked up towards him her top slipped down a fraction and he was so entranced by the tiny tattoo of a blue butterfly on her shoulder that he forgot what he was about to say.

'Now, I'm going to take a leap here, but would it be fair to say that you haven't actually made much progress on the biography itself? Actual words on paper? Am I right?'

'Not quite,' Mark replied, stepping away to escape the tantalisingly smooth creaminess of Lexi's bare shoulder and elegant neck. 'My mother started working on a book last summer when she was staying here, and she wrote several chapters about her earlier life as well as pulling together those bundles of papers over there. But that's about it. And her handwriting was always pretty difficult to decipher.'

'Oh, that's fine.'

'Fine?' he replied, lifting his chin. 'How can it possibly be *fine*? I have two weeks to get this biography into shape, or I miss the deadline and leave it to some hack to spill the usual tired old lies and make more money out of my mother's death.' Mark picked up a photograph of Crystal Leighton, the movie star, at the height of her career. 'Have you any idea how angry that makes me? They think they know her because of the movies she worked on. They haven't got a clue.'

He shook his head and shuffled the photograph back into the same position, straightening the edges so that each of the clippings and photographs were exactly aligned in a neat column down one side. 'I don't expect you to understand how important this biography is to me, but she is not here to defend herself any more. Now that's my job.'

Lexi stared at Mark in silence for a moment, the air between them bristling with tension and anxiety.

How could she make him understand that she knew exactly what it was like to live two lives? People envied her her celebrity lifestyle, the constant travel, the vibrancy and excitement of her work. They had no clue whatsoever that under the happy, chatty exterior was a girl doing everything she could to fight off the despair of her life. Her desperate need to have children and a family of her own, and the sure knowledge that it was looking less and less likely ever to happen. Adam had been her best chance. And now he was gone... Oh, yes, she knew about acting a part.

'You think I don't understand? Oh, Mark, how very wrong you are. I know only too well how hard it is to learn to live with that kind of pain.'

She watched as he inhaled deeply before replying. 'How stupid and selfish of me,' he said eventually in a low voice. 'I sometimes forget that other people have lost family members and survived. It was especially insensitive after what you've just been telling me about your father.'

'Oh, it happens in the very best of families,' she said with a sad smile. 'Your mother died a few months ago, while I've had almost twenty years to work through the fact that my father abandoned us. And that pain does not go away.'

'You sound very resigned—almost forgiving. I'm not sure I could be.'

'Then I'm a very good actress. I've never forgiven him and I don't know if I ever can. A girl has to know her limitations, and this is one of mine. Not going to happen. Can we move on?'

Lexi looked up into Mark's eyes as she asked the question, just as he looked into hers. And in the few seconds of complete silence that followed something clicked across the electrically charged space between them.

'And just when I thought you were perfection,' he whispered, in a voice which was so rich and low and seductive that the tingles went into overdrive.

Lexi casually formed the fingers of both her hands into a tent shape, raised an eyebrow and stared at him through the triangular gap between her fingers.

'There you have it. I have flaws, after all. You must be incredibly disappointed that a respectable agency sent you a defective ghost writer. You should ask for a discount immediately. And I shall officially hand back my halo and declare myself human and fallible.'

Mark smiled. 'I rather like the idea. Perhaps there *is* hope for the rest of us?'

'Really? In that case,' she breathed in a low, hoarse voice, 'let's talk about your baby photos.'

And Mark immediately swallowed the wrong way and sprayed coffee all over his school reports.

They had hardly stopped for over three hours. He had made coffee. Lexi had made suggestions, dodging back and forth to the kitchen to bring snacks.

And, together, somehow they had sorted out the huge

suitcase bursting with various pieces of paper and photographs that he had brought with him from London into two stacks, roughly labelled as either 'career' or 'home life.' A cardboard box was placed in the middle for anything which had to be sorted out later.

And his head was bursting with frustration, unease and unbridled admiration.

Lexi was not only dedicated and enthusiastic, but she possessed such a natural delight and genuine passion for discovering each new aspect of his mother's life and experience that it was infectious. It was as though every single scrap of trivia was a precious item of buried treasure—an ancient artefact that deserved to be handled with the ultimate care and pored over in meticulous detail.

It had been Lexi's idea to start sorting the career stack first, so she knew the scope and complexity of the project right from the start.

Just standing next to her, trying to organise newspaper clippings and press releases into date order, made him feel that they might *just* be able to create some order out of the magpie's nest of thirty years' worth of memorabilia.

He couldn't remember most of the movie events that his mother had attended when he was a boy, so photographs from the red carpet were excellent markers—and yet, for him, they felt totally repetitive. Another pretty dress. Another handsome male lead. Yet another interview with the same newspaper. Saying the same things over and over again.

But Lexi saw each image in a completely different way. Every time she picked a photograph up she seemed to give a tiny gasp of delight. Every snippet of gossip about the actors and their lives, or the background to each story, was new and fresh and exciting in her eyes. Each line provided a new insight into the character of the woman who'd been a leading lady in the USA and in the British movie and TV world for so many years that she had practically become an institution.

Dates, names, public appearances, TV interviews—everything was recorded and checked against the film-company records through the power of the internet, then tabulated in date order, creating a miraculous list which they both agreed might not be totally complete, but gave the documented highlights.

And from this tiny table, in this small villa on Paxos, in only three hours, they had managed to create a potted history of his mother's movie career. All backed up by photographs and paper records. Ready to use, primed to create a timeline for the acting life of Crystal Leighton.

Which was something very close to amazing.

He wondered if Lexi realised that when she was reading intently she tapped her pen against her chin and pushed her bottom lip out in a sensuous pout, and sometimes she started humming a pop tune under her breath—before realising what she was doing and turning it into a chuckle because it had surprised her.

Every time she walked past him her floral fragrance seemed to reach out towards him and draw him closer to her, like a moth to a flame. It was totally intoxicating, totally overwhelming. And yet he hadn't asked her to wash it off. That would have been rude.

The problem was, working so closely together around such a small table meant that their bodies frequently touched. Sleeve on sleeve, leg on leg—or, in his case, long leg against thigh.

And at that moment, almost as though she'd heard his

innermost thoughts, Lexi lifted up the first folder of the second stack and brushed his arm with her wrist. That small contact was somehow enough to set his senses on fire.

Worse, a single colour photograph slipped out from between the pages and fell onto the desk. Two boys grinned back at Mark from the matte surface—the older boy proud and strong, chin raised, his arm loosely draped across the back and shoulder of his younger brother, who was laughing adoringly at the person taking the photograph.

Mark remembered the football match at boarding school as though it were yesterday. Edmund had scored two goals and been made man of the match. Nothing new there. Except that for once in his life nerdy Mark Belmont had come out from the wings and sailed the ball past the head of the goalkeeper from a rival school.

And, best of all, his mother had seen him score the winning goal and taken the photograph. She had always made time in her schedule if she could to attend school sports days.

Edmund had called him a show-off, of course. And maybe he'd been right. Mark had wanted to prove to at least one of his parents that he could be sporty when he wanted.

He inhaled slowly through his nose, but just as Lexi stretched her hand out towards the photograph he picked it up and pushed it back on the pile.

Not now. He was not ready to do that. Not yet.

But there was no escaping his companion's attention to detail. Lexi instantly dived into the stack and retrieved the photograph.

'Is this your brother?' she asked.

He took a moment and gave a quick nod. 'Yes. Edmund was eighteen months older than me. This was taken at our boarding school. The Belmont boys had just scored all three of the goals. We were the heroes of the hour…' His voice trailed away.

Out of the corner of his eye he realised that she was standing quite silent and still. Until then it hadn't dawned on him that her body was usually in constant motion. Her hands, shoulders and hips had been jiggling around every second of the day, which was probably why she was so slender. This girl lived on adrenaline.

But not now. Now she was just waiting—waiting for him to tell her about Edmund.

He picked up the photograph and gently laid it to the far right of the table. Recent history. Too recent as far as he was concerned.

'He died seven years ago in a polo accident in Argentina.'

If he was expecting revulsion, or some snide comment, he was wrong. Instead Lexi gently laid her fingertips on the back of his hand in a fleeting moment of total compassion. And he felt every cell of his skin open up and welcome her in.

'Your poor mother,' Lexi whispered, only inches away from him.

He turned his head slightly. Her eyes were scanning his face as if she was looking for something and not finding it.

'That must have been so heartbreaking. I can't imagine what it's like to raise a child to manhood and then lose him.'

Her gaze slid down his face and focused on a family snap of his mother. Not a studio press release or a publicity shot. This was a photo he had taken with his pocket camera when his mother had been manning the cake stall at a local garden fête. She was wearing a simple floral tea dress with a white daisy from the garden stuck behind one ear. But what made her really beautiful was the totally natural expression of happiness she wore.

It was just as hard as he'd thought it might be, looking at the photograph and remembering her laughing and chatting and waving at him to put down the camera and enjoy himself.

Lexi ran a fingertip ever so gently across the surface of the print. He steeled himself, ready to answer her question about how the famous actress Crystal Leighton had come to be working behind the counter of a country village fête.

That was why, when she did ask a question, it knocked him slightly off-balance.

'How old is your sister?

'Cassie? Twenty-seven,' he replied, puzzled. 'Why do you ask?'

'Because I'm going to need to talk to her about Edmund. I know she's a lot younger, but I'm sure she can remember her eldest brother very clearly.'

'So can I,' he retorted. 'We were at school together—more like twins than brothers.'

'And that's the point. You're too close. You can't possibly be objective, and I wouldn't expect you to be. He was your best friend and then you lost him—and that's hard. I'm so sorry. You must miss him terribly,' she whispered, and her teeth started to gnaw on her full lower lip in distress.

The deep shudder came from within his chest, and it must have been so loud that Lexi heard it. Because she smiled a half smile of understanding and regret and looked away. As though she was giving him a moment to compose himself.

Just the thought of that generous gesture flicked a switch inside his head that went from the calm controlled setting straight to the righteous anger mode.

This woman, this *stranger* who had walked into his life

less than twenty-four hours earlier, was giving him a moment to bring his pain back under control.

Nothing she could have done would have made him more furious.

How *dared* she presume that he was unable to control himself?

That he was unable to do the job he had set himself because of the foolish, sensitive emotions in the gentle heart he had suppressed for all these years?

He'd learned the hard way that the Belmont men did not talk about Edmund and how his death had wrenched them apart. No. Instead they were expected to shoulder the extra responsibilities and obligations and carry on as though Edmund had never existed.

Lexi pressed both hands flat against the table, lifted her head and looked into his eyes.

And, to Mark's horror, he saw the glint of moisture at the corners of her own eyes—which were not violet after all, he realised, but more of a grey colour in the diffused warm light coming in through the cream-lace curtains from the sunny garden outside. Her eyelashes were not black, like his, but dark brown, with a tint of copper. The same colour as her hair—well, most of it. The places that weren't streaked with purple highlights.

But it was those amazing eyes that captivated him and dragged him helplessly into their depths. Multiple shades of grey and violet with blue speckles gazed back at him, with the black centres growing darker and wider as her eyes locked onto his and refused to let go. And he simply could not look away.

Those were the same eyes that had stared up at him in total horror that morning in the hospital. The same eyes that were now brimming with compassion and warmth and delight. And he had never seen anything like it before.

His mother had used to say that eyes were the windows to the heart.

And if that was true then Lexi Sloane had a remarkable heart.

But the fact remained—just looking into those eyes took him back to a place which shouted out, loud and clear, one single overpowering word.

Failure.

He had failed to protect his mother.

He had failed to replace Edmund.

He had let his parents down and was still letting them down.

And just the sight of his mother's pretty face looking back at him from all these photographs was like a knife to the heart.

'How do you do it?' he demanded through clenched teeth. 'How do you do this job for a living? Poring over the pain and suffering of other people's lives? Do you get some sick pleasure out of it? Or do you use other people's pain in order to make your own life feel better and safer in some way? Please tell me, because I don't understand. I just don't.'

He was trembling now, and so annoyed by his own lack of self-control that he brusquely slipped his hand out from under hers, turned away and strode downstairs to the patio doors, pulled them open sharply and stepped outside onto the cool shaded terrace.

Well, that was clever. Well done, Mark. Very slick. Taking your problems out on the nearest person, just like your dad would.

He closed his eyes and fought to control his breathing. Minutes seemed to stretch into hours until he heard the gentle tapping of Lexi's light footsteps on the tile floor behind him.

She came and stood next to him at the railing, so that they were both looking out across the pool towards the cypress trees and olive groves in total silence.

'I don't do this job out of some sick pleasure or self-gratification. Well...' she shrugged '...apart from the fact that I get paid, of course. No. I do it to help my clients record how they came through the traumas of their lives to become the person they are now. And that's what other people want to read about.' She half turned at the railing. 'I was serious when I told you how much I loved reading about other people's lives. I love meeting people. I love hearing their life stories.'

Her fingers tapped on the varnished wood. 'Just in case you haven't noticed, every family in this world suffers pain and loss, and every single person—every one—has to survive horrible trauma which changes their lives forever. That includes me, you and all our families and friends. There is no escape. It's how we deal with it that makes us who we are. That's all.'

'That's *all?*' He shook his head. 'When did *you* become an expert in sorting out other people's lives and their histories for them? You're hardly perfect yourself—not with *your* father.'

The temperature of the air dropped ten degrees, and the icy blast hit Mark hard on the forehead and woke him up.

He hadn't meant to sound bitter or cruel, but suppressed emotion and tiredness swept over him like a wave and he needed a few moments before he could very, very slowly relax his manic hold on the railing and start to breathe again. He was only too aware that Lexi was watching his every move in silence.

'I apologise for that outburst, Miss Sloane. It was un-called for and unnecessary. I thought that we could get past what happened at the hospital but apparently I was mistaken. I can quite understand if you would prefer not to work with me after my rudeness. In fact, if you pack your bags now, you should be able to catch the ferry which leaves at four. I'll make sure your hire car is picked up at the harbour, and that the agency pays your full fee. Thank you for your help this morning.'

CHAPTER SIX

Lexi stared at him as the hot sun beat down on her shoulders.

Yesterday Mark had listened to the truth about her father and still given her a chance to work with him. Now he had thrown her heritage back in her face—and then apologised to her for it.

He was the most contrary, annoying and confusing man she had met in a long time. But under that bravado something told her that he was okay. Intensely private, ambushed into having her at his house, but okay.

And she was not giving up on him.

'Oh, I'm well aware that I am very far from perfect. Stubborn, too. Put those two things together and the result is that I'm not going anywhere,' she replied with a lilting voice, and raised both hands, palms forward. 'This happens all the time. Who in their right mind wants to talk about the pain of the past? It's human nature to push all this turmoil into a box and lock the lid down tight so we can get on with our daily lives.'

And I should know.

She glanced from side to side, but the only living creatures within sight were the four cats along the wall. 'I'm not allowed to talk about other clients, because those confidentiality agreements I sign are completely watertight, but believe me—I've worked with some people and I don't know how they get through the day with all the baggage they're carrying. I thought I had problems until I worked with *real* survivors.'

'Is that what we are? Survivors?'

'Every single one of us. Every day. And there's nothing we can do about it. Although I do know one thing.'

He slowly exhaled. 'I can hardly wait to hear it.'

'I'm famished!' she exclaimed with an overly dramatic sigh, in an attempt to break the tense atmosphere with a change of topic. 'Can I suggest we break for lunch before we start on your mum's personal life? Because I have a feeling…' she looked at him with a grimace '…that we may need some fortification to get through it. And my body armour is back in London.'

'Famished?' Mark replied, blinking for a few seconds as though his brain was trying to process the words. Then his shoulders seemed to drop several inches, his back straightened and his head lifted. 'Of course. In that case it's my turn to provide lunch. Prepare to have your taste buds tantalised by one of the excellent tavernas on the coast. How does a big bowl of crisp Greek salad followed by succulent freshly caught sea bass and chips sound? But there's one condition. We don't talk about our jobs or why you're here. Do we have a deal?'

Lexi's mouth watered at the thought of it. Her last proper meal had been in Hong Kong two days earlier. Although lunch for two in a beautiful restaurant by the ocean could be mighty distracting if it meant sitting across the table from Mark for several hours, sharing delicious food.

'Lunch in a restaurant?' She baulked. 'Do we have the time?' She thought in panic of the mountain of paperwork they'd just left behind. 'There's a lot of work to do here.'

'Which is why the fresh sea air will do both of us a

world of good. I've been cooped up inside for the last three days. I need a break and a change of scene.'

'Why don't you go on your own?' She smiled, nodding her head. 'It'll take me a few hours to read through these typed pages in detail. I'll be quite happy with bread and salad.'

'You can do that later,' he shot back and looked at her through narrowed eyes. 'Unless, of course, there's another reason why you'd prefer not to eat lunch in public with me. Jealous boyfriend? Secret fiancé? Or simply worried about my table manners?'

He tilted his head and the tingles hit her the second those blue eyes twinkled in her direction.

'Just say the word and I can provide excellent references for both my sobriety and my familiarity with cutlery.'

Lexi rolled her eyes. Mark was clearly determined to avoid what they had left behind in that suitcase of memories, so she relented enough to step back from the balustrade and shake her head.

'No jealous boyfriends—or girlfriends, for that matter— no secret fiancé, and I'm confident that your table manners will be excellent. Okay, we have a deal.' Her face softened. 'However, there is one tiny problem.'

His eyebrows lifted.

'Oh, yes, I know it's hard to believe. I hate to admit this, but I didn't have the heart to move the kittens out of the car last night. Can we walk there? Catch the bus?'

Mark pushed his right hand into his pocket and took a step closer, filling the air between them with a few inches of warm masculine scent. He pulled out a set of keys and swung them into his left hand. 'No problem. I'm ready to go. How about you?'

'You mean now? I need a few minutes to get changed and grab a bag,' Lexi replied and twirled her forefinger towards her head. 'And do my hair and put some make-up on.'

He looked at her open-mouthed for a few seconds, and then did a complete head-to-toe scan of every item of clothing that she was wearing. And actually smiled as he was doing it.

Lexi crossed her arms and glared at him. She felt as though his X-ray vision actually bored right through her trousers and the off-the-shoulder tunic to the brand-new red-lace lingerie beneath. Her neck was burning with embarrassment, her palms were sweating, and the longer he looked the more heated she became. This was not doing much good for her composure.

'Oh, I really wouldn't worry about that,' he murmured. 'Especially about your hair.'

'What's wrong with my hair?' Lexi asked, flicking her hair out from inside her collar and away from the back of her neck. 'Is there a dress code where we're going?'

A peal of pure exuberant laughter came out of Mark's mouth and echoed around the garden. The sound was so astonishing, so warm and natural, that Lexi blinked twice to make sure she was looking at the same person. *Where had that come from?*

And could she please hear it again? Because his whole face had been transformed into a smiling, almost *happy* version of the usual handsome-but-stern exterior. And her poor foolish heart jumped up and did a merry jig just from looking at him.

She'd thought Mark handsome before, but this was taking it to a new level.

'You'll be fine,' Mark replied, looking rather sheepish at his outburst of jollity. And then he held out his hand towards her, as though he was daring her to come with him.

'I'm going to need five minutes,' she said, trying to

sound bright and enthusiastic as she slid past him and tried to ignore his hand. 'Just enough time for you to bring the car around.'

'You don't need five minutes,' he replied with a grin, grabbing her hand and half dragging her off the patio and onto the gravel drive. 'And who said anything about a car?'

'Your carriage awaits, madam.'

Lexi stared at the motorcycle, then at the boyish black crash helmet Mark was holding, then back to the motorcycle. She stepped out onto the gravel and walked slowly around the vehicle, examining it from a number of angles.

Mark waited patiently for a few seconds as Lexi stopped and nodded her head several times, before declaring, 'This is a scooter.'

'Your powers of observation are quite superlative,' he replied, fighting the urge to smile and thereby shatter even more of her expectations.

'It's a very nice scooter,' she continued, 'and very clean for a boy, but…it's still a scooter.'

She seemed to suck in a breath, then shook her head twice and looked up at him with total bewilderment on her face.

'But *you* can't ride a scooter! It must be against the rules for English aristocrats to ride scooters. At the very least I expected some swanky sports car worth more than my house. This is incredibly shocking.'

'I take delight in thwarting your expectations. For where we're going, two-wheeled transport is definitely the best option.'

And with that he calmly unfastened a second crash helmet from the back seat and presented her with it. The helmet was red, with a white lightning arrow down each side and the words *Paxos Pizza* in large black letters across the front. Not something you could easily miss.

'Ah. Yes. Cassie's helmet came at a bargain price. That was the only one my pal Spiro had left in a medium.'

She looked dubiously at the helmet that he was holding out to her.

'The only one? I see. And you're quite positive that we shouldn't take my hire car?'

'Quite,' he replied. 'I would hate to disturb the cats.'

'Ah,' she said, 'of course. The cats. A man clearly has to have priorities.'

Without saying another word she slid her shoulder bag over her head and across her chest, took the helmet out of his hands, swept back her hair and slipped the helmet on. All in one single sleek movement. She fastened the chin-strap as though she had been doing it all her life.

His silent admiration just clicked up two points.

'Don't say a word,' she murmured, glaring at him through slitted eyes.

'I wouldn't dare.' Mark patted the seat behind him. 'You might want to hold on to me when we set off.'

'Oh, I think I can manage. Thank you all the same.'

She was standing next to him now, one hand planted firmly on each hip, weighing up her options. Although she was only two feet away, he could hear her mind ticking. The air crackled with tension.

'You should be warm enough,' he said quite calmly. 'We're not going far.'

And with that he started the engine and clicked down into first gear.

Then he checked the chinstrap on his helmet, wriggled his bottom into the driver's position and faced directly ahead. Without looking back even once to check what she was doing.

Send For
2 FREE BOOKS
Today!

I accept your offer!

Please send me two
free Harlequin® Romance
novels and two mystery
gifts (gifts worth about $10).
I understand that these books
are completely free—even
the shipping and handling will
be paid—and I am under no
obligation to purchase anything, ever,
as explained on the back of this card.

❏ I prefer the regular-print edition
116/316 HDL FJD2

❏ I prefer the larger-print edition
186/386 HDL FJD2

Please Print

FIRST NAME

LAST NAME

ADDRESS

APT.#   CITY

STATE/PROV.   ZIP/POSTAL CODE

**Visit us online at
www.ReaderService.com**

Ten seconds later the bike lurched slightly to one side as she settled herself on the small pillion passenger seat.

That was his cue to enjoy a totally secret wide-mouthed smile, which he knew she wouldn't see.

'Hang on!' he called, and without waiting for a reply opened up the throttle and set off slowly down the drive. He checked the road was clear and they were on their way.

Warm summer air, thick with pollen from the olive trees and scented with pine resin, caressed Lexi's arms and bare legs as the scooter tootled down the main road heading for the coast.

She leaned back on her arms and gripped on to the grab-rail behind her seat, her muscles clenching and rattling with every bump in the road. Strange how she hadn't noticed the potholes in the comfort of her hire car. She was certainly feeling every one of them now.

She hated being a passenger. But she had to admit that the view in front of her was impressive enough. Mark's broad shoulders filled his shirt, and as he stretched forward on the scooter she could see the muscles in his arms move effortlessly through the controls. His top wasn't quite long enough, which meant she had occasional tantalising glimpses of the band of skin above his snug-fitting trousers.

Far too tantalising.

Dratted tingles.

Lexi turned her head slowly from side to side, looking for distraction in the stunning Greek countryside as they sped along at about twenty miles an hour. Lemon trees, bright purple and pink bougainvillaea, and pale oleander bushes filled the gardens of the houses they passed on the small country road. Dark green cypresses and pine trees created a perfect skyline of light and shade under the deep azure blue of the sky.

And all the time she could glimpse a narrow line of darker blue in between the trees, where the Ionian Sea met the horizon.

The sun shone warmly on her exposed skin and she felt free and wild and ready to explore. She felt so completely liberated that, without thinking about it, she closed her eyes and relaxed back to let the wind cool her throat and neck. Just as she did so the bike slowed, making a sharp turn to the left off the main road onto what felt like a farm track.

Lexi snapped her eyes open and instinctively grabbed Mark around the waist, her heart thumping. She could feel his muscles tighten under her hands, warm and solid and mightily reassuring.

He glanced back just once, to give her a reassuring smile, before reducing his speed and leaning the scooter through bend after bend of steadily narrowing and even more bumpy road until they came to a passing point outside a stunning tiny white church and he came to a slow, graceful stop.

They had arrived. At the end of the road.

'Did I mention that the rest of the way is on foot?' he asked in an innocent voice.

Lexi replied with a scathing look and glanced down at her gold wedge sandals. 'How far do I have to walk?'

'Five minutes. Tops. It's just at the end of the donkey trail and then through the olives.'

'Five minutes? I'll hold you to that. Of course you *do* realise that your terrible secret is now out in the open?' Lexi grinned, heading down the rocky path between the high drystone walls that separated the olive groves. Pine needles from the conifers softened her tread.

Mark swallowed hard. 'Any one in particular? I have so many.'

'This is undoubtedly true. I was, of course, referring to the secret life of The Honourable Mark Belmont, Company Director. The outside world knows him as the suave financial wizard of the London stock market. But when Mr Belmont comes to Paxos? Ah, then the other Mark emerges from his chrysalis. *This* version enjoys riding his scooter—in public—drinking the local wine and entertaining cats. So that only leaves one question. What other hidden talents are yet to emerge?'

His reply was a quick snort.

'Landscape painting, perhaps? No. Too sedate. How about speedboat-racing?' Lexi stretched up and ran her fingers through the low-hanging branch of an olive tree. 'Or perhaps you're the olive king of the island and have vats of the stuff back at Belmont Manor, ready to challenge the Greek olive-oil market? That'd suit your aristocratic swashbuckling style.'

He chuckled out loud now. A real laugh, displaying his perfect teeth. 'Swashbuckling? Not exactly my style. And, in answer to your question, I'm no water baby. But I can heartily recommend the local olive oil.'

'You don't swashbuckle *or* swim?'

'Never.'

'Seriously? When you have that lovely pool at the villa?

He froze, half turned and then looked at her for a split second, still smiling. 'Swimming was for pupils who preferred sport to studying. Apart from my stellar football experience, which was definitely a one-off, sport was not on my timetable. And it strikes me that I've been answering a lot of questions. Your turn. What hidden talents does Lexi Sloane have up her sleeve? What's *her* guilty pleasure?'

Now it was Lexi's turn to smile, but she shot him a quick glance as they walked along before speaking again.

'Apart from good food and wine, you mean? Ah. Well, as a matter of fact I *do* have a guilty pleasure. I write children's stories.'

Mark made a strange strangled sound but carried on walking.

'Children's stories? You mean teen vampire love and schools for wizards?'

She sniggered. 'Mine are meant for a much younger audience. Think talking animals and fairies.' She stopped walking, dived into her shoulder bag, brought out her favourite notebook and flicked to a particular page. 'I worked on this one during the night when I couldn't sleep.'

Mark turned around on the narrow path and took a step towards her, peering at the notebook she held out.

To Lexi's delight his eyes widened and a broad grin warmed his face, as though she'd lit a fire inside him which drove away the darkness of the morning with its brightness.

'That's Snowy One and Snowy Two.' He laughed, flicking over the page. 'These are wonderful! You didn't mention that you did the illustrations, as well. When did you find the time to draw the kittens?'

'I cheated and took some photos before dinner yesterday. They were perfect models and quite happy to stay in position for at least a couple of seconds while I found a pose I liked. Then I worked the photos into the stories.'

She took the notebook back and just for a fraction of a second her fingertips made contact with Mark's hand. And, judging by his sharp intake of breath, he felt the connection just as powerfully as she did. He immediately started gabbling to cover it up.

'Well, I am impressed. Are you planning to have your

stories published or keep them for your own children to enjoy?'

And there it was. A direct hit. Bullseye. Right between the eyes!

My own children? Oh, Mark, if only you knew how much I long to have children of my own.

Tears pricked at the corners of her eyes. *Stupid.* She should be able to handle the question better than this. But he'd hit her with it out of the blue. That was all. She could cope.

'Published, I hope,' she replied through a burning throat. 'One day.'

'Excellent,' he replied, his warm voice brimming with feeling. 'In that case I look forward to reading your stories to my nephews at the earliest opportunity.'

Lexi picked up his lighter mood and went with it gladly. 'Ah. Do I have to add bedtime story-reader to your long list of accomplishments?'

He smiled. 'I try. Actually…' He paused long enough for Lexi to look at him, then shrugged. 'Sometimes reading those stories is the best part of my day. We have a great time.'

With startling suddenness he turned away from her and started down the track, but the sadness and need in his voice were so powerful that Lexi stayed frozen to the spot.

Two things were clear. He loved those boys. And Mark Belmont was going to be a wonderful father to the lucky children he so clearly wanted in his life.

And her poor heart cried at the thought that she would probably never experience that joy.

Just as the thought popped into her head Mark glanced back towards her, and Lexi slid the book back into her bag and pretended to rummage around as she casually replied, 'I don't have any food with me except breath mints.'

Then she looked around her and raised her eyebrows. 'And, while I appreciate that this is a lovely spot, and I'm enjoying the countryside, something tells me that there won't be a restaurant at the end of this very winding footpath. Am I right?'

'Perhaps.'

'Sorry?'

'It's a long story.'

He gestured with his hand down the path and set off slowly. 'You were talking earlier about collecting impressions about a person by where they liked to live and what they read. And it struck me that you might find it easier to understand who Crystal Leighton was when she wasn't being a famous actress if I showed you her favourite place on the island. I haven't been here in a long time, but this is very special. If we're lucky it won't have changed that much.'

'What kind of place are you talking about?' Lexi asked, astonished that Crystal had chosen somewhere other than her lovely villa. 'And what makes it so special?'

'Come and see for yourself,' Mark replied in a hushed voice that she had never heard him use before.

Lexi followed him through a cluster of pine trees, pushed through some fragrant flowering bushes next to a stone wall, and stepped into a private garden.

And what she saw there was so astonishing that she had to clutch on to Mark for support. His reaction was to instantly wrap one long muscular arm around her waist to hold her safe against his body.

They were standing about six feet from the edge of a cliff. A real cliff. As in the type of cliff where, if you stepped forward one inch, you'd find yourself flying through space for a long time before hitting the sea below.

Their only protection from the dizzyingly close edge

was a waist-high stone wall, which had been built in a wide curve in front of a low stone bench.

But it was the view that grabbed her and held her even tighter than Mark. All she could see in each direction was an unbroken band of sea and the azure sky above it. She felt like an explorer standing on the edge of a new world, looking out over an ocean no one had ever seen before, with nothing but air between her and the sea and the sky. And all she had to do was reach out and it would be hers.

To her right and left were high white cliffs of solid rock, studded with occasional stunted pine trees like the ones she was standing next to now. Far below, the sea crashed onto a collection of huge boulders at the foot of the cliffs.

'There are huge caves under the cliff here,' Mark said as though he was reading her thoughts. 'Big enough for the tourist boats to go into. But we're quite safe. There are hundreds of feet of solid rock below us.' As if to prove the point he grabbed her hand and practically dragged her to the stone wall, so that they could look out together over the tops of the hardy bushes and bright flowering plants clinging to the cliff face at the open sea.

'This is the nearest I've ever come to being on the prow of a ship,' Lexi breathed. 'Oh, Mark. This is...wonderful. I can see now why she chose this spot.'

'You should come back at dusk and watch the sun setting. It turns the whole sky a burning red. It's a wonderful sight. And, best of all, it's totally private. No cameras, no people, just you and the sea and the sky. That was why she loved it so much here. That's why she spent hour after hour on her own up here with just a picnic and a book. Alone with her thoughts. Away from the press and the movie business and everything that came with it.'

Lexi glanced up at Mark's face but his attention was totally fixed on the horizon, where the sky met the sea.

His eyes were the colour of the ocean. His fingers were still locked on to hers and she could feel his heart pound with each breath.

And her heart melted like cheese under a grill.

She had not intended it to. *Far from it.*

She couldn't help it. The fire in his voice and in his heart burned too hot to resist.

Which was why she did something very foolish. She squeezed his hand.

Instantly he glanced down at his fingers, and she caught a glimpse of awareness and recognition that he had revealed a little too much of himself before he recovered and released her with a brief twist of his mouth.

'Last Christmas she tried to persuade me to take some time off to celebrate Easter with her on the island. Just the two of us. But I said no. Too much work.' He sniffed, looking out towards the islands in the distance. 'Ironic, isn't it? I have the time now.'

'She knew you wanted to come back. I'm sure of it. How could you not? When you write about the last few months of her life you should put that in. It would be a lovely touch to end her story.'

She instantly sensed his solid-steel defences moving back into place.

'I'm not ready to write about how her life ended. I'm not sure I ever will be.'

'But you have to, Mark,' Lexi urged him softly, ignoring just how close the cliff edge was so she could step in front of him, forcing him to look down at her face. 'You're the only one who can tell the truth about what happened that day. Because if you don't someone else will make it up. I know that for a fact. Your mother is relying on you. Don't you want the truth to come out?'

'The truth? Oh, Lexi.'

She lifted her hands and pressed her fingertips to the front of his shirt.

He flinched at her touch, but she didn't move an inch and locked her eyes on to his.

'I was only there for a few seconds that day, but you saw what happened in its entirety, and you know why it happened. That makes you unique.'

'What happened?' he repeated, his eyes scanning her face as though he was looking for permission to say what needed to be said and finding it. 'What happened was that I was half a world away from London when my mother collapsed with a brain aneurysm. Dad had sent me over to Mumbai to negotiate with the owners of a start-up technology firm, so I was in India when Mum's friend called me out of the blue. It was the middle of the night, but there's nothing like hearing that your mother's been rushed to hospital to wake you up pretty fast.'

'How awful. No one should have to take a call like that when they're so far away.'

'The next twenty-four hours were probably the longest and most exhausting of my life. But if anything it got worse when I finally arrived. Cassie had met me at the airport. I'll never forget walking into that hospital room. I hardly recognised her. She had tubes coming out from everywhere, she was surrounded by medical staff, and I couldn't understand why she was still comatose. She looked so lifeless, so white and still.'

He shook his head and closed his eyes as Lexi moved closer towards him.

'I think I must have been too exhausted at that point to take things in, because I remember asking Cassie if she was sure there hadn't been some terrible mistake—this wasn't our mother after all. But then the doctors whisked us all out to one of those beige and green so-called relatives' rooms and the truth finally started to hit home.'

He half opened his eyes as Lexi looked into his face. 'Our lovely, beautiful mother hadn't come to London to stay with her old friend and talk charity fundraising. She'd come to have plastic surgery. She didn't tell us in advance because she knew we'd try and talk her out of it. According to her friend, she'd planned the surgery months earlier, as a Christmas present to herself. Because she needed the boost to her confidence.'

'Oh, Mark.'

'She had the operation Monday morning, collapsed on the Monday evening, and slipped away from us on Thursday morning. While I was standing in a police station in central London, being cautioned for attacking a member of the press. Your father.'

Mark snapped his fingers, and the sound ricocheted out into the serene calm air and seemed to penetrate Lexi's body. She jerked back in shock.

'*That's* how fast your life can switch.'

Lexi felt tears roll down her cheeks, but she couldn't speak. Not yet. Not until he was ready.

'The surgeon kept telling us that if she'd survived the aneurysm she could well have been brain-damaged or disabled, as if that would help in some way. It didn't.'

'How did your dad get through it?' Lexi asked.

'He didn't,' Mark whispered. 'He fought off cancer a few years ago, and was in remission until her death destroyed him. He's never been the same since. It's as though all the light went out of his world. He's fighting it, but he's determined to do it alone and there's not one thing Cassie or I can do except make his days as bright and positive as possible.'

'And do you think this book will help? Is that why you agreed to do it?'

'Cassie thinks it's the one thing keeping his spirits up. He wants it to be a celebration of her life instead of some nonsense tabloid journalists will put together from media press kits to make a profit from some scandalous headline.'

'But what about you, Mark? What would help *you* to grieve for her?'

'Me? I don't know where to start. Sometimes I can't believe that I won't ever see her again or hear her voice. I don't want to think about all the future events and special occasions in my life where there will be an empty chair with her name on it. And then there's the guilt. That's the toughest thing of all.'

'Guilt? Why do you feel guilty?'

He closed his eyes. 'Let me see. Never having time to spend with my own mother one-to-one because of the obligations I took on when Edmund died. Always cancelling lunch dates with my biggest fan at the very last minute or having to cut short telephone calls because of some business meeting. Oh, yes, and let's not forget the big one. The reason she had plastic surgery in the first place.'

Mark lifted his head and looked directly at Lexi. She could see moisture glistening at the corners of his eyes, but was powerless to speak in the intensity of his gaze.

'She told her friend that she was having the surgery because she didn't want to let me down at my engagement party. She didn't feel beautiful enough to stand next to me and my future bride's aristocratic family. So she went to London on her own and went through surgery on her own. *For me.* Have you ever heard anything so ridiculous in your life?'

CHAPTER SEVEN

'OH MARK,' Lexi whispered in amazement. 'Why do you think your mother felt that way? She was stunningly beautiful.'

Mark looked up as a flock of seabirds circled above their heads before flying over to the cliffs to nest. 'Pressure. Competition from other actresses for work in TV and movies. Every time we met she talked about the disappointment of being turned down for the roles she really wanted to play.' Mark sighed. 'She couldn't get work, and it was obvious she was finding it tougher and tougher to bounce back from each new rejection. Her agent gave up even trying to interest the movie studios. There was always another beautiful starlet just waiting to be discovered, and in the end it wore her down.'

'But Crystal Leighton was still a big star. People loved her.'

'Try telling that to the casting directors. The truth is she'd been desperately unhappy for a very long time and it showed. She'd lost her spark. Her vitality. Her joy. And it was there on her face for the world to see.'

'So it wasn't just about your engagement party, was it? That was just an excuse for having the work done. Please don't feel guilty about something you have no control over.

From what you tell me, it doesn't sound like you would've been able to change her mind.'

Mark exhaled slowly and Lexi felt his breath on her face. She lifted her right hand and stroked his cheek with her fingertips as his eyes fluttered half-closed. 'I didn't realise you were engaged,' she whispered, desperate to prolong the sensation of standing so close to him for as long as possible. Even if there *was* a fabulous fiancée waiting for him back in London.

'There's no reason why you should. It never happened. It's over now,' Mark replied, his brow furrowed and hard. 'We'd known each other for years, we mixed in the same circles, and I think it just became something other people expected us to do. I never proposed and she didn't expect me to. It was simply a convenient arrangement for both of us. We were friends, but I wasn't in love with her. Two months ago she found someone she truly cares about, which is how it should be.'

'Did your mother know you felt that way?'

'I don't know. We never talked about it. We don't talk about things in our family. We skate over the surface for fear of falling into the deep icy water below. And all my father cared about was making sure there'd be another Belmont son to inherit the title.'

Mark shook his head, his mouth a firm narrow line. 'I thought for a while that I wanted the same thing. That perhaps having a wife and a family might bring the Belmont family back together again. But it would only have made two more people miserable and led to an embarrassing divorce down the line. I can see that now.'

Lexi's brain caught up with what Mark was saying and a cold hand gripped her heart in spite of the warm breeze. 'You were prepared to do that?' she asked, trying to keep the horror of his situation out of her voice and failing. 'To

marry a girl whom you didn't love? Then have a baby with
her to provide a son to inherit the estate?'

'Oh, yes. The old rules are still in force. Even Cassie's
boys don't stand a chance. Unless I persuade some poor
girl to give me a son, the next Baron Belmont will be my
least favourite cousin. And both of *his* boys are adopted, so
they can't inherit, either. So that's it. Nine hundred years,
father to son, and it all comes down to me.'

Lexi sucked in a breath and exhaled slowly. 'How can
you stand it? How can you live like that?' she asked in a
trembling voice. 'Bringing a child into this world should
be something for two people to celebrate—not an obligation you can tick off the list.'

*And at least you're able to have a son. Have you no
idea how lucky you are?*

Then she looked into Mark's sad eyes and all of her fight
drifted away. 'Sorry. That was unfair. You have a duty to
your family and they need you.'

His response was to rest his forehead against Lexi's
and take her hand in his, stretching out each of her fingers
in turn, as though they were the most fascinating objects
he'd ever seen.

'Now do you understand why I'm struggling to finish
her biography?' he asked, his voice low and trembling.
'People will expect my mother to have enjoyed a fabulous
life full of fun and happiness and excitement. Movie stars
like Crystal Leighton aren't supposed to end up living a
bitter, cold existence, racked with disappointment and low
self-worth. With a son who was never there for her.'

He clasped both her hands between his and held them
prisoner before asking the question Lexi had been dread-
ing but had somehow known would come.

'How will you write *that* story, Lexi? How do you tell

that kind of truth without destroying my father and my family at the same time?'

'That has to be your decision, Mark,' she replied, in as low and calm a voice as she could manage. 'I can tell you how to make this book a true celebration of her life. And I know that the dark and the shade only make the happy times seem brighter. That was a part of her life and you can't avoid the truth.'

'The truth? That's a strange concept from someone who writes stories for a living. Let me tell *you* the truth,' he murmured, his voice trembling with emotion. 'The truth is that I need to get back to London. Away from the manor. I have to focus on the future and learn to live my own life, not a second-hand one—that's precisely what she would want me to do.'

And then Mark released her fingers, pressed one hand to her cheek, tilted his head and, with the most feather-light touch, kissed her.

Lexi was so startled that she was rendered speechless. The pressure of his lips was so warm and soft that her eyelids fluttered closed and she almost leant forward for more—only to find him gone. And she immediately cursed herself for being so weak and foolish.

'Thank you for listening. I can't finish this book, Lexi. I can't put my family through the pain.' He took a step back and looked out over the cliffs to the wide blue ocean in front of them. 'Sorry, Lexi. The biography is cancelled. I'm going to return the advance to my publisher. I can deal with the fallout with my family, and it's better to do it now rather than later, in the full face of the media. Thank you for helping me to decide to move forward in my life, not backwards, but I don't need your help any more. You can go back to London. Your work here is finished.'

* * *

Lexi fought to bring her heartbeat back to normal before stomping up to Mark, who was standing at the stone wall looking out towards the islands on the horizon.

'Finished? Oh, no, you don't, Mark Belmont.'

Mark turned back to face her, startled. 'I beg your pardon?'

'And so you should. Because right now it seems to me that you are running away from a challenge just at the point when it starts to get interesting.'

He smiled and shook his head. 'I've already told you that you will get your fee. Don't worry about it.'

She stepped forward, grabbed his arms and turned him sideways, so that he was not quite so scarily close to the edge of the precipice.

'I'm really not getting through to you, am I?' She rolled her eyes. 'I refuse to let you walk away from the only chance you'll ever have to put the record straight about Crystal Leighton. Yes, that's right. I am not going anywhere. And neither are you. I've been hearing a lot about family obligations, but nothing about how the real Mark would choose to celebrate his mother's life and work if left to himself.'

'That option is not available. I don't have a choice.'

Lexi clamped her hands over her ears. 'Not listening. Of course you have choices. You're the one who decides what to do with the life you've been given. So you're going to be the next Baron Belmont? That's amazing!'

She lowered her hands and smiled at him. 'Think of all the good you can do in your position. Starting with celebrating the life of your wonderful mother.'

One more step pressed her against his chest. 'Take the risk, Mark. Take this week out of your life and do the best you can. Because together I know we can create something stunning and true and authentic. But I need you on my team. Come on. Take the risk. You know you'll always regret it if you don't. And I never took you for a quitter.' Her voice softened. 'Do it out of love, not out of obligation. Who knows? You might actually enjoy it.'

His finger traced a line from her cheek to her neck and the tingles made her want to squirm.

'One week?' he whispered, his breath hot on her face.

'One week.' She play-thumped him on the chest. 'Now. Where's that lunch you promised me? I've been desperate for Greek salad for the last hour.'

It was a very silly hour of the morning when Lexi finally gave up tossing and turning, pulled her pillow from under her head and attempted to throw back the covers from her comfortable double bed.

Only she'd twisted so much that the fine cotton sheets had wrapped around her like an Egyptian mummy, and after a few minutes of kicking and elbowing her way free she knew what silkworms must feel like. She felt so hot that even the single sheet was a weight on her skin. The simple air-conditioning unit was trying its best, but with the double glazed windows closed the bedroom felt airless and stuffy. And so desperately, desperately quiet.

Somewhere in the house a clock was striking every quarter-hour with a musical chime, but apart from that comforting sound the house was completely silent—as though it was a sleeping giant waiting for some magical spell to be broken to bring him back to life.

It was such a total contrast to the background hubbub of the large international hotels she usually stayed in and the city noises that surrounded them.

Lexi tiptoed over to the balcony door and peeked out through the hand-worked lace curtain. Slowly and quietly sneaking open the door, she stepped outside, closing it behind her.

She could see light coming from the living rooms of the house on the other side of the olive grove. Moths fluttered against the light above her head, but no mosquitoes, thank goodness. Down below in the garden, solar-powered lights illuminated the pathway to the pool and a barbecue area. A white cat pattered across the patio tiles towards the swimming pool—probably the Snowys' dad Oscar, going for a drink. But apart from that all was still, calm and serene.

Lexi looked out over the treetops and soaked in the silence as though she was drinking the contents of a deep well of cool, refreshing water. True silence like this was so rare in her life that when it happened she took the time to appreciate the tranquillity, no matter how temporary it might be.

Especially after today's scooter ride to the viewpoint.

It was going to take a while to process everything that Mark had told her. And what about that fleeting kiss? Oh, boy. Had he really no clue as to how totally tantalising it was to have had a taste of his mouth, so tender, even for such a fleeting second?

He'd made an effort to keep their conversation on neutral ground during their brief lunch at the lovely harbour at Lakka before going straight back to work. And this time they had both been enthusiastic and motivated. The tide had turned. Now Mark wanted this book as much as she did.

Perhaps it was this villa that had made the difference.

Everything seemed so still. So full of possibility. A white clean space just begging to be filled with activity and life and—

A loud clattering, quickly followed by a low mumble, banged out on the wooden floorboards and she practically jumped over the railing. The sound ricocheted like a bullet around the terrace, shattering the deep silence.

Holding her breath, she clung on to the railing and listened for any further indication of movement. Or for the sound of his voice.

He did have a remarkable voice—deep and intense, yet quiet. With that faint touch of an American accent. It truly was quite delicious.

She wondered for a moment what it would be like to hear that voice speaking her name with intimate, loving tenderness. To fall into those strong arms and not let go for any reason.

No! Wipe that image from your brain!

If she wanted a fantasy she would stick to thinking about her mother's engagement party and all the work they needed to do to make it as magical as possible.

So what if she was attracted to him? It was only natural. But there could never be anything between them. And she had better remember that.

Lexi took another step along the small balcony, gazing out over the olive groves towards the sea.

A ship was sailing on the horizon, the rows of coloured lights on its decks bright and sharp against the darkness of the night. Perhaps it was a cruise ship, or a large ferry from Italy. And above the ship the sky was a breathtaking blanket of stars. She leant on the balustrade and stood on the tips of her toes, but the overhanging wooden eaves were blocking her view.

There was only one thing for it: she would have to go outside to get the full benefit of the night sky.

Lexi skipped lightly down the staircase, carefully turned the creaking handle of the heavy door that opened onto the patio, anxious not to disturb Mark, and stepped out onto the stone floor.

She stood silently with her head back for a second, lost in the bliss of cool air against her skin. A gentle breeze was blowing in from the sea between the pine trees, and Lexi could smell flowers and pine resin mixed in with the slight whiff of chlorine from the swimming pool.

A tiny sliver of new moon peeked out from behind one of the cypresses across the lane, and the only light was from the solar-powered lamps around the car park and stone steps leading to the house. But as she made her way gingerly towards the side garden in her bare feet even that background light was blocked by the house.

Perfect! Lexi stopped, pressed her back against the wall, and looked up towards the night sky.

Without streetlights or a city glow, the sky was wonderfully dark and clear of cloud. Spread out above the trees was a magnificent display of stars which seemed dazzlingly bright in the unpolluted air. She even recognised a few of the constellations, although they were aligned in slightly different shapes from the ones she knew in England.

It was stunning. Without realising it Lexi exhaled a long, slow sigh of deep satisfaction and relaxation. Her shoulders slumped with pleasure.

'Stargazing? Can't blame you. It is rather spectacular.'

She practically jumped out of her skin.

There was a creak from the sun lounger at the far end of the patio, and as Lexi's eyes became more accustomed to the low light she saw Mark stretched out flat, hands behind his head. He seemed to be fully dressed, and she could only hope that her thin pyjamas were not too transparent.

'Well!' She tried to keep her voice light, jovial and her heart from exploding. 'This is a surprise. The famous businessman Mark Belmont is actually a closet astronomer. One more attribute to add to your résumé.'

He chuckled, and his voice was low, deep and resonant in the absolute stillness of the night.

'Guilty as charged,' he replied. 'Always have been. Even had a telescope at one time—much to my family's amusement. My sister could probably find it somewhere in the attic if needed. How about you? Long history of solar exploration in your family?'

'Oh, just one of my many talents,' Lexi replied and was just about to make some dismissive quip when it struck her that from the tone of his voice he sounded relaxed and comfortable. At home. Unencumbered with responsibility.

So she fought back the urge to be sarcastic and strolled over towards his lounger in the dark. Except that her bare toes connected with something solid on the way.

'Ouch!' She winced. 'What have I just banged into?'

'That would be the other lounger,' he replied, sounding concerned. 'Any damage done?'

'To my toe or your furniture?' she asked and flexed her toes. 'No, I don't think so. I still have some movement. I can't speak for the other party.'

'Excellent,' he replied. 'Then please feel free to sprawl and enjoy the free floorshow. No charge.'

'Well, in that case, I think I might just do that.' Lexi smiled as she sank her bottom into the sumptuous cushion and stretched her legs out. 'Oh, that's better.'

They lay there without speaking for a few minutes, disturbed only by the sound of the cicadas in the olive groves and the occasional car horn from miles away. It was so bizarrely quiet that when a weird whooping, screeching noise broke the silence Lexi sat bolt upright and clutched the sun lounger in alarm.

'What was that?' she whispered.

'An owl. They nest in the trees,' Mark replied. 'So, tell me more about your star-watching.'

Lexi knew from the warmth of his voice that he was smiling as he said it. 'I can't say it was a popular hobby in my family, but I've always been fascinated by the stars.' She snuggled deeper into the lounger and tried to find a comfier position. 'I can still remember the first time one of the teachers at school told us that each star was actually a sun and probably had a moon and planets going around it.'

Lexi chuckled. 'He had no idea what he'd started. I dragged my poor mother out on cold winter nights, huddled up outside the back door of our little London house, just to stare up at the sky. I remember asking her if there were people like us living on those planets around those stars, looking back at us at that very minute.'

'What was her reply?' Mark murmured in the dark.

'She said there probably were creatures and possibly even intelligent beings living on those planets, orbiting around suns we can't even see because they're so far away that the light hasn't reached us yet from those distant worlds.' She paused for a second. 'Which totally made my head spin. Clever woman, my mother.'

Except when it came to choosing husbands. Then she was a disaster.

'Do you still live with her? In your little house in London?'

'Mum? No. I moved out earlier this year—although we still live in the same part of London. I spend a lot of time overseas, but we make the time to catch up with each other every few months. Our telephone bills are pretty enormous. It works well. She recently got engaged, so the next few months are going to be a bit wedding-crazy.'

Lexi pursed her lips for a second. The conversation was starting to get a little personal, and way too close to home for this audience. Especially when it came to her parents.

'How about you, Mark? Tell me about your place in London.'

'I have the penthouse apartment in my office building.'

'You live in your office building?' she replied, realising even as she spoke that her voice was stinging with criticism.

A low snort came from the other lounger, but when he spoke Mark's voice was clear and honest, rather than embarrassed or apologetic for living above the shop. 'It suits me very well. I'm single and busy. And the views across the city are pretty spectacular from my balcony. But the stars? Ah. Not so spectacular.'

Lexi exhaled slowly. 'It must be wonderful to have this house to come back to any time you want and look at the night sky. You do know that this is every writer's dream? A quiet rural retreat where they can focus on simply being creative. It's magical.'

The silence seemed even more intense and Lexi squeezed her eyes closed. Why had she said that? *Stupid girl.* He might think she was angling for an invitation. Or more.

'That's the problem,' he replied in a very quiet voice. 'It is magical, but most of the year the place stays empty and the only people who benefit are the cats and my housekeeper. We're always so very, very busy. Always so much to do just to stand still.'

The sadness in his voice pierced Lexi's gentle heart.

She hadn't expected to like him or care about him, but she did. More than was good for her. She knew now that his family life wasn't perfect and happy after all, and she was sorry for that. So much loss and pain changed people, and not always for the better. But Mark? Mark still had that spark, even if it was hidden deep inside.

And the thought that he might lose that spark sent a shiver down her back. She quivered and rubbed her arms.

'Feeling cold?' he asked.

'A little,' she replied. 'Probably time for me to head back inside.'

She heard a low grunt and a shuffle as Mark swung himself off his lounger and took the two steps towards her. Before she had a chance to speak he had taken both her hands in his and was lifting her to her feet.

'We stargazers have to stick together,' he murmured, pressing his body against the length of her back with his arms around her waist. A delicious glow of warmth and strength filled Lexi's body and she instinctively leant back to enjoy the heat from his closeness.

Mark raised one arm and pointed to a bright star on the horizon below the new moon. 'I used to read all those exciting comics about mysterious invaders from Venus or Mars. Scared myself silly. I suspect that's why my dad bought me the telescope. So that hard science could replace dreams and fantasy stories about aliens and spaceships.'

'And what about your mum? What did she say?' Lexi struggled to keep her voice steady in the face of this sudden intimacy.

'Oh, she kept bringing me the comics. Keeping my mind open to every option. I loved her for that.'

'She must have been quite remarkable,' Lexi whispered into the night.

'Yes. Yes, she was.' He paused before going on. 'Thanks for talking me into carrying on with her biography. I think it's going to be a grand celebration.'

Lexi lowered her head and turned around so that she was facing Mark.

'You're most welcome. Good night. I hope you sleep well.'

She touched her cool fingers to either side of his face, and brushed her lips against his in a light kiss which was just a tiny bit longer than the one he had given her at the viewpoint. His lips were warm and full and inviting, and she hesitated for just a moment in the darkness before moving away.

Mark seemed to freeze. Then he took hold of her shoulders, pulled her tight into his body, stepped forward until her back was resting against the wall of the house, cushioned by his arm, so that when he kissed her, her pliant body had somewhere to go.

This was nothing like that first hesitant kiss in the sunshine. This was the kiss of a man determined to drive logical thought from her mind as he pressed harder, exploring her tongue and lips while taking the weight of her body in his muscular arms.

Her hands moved up from his shoulders and into his hair, which was as wonderful and sensual as she had imagined.

But she had broken the spell by moving. And he eased back, drawing her on wobbly legs away from the wall.

She hung on to him, her head against his chest until her breathing calmed, then looked up into his smiling face. His thumb brushed against her lower lip, sending tingles to places she really did not want to be tingling.

'You are really quite irresistible. Do you know that?' he whispered.

She managed a nod. 'You, too.'

He stifled a grin. 'But probably not a good idea. All things considered.'

Then he tapped her on the nose. 'It won't happen again. Good night, Lexi. Sleep well.'

She watched him stroll into the house. Sleep? After that kiss? Was he *kidding?*

CHAPTER EIGHT

'You bought me shoes?' Lexi stared at Mark open-mouthed, dangling the plain tan-leather flat sandals from one finger so that she could ogle them from every angle.

He winced, and nodded his head towards the local shop only a few feet away from the waterside restaurant where they were sitting.

'If you really hate them I won't be in the least offended. Take them back for an exchange. But the range is rather limited compared to what you're used to.'

Her eyes widened in disbelief. 'Hate them? What are you talking about?' She leaned forward over the remains of their lunch of kebab, Greek salad and hot grilled herb pitta. 'You're the first man ever to buy me shoes. This is an historic occasion. They're even the right size. I am amazingly, stunningly speechless. And I have no intention of taking them back. I may even wear them. How about that?'

He raised his water glass to her in tribute. 'The cats and I thank you for your understanding. I had a stern word with both kittens and they promise never to pee on your shoes again.' He played with a piece of bread before asking, in the most seductive voice Lexi had ever heard in her life, 'Do you really like them?'

'They are totally awesome sauce,' she murmured across the table in an equally low voice. 'Yes. I like them.'

She sat back under the sun umbrella and sipped her wine as she looked around at the harbour and the line of yachts moored in the marina in the warm bright sunshine.

'I must say, Mr Belmont, that you treat your lady guests remarkably well. A waterfront location only feet from the Mediterranean, a delicious meal, splendid local white wine—and shoes. I am impressed.'

'Thanks. I thought it was only appropriate since I have a pre-published children's author with me—that, and the small fact that we've been slaving away in that stuffy study for two days and hardly coming up for air.'

She looked at Mark over her glass.

Slaving was one way of putting it.

The constant struggle to avoid touching his body as they negotiated around each other in the small space had driven her mad with frustration.

Sometimes she could almost feel the tension between them.

But he had kept his word and not made any moves on her. And she was grateful…wasn't she? She couldn't give in to the feelings. That would mean trouble for both of them and would only end in heartbreak. She had to hold it together and fight temptation for a few more days. Just. A. Few. More. Days.

In the meantime she could enjoy his company. Memories of meals like this were going to have to sustain her on many a lonely night in a foreign hotel for a long time to come.

'It's been worth it, Mark. The book is shaping up really well, and the work we were doing this morning on your village school was lovely.' Lexi clinked her wine glass against his water beaker in a toast. 'To team work.'

'I'll drink to that. Speaking of which, I have a mission to accomplish—and you are the ideal person to advise me.'

'Ah,' Lexi replied, rubbing her hands together. 'Business or personal?'

'Personal. I have to buy a present for my nephew Freddie before I head back. Two years old and already interested in everything animal-related. I was thinking of a soft toy, but he has a room full of those already. Any ideas?'

Lexi rested her arms on the table and chuckled. 'I am no expert on toddlers. But tell me what sort of things he likes to do. What kind of games does he enjoy?'

Mark's face instantly relaxed into an expression of pure delight. 'Here. This might help. They are both total scamps, but you have to admit they're adorable.'

He dived into his trouser pocket and pulled out a state-of-the-art smartphone which made Lexi drool with envy. His fingers moved swiftly over the keyboard and a few seconds later he scooted his chair closer to hers so that she could watch the surprisingly clear images come alive on the small screen.

His body was pressed tight against hers all along one side of her capri pants and sleeveless top, and at another time and another place she would have called it a cuddle. He was so close that she could feel the golden hairs on his tanned arms against her bare skin, the heat of his breath on her neck, and the smell of his expensive designer cologne filled her head.

The overall effect was so giddying that it took her a moment to realise that he was looking at the phone rather than her, and she forced her eyes to focus on the video playing on the screen.

It was Mark. Playing with two of the cutest little boys on a sandy beach. They were making sandcastles and Mark, dressed in shorts and a T-shirt, was helping the youngest to tap the sand into his bucket with great gusto while his brother danced around with a long piece of seaweed. All three of them were laughing their heads off, and seemed to be singing silly, glorious nursery rhymes. Pure childish joy and delight beamed out from the brightly coloured images in front of her. They looked so happy.

Mark with his nephews. Caught in the moment. Living. Showing his love in every single laugh and smile and hug.

She glanced up at this man whose face was only inches away from hers. He was the real deal. He had taken time out from his international business to go to the beach with his nephews and simply enjoy them.

Her heart broke all over again.

Only this time it was not for Mark. It was for herself.

When had she ever done that? When had she made the effort to spend time with her mother's soon-to-be step-grandchildren or her friends' children? Or her neighbours? She hadn't. She'd chosen a job where the only children she met belonged to her clients—that way she could share their family life second-hand.

The truth of the life she had created for herself jumped out from that simple holiday video that Mark kept on his phone because he loved those boys so very much and it slapped her across the face. Hard.

She'd told herself that she wasn't ready to adopt a child as a single mum, after seeing what her mother had gone through, but the truth was simpler than that.

She was a fraud. And a liar. And a coward.

She was too scared to do it alone. Too scared to take the risk.

And here she was, trying to tell Mark Belmont how to live his life, when he was already way ahead of her in every way. He had chosen to fill his life with real children who loved him right back. Damn right.

'I think the best thing is probably to trawl the shops and throw myself on the mercy of the lovely ladies who work there.' Mark smiled, totally unaware of the turmoil roiling inside her head and her heart.

And she looked into those eyes, brimming with contentment and love for those two little boys, and thought how easy it would be just to move a couple of inches closer and kiss him the way he had kissed her under the stars. And keep kissing him to block out the hard reality of her empty life.

Bad idea. *Seriously* bad idea.

She could never give him, or any man, the children he wanted. And nothing she could do was going to change that.

Suddenly it was all too much. She needed to have some space from Mark. And fast.

'Great idea,' she gushed. 'I think I'll take a walk and meet you back here.'

Throwing her new sandals into her bag, Lexi stood up and, with one quick wave, took off down the stone wall of the harbour towards the port before Mark had a chance to reply.

White-painted wooden fishing boats with women's names lined the harbour between the marina and the commercial port, and Lexi forced herself to try and relax as she sat down on a wooden bench under the shade of a plane tree and looked out across the inlet to the open water between Paxos and Corfu.

The hydrofoil was moored at the dock and had just started loading passengers. For one split-second Lexi thought about running back to Corfu so she wouldn't have to face Mark again. All she had to do was buy a ticket and she could be on her way before he even knew she was gone.

Leaving Mark and his life and Crystal Leighton's biography and everything that came with it behind her.

Stupid, self-deluded girl. Lexi sniffed and reached for a tissue.

Other passengers had started to mill about. A taxi pulled up and a gaggle of suntanned tourists emerged, loaded down with holiday luggage, laughing and happy and enjoying their last few minutes on Paxos. Local people, children, workers, a few businessmen in suits. Just normal people going about their normal business.

And she had never felt lonelier in her life.

A stunning sailing yacht with a broad white sail drifted across the inlet on the way into the long safe harbour at Gaios, and Lexi watched as it effortlessly glided through the water.

She was simply overtired, that was all. Too many sleepless nights and tiring days. She would be fine once this assignment was finished and she was back in London with her mother.

And what then?

Tears pricked the corners of her eyes. Her mother had found a lovely man who was almost good enough for her. And even better, he had given her the grandchildren—*his* grandchildren—that she longed for, whom she already worshipped and spoilt terribly.

So where did that leave Lexi?

Alone. Directionless. Existing rather than living. Filling her life with frenetic activity and people and places and travel. On the surface it looked exciting—a perfect job for any single girl.

How had she become the very thing that she despised?

A parasite, living her life through second-hand experiences, listening to lovely people like Mark talk about their families, sharing their experiences because she was too pathetic and cowardly to have her own love affairs, her own family.

The people on that boat were free to go where they wanted. Moor up anywhere, take off when they wanted. And she felt trapped. No matter how far she travelled, or whatever she had achieved in her life, she simply could not escape the fact that she was childless and would probably be so for the rest of her life.

So why had she not done something to change that fact instead of blocking it out? When had she turned her back on her dreams and thrown them into the 'too hard to deal with' box?

She had talked to her mother about giving up full-time work and writing her own stories, but it had always seemed like a dream.

Well, the time for dreaming was over. She had her own home and could work part-time in London to pay the bills. Surely there was some publisher who'd like to work on her children's books? It would probably take years to be a financial success, but she could do it. If she was brave enough.

Couldn't she?

Lexi was so distracted by the yacht as it sailed past that when her cell phone rang she picked it up immediately, without even bothering to check the caller identity.

'Lexi? Is that you? Thank goodness. I'm so pleased to have caught up with you.'

Great. Just when she thought things couldn't get any worse. It was the talent agency. Probably checking up on her to make sure that the project was on track.

'You're not going to believe who we have lined up for your next writing assignment, Lexi. Think America's favourite grandmother and cookery writer. It's the most *amazing* opportunity, but we do need to get you out to Texas on Sunday, so you can interview all of the darling children who are staying at the ranch. Of course it'll be first class all the way and... Lexi? Are you there? Hello?'

Mark flicked down the prop stand on his scooter, whipped off his crash helmet and looked out across the road towards the hydrofoil, then breathed a huge sigh of relief

Standing on the edge of the pier, on the harbour wall, was Lexi Sloane.

And as he watched Lexi drew back her arm and threw her purple telephone with all her might over her head and into the air.

She simply stood there, panting with exertion and the heat and horror as her precious link to the outside world, her business contacts, her lifeline to business that never left her side, made a graceful arc into the sea.

It hit the waves with a slight splosh and was gone.

Well, that was interesting.

Lexi hardly noticed that someone had come to sit next to her on the bench until he stretched out his legs and she saw the sharp crease on his smart navy trousers, and the black crash helmet cradled on his knee.

'Hi,' she said.

'Hello,' Mark replied. 'I didn't have much luck in the shops so I thought I'd join you, instead. Much more entertaining.'

They sat in silence, watching the hydrofoil crew help passengers onto the deck.

Lexi lifted her head and frowned, as though she had just woken up from a deep sleep.

'Did I just throw my phone into the sea?'

'Yes. I watched you do it from the car park. For a casual overarm technique it made a very nice curve for the few seconds it was airborne. Have you ever thought of playing cricket? Not much of a splash, though.'

'Oh. I was hoping I had imagined that bit. No chance I could get it back, I suppose?'

'Sorry. Your phone is probably covered by about thirty feet of salt water by now.'

'Right. Thirty feet.'

Mark sidled up to her on the bench. 'When I take an awkward call I often find it better to wait a few moments before replying. How about you?'

She shook her head. 'You see what people do to me? They make my head spin so fast that I throw my phone, that I need for my job and has all my numbers, into the sea.' She gesticulated towards the open water. 'There's probably a law against polluting the Mediterranean with small electrical items. Perhaps you could direct me to the local police station? Because I have to tell you, handing myself in and spending some time in solitary confinement sounds pretty good to me right now.'

She swallowed hard but no more words would form through the pain in her throat.

'Attractive though that option might sound, I have an alternative suggestion. I have a spare phone and a number of spare bedrooms which you are welcome to use any time you like. And I still owe you dessert. If you are available?'

'Available? Oh, yes, I am available. I'm always ready to step in at a moment's notice when they can't find anyone else. Why not? After all, I don't have a life.'

'Don't say that. You know it isn't true.'

'Do I? Then why is it that I choose to live through other people's experiences of a happy family life, and other women's children? No, Mark, I do it because I want to forget for just those few days that I am never going to have children of my own. But it's crushing me. It is totally crushing me.'

And then lovely Lexi, totally in control as ever, burst into hysterical tears.

CHAPTER NINE

LEXI sat back on the sofa with her eyes closed. The patio doors were wide open and a gentle breeze cooled the hot air. It was evening now, and the only sounds were the soft hum of the air-conditioning unit on the wall, the cicadas in the olive grove and somewhere in the village some chickens being put away for the night.

The gentle glug of wine being poured into a crystal goblet filtered through Lexi's hazed senses, and she opened her eyes just in time to see Mark smiling at her.

'Feeling better now?'

She nodded. 'Almost human.'

And she meant it. She'd enjoyed a luxurious bath, with some amazingly expensive products Mark's sister had left behind from her last visit, and was now being cosseted and pampered by a handsome man.

The day was turning out a lot better than she had expected.

'I'm sorry about what happened at the harbour earlier, Mark. I don't usually burst into tears. But do you remember we'd been talking about how your mum had given up her career for a few years when you were small? So that she could take you to school in the morning and take you to see your friends and make cakes for your birthday parties?'

'Yes, of course. We loved it.'

'Well, sitting on that harbour this afternoon it hit me out of the blue that somewhere deep inside my head I know I'm never going to have that life—and like a fool I've been living through other people's stories.'

'What do you mean other people? You have a perfectly good life of your own.'

'Do I? All those celebrities I work with? I've been making a life for myself through their love affairs, their pregnancies, their children, their families—the good and bad and all the joy that comes with being a parent. That's what hurts. I've been using their lives as some sort of replacement for the family I'll never have—for the children I'll never meet. And that's not just sad, it's pathetic. Wake-up call. *Huge.* Cue tears.'

Her voice faded away and she tried to give Mark a smile as he kissed her on the forehead and pressed his chin into her hair.

'I think you would make a wonderful mother.'

Lexi squeezed her lips together and shrugged her shoulder. 'That's not going to happen Mark. That illness I was telling you about? I was diagnosed with leukaemia two months after my tenth birthday.'

Mark inhaled sharply, and his body seemed to freeze into position next to her on the sofa but he said nothing.

'I know. Not good. But I was lucky. I lived in central London and had a very quick diagnosis and treatment at one of the best children's hospitals in the world. I was in hospital for what seemed like forever. It was…painful and difficult to endure. My mum was there every day, and my dad phoned me now and then, but I knew he would never come.'

Her head dropped onto her chest and she twiddled the ring on her right hand. She paused and took a moment to compose herself before going on, and to his credit, Mark didn't interrupt her but gently stroked the back of her hand, as if reassuring her that he was there and ready to listen to anything she had to tell him.

'The day I was due to be discharged from hospital I remember being so excited. I can't tell you how wonderful it was to see my own home again, and my own room with all my things in it. Best of all, my dad was there. Waiting at the front door. With his suitcases. For a few precious moments I thought we were going on holiday somewhere warm, so I could get better. And then he closed the door, and he wouldn't let me hug him or kiss him because he said I was still getting better and he had a cold. Then he turned to my mother and told her that he had met someone on location in Mexico and had decided to make a fresh start with this girl and her daughter. He picked up his suitcases, opened the door, walked down the path to a huge black limousine and jumped inside.'

Her brows twisted and she had difficulty continuing. 'I couldn't walk very fast, and my mother... She was running after the limo, screaming his name over and over. Telling him to stop, begging him to come back. But the car didn't stop. It went faster and faster. When I caught up with her she was kneeling in the road, watching the car speed round the corner, taking my dad away from us.'

Bitter hot tears pricked the corners of her eyes and Lexi blinked them away.

Mark sat next to her on the sofa and wrapped his arm around her shoulders. 'You don't have to talk about it.'

'Yes, I do,' she answered. 'Because the past never goes away. There's always something there to remind you, and just when you think you're on a happy track and can forget about it and move on—*smack!* There it is again. Staring you in the face.'

'How did you ever get over that betrayal?'

'Oh, Mark. You never get over it. My mother taught me to focus on the best memories we had as a family. But she never really understood why I felt so guilty, and that guilt consumed me for years. Until I saw what he was really like.'

'You felt *guilty?* I don't understand why the ten-year-old Lexi would feel guilty about her father leaving.'

'Can't you see? I was the one who got the cancer. I was the one who forced my dad to have an affair with a beautiful actress on a movie set because it was too upsetting and painful for him to come back and deal with my illness and pain. I was the one who drove him to find another daughter who was prettier than me and healthier and cleverer and more talented and...'

Her voice gave way, unable to sustain the emotion any more.

'Parents aren't supposed to abandon their children,' Mark whispered. 'Sometimes I regret going to university in America. I loved being with my friends in a wonderful country where the world seemed open and full of opportunities to explore and to do business. I just forgot that my family needed me back in England. I could never have imagined that one day my mother wouldn't be there at the airport to take me home. We missed so many weekends and holidays together.'

'Young people leave home and follow their hearts and careers. Your mother knew that. Her little boy had grown up, with his own life to lead. She must have been so proud of you and what you've achieved.' Her voice faltered and she stroked his face with her fingertip as she went on. 'We're so very similar in many ways. We're both survivors. I came through cancer. I watched my mother going through torment as my father cheated on us both, then struggle to balance life as a single working mother with a sickly child.'

'Is she happy now?'

Lexi nodded. 'Very. She's taking a chance and getting married again. Brave woman!' She grinned at Mark. 'I think that's why finding out Adam cheated on me was so hard. In the past I could have laughed it off. Joked that it was his loss. But somehow this time it really did feel as though I was the one who'd lost out. He didn't have the courage to tell me what the real problem was. Apparently he wanted children after all.'

'Had you spoken to him about children?'

'Of course. That was why I was in the hospital. Having tests to find out if there was anything I could do to improve my chances. I do have more options than I ever thought possible, but they made it clear that the treatments are very gruelling and there's no guarantee of success.'

'So it didn't bother him that you couldn't have his children?'

Lexi turned and looked at Mark. There had been a touch of coldness in his voice.

'He said he would be happy to adopt at some point, but it was never going to happen. Adam was doing loads of location work, and I was travelling more and more. These past few months we hardly saw each other.'

'I'm sorry that it didn't work out. It's hard on you. So very hard.'

'Perhaps that's why I want to write children's stories— I can make up a happy ending and send a child to sleep knowing that all is well with the world and they are safe and happy, with loving parents who care for them. Maybe all of the love I have will filter through to those children

I'll never get to meet or hug through my words on the page.'

Lexi swallowed down her anguish and looked into his eyes.

Fatal mistake.

It meant she was powerless to resist when Mark shifted closer to her and reached up to hold her face in his hands, gently caressing her skin, his eyes locked on to hers.

And then he tilted his head to kiss her.

His full mouth moved in delicious slow curves against hers, and she closed her eyes to luxuriate in the tender kiss of this warm, gentle man she'd soon have to say goodbye to.

She put her arms around his neck and kissed him back, pressing hotter and deeper against his mouth, the pace of her breathing almost matching his. It was a physical wrench when his lips left hers and she gasped a breath of air to cool the heat that threatened to overwhelm her.

'I was hoping there was another very good reason why you might want to stay on Paxos instead of heading back to London so soon,' he whispered in her ear, before his lips started moving down towards her throat, nuzzling the little space under her ear.

At which point the sensible part of her brain admitted defeat and decided to have some fun, instead.

'You mean apart from the excellent accommodation and room service?' She batted her eyelashes.

'Absolutely,' he replied with a grin. 'I'm talking about the full package of optional extras here.' He tapped her twice on the end of her nose and lowered his voice. 'I don't have to go back for a few days. And there's nowhere else I would rather be than right here with you. Take a chance, Lexi. Stay. Let me get to know you better. Who knows? You might like me back.'

He shifted slightly and looked away. 'Besides, the cats would miss you terribly if you left now. They're waiting to—'

Lexi silenced him with one fingertip pressed against his lips.

'It's okay. You had me at the word *cats*.'

Lexi turned over and tried to find a comfy position. Only something solid and man-shaped was in the way. She cracked one eye open, then smiled with deep satisfaction.

Warm morning sunlight was flooding into the living room and reflecting back from the cream-coloured walls in a golden glow that made everything seem light and fresh.

It had not been a dream.

She really had just spent the night on the sofa with Mark Belmont.

At some point Mark had suggested going into the bedroom, but that would have destroyed this precious connection, which was so special and unique. She didn't need to take her clothes off and jump on him to show how much she cared.

Lexi snuggled into the warmth of his chest, and Mark's arm wrapped around her shoulders and drew her closer into his body.

Lexi's hand pressed against the long tantalising strip of bare chest she'd created by unbuttoning his shirt in the night. She closed her eyes and moved her forehead against the soft fabric of the shirt, inhaling its fragrance. It was musky, deep and sensuous, and totally, totally unique to this remarkable man.

'I have a question,' she murmured, her eyes closed.

A deep chuckle came from inside Mark's chest, and Lexi could feel the vibrations of his voice under her fingertips. It was weird that such a simple sensation made her heart sing with delight at the fact that she could be here, in this moment, enjoying this connection. No matter how fleeting or temporary it might be this was very special, and she knew that Mark felt the same.

'Out with it,' he growled, 'but it had better be important to disturb my beauty sleep at this hour of the morning.'

'Indeed,' she replied, trying not to give him the satisfaction of a grin. But it was too hard to resist, and she slid out of his arms and propped herself up on her elbow to look at Mark's face.

'Do you know that you have two grey hairs on your chest?' she asked in a semi-serious voice. 'And one just here.' Her forefinger stroked down the side of Mark's chin against the soft stubble, then tapped very gently at the offending hair.

'Are you offering a personal grooming service?' He smiled.

'Oh, if required a freelance writer should be ready to carry out any duties necessary to complete a task. No matter how odd or dangerous or *icky* the task.'

'I had no idea,' he said gravely, 'of the horror you must face on a daily basis.'

'Explorers going out into the unknown,' Lexi replied, her left hand making a sweep of the room. 'Armed only with a designer wardrobe and a make-up bag. Not for the faint-hearted. And that's just the boys.'

She lowered her head and rubbed her nose against his. 'It is, of course, essential that a writer should investigate local customs, which must be observed wherever possible,' she whispered in a low, sensual voice as her lips made circles around his mouth. 'So important. Don't you think?'

'Absolutely,' he replied, his mouth moving down the side of her neck.

Lexi closed her eyes and lifted her chin so that he could fit more closely into her throat.

'Were you thinking of any in particular?'

'Actually, I was… Oh, that's good.' Lexi sucked in a breath as Mark nuzzled aside the neck of her stretchy T-shirt and started kissing along the length of her collarbone. 'I was thinking about how people celebrate important dates in the year.' Her words came out in a rush as her breath suddenly seemed to be much in demand. 'Wedding anniversaries, Christmas, Easter and…' She slid down a gulp of anxiety and uncertainty before she said the word which would either be a horrible mistake or a wonderful way to connect them even more.

'And…?' a low husky voice breathed into her ear.

Lexi opened her eyes. She wanted to see how Mark responded to what she was about to say.

'Family birthdays,' she replied gently, hardly daring to say the words in case they brought back bad as well as wonderful memories. 'Like today, for example. Your mum's birthday.'

Mark was silent for a moment, and then he smiled and lay back on the sofa cushions. He looked at her—really looked at her—his eyes scanning her face, looking for something. For a few terrible moments Lexi felt that she had made a terrible mistake. But the words were out and couldn't be taken back.

'Clever girl. Mum would have been sixty today.'

He stretched out the full length of the sofa with a sigh, his head on her lap and one of his arms flailing onto the floor, his eyes staring at the ceiling. Mark seemed so totally natural and relaxed in her presence that it made her heart sing.

'Would she have hated turning sixty?' she asked quietly. 'Or would she have taken it in stride? Just another day?'

Mark was silent for a moment, before he looked up at her and gave a small shrug.

'Hated it. With a passion. I remember her fiftieth birthday party in London. She went to the gym every day for six months. Facials, Botox, hairdressers galore. Trips to Paris for flattering outfits. The works. Just so she'd look amazing in the photographs on that one night. And it worked. I remember those photos appearing across the world in every newspaper and gossip magazine. Crystal Leighton looking ten years younger. Or was it twenty? She made headlines at that party. She even announced a new contract with a make-up company at the same time. All part of the plan to revitalise her career and keep her name on the front page.'

He broke into a lopsided loving grin. 'She loved being the centre of attention at big events. The adulation, the crowds, flashguns, photographers. Mum could sign autographs for an hour and not get bored with it. There was no way she'd ever allow herself to be anything less than spectacular.' His grin faded. 'But that was in public.'

He reached up and pushed a lock of her hair back behind the ear with two fingertips, as though he'd been doing it all his life, and she revelled in the simple touch of his skin against hers.

'Crystal Leighton was totally professional in every way when she was at work. But her fans forgot that when she got home at night she took off her war paint and designer clothing and Crystal Leighton became Baroness Belmont. Wife and mother. And I don't think anyone truly saw her for the remarkable woman that she was.'

'Then tell them. Help them to understand.'

Mark started to sigh with exasperation, but Lexi pressed her hand hard against his chest and he stilled under her touch.

'You and your family are the only people who knew who she truly was. And now you have the power to celebrate that wonderful woman who was your mother.'

'I don't—'

'I know.' Lexi smiled. 'You don't want to hurt your family by revealing how very unhappy she was at the end. That's why I'm here. I'm helping you write a memoir. Not a dry list of dates and all the films she was in—anyone can get that from the internet. No. This is going to be a personal memoir.'

Lexi tapped a finger against his forehead. 'I want to release all those wonderful stories and precious memories you have inside your head and make this a *real* memoir which only you and your family could write. That's what is going to make this book so remarkable and real. And that's how you're going to give your mother the best birthday present she could ever have had. Because you know homemade presents are always the best.'

'A birthday present? I like that idea. Can we have birthday cake and bubbly?'

'I'm astonished that you have to ask. And a monster-sized birthday card. Just tell me what kind of cake takes your fancy and I'm your girl.'

'My girl? Is that right? Well, how could I possibly resist an offer like that?' His face relaxed and he blinked several times. 'Lemon drizzle. She liked lemon-drizzle sponge. With a dusting of icing sugar. No fancy cakestands or anything. Just an ordinary lemon-drizzle sponge. And a gallon of boiling hot tea to wash it down with. I'd completely forgotten about that until this minute.'

'Crystal Belmont's lemon cake,' Lexi replied in a faraway voice. 'Oh, my. That's lovely.'

Lexi sat up so quickly that she felt dizzy, and Mark's

head dropped onto the cushion. 'That's it! You are *so* clever.' She bent forward and touched her lips against his.

'It's been said before, but not frequently in this particular situation. Please explain before my head explodes.'

'The title for the memoir! I've been racking my brain all week to come up with an interesting title which will make your book stand out on the shelves.' She beamed down at Mark and shook her head slowly from side to side. 'I hate to say I was right, but sometimes I amaze myself. You have everything you need to write this story inside your head. My job is to make it into a book. And I can't wait to get started.'

Lexi flung back the light cover from her legs, swung her body off the sofa, and was on her feet and reaching for her sandals in an instant.

'Right. Time to make a list. So much to do and so little time.'

'Lexi?'

She looked back at Mark, still lying flat on the sofa with a certain smile on his face.

'Can't we do that later?' he implored. 'Much later?' And he waggled his eyebrows at her.

She sniffed at his cheeky grin. 'Work now, cuddle later, you scamp. You have a lot to do today. I'll get the coffee started while you're in the shower—then straight to the computer so we can start dictation. This is going to be *so* much fun!'

Lexi skipped out of the door before Mark could grab her and employ his best powers of persuasion to make her stay.

He could hear her humming happily as the plain leather sandals he'd bought her clapped along the tiled floor towards the ground-floor bathroom.

Telling Lexi about his mum's birthday parties? That

was new. But maybe she was right? Maybe there was a chance he *could* write this biography as a celebration of her life and make it a positive, happy thing, with only a tinge of sadness.

Mark linked his hands under his head and lay back as the sun filled the room with bright morning light. It was going to be another hot sunny day on Paxos, and from deep inside his body came a warm feeling of contentment that bubbled up and emerged as a smile that surprised his face.

He had slept for eight hours straight on a very uncomfortable sofa with a woman in his arms. For the first time in many years he hadn't snapped awake to reach for some electronic gadget and check his email, compulsively making sure he hadn't missed an important message about the business while he wasted time sleeping.

He could hear Lexi moving around in the kitchen. The hiss of water into a kettle. Cups rattling on the worktop and metal spoons hitting the olive wood tray. Was this the soundtrack to happiness he'd been looking for all his life? Or simply the joyful noise that came with sharing your home with this whirlwind of a girl?

He had found someone he wanted to be with in the last place on the planet he'd ever expected to. In this wonderful house that held so many memories of his mother and happy childhood holidays.

How could he have known that the path to happiness would lead right back to where he'd once been so happy? How ironic was that?

Belmont Investments and the manor were not important any longer.

This was where he wanted to be. *Needed* to be. With Lexi.

And now she was here. And he felt an overwhelming, all-powerful connection.

Finally. It had happened. He'd known lust and attraction. But this sensation was so new, so startling, that the great Mark Belmont floundered.

He was falling for Lexi Sloane.

'Mark?' Lexi popped her head around the door. 'Perhaps you should telephone your dad. He might need to hear your voice today of all days.'

And then she was gone, back to the kitchen before he had a chance to answer, singing along to a pop song, oblivious of the fact that she had thrown him a bomb and he'd caught it single-handed.

Telephone his dad? On his mother's birthday?

Oh, Lexi.

This lovely girl really had no idea whatsoever just how much it would take for him to lift the telephone and make that call. What would he say to his father? What *could* he say?

All his father cared about was the heritage of the estate and how his only remaining son was going to ensure their lineage was carried on. And Mark's failure to get married and produce an heir was starting to become a problem.

Mark swung his legs over the sofa and ran his hands down over the creases in his trousers.

His engagement had been a catastrophe—a disaster meant to placate his parents. He knew that his father blamed him for letting his fiancée go.

Failure. Yet again.

And here he was, falling for a girl who couldn't give him children. Couldn't give him the heir that he was supposed to provide.

More failure.

What was he doing with Lexi? What was he *thinking?* The answer was only too clear. He wasn't thinking at all. He was living and reacting and loving life, and he had Lexi to thank for that.

It didn't matter what happened in the future. It didn't matter one jot. He'd have to deal with the consequences when they happened. They both lived in London. They were both single. And, unless he had completely misread the signals, she felt the same way about him. And that was too special to give up.

Since Edmund had died Mark's life had been filled with obligation and duty. He loved his family too much to let them down. But Lexi was right. They were both living second-hand lives.

All that mattered was right here and right now.

Living in the moment. He quite liked the sound of that.

Without a second's further delay, Mark stretched up to his full height and headed off to the kitchen. Time to entertain the cats and drink coffee on the terrace with the woman he simply couldn't bear to be apart from.

CHAPTER TEN

'You have a whole hour to titivate yourself,' Mark joked, jumping into Lexi's hire car and cranking down the anti-cat-invasion window, 'while I'm on my perilous, swash-buckling mission to track down two bottles of champagne and the local version of lemon-drizzle cake. I'll be back with the swag before you know it.'

Lexi stuck her head through the window and kissed him swiftly but firmly on the lips. 'You'd better be.' She grinned. 'I have my favourite dress ready and waiting, and matching shoes that the cats haven't peed on yet.' She winked at him. 'It's going to be a lovely birthday party. And please bring back more doughnuts for breakfast.'

She kissed him again, and again and one more time for luck, before waggling her nose against his with a giggle, then standing back and waving as he sped off down the road towards the biggest town on the island.

Lexi stood and watched the car until it turned the corner onto the main road, carrying inside it the man she was already longing to see again. She felt as though part of her was somehow missing without Mark by her side.

The cool and unhappy man she had met only a few days earlier was gone, replaced by a remarkable, talented, gentle-hearted man who loved to laugh and enjoy himself.

He knew her faults, her history and he certainly knew

about her dad. And yet he still wanted to be with her. Which was so very amazing that it made her head spin.

And now she had a lovely birthday-party dinner to look forward to, followed by drinks on the terrace watching the sun go down, and then maybe a little stargazing. If they weren't otherwise occupied.

Delicious!

Was it any wonder that she adored him? Perhaps a little too much, and way too fast... But she adored him all the same.

Well... Now it was her turn to dazzle and give him a treat in return.

Lexi skipped up the steps to the house, waving at the sun-kissed cats on the way, and took the stairs to the first floor two at a time.

Clothes first. Then hair and miracle make-up. Mark Belmont would not know what had hit him—because tonight he was going to get the full works.

Let the titivation ensue.

Twenty minutes later Lexi was still humming a pop song under her breath as she jogged from the shower to her bedroom and flung open the wardrobe door.

Her designer cream-lace lingerie would have to do. But she hadn't been kidding about her favourite dress.

No wild patterns, flowers or multi-coloured designs this time. Just a completely sweet confection of flowing gold lace over a plain cream-silk shift dress picked out by her mother with her expert eye.

Elegant. Understated. Knockout.

She had only worn the dress once before, at the Valentine's Day party when her mother had announced her engagement. Somehow it had never seemed lively or colourful enough for any of the movie functions in Hong Kong, but now—in this villa, on this tiny island, with only Mark and the cats to see it—yes. She was glad she had hauled it through so many airport departure lounges.

The cream silk felt cool and luxurious against her moisturised skin. Sensuous and smooth and just what she needed. She smoothed down the lace overskirt and admired herself in the full-length mirror, turning from side to side for a few seconds before smiling and giving herself a quick nod in admiration.

'Not too bad, girl,' she whispered to herself with a wink. 'You'll do nicely.'

But now for the killer touch. Lexi reached into a shoe bag with the name of a famous Asian shoe designer on the front and pulled out a pair of pale gold kitten-heeled satin mules.

They were limo shoes and always would be. No excuses. These shoes were designed for fine wool and silk carpets, not country stone patios, and had cost more than she'd ever paid for shoes in her life even if they had been on sale. But she didn't care.

So what if they'd only ever seen red carpets before now? She was wearing them for Mark, who was all that mattered.

A little giggle of happiness bubbled up from deep inside her chest and Lexi bit her lower lip in pleasure as she slipped on the mules and posed in front of the mirror.

It had been such a long time since she had felt so light. So joyous. So very happy.

Yes. That was it. *Happy.*

This was so strange. Before this week, if anyone had asked if she was happy she would have answered with some glib statement about her magical, awesome life.

Not now. Not any longer. In a few short days Mark had shown her what real happiness could be like.

Until now she'd been living her life through other people's experiences, and now it was her turn to love. Not simple contentment, not settling for the best she could but true happiness with someone she loved.

Lexi inhaled sharply and pressed her fingertips to her throat.

Loved?

Was that it? Was that why she felt that she had been waiting for Mark all her life?

Breathing out slowly, Lexi tottered the few steps across to Crystal's library and ran her fingers down the rows of photographs Mark had chosen to feature in the opening chapters of the book.

They'd spent three glorious days together, laughing and chatting, and all the while Mark had dictated wonderful anecdotes, happy memories of his mother's life and the people she'd met, the things she'd done.

If only he could come to terms with the sad moments. Then it would be a remarkable biography. And she was happy to help.

Happy to do anything that meant she spent as much time with him as she could.

Looking at the photographs now, she could see that each image captured a moment in time when the young Belmont family had been happy together. Before things had changed and they'd lost that easy familiarity.

Her fingers rested on the photo she'd picked up on her first morning at the villa. The schoolboy Mark and his brother Edmund, arms around each other, muddy, happy and proud on the football pitch.

There was so much love shining out from the flat matte surface.

Edmund the older brother. Heir to the estate. The next Baron Belmont.

A shiver of unease ran across Lexi's shoulders and she

scanned the photographs, looking for some sign of where things had changed.

And there it was. Mark must have been in his early twenties when this photograph had been taken at some movie award ceremony. He was standing next to Crystal, who looked stunning, but that spark, that easy, relaxed expression that Lexi had come to know on Mark, was missing. Snuffed out.

It was more than grief at losing his brother. It was as though the heavy weight of being the only son and heir to the Belmont estate was sitting on his shoulders, pressing him down.

It truly was a shame that Cassie's boys would never inherit the title.

An icy feeling quivered and roiled inside Lexi's stomach and she slumped down onto the nearest hard chair.

Bad choice. Because the chair faced a small round mirror on the wall opposite. And as she glanced at her reflection all the energy and fun and joy of the day drifted away, leaving behind the cold, hard reality she'd managed to stuff deep into the 'too difficult to handle today' box.

Shame that she'd chosen this minute to let it out.

Because suddenly her lovely dress and shoes felt like a sad joke.

She did not have any future with Mark. How could she when she was unable to give him the son he needed to carry on his family name and title?

Sniffing away the tears, she stared at photo after photo through blurred vision.

His family meant everything to him.

It was so unfair. So totally unfair. Just when she thought she'd found the love of her life. Staying with Mark, loving Mark, sharing her life with Mark would force him to decide between his family and her.

And she couldn't do that to him. She loved him too much to put him in that position.

What was she going to do?

The sun was already low in the apricot-tinged sky when Mark pushed through the cypress and olive trees onto the secluded circle of stones facing the cliffs and the open sea.

But at that moment not even the view from this special place his mother had used as her escape could compare with the lovely woman sitting so quietly with her eyes closed and her head leaning back on the sun-warmed bench.

It staggered him that one look at her beautiful face could send his senses into a stomach-clenching, mind-reeling, heart-thumping overdrive.

What was it about her that made him feel like a schoolboy on a first date?

His heart raced just at the sight of her, and it was as if he'd dreamt this marvellous creature up out of his imagination—because she was too special to be real.

Lexi's skin and dress were lit by golden and pink sunlight, creating the illusion that she was lit from within, that she was the source of the light. Shades of gold. Apricot and pink.

She looked stunning.

No amount of clever studio lighting would be able to recreate this unique combination of place and time, and Mark instinctively knew that this image would stay locked in the safe and secure place where he kept his most treasured possessions: wonderful memories of love and happiness forever.

Not in printed photographs which could be recreated inside the pages of a biography for others to read. But inside his head and heart, where the real Mark Belmont had been kept safe until now.

Waiting for someone to release him from the constraints he'd made for himself to get him through the obligations he'd accepted for his family.

That someone was Lexi Sloane.

And he loved her for it.

Time to step up and prove that he was good enough for her.

But as he moved the dry pine needles covering the stones on the gravel path crunched beneath his smart shoes, and her eyes flicked open and she looked at him.

And in that one single glance any doubt he might have had was wiped away.

He was in love. Not for the first time—but for the last.

She was the one he wanted. For good.

Lexi stretched her arms out so that they rested on the back of the bench and smiled. Waiting for him to speak. As he came closer he saw something more than relaxed confidence in that smile. Confusion, regret. And apprehension. She was nervous.

Oh, yes. He recognised *that* look only too well. His stomach was suddenly ice.

She was leaving him and she didn't know how to do it without hurting his feelings. He was grateful for that sensitivity, but it wouldn't make the next few minutes any easier.

Her fingers started to curl into tight knots of tension, but she instantly blocked the move, stretched out her fingers and turned it into the casual brush of a stray dry leaf from the stonework as he strolled closer.

'Hello,' she said with a small smile. 'I hope you don't mind, but I couldn't bear to miss my last sunset. Looking for me?'

Here it comes, he thought, *and she doesn't know how to handle it.*

'I'm not used to being stood up,' Mark replied. 'Came as quite a shock. Especially since my mission was completely successful, and our party food is ready and waiting back at the villa.'

She raised her eyebrows. 'Congratulations. I…er… waited for you.' Her fingers waved in the direction of the main road. 'But I got lonely.'

He winced. 'Ah. Thanks for the note. It was good to know that you hadn't been kidnapped by pirates or called back to write some other biography at the last minute. Sorry I was late. I was tied up on the phone to Cassie, trying to organise a surprise thank-you present for you.'

Her mind reeled with the impact of what he'd said, and she slid back down onto the hard stone bench and looked up at him in astonishment.

'A thank-you present? I don't expect a present, Mark. I'm just doing my job—your publisher is already paying me a great deal of money to be here.'

'Then think of it as a bonus. From the family.'

'The family? You mean the family who doesn't know who my father is? *That* family?'

Mark tapped his forefinger against his lower lip as he nodded, and then broke into a smile at her stunned face. 'Yup. I loved what you said about having your own writer's cottage, hidden away in the woodland. Well, I have woodland on the Belmont estate. Beech woods, oak, maple and hornbeam. And they are beautiful. Stunningly beautiful, in fact. Which got me thinking that clever people who write children's stories—' he tapped her on the end of the nose '—might care to test out one of the cottages to see if they work as country retreats for artists and writers. What do you say, Lexi? Are you willing to take the risk and give it a go?'

In the absolute stillness of the secret place the air was filled with the sound of nature: flying insects in the olive groves on the other side of the footpath, and birds calling on the clifftops where they nested. But Lexi did not hear the sea-birds. She was way too busy fighting to keep breathing in a controlled manner.

Because they both knew that he wasn't just talking about renting a cottage. Oh, no.

Mark lowered his body onto the bench next to her and stretched out his long legs towards the sea wall, his splayed fingers only inches from hers.

One side of his throat was lit rosy pink by the fading sun as he twisted his body to face her, apparently oblivious to the damage he was causing to the fine fabric of his trousers, which stretched to accommodate the muscled thighs below.

'What do you say?' he repeated, his blue eyes locked on her face, his voice low and intense, anxious. 'Would you be interested in moving into my world? Say yes. Say you'll run away from the city and come and write your children's stories in one of my cottages. Trust me, I will make sure that your new home has everything you could possibly want. It'll be so perfect that you'll never want to leave.'

Trust him? Trust him with her life? Her future? Her love?

'Why me?' she asked, her voice almost a whisper.

His response was to slide his long, strong fingers between hers and lock them there. Tight. A wide grin of delight and happiness cracked his face.

'For the last five months I've done everything I can to avoid going back to my home. You've helped me see that

Belmont Manor is where I belong. I can't run away from home forever. But it's missing one thing which would make it truly special.' He flashed a cheeky smile. 'The woman I'm looking at right now.'

Her dream of finishing her stories.

Her own home with someone who loved her.

This amazing man was offering her the chance she had been waiting for, working towards every second since she'd started writing down her grandmother's children stories all those years ago. This man she'd met only a few days ago, yet she felt she'd known him all her life.

He was holding her dream out to her, confident that she could do it. All she had to do was say yes and it would be hers.

Lexi leaned back and her sides pressed against the stone.

She inhaled a deep breath, trying to process words when his body was only inches away from her own, leaning towards her, begging her to hold him, kiss him, caress him.

She swallowed hard down a burning throat and tried to form a sensible answer.

'Belmont Manor? I don't understand. I thought you couldn't wait to leave your father and run your own life in the city?'

'It dawned on me that I have to *talk* to my family about the important things in my life now and then. Strange concept. But I'm getting used to the idea and it might just work. And of course there is one final reason why you are the only writer I would ask to test out my writers' retreat.'

Lexi let out a long slow breath as his fingertips moved over her forehead and curled around the layers of her hair before caressing her neck in slow, languorous circles.

'Why is that?' she whispered, almost frightened at what he might say next.

'It's not every day that I get the chance to make a girl's

dream come true. I want to read your stories to my nephews one day. Will you let me into your life to help you do that?'

Suddenly it was all too much for her to take in.

Let her into his life? Make her dream a reality because her cared for her?

She looked out towards the distant horizon, where the calm ocean formed a line with the apricot sky, and was instantly transported into her happy dream of what life could be like. Writing in her little wooden retreat in the forest all day. And then maybe the tantalising prospect of being with Mark every evening, sharing their lives, their dreams and their hopes for the future.

Future. The reality of what he was proposing hit her hard.

Idiot girl! Who was she kidding? They *had* no future.

By looking down and taking both of Mark's hands in hers she managed to regain some composure so words became possible.

'This is a wonderful offer, and I'm sure that I would love it there, but you know I have to work as a contract writer to pay the bills, and I can't accept your charity. Or your pity.'

His fingers meshed into hers and he raised one hand to his lips, gently kissed her knuckles before replying.

'Last I heard writers can work from home and be quite successful. You're so talented, Lexi—you can do this. I know you can.'

The pressure in her chest was almost too much to bear as she looked into his face and saw that he meant it. He believed in her!

'You'd do that? You'd put up with having me hanging around the place? Even with my horrible taste in music and annoying habits?'

'If it meant I could be with you? In a heartbeat.'

Mark's words seem to echo inside her head. Her chest and her whole body were filled with their overwhelming joy and deep love.

She forced herself to look up into his face, and what she saw there took her breath away. Any doubt that this man cared about her was wiped away in an instant.

No pity, no excuses, no apologies. Just a smouldering inner fire. Focused totally on her.

'And now you've gone quiet. I find this worrying,' he joked.

'I can't think, Mark. This is all too new and terrifying. I need to try and get my head around what's going on, make sense of it all. Can you understand that?'

'What's going on is that you have come to mean a great deal to me—more than I could ever have expected. Not for one minute did I believe that anyone could reach inside me and open up my heart, make me vulnerable again.' He grabbed hold of both her hands and held them tight against his chest. 'It's taken me years to build up so many layers of defences. This suit of armour I've created is even more impressive than the one standing in the hall at Belmont Manor. But I needed it so no one could hurt me and break my heart again. And then you walked into my life—my empty, busy and on-the-surface so-successful life—and you smiled at me. And ever since that moment my life hasn't been my own any more. It just took a while for the message to get through.'

He must have seen the terror in her eyes and felt her fast breath on his neck, because Mark took a second before smiling and lowering his voice.

'And now I'm doing it again. Rushing ahead of myself just to keep pace with you.'

He kissed her fingertips one by one.

'Don't you understand, Lexi? You've taken me hostage.

Heart and soul and mind. You've become part of me. And you feel the same. I hope—no, I *know* that I am part of you, so please don't try and deny it. Because I can see it in your eyes and feel it in your touch.'

And suddenly she couldn't stand to look into his eyes and say what she had to. It was just too painful.

His presence was so powerful, so dominating, that she slid her fingers away from his and pushed herself off the stone bench and across a few steps to the cliff wall.

Sucking in cool air, she looked down the steep bank towards the sea below, to the crashing waves on the boulders at the foot of the tall white cliff to her right.

She could jump into Mark's arms and leap into the deep, warm ocean of life with him, knowing that he would hold her up and not let her drown. But one day the waves of his obligations would crash over their heads and they would both drown in a sea of bitterness and despair from which there was no going back.

She couldn't bear it. Not when Mark had a chance to find someone else and have a happy married life with children to carry his name and his heritage to more generations.

She loved this man too much to allow him to sacrifice everything he held sacred. Just to be with her.

The very thought that he'd offered her that amazing gift filled her heart and soul with happiness and a sweet contentment that they'd at least shared these few precious days together. That was going to have to be enough.

Mark was standing behind her now, and she felt the light touch of his hands on each side of her waist.

Lexi immediately pulled his hands closer to her body, so that she could grasp them to her chest as it rose and fell. His knuckles rested on the exposed skin of her throat and neck, and the heat of the delicate touch and the gentle

pressure of his chest against the back of her dress warmed
her body as nothing ever had before.

He was the flame that had set her world on fire, and
she knew beyond any measure of doubt that no man could
ever touch her heart the way Mark had.

He was the love of her life.

Which was precisely why she was going to have to walk
away from him.

All she had to do now was turn around and tell him
to his face.

Slowly, inch by inch, she lowered his hands and slid
her fingers out, one by one, until they were only in contact at the fingertips, before turning around within the
circle of his arms.

But she couldn't do it. She surrendered to her desire
for one last time and pressed her head onto his chest, her
arms around his neck, hanging on for dear life, pulling
his head lower.

His eyes flickered at her touch, and she had to blink
away tears as his nose pressed against her cheek, his mouth
nuzzling her upper lip as his fingers moved back to clasp
the back of her head, drawing her closer to him.

His hard body was against her, rock-solid, safe and secure, and so loving that the overall effect was more than
intoxicating.

And then his mouth was pressing hotter and hotter onto
hers, his pulse racing below the fine cloth as he pushed
her lips apart and explored her mouth. One of his hands
made slow circles on the small of her back, then higher,
while the other caressed the skin at the base of her skull
so gently that she thought she would go mad with wanting
Mark so much, needing him to know how much she cared.

She felt carried away on a sea of love and deep connection that she could happily drown in and not regret for a moment.

Maybe that was why she broke away first, leaning back just far enough so that he could brush away the glint of tears away from her cheeks.

'Hey. Don't cry, gorgeous. I'm going to be right there with you, every step of the way.'

And he was kissing her again, pressing his soft lips against her throat and tilting his head so he could reach the sensitive skin on her neck.

Her eyes closed and she leant back just a little farther, arching her spine, supported by his long fingers as they slid down to her hips. Lexi stopped breathing and inwardly screamed in frustration because her body was enjoying itself far too much for her to reply. And her heart and mind sang.

She closed her eyes tight shut and focused on the sound of her own breathing. Only it was rather difficult when the man she wanted to be with was holding her so lovingly, keeping her steady on her wobbly legs, her toes clenched with tension inside her shoes.

Tempting her. Tempting her so badly she could taste it. She wanted him just as much as he wanted her. This was going to be their last night together, and…

No. If she gave in now there would be no going back. She would never be able to walk away. And neither would he. No matter how much she wanted to stay in his arms, she had to be brave for Mark's sake.

She just had to find the strength to get through this.

Lexi inhaled slowly, then whispered into Mark's shoulder, 'I don't think that would be a very good idea.' She dropped back so he would have to stop kissing her. 'In fact,' she continued in a trembling voice, 'it might be better if I started packing. I have an early flight tomorrow.'

The air escaped from his lungs in a slow, shuddering hot breath against her forehead.

It took her a few seconds to form the words she had to say. She was almost too afraid.

Her voice stayed calm, despite the thumping storm of confusion and resignation building in her chest. 'You know why we don't have a future together, Mark. You need to have a son to inherit your title and I can't give you one. And nothing we say or feel is going to change that fact.'

As soon as the words left her mouth she regretted them. The man who had been holding her so lovingly, unwilling to let her move out of his touch, stepped back. Moved away. Not physically, but emotionally.

The precious moment was gone. Trampled to fragments.

His face contorted with pain and closed down before her eyes. The warmth was gone, and she cursed herself for being so clumsy.

She had lost him.

'I was never supposed to be Baron Belmont,' Mark replied, his voice low and rough. 'That was my brother's job. Ed was the heir apparent, my parents' pride and joy. As far as my parents were concerned Edmund was the golden boy, the eldest son, whom they'd groomed since junior school to take over the company business and the estate. So when he died…it destroyed the family plans completely. And broke my mother's heart forever. It was as simple as that. The entire family collapsed.'

He looked into Lexi's face and smoothed back her hair with his fingertips.

'I was the second son, Lexi. As different from Edmund and my father as it was possible to be. I had to leave my world behind and take over the obligations that came with being the next Baron Belmont. I had no choice. I *had* to take over as the next heir. And everything that comes with it. Including making sure that I married early and produced a son to carry on the name.'

He closed his eyes. 'Working on my mother's biography has shown me just how much I've sacrificed to take his place—and how much I need to claw back my right to personal happiness. And that means *you,* Lexi.'

'You know that I can't have children.' Her voice quivered as she formed the syllables, and she only just managed the words before her voice failed. 'But you can. And that is why I have to let you go.'

Mark shook his head slowly and his chin dropped so their foreheads were touching. His breath was hot against her skin as the words came stumbling out. 'I can see where this is going, but you are *so* wrong. I want you and only you. Can you understand that?'

Lexi took a slow breath and squeezed her eyes tight shut, willing away the tears. 'And I want you. So very much. I'd given up hope of ever finding someone to love. But you need to have a son of your own. Somewhere out there is a very lucky woman you can cherish and who will be able to give you that son. And it's not me.'

'Another woman? Oh, Lexi.'

He straightened and drew back, physically holding her away from him. Her hands slid down his arms, desperate to hold on to the intensity of their connection, and her words babbled out in confusion and fear.

'We had a wonderful few days together, Mark. And I am so grateful to you for that.'

He'd turned away from her now, and paced back towards the bench, one hand clenched onto the back of his neck

'Grateful? Is that it? You're *grateful?* How can you walk away from what we have? I know you care about me, Lexi—please don't try and deny it.'

The bitterness in his voice was such a contrast to the loving man she'd just been holding that Lexi took a breath before answering. 'I do care about you—more than I can say. Can't you see? That's why the last thing I want to do is trap you into a relationship which will end in bitterness and disappointment, no matter how hard we both try.' She stepped forward and gently laid her hand on his arm as she looked into his face. 'You know I'm right. You're going to be a wonderful father, Mark. I just know it.'

She gulped away the burning sensation in her throat and looked into those wonderful eyes, so full of concern, and told him the truth—because nothing else would do.

'This is breaking my heart, Mark. I can't be with you any more. It's time to escape this perfect fantasy and get back to our ordinary lives. And if you love me then you have to let me go, Mark. Let me go. While we still have our precious love intact.'

'Lexi!'

The only thing that stopped Mark from running after her down the gravel footpath that led back to the villa was the heartbreak in her words and the unavoidable truth that he *did* love her—enough to stand, frozen, and watch her walk away.

Lexi sat in the very front row of the hydrofoil, facing the bow window at the front, so that her head was right in front of the TV showing cartoons with the sound off.

Her once-white linen trousers were a total mess, her blouse worse, and the only shoes she had with her were the flat tan leather sandals that Mark had bought her after they'd shared lunch that day in Gaios.

The elegant Greek woman sitting to her left was totally absorbed with cuddling and kissing a black toy poodle with red bows in its curls, which was getting ready to doze off for the hour-long journey.

Lexi was vaguely aware of tourists with their suitcases being loaded on at the harbour, filling up the seats behind her, their voices a blend of English and Italian accents. Some were yawning with the happy contentment of a sunny early morning call, but most were chatting away, couples and families enjoying the last day of their holiday before flying home.

She envied them that serenity. Her mind was a maelstrom of confused emotions and regret and loss, and she hadn't even left the island yet.

She felt as though time had stood still since she'd last spoken to Mark at the viewpoint.

It had taken only minutes to strip off her dress when she got back to the villa alone, to throw on the same trousers and loose blouse she'd been wearing that morning and cram everything from the wardrobe and drawers into her bags. He had not returned by the time her luggage was loaded into the car.

The cats had been sitting on the wall of sun-warmed stone as she'd turned the car around and driven through the wide entrance and onto the main road. When Snowy One had sat up and called to her she'd almost lost the will to go ahead with it.

Coward! She should have waited for him to come back. But that would have meant staying the night in the villa. And she was just not up to it. She would have given in and spent the night in his arms. And not regretted a second of it. That was the hard part.

Instead she'd held herself together long enough to drive down a country sideroad near Loggos and park her car well off the road, under the trees and away from the traffic and houses, before finally surrendering to the tears and anguish and exhaustion of the day. At some point in the night she'd fallen into an uncomfortable sleep for an hour or two before light broke through the trees above her.

She'd dropped her luggage off at the travel agent in Gaios when she'd handed back the hire car just as soon as the office opened that morning. She didn't need her expensive gowns and shoes for where she was going. This time her suitcases would be travelling cargo by themselves, and at this precise moment she really couldn't care less if they made it back to London or not. Everything she needed, everything she could not replace, was either in her huge shoulder bag or carried safe inside her heart. Where it would be locked away forever.

The burning in her throat emerged as a whispered sob, muffled by the sound of the hydrofoil engines starting up.

The sea was as smooth as a mirror, with only a gentle ripple to reflect back the jewelled sparkling of the rising sun. It was stunningly beautiful. A new hot sunny morning had dawned and her heart was breaking. She looked out of the hydrofoil windows, streaked with droplets of salt water from the seaspray.

The dew on the windows reflected back the fractured image of a woman who'd thought she knew what she wanted and had been proved completely wrong by someone so remarkable, so talented and so very lovable, that it took her breath away just thinking about him.

He would be awake now—if he had managed to sleep at all.

She wiped at the glass as the hydrofoil moved out into open water and headed towards Corfu, leaving behind the narrow green strip of the island with its white limestone cliffs that formed her last sight of Paxos. And the man she loved.

CHAPTER ELEVEN

Mark stood under the shade of the huge oak tree at the bottom of the drive as Cassie's golden retriever went tearing off across the lawn in search of a squirrel.

He looked up into the flame-tinged dark green and russet oak leaves above his head, so familiar to him that he sometimes forgot that tall oak trees from Belmont had been used to build the great wooden sailing ships that had made up the navy for so many kings and queens over the centuries.

Belmont's heritage. *His* heritage. And now he was paying the price for that.

Mark turned and started walking down the driveway between the two rows of mighty oak trees, back towards the magnificent Elizabethan manor house that was his family home. Belmont Manor.

The September late-afternoon sunshine had turned the buff old limestone to a warm, welcoming glow that brought to mind old hearths and the long history of the generations who had lived there. Purple and red ivy tinged with green clambered up the right block of the E-shaped house, but ended well below the curved stone decoration on each turret.

It was a solid house, almost six hundred years old, and barely changed over the centuries because the men had either been in London at court or busy fighting for their country. The heavy stone walls were broken up by rows of narrow mullioned windows which filled the rooms with coloured light, but never quite enough.

Looking at it now through fresh eyes, he couldn't fail to be impressed by the grandeur of the huge house. And yet this was his home. The place where he'd spent the first ten years of his life until he was sent to boarding school. But even then he'd come home to Belmont most weekends and every holiday. And he'd totally taken it for granted—just as he had with so much else in his life. Such as parents who would always be there to welcome him home, and a brother who would inherit the title and the house and all the obligations that went with it. Leaving the second son free to live his own life.

That was then. This was now.

Time to make a few changes.

Mark walked slowly through the beautiful timbered hallway and chuckled to himself at what Lexi would make of the suit of armour standing in the corner, and the family shields over the huge stone fireplace. She would probably want to wear the armour and invent some entirely inappropriate alternative descriptions for the heraldic symbols on the shields.

But as he strolled down the narrow oak-panelled corridor towards his father's study his smile faded. Everywhere he looked there was something to remind him of his mother. A Chinese flower vase or a stunning Tudor portrait, perfectly matched to the oak panelling and the period of the house. Right down to the stunning needlepoint panels which decorated the heavy oak doors. She'd always had the knack of finding the perfect item to decorate each room with such loving care and detail. It had taken her thirty years to do it, but in the process she'd transformed the dark and gloomy house he'd seen in family photographs into a warm, light family home.

This house was a celebration of her life, and Lexi had helped him to see that. Helped him to see a lot of things about his life in a new light.

He didn't need to be here in person today. He could have simply telephoned. But that was the coward's way out and he was through with that way of life. He had left that behind on Paxos three months ago.

Lifting his chin and squaring his shoulders, Mark strolled up to the half-open door and pushed it wide. His father looked up from his usual leather chair and waved at him to come closer. The gaunt look following his cancer treatment had faded. Charles Belmont was still slight, but he'd put on weight and was looking much more like the towering captain of industry and natural leader he had always been.

'Mark, my boy. Great to see you. Come and take a look at this. The advance copies of your mother's book arrived this morning. The printers have done a half-decent job.'

His father lifted up the hardback book and passed it to Mark, who had chosen to stand, rather than sit in the chair on the opposite side of the desk from his father as though he had come for a job interview.

'Excellent choice of photographs. Natural. I could not have chosen better myself. You did a remarkable job, Mark. Remarkable.'

And to Mark's horror Charles touched his nose with his knuckle to cover up his emotion. Strange: Mark did exactly the same thing and had never noticed it before.

Mark looked away and made a show of examining the cover's dust jacket and flicking through the first pages of his mother's biography. The publishers had chosen the very first photograph that Lexi had picked up that day on

Paxos, of his mother at the village fete. She looked happy and natural and full of life.

The photo worked brilliantly.

'Thank you, Father. But I can't take the credit for going with this particular photograph. That was Lexi's Sloane's idea. She thought it might help if people saw the real Crystal Leighton instead of some shallow movie star.'

'Damn right.' His father nodded. 'The girl's got a good head on her shoulders. And it did you good to meet someone outside the business world.' He nodded towards the book. 'I didn't just mean the cover. The stories you tell and your memories of happy and not-so-happy times brought her back to me in a way I didn't think possible. I don't have the talent for it. You clearly do.'

His voice dropped and he sat back in his chair, legs outstretched, tapping his fingers on the desk.

'Your sister is worried about you, Mark. When your mother was alive you would talk about what was happening in your life. But now…? I don't know what's going on in your head. We talk about the business—yes, sure. You even convinced me to go ahead with converting the cottages, and so far we're right on track with that risky business plan of yours. But since you got back from Greece you haven't been the same man. What do you want? More control of the business? The manor? Shout it out, son.'

'What do I want?'

Mark put down the book, strolled over to the window and looked out across the sunlit lawns. This was the first time in many, many years that his father had even asked him how he spent his day, but it was true that he had changed. They both had.

'Actually, I've been asking myself the same question an awful lot since I got back from Paxos. And the answers are not always comfortable,' he replied.

'Tough questions demand tough answers,' his father muttered dismissively. 'Let's hear it.'

Mark half turned back towards him. 'I want to stop feeling guilty for the fact that my mother couldn't tell me she didn't feel pretty enough to stand by me at my engagement party. That would be a start. I know now that there was nothing I could have done differently at the time,' he added softly, 'but it still makes me angry that she didn't trust us enough to share her pain.'

'Of course it makes you angry,' his father replied with a sniff. 'She didn't tell me, either. I thought she was perfect in every way. I can't understand her decision any more than you can. But she was an adult, intelligent woman who knew what she was doing. And don't you *dare* think it was about your blasted engagement. Because it wasn't. It was about her own self-worth. And if you're angry—fine. We can be angry together.'

The tapping continued.

'What else is on that list of yours? What about this girl who helped write the book?'

Mark took a moment to stay calm before making his reply. 'Actually, she's the reason I'm here today. Lexi has it in her head that marrying a girl who can give me a son is more important to me than finding someone I want to spend the rest of my life with. Three months ago she might have been right. Not any more. Not now.' He looked over his shoulder and made eye contact. 'I'm sorry, Father, but chances are that Lexi and I will *not* be able to give you the grandson you were hoping for. The Belmont line will probably end with me.'

The air between Mark and his father almost crackled with the fierce electricity of the tension between them.

'Even if it means that the title passes to your cousin Rupert? The spoiled brat who threw you out of a boat on the lake when you wouldn't let him row? This girl must mean a great deal to you.'

'She does. More than I can say.'

Mark heard the creak of the leather chair behind him, but didn't turn around to his father because of the tears in his eyes. A strong, warm arm wrapped around his shoulders and hugged him just once, then dropped to the window frame so they were both looking out in the same direction.

The intimate contact was slight, but so incredibly new that it seemed to break down the final barrier Mark had been holding between himself and his father for so many years. They had made real progress over these past three months, but this was new. He turned his head towards him.

'I'm pleased to hear that you've met someone at long last. I had almost given up on you. From what Cassie tells me, Alexis is not responsible for what her father did. She loves you enough to do the right thing, and sacrificed her personal happiness for yours. In my book that makes her someone I would like to meet. You deserve to have some love in your life, Mark. Your mother was right. You should get out more.'

He nodded once, then gestured with his head towards the book on his desk.

'If there's one thing your mother's story tells us it's that we loved her and she loved us. More than we knew. And in the end that's the only thing that matters. I am jolly glad that Crystal Leighton came into my life and made me the happiest man alive for so many wonderful years. And gave me my three wonderful children. I blame myself for what happened after Edmund. Tough times. Hard to deal with. I was not up to the job.'

Then he looked up into the sky and his voice turned wistful. 'I should be the one apologising to you, not the other way round. You're right. Don't give your inheritance another thought. The future can take care of itself. You're the man I always knew you could be, and I'm proud to have you as my son.'

Mark took a deep breath and startled his father by giving him a slap on the back. 'I'm pleased to hear it—because I'm heading off to London tomorrow to try and persuade her to give me another chance. Thanks, Dad. I'm pleased you like the book. And thank you even more for bringing Lexi Sloane into my life.'

'What are you waiting here for? Go get your girl and bring her home so she can meet the family. And don't you frighten her off with all this pressure about having sons. It's about time we had some fun around here.'

Dratted device. Lexi shook the small battery-powered sander in the vain hope that playing maracas with it would actually squeeze out enough power to finish the living-room wall.

No such luck. The sander gave a low whine and then shuddered to a halt as the battery gave out.

'Oh, come on, you stupid thing,' she snapped. 'I charged you for three hours this morning. The least you could do is work.'

She sat down on the arm of the sofa in the middle of the room. It was covered with a dust sheet and had been for weeks, while she stripped off the old wallpaper and repaired the holes in the plaster. Now came the dusty part. Sanding away the bumpy walls until they were smooth.

For the last twelve weeks Lexi had filled her days and nights with work that should have provided the perfect distraction.

But it was no use.

Apparently no amount of physical hard work on the

house could replace her obsession for Mark Belmont. He filled her days and nights with dreams and fantasies of what could have been; what had been lost. Worse, every time she looked at her children's stories of kittens having great adventures she was transported back in her mind's eye to the original inspiration and the sunny garden of Mark's villa on Paxos. The wonderful house and the man who owned it.

She could only hope that he wasn't as miserable as she was. Even if the view was particularly delightful from the balcony of his no doubt sumptuous penthouse apartment.

With a low sigh, Lexi replaced the sander on its charger and turned off the trance music that was giving her a headache.

She needed air.

Lexi walked the few steps from the living room to her freshly decorated kitchen, grabbed some juice out of the refrigerator and stepped out onto the tiny patio where she had replaced the traditional redbrick paving with buff-coloured sandstone slabs. Bright red geraniums and herbs spilled out from terracotta pots close to the kitchen door, and a simple wooden trellis still carried the last of the climbing roses.

A precious ray of September sunshine warmed her face and the tiny olive bush in the brightly coloured pot she had painted next to her wooden chair. The colour on the paint tin had been described as 'Mediterranean Blue.' But it was not the same. How could it be? Nothing in her life could be the same again.

She was still standing in the sunshine watching the sparrows on the bird table ten minutes later, when the front doorbell rang. She jogged back to fling it open, a pencil still logged behind one ear, expecting to see the postman.

It was not the postman.

'Mark?' she gasped, staring at him, hardly able to believe her eyes. 'What are you doing here? I thought you'd moved to—'

'No. I changed my mind about New York. I'm having way too much fun right here in Blighty.'

She swallowed and then gave a low sigh, blinking away tears.

He was here. On her doorstep. Tall, gorgeous and overwhelmingly tinglicious.

'Is your dad okay? I saw the pictures from the film festival when he accepted that lifetime achievement award on behalf of your mum. He looked a bit shaky.'

He reached out and touched her arm, his fingers light on the sleeve of her boiler suit. 'Dad's fine. He's still recovering, but he'll stick around long enough to make my life interesting for some time to come. Thanks for asking. The emotion of the night got to all of us. I'm sorry you weren't there to help us celebrate.'

There was an awkward pause, and just when her resolve gave way and she felt that she simply had to say something, *anything,* to fill the silence, Mark suddenly presented her with a gift-wrapped square package tied with a silver ribbon.

'I know that you'd prefer me not to contact you, but I thought you might want to have your personal copy of the biography. Signed, of course,' he said, his voice dry and hesitant. 'My dad is planning a private launch party in a few weeks, so this is a sneak peek. And, by the way, the Belmont family would love to have you there. It wouldn't be the same if I couldn't thank you in person on the big night. I haven't forgotten what you said. You deserve the credit for making this book a reality.'

She looked at the package, then back to Mark in silence, and then her shoulders dropped about six inches and she slid the yellow washing-up glove from one hand and wrapped her fingers around the book. She pulled it towards her for a second, then looked down at the paint splattered overalls and socks she was wearing and shrugged.

'Sanding. Plastering. Bit of a mess. Not sure I'm ready for smart book-launch parties.'

'You look lovely,' he replied in a totally serious voice, but his eyes and mouth were smiling as his gaze locked onto hers. 'You look like *you*.'

He tilted his head to one side and gave her a lopsided grin which made him look about twelve years old.

And her poor lonely heart melted all over again.

'What have you been doing with yourself these past few months?' he whispered. 'Travelling the world? Seeing the sights? Tell me about all the wonderful exotic locations your clients have whisked you away to. Africa? Asia?'

She smiled back, her defences weakened by the wonderful charm and warmth of this man who was standing so very close and yet seemed beyond reach.

'Actually, I've been working on my own projects right here.' She waved her right hand in the air and looked up at the ornate plasterwork ceiling of her hallway. 'I thought that I might stay in one place for a while.' Her voice quivered a little and the silver bow on the gift-wrapping suddenly became the focus of her attention. 'Try and get my bearings after…'

She swallowed, almost losing control at the thought of Paxos, and quickly changed the subject. 'But I can see what *you've* been doing,' she whispered, giving him a half smile. 'You finished the book. Does you dad love it as much as you hoped?'

'He does. He had to go back into hospital for another round of chemotherapy. It was tough. But when I brought the manuscript in to check on a few details… It was one of the few times in my life that my father has held my hand and cried. Going through the chapters together changed us. Made us talk about things I had put off for way too long. It was good. Actually, it was better than good. It was grand. What was the phrase you used? Oh, yes. *Awesome sauce.* The book is awesome sauce. And I have you to thank for making that happen.'

'Not just me. He should be proud of you.' Lexi stroked the wrapping and pressed her lips together, her mind reeling from the fact that Mark was so close. She longed to touch and hold him and tell him how much she had desperately missed him… But she knew that would only make things a lot worse.

'I'll read it later, if you don't mind. I need to get back to my decorating.' She waved her yellow glove back inside the hallway. 'Lots to do.' She half turned to step back inside, then glanced back at him over her shoulder. 'But thank you for bringing me this in person. I hope it gets stunning reviews and puts some ghosts to bed. For all of us. Good luck, Mark. To you and your family.'

Time stood still for a few seconds as Lexi remained in the doorway, hating to say goodbye.

'Lexi. Can I come in? Just for five minutes? I really do need to talk to you.' Then he pulled back his arm and shook his head. 'Forget that. That's what the old Mark would have said.'

He stepped forward so quickly that Lexi was still taking in a sharp breath when he wrapped his arms around her back and pulled her sharply towards him. Looking into her startled eyes, Mark smiled and pulled her even tighter, so that the only thing separating their bodies was the book he had just given her.

'I would much rather have this conversation on your doorstep, so that the whole of London can hear me tell you that I've been totally miserable these past few months without my sparkly Lexi by my side. In fact I missed your irritating sparkliness so much that I stopped being grumpy and decided to be a better man, instead.'

Her heart turned a somersault. 'Oh, you were grumpy. But I wasn't always sparkly, so I think we're about even.'

'Sparkly enough for me. And please don't make me lose my place in my speech. I was just getting to the apology—where I grovel at your feet and beg your forgiveness for being such an idiot that I let you go without fighting harder to persuade you to stay.'

'In that case I shall try not to be sparkly. Because I quite like the sound of that part.'

'I rather thought you might. Only I'm a bit out of practice when it comes to grovelling. In fact, this is a first, so you'll have to forgive me if I get it wrong.'

Lexi tugged off her other glove and pressed her free hand onto Mark's chest. He inhaled deeply with pleasure at her touch.

'On the contrary.' She smiled. 'I think you grovel quite beautifully. But you can stop now. There's something I'd like to show you.'

She grabbed his hand and half dragged him down the narrow hall and into the kitchen of her tiny terraced house.

'Do you remember all the photographs I took of your kittens on the terrace at the villa? Well, here they are.'

She pointed to the row of printed pages which ran the full length of the kitchen wall. 'On the left side of the page is a photo of the kittens, and then on the right side are a few lines of the story.'

'Is that Snowy One peeping his head out from my stone wall?' Mark asked, laughing at the cutest white kitten with pink ears, pinker tongue and a cheeky grin. 'It is—and here's Snowy Two, halfway up the trunk of the olive tree next to the table-tennis table. I think it was the moment when it dawned on him that going down might be slightly trickier than climbing up. "Once upon a time in the land of sunshine there lived a family of positively pampered cats,"' Mark read slowly, then snorted and looked back at Lexi. 'Well, that certainly is true. My housekeeper feeds them chicken when I'm away!'

Lexi took a step to his side and read out the rest of the page. '"There was a mummy cat, a daddy cat and two kittens. Their real names were Snowy and Smudge, but most days they ended up being called other names—like rascal, scamp, trouble and mischief."'

'Oh, that is perfect. These are wonderful, Lexi.' He sighed warmly and walked, with her hand still held in his, from photograph to photograph. 'I knew you were talented. But these are magical. Truly wonderful. Cassie's boys would adore these stories.'

Lexi paused and looked up into his face. 'But not *my* boys, Mark. I know there's a small chance that medically I could have your son, but lurching from month to month with hope and then disappointment is no way to live. It wouldn't be fair on either of us. And that hasn't gone away.'

'No, it hasn't,' he replied, lifting a strand of hair and pushing it back over her forehead as he slid away her bandanna. 'But I know now that a life without love in it is no life at all. *You* are the only woman I want in my life. Plus I'm going to need some help with childcare. Ah…yes.' He smiled at her stunned face. 'That reminds me. I should probably mention that I plan to adopt. Two girls and two boys would work well, but I'm flexible. There are an awful lot of children out there who need a loving home where they can be spoiled rotten, and I suspect that we would be very good at that.'

'Adopt? Four children? You would do that for me?' Lexi

asked, suddenly feeling faint, horrified, stunned, amazed and thrilled to the core.

'In a heartbeat.' Mark shrugged and drew her closer. 'You are the girl for me. And that's it. Those children will be blessed with the most wonderful mum. And I'm going to be right there every step of the way. In fact, I'm rather looking forward to being a dad.'

'Wait a minute,' Lexi replied and shook her head. 'You seem to be forgetting something very important here. I was the one who couldn't face the hard time ahead of us. Not you. I was the coward. You made me feel loved and treasured, and it was so intense and so beautiful I couldn't deal with it, Mark. I just couldn't believe it was possible that any man could love me so much. And I ran. And I shouldn't have. I should have stayed and fought harder to make it work. I am sorry for that. I just couldn't believe it was real. I couldn't believe you wanted me.'

Her head lolled forward so that her dirty, dusty forehead was resting on his beautiful dark suit.

'Believe it,' he murmured, his chin pressed on top of her hair. 'Because it's true.'

He tipped her chin up so that she could look into his eyes, and the intensity and depth of what she saw there choked her so much that her breath came out in deep sobs.

'I telephoned your mother yesterday and personally invited her to the book launch. She was a tad surprised to hear from me, but we got along splendidly after I mentioned that I am completely besotted with her daughter and my sole objective in life from this moment is her complete happiness.'

'You said that to my mum?' Lexi gasped. 'Wow. That must have been an interesting conversation. You do know that she'll hold you to it? Wait a minute… I spoke to her last night and she never said a word.'

'Um… We made a pact. She wouldn't tell you that I was coming round so long as I promised to kidnap you from your world of plastering and whisk you off to a luxury hotel for an afternoon of pampering in the spa, a fine meal and hopefully some debauchery.'

She slumped against him. 'Oh, that sounds so good.'

'There's more. Your delightful and charming parent happened to mention that your home-decorating project was sucking time away from your writing. This cannot be permitted to continue. Children everywhere need to see these stories as soon as possible.'

He grinned and winked. 'The Belmont estate has a wonderful team of builders and decorators who will be happy to help my girlfriend in her hour of need. They are currently on standby, ready to burst into action at a moment's notice and get busy on your charming London house while you spend the weekend with my family at the manor.'

'That's—that's very generous, but I couldn't possibly accept… And…girlfriend? What manor? And you winked at me. You *winked*. Things really have changed.'

'I thought it was about time I started to be spontaneous. And I was hoping that if I played my cards right you might let me share this bijou gem of a home with you. It's far better than any clinical, empty penthouse. And, best of all, you are in it.'

He cupped Lexi's head between his hands, his long fingers so gentle and tender and loving that her heart melted even more.

'I love you, Alexis Sloane. I love everything about you. I love that you are a survivor. I love that you have come through so much and still have so much love to give to the world. I am so proud of everything you have achieved, and I want to be there when you go on to even greater things. I believe in your talent and I want to share my life with you.'

'You love me?'

He nodded. 'Yep. I love you. All of you. Especially that part of you that doesn't believe that she deserves to be loved. Because that's the bit I fit into. Say yes, Lexi. Say *yes*. Take the risk and let me into your life. Because you are not a coward. Far from it. You are the bravest woman I have ever met.'

'I would have to be brave to be *your* girlfriend,' she sobbed, spreading tears and plaster dust all over his suit. 'But give me ten minutes to get packed and I'll show you how much I've missed you every second of every day we have been apart.'

'You don't need to pack. Where we're going clothing is entirely optional.'

'Oh, I *do* love you,' she replied, flinging her arms around his neck and kissing him with every ounce of devotion and passion and repressed longing that she could collect into one kiss—a kiss that had them both panting when she released him.

'Wow.' He grinned, blinking, gasping for breath, his eyes locked on hers. 'Really?'

'*Really,* really. I love you so very, very much. Enough to stand up to anyone who even tries to break us apart. No matter who it is. Oh, Mark, I've missed you so much.'

His hands stroked her face and he grinned, his eyes sparkling with energy and life. 'Excellent. Because I've already invited your mother and her fiancé to meet the Belmont clan at the manor tomorrow. I cannot wait a moment longer to show you off.'

She gasped. 'My mother? And Baron Belmont? Now, *that's* something I want to see. He won't know what's hit him.'

'I have no doubt. But they're all going to have to get used to the idea. This is the first day of the rest of our lives,

Lexi. Tell me what you want to do and where you want to go and I'll take you there.'

Lexi took in a long breath and looked into the face of the man she loved—the man who loved her in return and was offering her the world on a golden platter. 'Then take me back to Paxos and that secret garden on a clifftop. And this time we are going to watch the sunset together. Forever.'

EPILOGUE

LEXI strolled into the luxurious reception room of one of London's most exclusive gentlemen's clubs and paused to take in the sumptuous interior which had already sent her mother into raptures over the ornate plasterwork, stunning Art Nouveau statuary and hand-painted Chinese wallpaper.

Deep brocade-covered sofas and crystal chandeliers added to the opulence—but they were lost on Lexi. Her high-heeled sandals sank into the fine Oriental carpet as she stood on tiptoe to find the one person she needed and wanted so badly to be with on his special day.

And there he was. Elegant in his favourite charcoal cashmere suit and the pale pink shirt she had ironed for him that afternoon, chatting away to Cassie and his mother's showbiz friends in front of a huge white marble fireplace. His father had one arm around Mark's shoulder and was laughing out loud, his head back, relaxed and happy, as one of London's most famous theatre actors shared an anecdote about the old days when he worked with Crystal.

The love and the warmth of the scene added to the familiar heat that flashed through her body the moment she saw Mark's eyes focus on her from across the room, inviting her to join him.

Clusters of elegant people were gathered around the tables, flicking through the pages of *Mrs Belmont's Lemon Cake,* some smiling and some wiping away tears. All affected by the woman Mark had captured so brilliantly in the pages of a book that was surely going to soar up the best-seller lists.

Her reward for wending her way across the room was a warm hug from Cassie and a kiss on the cheek from Charles. But it was Mark who gathered her to him, his arm wrapped tightly around the waist of her simple pleated silk plum cocktail dress so that she was locked into his side.

'You look even more amazing than normal, Miss Sloane. And that is saying something!' he whispered into her hair.

'Well, thank you, Mr Belmont, but I think the jewellery might have something to do with that.' She grinned, pressing one hand to his mother's stunning diamond-and-sapphire necklace which Mark had placed around her neck only minutes before they'd been due to leave her house for the party.

'Oh, no. You are already sparkly enough for me. This is just a finishing touch for the rest of the world to see.'

The sides of his mouth lifted into an intimate smile that made her heart soar as he tapped the end of her nose.

'Ah. Lexi. There you are.' The smiling owner of Brightmore Press charged forward, waving the biography in his hand. 'Splendid job. Just splendid. Huge success. I need to say a few words to our guests, but I'll be right back.' He looked at her over the top of his black spectacles. 'And don't you *dare* leave before we have a chat about that series of children's books you've promised me. I've already booked a page in our Christmas catalogue. Catch you later!'

He sped off to grab Baron Belmont.

Mark squeezed Lexi's waist as she smiled up into his

face. 'Well, I suppose I shall have to get used to having my own name on the cover for a change.'

'This is only the start,' Mark replied, then laughed out loud. 'They already know that I couldn't have written this book without you. Get ready for the time of your life, Miss Awesome Sauce. There's no holding you back now—and I am going to be right there by your side, cheering you on. All the way.'

* * * * *

COMING NEXT MONTH from Harlequin® Romance
AVAILABLE OCTOBER 2, 2012

#4339 THE ENGLISH LORD'S SECRET SON
Margaret Way
Seven years ago Ashe left Cate heartbroken. Now he's back...but is he prepared for a secret that will change *everything*?

#4340 THE RANCHER'S UNEXPECTED FAMILY
The Larkville Legacy
Myrna Mackenzie
Taciturn cowboy Holt turns his *no* into *yes* when Kathryn demands that he save the local clinic—and, annoyingly, also attracts his attention!

#4341 SNOWBOUND IN THE EARL'S CASTLE
Holiday Miracles
Fiona Harper
Faith has never found a man more infuriating *and* attractive than aristocrat Marcus! Trapped in his castle, she finds him suddenly hard to resist....

#4342 BELLA'S IMPOSSIBLE BOSS
Michelle Douglas
Babysitting your boss's daughter doesn't mean you have to like her! Dominic's risking his reputation, but does Bella know it, too?

#4343 WEDDING DATE WITH MR. WRONG
Nicola Marsh
There's something about her ex, Archer, that has always tempted Callie to throw caution to the wind... but hasn't she learned her lesson?

#4344 A GIRL LESS ORDINARY
Leah Ashton
Billionaire Jake knows the real woman beneath Ella's glamorous transformation, and sparks fly as the past evokes unforgettable memories!

You can find more information on upcoming Harlequin® titles, free excerpts and more at www.Harlequin.com.

REQUEST YOUR FREE BOOKS!
2 FREE NOVELS PLUS 2 FREE GIFTS!

Harlequin Romance

From the Heart, For the Heart

HARLEQUIN Romance

At their grandmother's request, three estranged sisters return home for Christmas to the small town of Beckett's Run. Little do they know that this family reunion will reveal long-buried secrets... and new-found love.

Discover the magic of Christmas in a brand-new Harlequin® Romance miniseries.

In October 2012, find yourself
SNOWBOUND IN THE EARL'S CASTLE
by **Fiona Harper**

Be enchanted in November 2012 by a
SLEIGH RIDE WITH THE RANCHER
by **Donna Alward**

And be mesmerized in December 2012 by
MISTLETOE KISSES WITH THE BILLIONAIRE
by **Shirley Jump**

Available wherever books are sold.

*Sensational author Kate Hewitt brings you
a sneak-peek excerpt from THE DARKEST OF SECRETS,
the intensely powerful first story
in her new Harlequin® Presents® miniseries,
THE POWER OF REDEMPTION.*

* * *

"YOU'RE attracted to me, Grace."

"It doesn't matter."

"Do you still not trust me?" he asked quietly. "Is that it? Are you afraid—of me?"

"I'm not afraid of you," she said, and meant it. She might not trust him, but she didn't fear him. She simply didn't want to let him have the kind of power opening your body or heart to someone would give. And then of course there were so many reasons not to get involved.

"What, then?" She just shook her head. "I know you've been hurt," he said quietly and she let out a sad little laugh. He was painting his own picture of her, she knew then, a happy little painting like one a child might make. Too bad he had the wrong paint box.

"And how do you know that?" she asked.

"It's evident in everything you do and say—"

"No, it isn't." She *had* been hurt, but not the way he thought. She'd never been an innocent victim, as much as she wished things could be that simple. And she knew, to her own shame and weakness, that she wouldn't say anything. She didn't want him to look at her differently. With judgment rather than compassion, scorn instead of sympathy.

"Why can't you get involved, then, Grace?" Khalis asked. "It was just a kiss, after all." He'd moved to block the door-

HPEX1012R

way, even though Grace hadn't yet attempted to leave. His face looked harsh now, all hard angles and narrowed eyes, even though his body remained relaxed. A man of contradictions—or was it simply deception? Which was the real man, Grace wondered, the smiling man who'd rubbed her feet so gently, or the angry son who refused to grieve for the family he'd just lost? Or was he both, showing one face to the world and hiding another, just as she was?

Khalis Tannous has ruthlessly eradicated every hint of corruption and scandal from his life. But the shadows haunting the eyes of his most recent—most beautiful— employee aren't enough to dampen his desire. Grace can foresee the cost of giving in to temptation, but will she risk everything she has for a night in his bed?

Find out on September 18, 2012, wherever books are sold!